Restitutions of the Blood

Lila Richards

Millwheel Press

Published by:

Millwheel Press Ltd

Eyrewell Forest, New Zealand

www.millwheelpress.co.nz

ISBN: 978-0-473-50205-8 - softcover

978-0-473-50206-5 - Epub

978-0-473-50207-2 - mobi

In 1890, when Alex Randall returns from university to his ancestral home of Shillington Hall, he finds his father remarried, less than a year after his mother's death. Dismay turns to anger when a son, Oliver, is born. Convinced the new Lady Randall means to steal his inheritance, Alex flees to London, where he meets and befriends Henri de Saint Clair, a charming, but enigmatic Frenchman. When Alex's friend Charles becomes involved in an illegal duel, and both parties are killed, Alex finds himself on the run from the law, and obliged to leave England. In Paris, he renews his friendship with the still strangely elusive Henri. After a series of misadventures that lead him to the very depths of Parisian society, Henri rescues Alex and restores him to health by means of a mysterious 'restorative' but, before long, Alex's determination to discover the truth about his friend plunges him into a world darker - and more addictive - than anything he could have imagined.

Dedication

With special thanks to Roy for his help with editing, his invaluable comments, his humour and, above all, for his continued faith in me and my creations.

All changes, even the most longed for, have their melancholy,
For what we leave behind is part of ourselves.
We must die to one life before we can enter another.
                                    Anatole France, 1844 – 1924

You know who have waited by the wall
The twilight certainty of an animal
Those midnight restitutions of the blood...
                              Ode to the Confederate Dead
                                    Allen Tate, 1899 – 1979

CHAPTER ONE

The story I am about to relate is a strange one, being, indeed, of a nature I had supposed to belong only in the realms of speculative and fantastical fiction—until events proved me all too wrong. Whether it was ignorance and naivety, or some fatal flaw in my nature or upbringing that led to my present condition, I leave to those more expert than I in the fields of philosophy and psychology. But I have resolved to set down my story, not just as a warning to others, but as an attempt to explain to myself the steps by which I reached the state in which I must now drag out what I still refer to as my life— although the word has little meaning for me now.

It is not easy for me to determine the moment when I first set foot on the path of my doom. It may be, as John Calvin believed, that it was predestined from my birth, although I shudder to think what appalling deity could have devised so hateful a plan for me. Or perhaps, as the Buddhists believe, I had doomed myself by evil deeds in a past life. I do not pretend to understand how these things happen. What I do know, however, is that when I came down from King's College, Cambridge, at the age of twenty-three, I was a well-educated, but—it seems to me now—hopelessly naïve and romantic young man.

My dear Mama had died the previous winter of influenza, and I had missed her long letters full of the minutiae of life back at Shillington Hall even more than the parcels of homemade cakes or sweets, or warm winter socks that were such a comfort to me in my meagre student lodgings. Nevertheless, I was looking forward to seeing my father again. He had never been much of a man for letters or chitchat, and I was looking forward to catching up on the affairs of the estate at last.

As Captain Nuttall, the estate manager, drew the family brougham to a halt before the wide steps of Shillington Hall, I glimpsed through the carriage window my father's beaming face, still fine-looking despite his sixty-seven years, although his hair was thinning, and even greyer than when I had last seen him. Hovering just behind him stood Barrett, the butler, grave-faced as ever; plump Mrs Dear, who had been my childhood nurse and now served as housekeeper; the two menservants, Holman and Cox; and a maid whose face was new to me. It was a sadly depleted household, I thought, recalling childhood days when the old house buzzed with activity—and Mama was still alive. Then Holman came to let down the carriage steps and I shook off my gloom, stepped down and hurried to greet my father.

Papa clapped me on the shoulder, exclaiming, "Good to see you again, my boy! I trust you've had a good journey?" which was a close as he ever came to effusiveness. He bustled me inside. "Will you have tea, Alex, or do you fancy something stronger?"

"Oh, tea, please, and perhaps some bread and butter?" After the jolting I'd received on the rutted country roads, the last thing I felt in need of was strong drink.

As Mrs Dear and the maid, Ellen, hurried off to make our tea, my father and I repaired to the drawing room, which I was pleased to see looked just as it had always done, from the faded green plush curtains to the great marble fireplace, its mantel laden with trinkets my mother had collected over the years. By the time Ellen came in with our tea, I felt almost as though I'd never left—almost, for the gracious presence of my dear Mama was almost palpable in its absence.

* * * *

It was several days before I realised there was something different about my father. He seemed to carry an air of suppressed excitement, although he vouchsafed nothing of its cause, and I avoided asking, not wishing to seem unduly inquisitive. A few days after my return, I came back from riding around the estate with Captain Nuttall to find my father in the hallway issuing animated orders to Barrett and Mrs Dear. He turned as I entered, his face warm and smiling.

"Alex, I've decided I must welcome you home in style!"

"That's very kind of you, Papa, but really, there's no need..." I began, but my father interrupted me with an

3

impatient wave of his hand.

"Of course there is! My only son has just graduated from one of the best universities in the country! Surely that's cause for celebration. No, no, Alex, I've made up my mind, I'm giving a dinner party on Saturday. Holman has already sent out the invitations."

"Well, thank you, Papa—" I smiled "—though it really wasn't necessary. I'm just happy to be home. But, since it's clearly a *fait accompli*, who have you invited?"

My father waved an airy hand. "Oh, just a few neighbours, and Doctor Phillips and his wife and daughter, the Reverend and Mrs Paull, and Colonel Havers. I hope they meet with your approval."

I nodded acquiescence, although most of the proposed guests were at least twice my age. I knew my father meant well, and old Colonel Havers was always good company with his tales of his years in India, although I expected he would need to expurgate them for the sake of the ladies present.

As the weekend approached, my impression became stronger that Papa was hugging some secret to his breast that seemed to cause him greater excitement than a mere welcome-home party for his son should do, but on the few occasions when I might have broached the subject, I balked at the idea. Although I loved him dearly, my father had never been the most approachable of men. As a child I had been in awe—and a certain amount of fear—of his energetic presence. He was never less than kind to either Mama or me, yet I found myself wary of crossing some ill-defined, but, I always suspected, fateful line with him. Whether or not this perception was true, I found my years at Cambridge had done little to ameliorate my reticence.

Saturday dawned as clear and bright as anyone could have hoped for, a summer day bathed in golden warmth, bright with flowers and buzzing with bees that flitted from bloom to bloom in the well-kept garden. After lunch, while the servants prepared for the dinner party and Papa ran hither and thither supervising their efforts—or rather, impeding them—I escaped to the orchard to spend the afternoon on my own, reading in the shade. Far from infecting me with his enthusiasm, Papa had managed only to irritate me, ungrateful wretch that I was. I must have dozed off. When I next looked at my watch it was almost a quarter to five. Feeling more than a little guilty, I hurried inside to wash and dress for dinner.

An hour or so later, I walked into the drawing room to find the Reverend and Mrs Paull and Colonel Havers had just arrived, having driven over together in the Paulls' barouche. Colonel Havers immediately strode across the room to meet me, his bony hand outstretched in greeting.

"Alex! It's good to see you again, and what a splendid young man you've grown into. Your father has just been telling us how proud he is of you."

A little embarrassed at this encomium, I shook his hand. "Thank you, Colonel. It's good to see you, too."

As I was greeting the vicar and his wife, the doorbell rang. A few moments later, Barrett announced Doctor Phillips and his wife, and their daughter Cicely, initiating another round of greetings. I hadn't seen Cicely for some years, as she had gone to live with an aunt in London shortly before I left for Cambridge. In the intervening years she had grown from a plump schoolgirl into a shapely and stylish young woman. I rather hoped I should be seated next to her at dinner.

5

My father, still with that air of barely concealed excitement, was offering sherry to his guests when the doorbell rang once more. He gave an audible gasp and stood holding his breath until Barrett ushered into the room a tall, dark, sallow-faced man of perhaps forty years. He was accompanied by a woman some ten years his junior, an elegantly dressed brunette, a little on the plump side for my taste, yet by no means unattractive. Papa, as one awakening from a trance, started forward, a great smile suffusing his face.

"Mr Fordham, welcome! I trust you're fully recovered?"

Mr Fordham gave a slight bow. "Yes, thank you, Sir John, I'm quite well again now, thanks to dear Mariah's kind ministrations." He bestowed a rather saturnine smile on the young woman beside him. "I'm very grateful you could spare her for so long."

"No, no, you're most welcome." My puzzlement at these words grew even greater as Papa turned a dazzling smile on Mr Fordham's companion and added, "Not that I haven't missed you greatly, Mariah, my dear."

Missed you greatly? Mariah, my dear? I felt a stab of anger at this apparent slighting of my mother's memory, accompanied by a vague, but disconcerting presentiment of I knew not what. I had not long to wait for enlightenment.

My father took Mariah's hand and bent to kiss it, then drew her and her companion towards where I stood.

"Alex, my boy, may I present to you our new neighbour, Mr Joseph Fordham. He's lately inherited Harrington Park, you know. And it's my very great pleasure to introduce his sister, Mariah, the new Lady Randall."

It was as much as I could do to stammer out a formal

6

greeting before turning away to conceal the wave of fury that surged through me at the thought of this—interloper— replacing my mother less than a year since her death, before we were even decently out of mourning. How could my father have done such a vile and heartless thing, and without so much as telling me?

Papa, however, seemed unaware of my feelings, announcing to the company at large, "It is my very great pleasure to tell you all that my dearest Mariah has made me the happiest man in all England by accepting my proposal of marriage. We were married six weeks ago in the private chapel at Harrington Park. Unhappily, for the past month Mariah has been obliged to remain there tending her brother through his illness. But, as you see, Joseph is recovered, Mariah has returned, and my happiness is restored."

Murmurs of congratulation came from the assembled company, although I noted expressions of surprise on their faces as well, except for the Reverend Paull, from which I deduced it was he who had done the deed.

How I contrived to make my way through dinner I scarcely know. Fortunately no one seemed to notice my poor appetite, or my automatic responses to their pleasantries. As for my father, he had eyes for no one but his new bride, hanging on her every word, and lavishing her with glances a love-struck schoolboy would have deemed ridiculous. The bride, for her part, played the loving wife in a manner that would have done credit to the great Ellen Terry and, try as I might, I could not rid myself of the suspicion that she was, indeed, play-acting.

* * * *

Over the ensuing weeks, I did my best to cultivate a more charitable view of Mariah, if only for my father's sake. But the more I came to know her, the more I mistrusted her motives in marrying a man more than twice her age, and one, moreover, still missing his wife of over thirty years. I could certainly see what might have attracted Papa; Mariah was a good-looking woman with a charming manner and smile—though I fancied I detected a certain shrewdness lurking in her hazel eyes. But what, I wondered, could she have seen in a man well past the prime of his life, and troubled with the ailments that come with age? I gathered she had been married to an army lieutenant, who had been killed during some skirmish in India several years previously, after which she had returned to England to keep house for her brother. I imagined this must have been quite a comedown after life as the wife of an army officer in India, and could quite see why she might wish to establish herself elsewhere. But in a quiet country manor with an elderly husband? Perhaps it was the lure of a title? To become the wife of a baronet—and a wealthy one at that—must, I supposed, hold a certain attraction for a widow past the first flush of youth, and with probably only an army widow's pension to sustain her. However, I could not shake the misgiving that there was more to this marriage than met the eye, and that my father had somehow been duped.

Some days later, Mrs Dear found me in the library, seated at the table under the window with my chin propped in my hands, staring unseeingly out at the garden. I had gone there to read for a while, hoping, in vain, to escape the mood of dejection that had settled over me since learning of my father's remarriage. She came to stand beside me and laid a hand on my shoulder.

"Master Alex, I know how upset you must be, but please try to understand how lonely your father has been these months since your poor, dear Mama passed away. Can you not find it in your heart to wish him well?"

How could I wish him well when he had cast aside everything that had given meaning to my life? And for what? A woman young enough to be my sister, who was clearly a social climber looking to better herself.

"Well, I won't be calling her Mama," I muttered ungraciously.

"Of course not," Mrs Dear soothed. "I'm sure no one will expect it. But for all it's not what any of us expected, or wished for, perhaps, you must allow that your father is happy with Lady Randall. And if she makes him happy, can that be such a bad thing?"

"It's nothing but an old man's foolishness," I opined bitterly. "He may be happy now, but you mark my words, Mrs Dear, it won't last long. It's not him she's interested in, but the social standing, not to mention the wealth the connection can give her."

Mrs Dear sighed and patted my shoulder. "I can't force you to like it, Master Alex, but I hope I taught you better manners than to say such things to your father."

I could not help smiling at these words; she sounded exactly as she had when I had been a wilful little boy. "Of course I won't, Mrs Dear. For all that I think Papa is making a fool of himself, I promise you I shan't tell him so to his face."

"There's a good boy. I've just this minute taken a loaf of

bread out of the oven. Why don't you come into the kitchen with me, and I'll make you a nice cup of tea as well?"

Contrary to my dire prediction, Papa and Mariah were very happy together, and continued to be so. I immersed myself more and more in the affairs of the estate, and my father seemed content for me to do this, his time being taken up with excursions and shopping trips and a hundred-and-one other activities designed to make Mariah happy. So involved did I become in my father's affairs that the news of his and Mariah's impending 'happy event' came as a considerable shock. I found myself fervently, if ignobly, wishing for the birth of a daughter, lest I lose the estate I loved so much.

In January of the following year, however, Mariah was brought to bed of a son, named by his doting parents Oliver Fordham Randall.

To say I was furious is to understate the case. Although Mariah could not inherit the estate on Papa's death, she would doubtless continue to live there, and I felt certain she would do her utmost to see to it that it went to her son, not to me, when she died. Seeing the two of them bent over their baby son, I felt cast off, like a piece of outdated furniture unwanted in their new life together. It is easy, in hindsight, to see how foolish this was, and how my own attitude stood to bring about the very outcome I most feared. At the time, however, I lacked the necessary insight, and so I made up my mind to pre-empt my inevitable fate and make my own future.

I would leave home.

But where should I go? Papa had offered to finance a Grand Tour of Europe when I finished my studies but, in my present state of mind, I was determined to accept nothing from him, so I banished that thought from my mind. He had a town house in Kensington, which had lain unused for some time, though I had happy memories of staying there with Mama and Papa each year during the London Season. Perhaps he would let me live there. But then it occurred to me that the new Lady Randall might well wish to stay there to enjoy the Season, and whatever the new Lady Randall wanted, it seemed Papa was only too delighted to provide. Fury gripped me at the thought of her presence defiling my mother's memory, her and her wretched usurper of a son.

Then I recalled my old university friend Charles Weston-Greer had written to me some weeks ago. Oliver's birth had driven it from my mind. Charles was in London for the Season, and had invited me to join him there. Well then, I would go, and for all I cared, Mariah and her brat could go straight to hell, where they belonged.

CHAPTER TWO

Having announced my intention to my father, I wasted little time in packing my bags. Papa agreed to my staying in the town house, although he warned me to expect no more than maintenance staff to be in residence. He also offered to drive me to Luton to catch the London train but, not wishing to be further indebted to one I viewed as the author of my misery, I asked Captain Nuttall to drive me instead. As we bowled along the road in the wintry sunshine, he made no reference to the reason for my sudden departure, although I knew he must have deduced it, even in the unlikely event no one had told him. He made a few commonplace remarks, but my monosyllabic replies were hardly conducive to conversation, and for the most part we travelled in awkward silence.

The journey to London did not take long, and by mid-afternoon I was standing on the platform at Euston Station surrounded by the clamour of human commerce and the smoky breath of trains, my baggage at my feet. Above the general hubbub I heard my name called, and Charles came sauntering towards me. At Cambridge, he had seemed a rather conservative young man. The approaching vision was dressed in the very height of gentlemanly fashion in cream-coloured trousers with the newly fashionable cuffs, a matching dress coat adorned with a large buttonhole of violets, and a white silk shirt with a tie swirling with mauve and pink roses and held with a diamond pin. His expertly coiffed brown curls shone with pomade and were crowned by the most amazing top hat I had ever seen; its curly brim was violet and the high crown boasted diagonal stripes of pink, purple and cream. His feet were clad in black patent-leather shoes. I felt positively dowdy in my dark-blue Norfolk jacket, grey trousers and plain blue tie.

But Charles seemed not to notice as he called out, "Hello, Alex old chap! So you finally got round to answering my letter. The Season's half over, now. Still, it's good to see you again. Let me get someone to carry your bags to the old jalopy."

The 'old jalopy' turned out to be a shiny new Rolls Royce motorcar in an aggressive shade of red. The porter Charles had commandeered to carry my bags stowed them in the boot and, before I could do anything about it, Charles handed him a handsome tip, saying as an aside to me, "My treat, old boy. Come on, hop in."

Once he had got the motor going—an energetic process that involved cranking the engine with a special handle—we sailed off into the London streets and, before long, reached Charles's club, the Cavendish, where he treated me again to a hearty lunch.

"You really must let me pay," I protested as we finished our meal.

Charles waved my offer aside. "No, no, I won't hear of it! It goes on my tab, and my accountant will settle it later. I'm a man of substance now, Alex. You remember I mentioned my Uncle Benjamin down in Sussex, rich as Croesus?" I nodded. "Well, he died last winter and left everything to me. He'd no children of his own," he added by way of explanation, "and no wife, so...behold, the new Croesus!" He drew a handsome gold watch from his pocket and consulted it. "I'll run you home now, Alex, and get you settled in. I'm off to the theatre this evening. You're more than welcome to join me."

"I should like that," I said. "My father's town house is in Kensington, Holland Park, not too far from here, I think?"

"Nonsense, old chap!" declared Charles. "You'll stay with me, of course. I'm staying at Uncle Ben's town house—well, mine now—in Brook Street for the Season, and I'm fed up with rattling round there on my own."

It was useless to protest, and if I'm honest, I was pleased to be relieved of the necessity of being beholden to Papa.

A short time later, I was being shown into an elegantly appointed room in Charles's fine Georgian house in Brook Street. When I had seen my bags unpacked, and changed into clean clothes, I repaired downstairs, where Charles waited for me in what the maid, quite appropriately, as I soon saw, referred to as 'the green sitting room'. As I entered, Charles stood up from his chair by the fire.

"Ah, Alex, would you care for some sherry? I've just had this particularly fine Amontillado imported directly from Spain."

He waved a languid hand towards a cut-crystal decanter and glasses on a small sideboard. In truth, I would just as soon have had tea, but it seemed churlish to refuse a wine imported directly from Spain, so I smiled and allowed Charles to pour me a glass, disposing myself in the fireside chair opposite his.

Charles sipped his sherry appreciatively, and then leaned towards me. "And what have you been up to since we came down from Cambridge? Surely you haven't merely been rusticating away in Bedfordshire?"

I laughed. "I'm ashamed to admit it, but I have. I've been helping to run my father's estate."

"Ah! Getting your hand in for when the old man shuffles off this mortal coil, eh? Very wise, Alex, an excellent stratagem." He fell silent for a moment as he saw the expression I could not hide. "Oh, I'm sorry, Alex. I didn't realise there was bad blood between you and your father."

"Not bad blood," I told him with a bitter laugh, "so much as foreign blood. I came down from Cambridge only to find Papa had remarried—mere months after Mama's death—and without a word to me. The new Lady Randall is an army widow half his age whose brother owns a neighbouring estate. And, if that wasn't enough, she's wasted no time in presenting him with a son. I tell you, Charles, the sight of the two of them cooing over the brat was more than flesh and blood could stand."

Charles nodded. "Ah, so that's why you've come up to London. I must say I don't blame you. Babies aren't much in my line, either."

"It's not just that, Charles. Ever since he was born, it's as though I don't exist any more. I've spent months learning to manage the estate—poured my heart and soul into it—but it seems that counts for nothing now there's a new son on the scene."

"Still, you're the eldest, aren't you, so you'll still inherit?"

"If the fair Mariah outlives Papa, and I should think she will, being at least thirty years his junior, then I dare say she'll be able to continue living at Shillington Hall. And since her brother owns the neighbouring estate, there's bound to be pressure on her to find a way to join the two together. In

15

fact, now I come to think of it, it wouldn't surprise me if that was their plan all along—her and her mealy-mouthed brother." I had not intended to tell Charles so much but, once started, I found myself unable to stop, and so the whole, sorry tale came tumbling out. "It's not the inheritance, *per se*, Charles," I concluded, "but Shillington Hall is my home! I was born there, and I've loved it ever since I was old enough to think about such things. I was brought up in the expectation of its being mine one day, and now... I feel betrayed, Charles, that's what it is. Betrayed!"

Charles nodded gravely, all his affectation gone. "I'm very sorry things have turned out so badly for you, Alex, and I can see why you didn't want to stay at Shillington. Look, you can stay here with me for as long as you want. I've oodles of lucre, I promise you. Uncle Ben left me exceedingly well provided for. I can live very comfortably indeed without ever touching my capital. We'll see out the Season here in London then, if you wish it, we can go to Compton, that's my estate in Sussex, you know, for the summer. There's excellent hunting and fishing to be had there, not to mention an extensive cellar. I'll invite a few others to join us. We'll have a famous time, I promise you!"

I could only smile at this veritable gusher of enthusiasm. "Thank you, Charles, I'll be glad to join you as long as you think you can stand my long face."

Charles laughed. "Oh, we'll soon do something about that! Let's dress for dinner now. I'm dining at the Savoy with Ferdy Smythe and a couple of other friends. You remember Ferdy, don't you? After that, we're going to the theatre— Gilbert and Sullivan— *The Pirates of Penzance*. I hear it's tremendous fun, and you're more than welcome to come with us, if you'd like it."

"You know, Charles," I replied, carried along, despite myself, by his enthusiasm, "I rather think I would!"

* * * *

Charles and I arrived at the Savoy to find Ferdy already there, and partaking of a whisky and soda aperitif. There were two men I didn't know sitting with him, no doubt the friends Charles had mentioned earlier. As soon as he saw us, Ferdy stood up, a smile lighting his face like a beam of sunshine.

"Ah, Charlie, here you are at last. And Alex! So glad you could join us. Charlie said you were coming to town."

With a smile, I shook his hand. "Hello, Ferdy, I see you've grown a beard. It suits you. You're a dead ringer for the Prince of Wales."

A look of pleasure suffused Ferdy's face. "You think so? Charlie doesn't like it, but I think he's just jealous because he can't grow a decent beard."

"I don't *want* to grow a beard," Charles retorted. "Besides, there's no such thing as a decent beard, don't you agree, Alex?"

"Leave me out of it," I demurred with a grin.

Ferdy suddenly clapped a hand to his brow. "Ah, where are my manners? Let me buy you both a drink. The usual, Charlie? Alex, what will you have?"

Charles's usual turned out to be whisky and soda. I wasn't in the habit of drinking whisky but, in my present reckless mood, this seemed as a good a time as any to start, so I told Ferdy I'd have the same. Having placed our orders, Ferdy

17

ushered us back to the table, and I was able to view the two strangers. One of these was a cheerful-looking man of around our own age, with thick, sandy hair and a freckled countenance. The other, some years older, was one of the most unusual-looking men I'd ever seen. Slim, and very elegantly dressed in a well-cut black suit and a waistcoat of grey moiré silk, his black hair, worn unfashionably long, fell in waves to frame a face all planes and angles, with moonlight-pale skin through which a faint tracery of veins was visible. His grey eyes were set deeply beneath straight, black brows. One could not have said he was handsome, but his face was certainly arresting. Its dramatic features called to mind a portrait I'd seen of the composer Franz Liszt.

As we approached the table, the two men got to their feet. Ferdy undertook the introductions. "Alex," he said, indicating the sandy-haired man, "I don't think you've met Eddie, have you? The Honourable Edward Montrose—Eddie to his friends. He was at Eton with me and Charles, though he went to Oxford afterwards. Eddie, Alex Randall, friend of ours from Cambridge. And this—,"he indicated the pale gentleman, "—is Henri de Saint-Clair, recently arrived from Paris."

Saint-Clair stepped forward to shake my hand. As his hand touched mine, I almost recoiled. His skin was as cold as ice. Perhaps, I thought, considering the pallor of his face, he suffered from some illness.

"Your servant, *M'sieu* Randall," he said. "It's a pleasure to meet you." His English was excellent, if perhaps a little old-fashioned, and his soft and melodious voice formed a marked contrast to his harsh features.

At that moment, our drinks arrived, and we all sat down

and made small talk while we waited for our meal.

Amidst much good-natured banter, we partook of a delightful dinner of buttered crabs and escallops of veal washed down with an excellent Pinot Noir, followed by strawberries and champagne, and finished off with brandy. Afterwards we strolled the short distance to the theatre, Ferdy puffing on the pipe he had presumably taken up to go with his beard.

The wit and humour of *The Pirates of Penzance*, and the company of old friends and new, were both just the tonic I needed to lift my spirits. By the time the curtain descended for the final time, all thoughts of my father's perfidy had been driven from my mind—at least for the time being.

"So," drawled Ferdy as we stepped into the chill night air, "what's next on the agenda?"

"We could go to the Cavendish," Charles suggested.

Ferdy's expression showed what he thought of that rather staid establishment. "No, no, let's go to Packham's. Bound to be a couple of good games going there."

"Packham's?" I queried.

"Poor Alex," said Charles with a grin. "You really have been out of circulation."

"I have heard of it, I just haven't been there," I replied, bridling a little at Charles's patronising tone. "Is it reckoned to be good?"

"I should say so!" Ferdy exclaimed. "It's not one of the older clubs, but that's all to the good, if you ask me, as it's not crowded with a bunch of old fuddy-duddies." So saying, he set off towards Piccadilly at a brisk pace, with the rest of us in tow.

Packham's, just off Piccadilly Circus, might not have been

one of London's more established clubs, but it was a respectable-looking establishment whose doorman could have been butler to any family of substance. He obviously knew Charles and Ferdy, as he greeted them by name.

"Mr Smythe, Mr Weston-Greer, gentlemen, good evening and welcome. I believe the Blue Room might be of interest this evening. May I take your hats and coats?"

Charles nodded. "Thanks, Chalmers."

From the vestibule, we passed into a commodious room stylishly decorated in cream and gold, and containing a roulette table and several tables set up for *vingt-et-un* and other games. Open double doors at the end of this room led to a further large room set about with card tables. Its décor proclaimed it to be the aforementioned Blue Room. Charles and Ferdy's unerring instincts led us to the whist table, where two young men were sitting.

"Evening, Butterworth, Harleigh," said Ferdy. "You know Charles, don't you?" He went on to introduce the rest of us.

"I don't suppose you'd be interested in a rubber of whist?" enquired Butterworth, whose golden curls formed a halo about a plump, pink face, giving him the look of a Botticelli cherub. "Algy and I were hoping to find someone to play with."

Charles showed immediate enthusiasm, but then his face fell. "There are too many of us for whist," he pointed out, adding in hopeful tones, "unless two of us are prepared to stand down, of course."

Since I had never much cared for whist, I offered to forfeit the rubber.

"I, also, shall be only too happy to sit the game out," offered Saint-Clair. "Mr Randall, would you care to join me?"

He asked one of the waiters to bring us a bottle of burgundy and two glasses, and led the way to a small table by one of the windows.

"You do not like whist, sir?" I asked as he poured the wine.

He shrugged, in that way peculiar to the French. "Oh yes, I like it well enough, but I think Charles and Ferdy like it more."

I smiled. Saint-Clair had read my friends only too well. "Have you been in London for long, Monsieur de Saint-Clair?"

"No, not long. But won't you please call me Henri? Monsieur de Saint-Clair is a trifle unwieldy, *n'est ce pas*?"

"Then you must call me Alex," I said.

He nodded his acquiescence, and sipped his wine. "Am I to understand you've recently completed your studies, Alex?"

"Yes, I've just come down from Cambridge—King's College."

"Ah, an excellent college, or so I've heard."

I nodded. "My father thought so. He didn't have the benefit of a good education himself, but he was determined that I should. And I must say I was glad to be shot of tutors and teachers at long last."

"So you weren't sent to school, then? It was my understanding that the sons of the English aristocracy were sent off to boarding school as soon as they were out of the nursery."

I suspected he was making fun of me, but decided to ignore it. "I was tutored at home for some years, because of what my mother called my 'delicate constitution', but I was, as you suggest, sent to boarding school when I was thirteen.

However, I'm sorry to disappoint you, Monsieur, but I'm afraid I'm not a son of the aristocracy. My father made his fortune in mining."

"A captain of industry, then." His tone was grave, but I was sure he was still teasing me.

"Precisely," I returned with a grin. "Though he's certainly a gentleman now, if not quite of the aristocracy. Having amassed his fortune, he bought an estate in Bedfordshire— Shillington Hall, where I was born and grew up—and a baronetcy to go with it."

"I see. I suppose one cannot but admire a society so pragmatic as to allow titles to be bought and sold. It grieves me to agree with such a man, but it seems Napoleon was right, the English really are a nation of shopkeepers."

I could not help feeling aggrieved by this disdainful dismissal of my countrymen. "Indeed," I retorted with spirit, "and I confess I'm very grateful for it, since it has allowed me a fine education and the ability to pass myself off as a gentleman."

"I do beg your pardon," he said quickly. "That was unforgiveable of me. I'm afraid old habits die hard, sometimes."

It was on the tip of my tongue to ask him what he meant by this, but I felt he might take it amiss and, for all that his casual arrogance had annoyed me, some instinct warned me against angering him. We sat in awkward silence for some minutes, sipping our wine, before he spoke again, in a more conciliatory tone.

"May I ask what you studied at Cambridge?"

"I read English literature and philosophy."

"Ah, then we have something in common. Tell me, did

you study the philosophy of Immanuel Kant? I find much to admire in his ideas, in particular his attempts to reconcile empiricism and reason."

"Oh, yes, we read him. I was much taken with him, too. I admired his bravery in pursuing his precepts, given the age in which he lived and, of course, his influence on subsequent thinking. But I'd have thought you'd be more interested in the French philosophers, Descartes, for example."

The awkwardness between us now dispersed, we became engrossed in an animated discussion of the relative merits of various philosophies, and it was with a feeling akin to disappointment that I looked up to see Charles and Ferdy standing by our table.

"Algy and Butters have left," Charles announced. "I think the play was becoming a trifle too deep for their pockets. Shall we make up a four for another rubber of whist? Or would you prefer to play something else?"

Henri took out a handsome silver pocket watch and consulted it. "I'm afraid I must also leave," he said.

"I've enjoyed our conversation tremendously," I told him. "I do hope we'll meet again while you're in London. I'm staying with Charles. Do you know his address?"

"Oh, yes," he replied with his odd half smile.

"Charles," I said, "would you mind if I ask Henri to call on us one day soon?"

"Oh, Henri doesn't go about during the day," Charles said with a dismissive wave of his hand. He turned to Henri, who had got to his feet and was showing evidence of wishing to leave without delay. "But do come and dine with us next week, say Tuesday? You too, Ferdy."

Henri nodded. "Thank you, I shall enjoy that very much."

He gave a slight bow and left.

It was only afterwards I realised that, although he now knew my background in some detail, not a single thing did I know about him beyond a few impressions gleaned from our conversation: namely, that he had a very perceptive mind, and appeared to have read widely. One thing I did know, however: I was very curious to learn more about the enigmatic Henri de Saint-Clair.

CHAPTER THREE

Over the ensuing weeks, my acquaintance with Henri de Saint-Clair developed into a friendship based on our mutual interest in philosophy and what I suppose I should call the psychology of human nature. The fact that we did not always agree lent a vigour to our discussions that perfect accord could never have achieved, since it led us to explore fascinating byways we might otherwise have ignored. Little by little, I came to admire Henri for his breadth and depth of knowledge, and to like him for his dry humour and unfailing cordiality—at least to me. Some of his comments showed a touch of the arrogance with which he had commented on my father's acquisition of his baronetcy, and it was clear Monsieur de Saint-Clair did not suffer fools gladly. For myself, I favoured a more conciliatory approach, but Henri, with a smile, declared that to be more due to my English devotion to good manners than to any innate charity. With a rueful smile, I had to admit he might very well be right.

As I grew to know Henri better, I discovered Charles's off-hand comment about his never going abroad during the day was quite literally the case. One morning at breakfast, I asked Charles where he lived, so I might call on him and leave my card.

Charles shrugged, and reached for another piece of toast. "I haven't the foggiest, old chap. Plays his cards pretty close to his chest, does Saint-Clair. In any case, he's made it clear to us he's not at home to visitors during the day. Fact is, I think he's a trifle eccentric. You know how these continentals can be. But, live and let live, you know, that's my motto."

"How did you meet him?" I asked. "I'd have thought he was little—um—serious for the likes of you and Ferdy." I'd been about to say 'old', but thought better of it, since I suspected my friends considered themselves rather more mature than they sometimes seemed to me.

"I believe he was an acquaintance of Ferdy's cousin Horace—the one who died suddenly just before Christmas. According to Ferdy, Horace met Henri while he was visiting Paris last summer, and invited him over for a visit. He'd not long arrived in London when poor old Horace cashed in his chips, so Ferdy offered to show him the town. You know how Ferdy is."

I nodded. It would have been hard to find a friendlier fellow than Ferdy, or a more gregarious one. It had been he who took me under his wing when I first arrived at Cambridge, introducing me to Charles and his other friends, and generally making me feel less like a fish out of water.

Conversation between us lapsed as we addressed ourselves to the last of our breakfast. When Charles's butler, Hetherington, brought in the coffee, along with the morning newspapers and the mail, Charles, after the briefest of glances at the latter, picked up *The Times* and began to leaf through it.

"Good Lord!" he exclaimed, thrusting the paper in my direction. "Look at this, Alex. They're saying the Whitechapel killer might be abroad again."

I took the proffered paper, which Charles had folded to

highlight an article headed: 'London Deaths Raise Spectre of Whitechapel Murders'. Intrigued, I read on:

'The bodies of two women lately discovered in London's East End have raised fears of a killer in the mode of the Whitechapel murderer popularly known as Jack the Ripper. However, the *modus operandi* bears little resemblance to the gruesome mutilations of 1888, and neither of the victims was a prostitute. The Police have identified the two women as Mrs Ada Thorpe, thirty-three, a shop assistant of Camberwell, and Miss Mary Miller, twenty-five, a barmaid of Shoreditch. Both bodies were found in areas close to where they lived or worked. In marked contrast to the Whitechapel victims, neither exhibited signs of violence, yet, in both cases, severe blood loss was evident. Both Police and medical investigators are baffled as to the cause of this, although they are certain it must have been the cause of death. Investigations are ongoing, and any members of the public privy to information that might help the Police are requested to contact Inspector Reginald Jolliffe at Scotland Yard.'

With a shudder, I handed the newspaper back to Charles, exclaiming, "How can people do such dreadful things? And what a shocking way to die."

"Do you think it can be Jack the Ripper on the prowl again?" Charles asked with ghoulish enthusiasm.

I shook my head. "I shouldn't think so. The paper says the method used is quite different, and neither of the victims was a prostitute, whereas all the Ripper's were."

"Hmm." Charles seemed almost disappointed. "Still, they might have been 'no better than they ought to be', as my Mama was wont to say. I wonder how the killer managed to drain their blood, though. I shouldn't think it would be easy without medical knowledge, and they do say Jack the Ripper was a medical man..."

I almost choked over my coffee. "Charles! How can you be so morbid? And no one deserves such a horrid fate, no matter how they may have lived."

"Sorry, Vicar," said Charles with an unrepentant grin. "Still, you have to admit it's an intriguing mystery."

"It is," I agreed, "and one best left to the Police, don't you think?"

"Never fear," said Charles. "I've no intention of visiting the East End, for that or any other purpose. But I'll keep an eye on the papers. You never know, they might manage to find out how a body can be drained of blood without any sign of violence." He set down his empty coffee cup and got to his feet. "Ferdy and I are driving out to Newmarket later this morning. His father has asked him to look out for a new hack for his sister, Julia. There's a very snug little inn nearby where we thought we'd have luncheon before driving home, so it should be an enjoyable outing. You're welcome to come with us, Alex, unless you have other plans."

I had been contemplating a trip to the British Museum to see the new exhibition of Egyptian artefacts, but a drive into the country in Charles's splendid motorcar, even on a winter's day, seemed more appealing, so I agreed to his proposal.

Shortly after eleven o'clock, Ferdy arrived at Brook Street along with Eddie Montrose, and the four of us, well wrapped up against the nipping air, set off. It proved, as Charles had predicted, an agreeable excursion. At the back of my mind, however, lurked the grisly thought of bodies drained of blood, yet with no clue as to how this could have been

28

achieved. What sort of creature could commit such a ghastly act—and why?

* * * *

A week or so after our excursion to Newmarket, Charles decided to give a party. He sent out what seemed to me an inordinate number of invitations or, rather, he had his secretary do this for him, and then set about giving orders to Hetherington for food and drink to be procured for the event.

When I queried such large-scale preparations, he gave an airy wave of his hand. "Pooh, nonsense, Alex! It's by way of welcoming you to London, so it's going to be a bang-up do. Oh, and while I think of it, we're going to have to get you some decent clothes. If I'm going to introduce you to the cream of London society, you don't want to be mistaken for Tony Lumpkin, do you?"

I couldn't help but laugh at this reference to the country-bumpkin from Oliver Goldsmith's play, especially as I'd played the role in a production by the Footlights Dramatic Society in our final year at Cambridge.

"Charles," I protested, "how can you bring up my ignominious past when I'm just beginning to be a man about town?"

"Not in those clothes, you aren't," he averred, eyeing the offending garments with disdain, albeit with a twinkle in his eye. "Get your hat and gloves, Alex. I'm taking you to see my tailor."

"I'll thank you not to cast aspersions on my father's tailor," I told him with a fair approximation of wounded dignity. "I consider my attire perfectly respectable and in keeping with the status of a gentleman, and I see no point in wasting good money on clothes I don't need."

"Oh, they're all very well if you want to look like a country parson," Charles said, "but I assure you they won't do for the city. And you won't need to pay a penny. I can take care of that."

"I'll go with you," I conceded, "but I insist on paying for my own clothes. And I won't have your man dressing me like a popinjay, either," I added, eyeing Charles's extravagant get-up.

"Pleb!" pronounced Charles, grinning. "Come along, then. We'll pick Ferdy up on the way and have lunch at the Cavendish afterwards."

An hour or so later, the three of us entered the portals of Frobisher and Sons, Gentlemen's Outfitters. This was not one of the august establishments of Savile Row, but respected, nonetheless, and—or so Charles assured me—very popular with the younger set. Naturally, there was no possibility of my bespeaking an outfit at such short notice, although Young Mr Frobisher, a rather frail-looking gentleman of some seventy years, measured me for future reference. However, I was able to purchase a very fashionable morning coat of charcoal-grey worsted and trousers of a lighter grey, two fine-linen shirts and a selection of silk ties, although nothing as flamboyant as those affected by Charles and Ferdy. To complement these I selected one of the modern trilby hats. I already had evening dress, but my friends insisted I needed a more up-to-date outfit.

"What on earth for?" I protested. "The one I have is only

two years old, and I can't have worn it above half a dozen times."

Charles and Ferdy looked at one another in horror. "Two years!" exclaimed Charles. "Good Lord, Alex, these days a suit is out of fashion if you've worn it for one season!"

Having listened to them thus far, however, I remained steadfast in ignoring their impassioned arguments, maintaining that, since men's evening attire had barely changed throughout the Queen's long reign, my black cutaway coat and trousers would be more than adequate. However, since first setting eyes on Charles at Euston Station, I had coveted a pair of black patent-leather shoes, so I duly purchased these. Charles, of course, wanted me to buy a tall topper such as he and Ferdy wore. I protested I already had a perfectly serviceable top hat. A pained expression came over Charles's face, but I was determined not to waste money on a hat for which I had no real need, and he contented himself with no more protest than sighing and rolling his eyes.

Charles having ordered my purchases to be delivered to Brook Street that afternoon, we were about to leave when he stopped suddenly in his tracks. "Wait, there's one more thing you must have, and I insist that it be my treat." After several minutes' conference in camera with Mr Frobisher, he returned bearing a small, dark-blue box. "Here you are, Alex, this will set everything off beautifully."

I opened the box to see a finely wrought gold tiepin set with a row of tiny diamonds either side of a garnet the colour of fine ruby port. "Charles, this is simply splendid! I'm very much in your debt."

"Nonsense, old chap. Half the fun of being filthy rich is

being able to treat one's friends. Call it a welcoming gift to your new life in London."

"Charles, you have an answer for everything!"

"And the question of the moment," put in Ferdy, who had been flicking through the pages of a style book in a desultory manner, "is when shall we eat lunch?"

His mission now completed, Charles took each of us by the arm and we set off together for the Cavendish.

* * * *

The night of Charles's party, though cold, was mercifully free of the rain that had fallen on and off for the best part of a week. As I dressed for the evening, I glanced out of my bedroom window to see a pale crescent moon sailing in a night sky clouded by the smoke drifting upwards from a million chimneys, and thought of the clear skies of home, teeming with stars all but invisible here in the city. A pang of homesickness shot through me, but then I recalled why I had come to London, gave a resolute shake of my head, and resumed the tricky task of tying my bow tie.

Satisfied at last that I met my own sartorial standards, if not those of Charles or Ferdy, I made my way downstairs to the drawing room. Charles and Ferdy were there, along with Eddie Montrose, George Butterworth, and Algy Harleigh, whom I'd met at Packham's. Charles had already told me we were to be an all-male party for dinner, assuring me with a grin that there would be ample female company for the party proper. As I greeted my fellow dinner guests, I found myself looking about me as though expecting another to be present, and realised I had been hoping to find Henri de Saint-Clair, whom I had not seen for almost a fortnight. I walked across to where Charles was dispensing sherry.

"Is Henri dining with us?" I asked.

Charles handed me a glass. "No, he had an appointment elsewhere, but I believe he'll be along later."

I nodded. "Just as a matter of interest, how did you get an invitation to him if you don't know where he lives?"

"Oh, I ran into him the other evening in Pall Mall. He has something of a knack for turning up just when one is hoping to see him."

I gave another nod, and wandered off to chat with Ferdy. A short time later, dinner was announced and we all filed into the dining room, where the dinner table sat resplendent with starched white damask, silver cutlery, and Royal Doulton china.

The first party guests began to arrive just as we were finishing our port, and an hour later, with the heavy oak dining table pushed back against one wall to provide more space, both dining and drawing rooms were packed with guests, their cheerful chatter and laughter all but drowning out the music of the string quartet Charles had hired for the occasion. A smaller room adjoining the dining room had been set aside for those who wished to play cards, but I was so filled with nervous excitement I lacked the concentration for such a pursuit. Instead, I wandered from room to room, observing the milling crowd. There were a number of men I recognised from either the Cavendish Club or Packham's, but many more I did not. Most were fashionable young gentlemen, with the odd smattering of rougher-looking characters, perhaps from the racing or fighting circles I knew Charles and his set frequented. As Charles had intimated, there were plenty of ladies in attendance. Many of them, I suspected from their dramatic attire and make-up, from the world of the theatre; indeed, I was sure I recognised two or three from the chorus of *The Pirates of Penzance*. Charles introduced me to several of them but, despite his having transformed me into a man about town, I felt more than a little intimidated by such worldly and confident young women.

It was quite late in the evening before Henri made his appearance. He was looking in particularly fine fettle, I thought. When I had first met him, I had noticed his pallid, almost unhealthy complexion, and a certain quality in his dark eyes that had made me wonder if he might be haunted by some deep sadness, or some lingering pain, perhaps. Now, his eyes sparkled with life, and his cheeks and lips were touched with a rosy glow. It occurred to me he might suffer from tuberculosis, which I had heard caused such effects, but of course good manners forbade my asking. In any case, we were soon deep in conversation, and my curiosity receded.

Next morning, over a very late breakfast, Charles teased me about my backwardness with the ladies.

"Really, Alex, after I take the trouble to introduce you to several particularly stunning young ladies, what must you do but ensconce yourself with Henri for hours on end." He paused, his toast halfway to his mouth. "I say, you're not...?"

"No, Charles, I am not!" I assured him, buttering my toast with unnecessary attention to hide my embarrassment.

"Thank God for that!" Charles exclaimed. "You wouldn't want to end up like that fellow Wilde, would you?"

"Have no fear, Charles," I said with the hint of a smile. "I lack both Mr Wilde's wit and his flamboyancy. My trouble, if such it is, is that I'm not very used to female company, and certainly not that of such dashing females as I met last night."

Charles nodded, his eyes belying his grave expression. "Well, we'll have to do something about that, won't we?"

At that moment, Hetherington brought in the coffee tray. Charles picked up his mail and flicked through it. "More dratted bills," he said, pushing them to one side. "Take them away, please, Hetherington. Jarvis can deal with them later." Robert Jarvis was Charles's secretary, although as far as I could see his only duties were writing letters and invitations and juggling Charles's many bills. Charles poured coffee for us both, and then picked up *The Times* and began to peruse the front page. "I see they've found another body," he commented, "though this one appears to have been killed some weeks ago."

An involuntary shudder ran through me. "Drained of blood, like the other two?"

"Yes, though this one was a man, a coachman called Bartholomew Wallace. His wife went to the Police when he didn't come home for his supper after work, and they found his body this morning in Hyde Park. So much for its being Jack the Ripper."

"We must be thankful for that, at least," I said, "though it must mean some other vile killer is on the loose."

"Well, I dare say the Peelers will soon have him safely in custody." I forbore to mention that Jack the Ripper had never been caught. "Unless it's a vampire, of course," Charles added, "you know, like Count Dracula, and that other chap— who was it? Oh, yes, 'Varney the Vampire'."

"That's just silly, Charles," I said with a grin. "You know as well as I do that vampires don't really exist."

He nodded, returning my grin. "Pity, though. It would be a lot more interesting than some boring old murderer."

I shook my head and addressed myself to my coffee while Charles continued to peruse *The Times*.

At length, Charles laid down the newspaper. "I see there's a new Gilbert and Sullivan playing at the Savoy," he said, "*The Mikado*. Why don't we get up a party and go along on Friday night?"

As I had enjoyed *The Pirates of Penzance* so much, I was happy to agree to this, and Charles said he would get Jarvis to deliver notes to Ferdy and a few other friends. "And I'll get him to book us a table for dinner at the Savoy as well. In the meantime, how would you like to visit the Tower of London this afternoon? I dare say you haven't seen it before."

"I haven't," I agreed. "Is it as gruesome as they say?"

"I should say so!" Charles exclaimed with enthusiasm. "You can see the Crown Jewels there, of course, and the rooms where all sorts of famous people were imprisoned, but the best bit is all the instruments in the torture chamber downstairs." He twisted his face into a ghoulish grimace and added, in a creaking voice, "If we're really lucky, we might even see the ghost of Anne Boleyn."

CHAPTER FOUR

The following evening, Charles and I repaired to the Savoy Hotel, where we found Ferdy waiting for us at our table, along with Eddie Montrose and another slightly older man in the dress uniform of a cavalry officer, who, from his appearance, I guessed was related to Ferdy.

"Evening, you two," Ferdy called to us. "Come and meet my cousin, Clarence. He's just back from India, and I've offered to show him around." A few moments later, another young man with sandy hair, whom I recognised from Cambridge, arrived.

"Ah, Forrest," said Charles, "I hoped you'd be able to make it." He turned to me. "You remember Tom Forrest, Alex? He was reading philosophy with you, I believe."

"Yes," I said, holding out my hand to him. "I remember. You have a sister, Charlotte, if I'm not mistaken. Pretty girl with red curls."

"Everyone remembers Charlotte," he said with a laugh. "I positively pale by comparison. But she's out of bounds, now, you fellows take note. Married the Honourable Frank Cottrell last spring, and they're expecting their first in January."

"Thanks for the warning," Charles said. "I was always very fond of Charlotte. Still, plenty more fish in the sea, eh?"

He winked at me in a way that made me wince. "Now, are

we all here? Let's order, then, shall we?"

He signalled a waiter, who brought us the menu and stood by while we made our choices. As we waited, I murmured to Charles, "I see Henri isn't here. Were you unable to get in touch with him?"

Ferdy, overhearing me, said, "Oh, hadn't you heard? I thought I'd mentioned it to Charlie. Henri's left London. I ran into him a few nights ago, Wednesday I think it must have been, because I was on my way to my Aunt Agatha's whist party, and he told me he was leaving next day."

I felt oddly bereft at these casual words. Although I had known him for only a short time, my conversations with Henri had been some of the most enjoyable moments I could remember. Indeed, for all I enjoyed the company of my other friends, with Henri I felt understood in a deeper way, as though we communicated soul to soul. Of course I could not express these feelings to my friends for fear of ridicule, so I merely observed, "That was rather sudden."

"That's what I thought," said Ferdy, "but he said something about urgent business in the north, of all places. What on earth anyone could find to do up there, I can't imagine. I must say, Charlie, this is an excellent Hock. I must see if I can get hold of some."

During dinner, Ferdy's cousin regaled us with tales of military life in India but, although he was an amusing raconteur, I found myself thinking of Henri, and wishing I had had a chance to say goodbye to him, and to ask him to keep in touch with me. Whether he would have done so, of course, was a moot point, and now I could only suppose he had not wished to continue our friendship. It was in an unexpectedly despondent mood that I left with the others for the theatre.

The play, however, cheered me up considerably. After all, who could fail to enjoy the wit and the music of Gilbert and Sullivan? During the second interval, Charles leaned across to me and whispered, "What did you think of the Three Little Maids, Alex?"

"I thought they were delightful. They sang rather well, too."

"Yes, well, Ferdy and I know them quite well, and we've invited them to supper after the show."

I nodded. "That sounds pleasant."

"What I mean is," continued Charles with a wink, "Ferdy and I are good friends with two of them— *very* good friends, if you take my meaning—and we thought you should meet the third."

I was spared the necessity thinking up a suitable response when the curtain rose for the third act. During the course of this, Charles nudged me and pointed out the young lady I was to meet, a redhead whose large, sparkling eyes seemed to hold the promise of fun. I found myself looking forward to making her acquaintance and nervous, both at the same time.

After the final curtain, while we were waiting for the Three Little Maids to change out of their costumes and come to Charles's box, we polished off the champagne Ferdy had ordered earlier. At length, we heard approaching footsteps.

"Ah, here they are!" Charles jumped up and went to hold back the curtain for our guests. Charles and Ferdy gave each of them a kiss. "Ladies," said Charles, his arm about the waist of a pretty blonde whose cornflower-blue gown matched her eyes, "may I introduce to you our good friend,

Mr Alex Randall. Alex, this is Miss Lucy Devereux, and this —" He indicated the slim, brown-haired girl whose arm Ferdy had taken "—is Miss Polly Marchant."

I bowed to each of them in turn.

Charles drew forward the redhead, who smiled at me in a friendly, unaffected way and held out her hand as the others had done. "And this," said Charles, with a surreptitious wink in my direction, "is Miss Emmeline Beaumont."

I found myself looking into smiling eyes of an arresting sea green, fringed with long lashes I suspected were artificially darkened. The red hair piled up on her head and held with a green ribbon probably owed at least some of its colour to henna, but it looked no less charming for that as it framed a quizzical face dusted with pale freckles. She had on a sea-green taffeta gown that admirably enhanced her neat figure. I had been nervous about meeting her, but her friendly manner put me immediately at ease, and there was no denying I found her attractive.

I took her proffered hand and gave a slight bow. "I'm very pleased to meet you, Miss Beaumont."

"Oh, please, call me Emmeline. 'Miss Beaumont' makes me sound like someone's governess."

"I can't imagine anyone mistaking you for a governess," I assured her, with a grin. "If my own governesses had been half as pretty, I'm sure I'd have paid far more attention to them."

"Yes," Charles put in, "but not to your lessons."

"At any rate," I said, "Emmeline is such a charming name I shall be only too happy to use it at every available opportunity."

"Oh, very prettily said!" exclaimed Miss Marchant.

"Don't you think so, Ferdy?"

"What I think," said Ferdy, giving her arm an affectionate squeeze, "is that we're all in need of our supper."

He led the way out of the theatre. Emmeline tucked her arm into mine and we all followed Ferdy to a small café not far from the theatre. The dapper little man who came to wait on us clearly knew Charles and Ferdy as well as the young ladies.

"Good evening, sirs and young ladies, I do hope you've had a pleasant evening. Would you care to order now?"

"We'll have a bottle of champagne to start with," said Charles, "and Oysters Mornay, I think."

"Ooh!" exclaimed Miss Devereux. "You know just what I like, don't you, Charlie?"

"I like to think so," Charles murmured with a look that made it clear he was referring to more than just food.

I smiled to myself. I was clearly in what my father would have referred to as 'fast company' and, a little to my surprise, I found I intended to enjoy every moment of it. The thought of earning his disapproval, even if he would never know of it, merely added to my gratification. Over oysters and champagne, followed by raspberries and cream, and more champagne, the six of us carried on an animated conversation punctuated by much laughter. I found Emmeline a charming companion with a ready wit, an infectious laugh, and a manner that was affectionate without being over-familiar.

All too soon, however, our supper came to an end. As Charles went off to pay the bill, Ferdy leaned back in his chair.

"Well, ladies, the night's still young. What would you like

to do now?"

"Let me see," said Miss Marchant in a teasing voice, "the music halls will be closed, and we dare not go to a club. It'd be more than our reputations are worth, even if those tyrants who keep the doors would let us in. Oh, I know! Why don't we go to Jonty's party?"

Ferdy eyed her suspiciously. "Who's Jonty?"

"Oh, Ferdy, I do believe you're jealous!" exclaimed Miss Marchant, leaning across to ruffle his beard. "Jonty is our stage manager, silly. He's giving a party at our lodgings—in honour of his *fiftieth* birthday."

She emphasised the gentleman's age presumably to reassure Ferdy he had nothing to fear from a man of such advanced years. I could have told him a different story, but refrained from puncturing his illusions. Charles returned and readily agreed to Miss Marchant's suggestion, so we all piled into two hackney cabs and set off for Soho, where the theatrical company was lodging.

The boarding house was one of those tall, narrow buildings often found in the older parts of the city, so crammed together they seem in danger of squashing one another. The narrow door led to a dark passageway that smelled, paradoxically, of dust and furniture polish. An even narrower staircase led up to what were presumably bedrooms on the upper floors, but the young ladies led us along the hallway and into a spacious sitting room with a quantity of old-fashioned furniture, and red-plush curtains with fringes. The room was a hubbub of colourfully attired people, all of whom seemed to be talking at the tops of their voices. An ancient pianoforte in one corner added to the clamour as a stick-thin gentleman in a black-velvet smoking jacket coaxed a selection of popular songs from its yellowed keys.

As we entered, a plump-faced older man with thinning, sandy hair broke away from his companions and came to greet us. Miss Marchant introduced him to us as Jonty Arbuthnot, and Charles did the honours on our behalf.

"Come and get a drink!" Jonty urged. "Will has made us some of his special punch, but we've plenty of wine, or there's gin and porter if you'd prefer them."

He led the way to a table on which stood a large silver punchbowl, a variety of bottles and jugs, and a quantity of glasses of all shapes and sizes. The ladies made a beeline for the punchbowl and I decided to join them, while Charles and Ferdy settled for sparkling wine. Whatever Will had put into his punch, it certainly lived up to its name. A couple of glasses of it had me convinced I must sit down for a while.

Emmeline took my arm and steered me towards a large chair. As I sank gratefully into it, she perched herself on its arm, draped an arm about my shoulders and leaned her cheek against mine. Her skin was soft and warm and smelt of powder and a sweet, spicy perfume. Any lingering nervousness left me as I breathed in Emmeline's heady scent. I slid my arm around her waist and, with a rustle of taffeta, she leaned down and kissed me on the mouth. Of course I returned her kiss—how could I help myself?—and soon we were twined together in an ardent embrace. Delicious sensations flooded my being, and a sweet longing overtook me. This was how the poets described love, I thought as I revelled in the sensation of Emmeline's lithe body against mine. Of course I knew it was not love I was feeling, poetic or otherwise; it was a far more basic human urge. But what did I care? Right now, all I wanted was Emmeline's soft lips against mine, and to feel her body's warmth through the silk of her gown. Thus I gave myself up with enthusiasm to the moment.

As the party wound down to its end, I realised with some surprise it was half past two in the morning.

Emmeline gently disengaged herself and murmured in my ear, "It's been lovely meeting you, Alex, but I need my sleep if I'm to perform well tonight."

I traced the line of her cheek gently with my forefinger. "May I see you again?"

"I don't see why not. You know where to find me."

"Yes." I kissed the corner of her mouth. "You'll not escape me now."

Her mouth curved up in a smile. "Who says I want to?"

"You're as intoxicating as wine," I murmured.

She smiled, her eyes teasing. "And I think you've had quite enough for now."

She kissed me lightly on the lips, and then jumped up and left the room, blowing me another kiss from the doorway.

As I followed Charles and Ferdy along the narrow passageway and out into the night, I thought: enough for now, perhaps, but I fully intended to drink again from that sweet cup.

The cold night air was almost like a blow to the face as I stepped out onto the pavement.

Charles, who was leaning against a lamppost looking elegantly dissolute, pushed himself upright and grinned at me. "Didn't I tell you they were charmers, Alex?"

I grinned back, or, rather, smiled beatifically. I could still smell Emmeline's perfume on my clothes. I felt light-headed, and it was not just from the alcohol I had drunk, though I had imbibed a prodigious quantity, for me.

As soon as the three of us reached Brook Street, I took myself off to bed, refusing my friends' offer of a nightcap. The rest of the night passed for me in a pleasant blur of dreams of soft red hair and warm, perfumed skin.

* * * *

I finally regained consciousness some time after noon the following day, with a splitting headache and a mouth that felt like a well-travelled, dusty road and tasted about as bad. Charles was already up and dressed when I staggered from my room in my dressing gown.

"Good Lord, Alex, you look like death warmed up! Not used to high living, eh?"

"Not since I left Cambridge, at any rate," I admitted with a grimace.

"Never mind, we'll soon set you to rights." He reached out and tugged on the bell cord. Almost immediately, his manservant appeared. "Ah, Hetherington, can you bring Alex one of your special restoratives? And ask Mary to draw him a bath, if you please."

Hetherington bowed and left to pursue his errands, returning a short time later carrying a tumbler filled with a viscous, chalky-looking liquid.

"What is it?" I demanded, eyeing Charles with suspicion.

"Don't ask, just drink it. It'll help, I promise you."

Whether it was the vile-tasting elixir or the long, hot bath that did the trick, by mid-afternoon I felt well enough to partake of some tea and bread and butter.

Charles, who was lounging in his favourite chair by the fire, looked across at me through half-closed eyes and drawled, "I had no idea what an *ingénue* you were, Alex."

I shrugged, not entirely pleased by this opinion of me.

"Ah, well, I trust you enjoyed last night's introduction?"

"Enormously, thank you, those parts I can remember, but I really shouldn't have drunk so much."

"Oh, you'll soon learn the knack of it. I'm glad I introduced you to Emmeline, though. The two of you seemed to be getting along quite famously—if you take my meaning."

I knew Charles was merely teasing me, but I was obliged to hide my blushes behind my teacup, furious with myself for appearing the innocent he thought me.

"Tell me, Charles," I said, as much to change the subject as anything, "what is it that's wrought such a change in you? At Cambridge, you seemed rather a serious young man, certainly not given to dressing—or behaving—as flamboyantly as you do now.'

"It's very simple, Alex. It's money that's changed me. When I left Cambridge, I imagined myself bound for a career in a legal office, or something of that sort. But when Uncle Ben died and left me his fortune, I very quickly realised I had other options. I've no need for a career now. And you know what, Alex? When you're as rich as I am, you can do almost anything and nobody gives a damn. And what I've chosen to do is to have fun—as much of it as I possibly can."

"Don't you wish for a wife, a family?"

"Good Lord, no! At any rate, not for a long time yet. Why should I want to settle down with one woman when I can have my pick of them, practically for the asking? Well, obviously not the sort my parents would approve of, but their approval is another thing obviated by the possession of a fortune. As for children, if you'd seen all my ghastly nephews and nieces, it would soon disabuse you of *that* idea."

I could not help smiling a little at the picture he drew, although it disappointed me to see he had become so selfish.

"Then you'd better take care your—er—enjoyment doesn't produce any accidentally."

"Oh, there are ways to avoid that," said Charles with an airy wave of his hand. "And if worse comes to worst, why, I dare say money will solve that, too."

"I dare say," I replied, more than a little shocked at his apparent callousness, and found myself wondering whether my friend's supposed good fortune had been as beneficial as he thought it.

CHAPTER FIVE

Although I thought of her often, I made myself wait for several days before calling on Emmeline. It would not do, I told myself, to seem desperate. At last, however, my desire to see her again overrode my wish to seem calm and collected. I decided to call on her in the afternoon in case she needed to sleep late after her performance, and whatever activities she might have undertaken afterwards, though I found I preferred not to dwell on these in case they involved other men. On a Wednesday afternoon, then, I set out for Soho, deciding to walk, since the weather was fine and I felt in need of the exercise. The day was clear and cool and, although I enjoyed walking, the dingy streets, with the grime of soot on every building, brought home to me just how much I missed the clean air of the countryside. The very sky seemed clogged with the constant outpouring of chimney smoke. When I reached Emmeline's lodgings, I realised I had no idea which room might be hers. The front door was unlocked, so I ventured into the dim hallway and stared about me as if hoping to find a clue.

As I stood there, an older man who looked as though he might be a porter came down the stairs carrying, of all things, a large, pink porcelain umbrella stand.

"Good day to you, sir," he said on noticing me, "and what was it you was wanting?"

"I was hoping to call on Miss Beaumont, if she's at home to visitors."

"I don't know about that, but her room's number sixteen, on the first floor."

"Thank you."

I waited only for him to quit the staircase before hurrying up it. Outside room sixteen, a sudden nervousness assailed me. Would Emmeline even want to see me? How did I know she was not, at this very moment, ensconced behind that door with another lover? Her free behaviour with me at Jonty Arbuthnot's party suggested this might not be beyond the bounds of possibility. Somehow, however, I managed to summon the courage to knock on her door.

Her voice called out, "Just a moment." I heard footsteps, and the swish of silk, then the door opened to reveal Emmeline, looking just as lovely as when I had met her. Did I say she looked as lovely as before? No, she looked lovelier— a nymph of the woods, wrapped in a leaf-green silk dressing gown, her russet curls flowing loose over her shoulders.

"Alex!" she exclaimed. "How delightful to see you! Do come in and I'll make us some tea."

Her room was not large, and was rendered even smaller by containing not only a large bed and a dressing table, but also a small dining table with two chairs, a couple of old armchairs, several occasional tables, and a pianoforte. Emmeline had contrived to render it less drab, however, by the artful draping of a number of colourful silk scarves. She bade me sit down in one of the armchairs, and then made tea over a small spirit stove that sat on the table. As I watched her graceful movements, my nervousness left me.

"I wasn't sure when would be a good time to visit you," I

told her. "I thought you might wish to sleep late."

She glanced round at me, pushing her hair back from her face, which was not made-up and was enchantingly freckled. "How thoughtful of you! The afternoon is perfect. I've been thinking about you, you know."

"So have I—of you, I mean."

She turned and smiled at me, then returned her attention to the teapot. "Now, how do you take your tea?" She brought it to me in an old china cup without a saucer, fetching one of the occasional tables to set it on. "I have some biscuits, too, if you don't mind eating them out of the tin. These lodging houses never have enough china, but it's scarcely worth buying my own as I've nowhere to store it when I'm on tour."

"I don't mind the tin," I told her with a smile. "If there's one thing a university education teaches one, it's not to be fussy about such niceties. In fact, this reminds me a little of my room at Cambridge, except that I shared it with three others, two of whom snored, and no one had bothered to make it look pretty."

She laughed. "I must be thankful for small mercies, then. At least I'm not obliged to share."

Something in her tone suggested that she might, nevertheless, be willing to do so, and my heart quickened at the thought.

Over tea and Garibaldi biscuits we chatted comfortably, me in one armchair, she perched on the arm of the other, as seemed to be her wont.

"Tell me," I asked, "how does a young lady come to have a career on the stage?"

Emmeline gave a little laugh. "Oh, purely by accident in my case. My father died when I was scarcely able to walk, and my mother kept us—me and my brother and sister—by taking in laundry. Then, when I was eleven, my mother and brother were carried off by diphtheria. How my sister and I managed to escape infection I have no idea, since the three of us shared a bed. Anyway, there being no family or relatives who could take us in, we were sent to live in the Strand Union Children's Home—that's in Edmonton, you know, here in London—until we were old enough to find work. Those who ran the home saw to our education, for which I'll always be grateful, and we were each taught a trade, for which I confess I was rather less grateful."

My heart went out to her as she confided her sad tale. I reached across to take her hand. "Did they make you do something you disliked?"

"Yes, we had no choice in the matter. I was taught the art of millinery, and later went to work for a milliner who had a shop in Drury Lane. She was by no means an unkind employer, but the workshop behind the shop was dreadfully small and cramped for the three of us who worked there, and I found the work unutterably dreary. I'd always loved singing, and sometimes I'd sing to my companions to make the day less wearisome. One day, a customer heard me and asked the proprietress if she might meet me. It turned out she was a patroness of the theatre and knew Mr D'Oyly Carte and other theatrical producers. She arranged for me to meet one of them and to sing for him. He must have liked what he heard, because from then on Mrs Romayne-Smith—that was the lady's name—took me under her wing, arranging for me to have tuition in singing and acting, and then finding me a position in the company I'm with now. To this day, I can't imagine why she was so kind to me."

"I can," I told her, kissing her hand, which I still held in mine, "and I'm glad of it, for I shouldn't otherwise have met you. But tell me, what happened to your sister?"

"Oh, Grace became a seamstress. Unlike me, she enjoyed the work to which she was apprenticed. She has her own business now, and is engaged to be married to a boot maker in Willesden."

"So, a happy ending for both of you." I smiled.

"Yes, but I don't wish to bore you with my history. Tell me about your life, if you please?"

"I can't imagine you could ever bore me," I replied. But I told her of my childhood at Shillington Hall, and of my university days, omitting the worst of the scrapes I got into with my friends. Then, since she listened with the most flattering attention, I went on to tell her what had brought me to London. She showed warm sympathy for my feelings about my father's remarriage, and was very taken with the mysterious Henri de Saint-Clair, and wanted to know more, but since, despite our ready friendship, I knew almost nothing about him, and now seemed unlikely ever to know more, I was unable to oblige her.

Throughout our conversation, I noticed she seemed completely sanguine about our different stations in life. I found this refreshing, and oddly affecting. I had never before met anyone so completely indifferent to social standing, and supposed it must have something to do with her profession. Actors, after all, play at being people from all stations in life and must, after a time, come to see their common humanity rather than the differences imposed by society.

As the afternoon drew to a close, so, alas, did my visit.

"I must dress now," she told me. "I need to be at the

theatre by six o'clock. Jonty dislikes us being late, as there's always such a lot to do before the performance begins."

"Of course, I'm sorry to have taken up so much of your time, but I was so enjoying your company I quite lost track of its passage."

"Alex, what a charming compliment!"

She came and laid her hand on my arm and stood on tiptoe to kiss my cheek.

Instinctively, I slid my arm about her waist and pulled her against me. "I'd very much like to see you again," I said.

"I'd like that, too. I'm committed elsewhere after tonight's performance, but I'll be free tomorrow night."

"Shall I be a stage-door Johnny, then?" I murmured, my lips against her hair.

She gave a soft, throaty chuckle. "No need for that. Just come backstage. Someone will show you where to find me."

"I'll be there, I promise."

"*Adieu*, then, Alex. I'll look forward to seeing you."

She kissed me once more and then ushered me out of the room. I walked home as though I were floating, unable to keep a smile from my face.

* * * *

The following evening, resplendent in my new finery, I dined with Charles at his club and, after playing several games of billiards with him in a futile attempt to calm my nerves, set off for my rendezvous with Emmeline. It was a half-hour walk from the Cavendish to The Strand, where the Savoy Theatre was situated, but I decided not to take a cab, hoping a walk might accomplish what billiards had not. Just why I was so nervous, I was unsure. Perhaps I found myself fearing the cup of delight offered by Emmeline might, at any moment, be summarily dashed from my lips.

I arrived at the theatre about twenty minutes before the final curtain and made my way through the Stage Door, and along a passageway cluttered with pieces of scenery and packing boxes. Several doors opened off this passage, probably leading to dressing rooms, but I had no way of knowing which of them was Emmeline's. Spying a skinny youth clinging to what I supposed to be part of the mechanism for opening and closing the stage curtains, I approached him and caught his attention.

"Can you please tell me which dressing room is Miss Beaumont's?"

"Oh, she don't rate a room to 'erself," he informed me, as one of the inner circle addressing a mere outsider. "She's in room three, dahn the far end, but yer'd best wait ahtside."

I thanked him, tipped him for his help, and went to do his bidding. I had bought some flowers for Emmeline, a bunch of violets from a flower girl outside the theatre. Now I began to worry that perhaps I should have bought chocolates as well. As I was thus tormenting myself, the dressing-room door opened and Miss Polly Marchant came out.

"Oh, it's—it's—Charlie and Ferdy's friend!" she exclaimed, patting my arm in a friendly gesture. "I'm so sorry, I've forgotten your name."

"Alex," I said. "Alex Randall."

"Of course, do forgive me. Have you come to see Emmeline?"

I nodded. "The young man over there by the curtain told me I should wait out here."

"Oh, don't mind Jimmy. Ever since he was promoted from sweeping the floors he thinks he knows everything. You pop inside and make yourself comfortable. There's some champagne if you fancy a tipple. We'll be back after we've taken our bows. I'll tell Emmeline you're here. She'll be so pleased."

"No, please don't tell her," I said. "I'd like to surprise her."

She gave me a conspiratorial grin and tapped the side of her nose with a forefinger.

"Right you are, then. I must dash or I'll miss the curtain call."

The dressing room was bathed in garish light from a row of bare electric bulbs set at intervals above a long mirror lining the far wall. Beneath the mirror ran a bench cluttered with stage makeup, jars of cold cream, brushes and combs and other accoutrements of transformation for the stage, including a number of wigs on wooden stands or simply lying crumpled on the bench like small, sleeping animals. Wooden racks filled with a variety of colourful costumes took up a fair part of the rest of the room, but there were also several worn but comfortable-looking armchairs surrounding a low table on which stood several champagne bottles and a number of glasses. I disposed myself in one of the chairs, but thought better of Miss Marchant's offer of champagne. The memory of recent events was still fresh in my mind.

As I sat nervously clutching my bunch of violets, a great roar of applause went up from the auditorium, and a few minutes later the dressing-room door burst open to admit a gaggle of laughing and chattering young ladies. I didn't recognise Emmeline at first, as her red curls were hidden beneath an enormous black wig decorated in the Oriental style, and she wore chalk-white makeup designed to make her look like a lady from a Japanese painting. However, as soon as she saw me, she came running to greet me, tugging off her wig and tossing it onto the bench, where an elderly dresser snatched it up, tut-tutting and shaking her head, and placed it on a stand, smoothing it lovingly with gnarled fingers.

"Alex! How good it is to see you! I wasn't sure you'd come, you know."

"I gave you my promise," I replied, catching up her hand and kissing it. "And a gentleman doesn't break his promise."

She smiled, her green eyes lighting up with mischief. "Well, you know, there are some who purport to be gentlemen who don't behave as such."

"I dare say that's true, but then I hadn't the slightest desire to break *my* promise." Suddenly remembering the violets, I offered them to her, saying, "These are for you. I thought they'd look well with your hair."

She held them to her nose to inhale their perfume. "Alex, they're lovely! I'm wearing my lavender gown this evening, so they'll be perfect!" She reached up to kiss my cheek and murmured in my ear, "Please excuse me for a little while. I must get rid of this makeup and change out of my costume. Will you pour me some champagne, please? And do have some yourself."

I took Emmeline's champagne and set it down beside her on the bench, before which she sat perched on a stool smearing cold cream onto her face. While she completed her ablutions, I sat watching her transformation from Japanese schoolgirl to titian-haired young Englishwoman. My upbringing, and perhaps my lack of worldly experience, caused me a few blushes when she and the other young ladies stepped out of their gowns, revealing their underclothes. But it was impossible to remain embarrassed when none of them seemed the slightest bit perturbed by my presence, or that of several other gentlemen who had arrived after the final curtain.

The best part of an hour passed before Emmeline had completed her toilette to her satisfaction, but, fascinated by my introduction to the feminine mysteries, I scarcely noticed. Finally, she pinned the violets at the neck of her gown, draped a grey velvet cape over her shoulders and came to sit on the arm of my chair, laying her cheek against mine as she had on the night of the party. With the utmost difficulty, I refrained from responding as I had then.

She said in her soft voice, "I must apologise for taking so long."

"Not at all," I replied. "It was well worth the wait to see you looking so delightful. If you have everything you need, though, may I please have the very great pleasure of taking you to supper?"

Having quizzed Charles and Ferdy extensively during dinner, I now knew of several good cafés in the vicinity of the Savoy Theatre, and took Emmeline to a small one just off The Strand in Savoy Street where, my friends had assured me, the food was excellent and the surroundings pleasing. Over a supper of crepes with orange sauce and strawberries, washed down with champagne, we conversed in the greatest amity until it became clear the restaurateur was anxious to close up for the night, then I walked Emmeline home to her lodgings, her arm tucked cosily in mine.

In the hallway of the boarding house, I drew her into the

shadows and kissed her and murmured, "Good night, sweet Emmeline."

"Oh, must you go so soon?"

I smiled and shook my head.

"Then, Alex, would you think me terribly forward if I invited you up to my room?"

"Oh, undoubtedly, but I'm not sure I'd have the fortitude to refuse you. Like Mr Wilde, I can resist anything except temptation, and you, sweet Emmeline, are temptation itself."

With a smile that sent thrills through me, she took my hand and led me up the narrow stairs.

In her room, she lit the oil lamp on the bedside table, unfastened her cape and cast it onto the bed. Now I was there alone with her, all at once I became acutely aware of my lack of experience in the art of romance. Of course I had had a few encounters with the fair sex while at university, but they had not been at all the same thing as this. I found myself uncertain as to what she expected of me or, even more important, what she might find acceptable, and I dreaded to overstep the mark lest I lose what I was fast coming to realise was what I wanted above all—the company of this delightful young lady.

She must have seen something of my uncertainty in my face, as she came to me and laid a hand on my arm. "What is it, Alex? Should I not have invited you here? If I've offended you or made you feel uncomfortable, please accept my apologies. I'll understand perfectly if you want to leave."

I caught up her hand and held it in mine. "I do feel a trifle uncomfortable," I admitted, "but it's none of your doing. To be here with you is what I want more than—than anything— but I couldn't bear it if I sullied your reputation in any way.

That's the last thing I want, believe me."

To my surprise, she threw back her head and laughed. "My reputation? That's a good one! Alex, I'm an actress. I'm already beyond the pale of society. Why do you think young blades like Charlie and Ferdy consort with the likes of me? It's not to seek our hands in marriage, I assure you. I thought you'd know that."

"I'm rapidly coming to see just how little I do know," I said, subsiding into the nearest chair. "I'm afraid I'm still not at all worldly."

Emmeline came and sat on the arm of my chair and began to stroke my hair. "Why do you think I like you so much? You aren't trying to use me, and you treat me like a lady, even though I'm not one." She flashed me a sudden grin.

"Well, apart from at Jonty's party, perhaps, but you were a little the worse for wear that night, and I thought you were the same as the others."

"If you could see into my mind," I told her, "I think you'd be sadly disillusioned. My thoughts when I'm with you are not at all those of a gentleman."

"But your actions are, and surely that's what distinguishes a true gentleman."

"'Manners makyth man'," I quoted. "Your name should be Sophia, for you're not only beautiful, but wise as well."

"Oh, Alex, you pay me such pretty compliments!"

"I mean every word, I promise you."

"Oh, Alex!" she repeated, leaning down to kiss me.

I pulled her onto my lap, put my arms about her and returned her kiss with a will, savouring her soft lips and the warm, sweet scent of her that mingled with the spicy perfume of the violets now crushed against her breast. At length she pulled away from me a little and fixed her shining eyes on mine.

"We could be more comfortable than this," she murmured, "if you'd like it."

"Madam, you are a temptress," I replied, assuming a tone of mock severity.

Her lips curved into a mischievous smile. "And you've already told me you can resist anything except temptation."

At that, I kissed her fervently, crushing her lips against mine until I could taste the champagne that lingered in her mouth. She stood up, pulling me to my feet and leading me to the bed. As I sat on the edge of the bed, she began to unbutton my jacket, saying, "You mustn't ruin your splendid clothes. That would never do." Gently, she eased the well-fitting garment from my shoulders, folded it and laid it across the back of a chair. Next, my waistcoat came off, followed by my tie and shoes. "Now," she said, standing before me, "can you help me unfasten my dress, please?"

My fingers were less adept than hers, but soon her gown was laid on top of my clothes. The little bunch of violets fell to the floor and she picked it up and held it to her lips for a moment before placing it on the table beside the lamp. At her instruction, I helped her to remove her petticoats and unlace her corset and these, too, joined the others. On her feet she wore kid boots that matched her dress, and I knelt and unbuttoned them.

So we sat side by side on the edge of the bed, me in my trousers and shirt, Emmeline in her white-linen chemise, its soft folds granting me tantalising hints of what lay beneath. I reached out a tentative hand and ran it down her neck to her small, soft breast, and she gave a little sigh of pleasure. In an instant, it seemed, we were lying on the bed locked in one another's arms and covering each other with kisses. More clothing needed to be removed, since it hindered our closeness. How we achieved this I cannot tell you, but achieve it we did, to lie, at last, skin touching skin, revelling in each other like two savages in paradise, oblivious to all but the sensations aroused in ourselves and each other. At length, our passion spent, we lay cradled in each other's arms until we began to feel cold. Then we slipped beneath the bedclothes and slept.

Some hours later, I opened my eyes to find Emmeline sleeping peacefully beside me, a shaft of early-morning sunlight, which had crept through a gap in the curtains, gilding her skin with its dusty light. Taking care not to waken her, I raised myself on one elbow and gazed down at her, taking in the soft curves of her face, her neck, her breasts. How I longed to feast my eyes on all of her, to drink in every line, every plane, each gentle curve of her. To me, at that moment, she was a very Venus, a goddess of love and beauty. Was I in love? I scarcely knew. All I knew was that I adored her with all my being.

As I gazed at her, her eyes fluttered open and she smiled as she saw me. "Oh, you *are* here. I thought I must be dreaming."

I bent to kiss her. "I'm no dream, my dear, but *you* are a vision!"

At that, she threw her arms about me and pulled me close. Our passion quickly rekindled, we made love once more, this time savouring one another as one might savour a cup of clear water once the original thirst has been slaked. When we eventually roused ourselves from our blissful torpor,

Emmeline wrapped herself in her dressing gown and went to fetch a pitcher of water for our ablutions. Of course I had no razor with me, so I took her out for a late breakfast feeling delightfully dissolute. We ate our bread rolls and drank our coffee almost in silence, content merely to be in one another's presence.

I arrived home some time after noon to find Charles and Ferdy tucking into a luncheon of bread, ham and cheese, with a pitcher of ale set between them.

"Ah, here he is at last!" cried Charles. "I suppose we needn't ask where *you've* been?"

"Nor what's kept him so long," added Ferdy with an arch wink.

Much good-natured ribbing followed before I finally took myself off for a bath and a shave and a change of clothes.

After that night, I saw Emmeline as often as I could. We took walks in Hyde Park on fine days, or wandered through London's various museums and art galleries, and several times we went to see the biograph, or to one of the music halls. And of course I attended numerous performances of *The Mikado*. I never tired of seeing her and hearing her sweet soprano voice and watching her graceful movements on the stage. Afterwards, we'd have supper together at our favourite café in Savoy Street before making our way back to Emmeline's room.

When I was unable to see Emmeline, I went out with Charles and Ferdy and others of their set, enjoying gaming (at which I became adept enough to provide a useful supplement to my financial resources), horse-racing, boxing matches: in short, all the kinds of enjoyment available to young men with money in their pockets. And so the next few months passed in what was, for me, a kind of idyll—until an incident occurred that changed everything.

CHAPTER SIX

As the days grew longer and warmer, the London Season began to wind down, and it became quite common to see coaches leaving town laden with the personal effects of those retiring to resorts such as Brighton, Bath, or Tunbridge Wells, or to their country estates for the summer. I, of course, had no desire to leave town, determining to brave the stifling heat of the London summer rather than forego Emmeline's company.

She was still engaged in what was proving a long and successful run of *The Mikado*. Charles made it clear he thought me a fool, but he knew better than to tell me so to my face, merely making his own travel arrangements, assuring me I might continue to live at Grosvenor Square, and I was welcome to visit him at Compton whenever it pleased me, and to bring Emmeline, too.

"In fact," he told me one evening as we dined at his club, "dashed if I don't invite Lucy and Polly as well, and any of the cast who care to join us, and make it a house party. The theatrical set are always such great fun, don't you think, Alex?"

Since I knew it was futile to point out to him the impossibility of their taking leave from their work before the end of their run, I went along with his suggestion. Charles in the grip of one of his sudden enthusiasms was not easily deterred, but I felt tolerably certain that by the time he'd ensconced himself at his country estate, some other passion would have taken its place.

I had come to have no very good opinion of Charles and Ferdy's feckless ways, and was pleased to be able to pursue what by now I readily acknowledged as my affair with Emmeline without having to endure their unsavoury jibes and inferences.

One morning, about a month after Charles's departure for Sussex, I was drinking tea in the morning room when his butler brought me a telegram. My heart leapt in sudden fear, thinking my father might be ill, or even dying. Then I realised such a missive would have been sent to his town house in Kensington, in which he must suppose I was living, since I had not seen fit to advise him of my change of plans.

I took the envelope from the silver salver on which it lay. "Thank you, Hetherington. I'll let you know if there's a reply."

"Begging your pardon, sir," he replied in his usual grave tones, "but an urgent reply is requested. The delivery boy is waiting in the hall."

I tore open the envelope and read: 'Need you here urgently stop repeat urgently stop please come soonest stop Charles.'

"I don't suppose you have any idea what this is about?" I asked Hetherington, showing him the telegram.

"I'm sorry, sir, I do not."

"No, of course not," I said with a sigh. "Please send an urgent telegram to let Charles know I'll travel down on the next train I can get."

"Very good, sir. To whom shall I charge the telegram?"

"Oh, to Charles. It serves him right for dragging me away like this."

Hetherington's lip gave a faint twitch. "Very good, sir. I shall send someone directly to pack your bags. Will you be wanting Mr Weston-Greer's carriage to take you to the station?"

"Yes, I suppose that would be best."

"Very good, sir, I shall tell Thomas to have it ready directly."

As I was attempting to decide what to take with me, I suddenly thought of Emmeline. I couldn't leave without letting her know. As Thomas was stowing my bags on the luggage rack of Charles's coach, I asked him to take me first to Soho. He looked a little surprised, but did my bidding. I hurried up the stairs and knocked on Emmeline's door. She was dressed in a sky-blue coat, with a straw boater perched atop her red curls, and was pulling on a pair of grey kid gloves. She was, of course, surprised to see me.

"Oh, Alex, I was just going out to lunch with Lucy and Alice—the lady who plays Yum-Yum, you know—but you're welcome to join us if you like. Perhaps we can go for a walk afterwards, since it's such a lovely day."

"I'm sorry, Emmeline dear, I should love to accompany you, but I've just received an urgent telegram from Charles, and I'm travelling down to Sussex on the one-forty train."

"Oh, dear! Is Charlie in one of his scrapes again? Still, I can see you must go to him. You never know, it might just be serious this time. How long shall you be there, do you think?"

I shook my head. "I've no idea, I'm sorry. But I promise

I'll write to you the moment I know." I tilted her chin up with my hand and bent to kiss her. "I shall miss you dreadfully, you know."

In reply, she put her arms about me and hugged me to her. "And I'll miss you, Alex dear. I don't know how I'll spend my time without our meetings to look forward to."

"Well, I dare say it's nothing serious. I'll return just as soon as I can, I promise."

"The promise of a gentleman." she smiled. "God speed, Alex. I'll look forward to your return."

"So shall I, sweet Emmeline!" I enfolded her in my arms and kissed her again and again until I suddenly remembered Thomas waiting outside. "I really must go now. I'll write to you very soon."

Then, with the greatest reluctance, I ran down the stairs and out into the street, aware of her sea-green eyes watching me go.

* * * *

Charles was at Petworth railway station to meet me, looking uncharacteristically pale and nervous.

As soon as the porter had stowed my bags in Charles's car and left, I voiced my concern. "What on earth has happened, Charles? Nothing too serious, I hope?"

"About as serious as may be," he replied in a sober tone. "But, please, let's not talk about it here. We'll be at Compton soon enough."

Compton, a massive manor house whose multifarious style suggested Elizabethan origins with several later additions, stood on the outskirts of the village of Fittleworth, only a short drive from Petworth. As soon as my luggage had been dealt with, Charles took me to a small parlour off the hall and poured us each a large brandy, waving aside my protestations that tea would be more than sufficient.

"You're going to need this," he said in grim tones, "and if you don't, *I* certainly do."

"Surely it can't be as bad as all that."

Charles took a gulp of brandy. "Oh, yes, it can!"

"Then for goodness' sake tell me what's troubling you. There must be something I can do to help."

"There is, but you won't want to do it."

"Charles, will you please stop talking in riddles and tell me plainly what the matter is?"

He took another mouthful of brandy, then, his eyes fixed on the floor, muttered, "I'm engaged to fight a duel—"

"A *what*?" I interrupted. "Don't be silly, Charles. You can't fight a duel. It's illegal, and has been for decades."

With a defensive hunch of his shoulders, Charles went on, "Nevertheless, I'm to fight one. I've agreed to it now, and I can't back out. It's a matter of honour, Alex. Not just mine, but that of a lady."

"Oh, God!" I groaned. "I might have known. Of all the stupid—"

"Yes, well, it's no use telling me that now. I may be stupid, Alex, but I'm a man of honour. I've engaged to fight, and that's what I must do."

With a sinking feeling in the pit of my stomach, I enquired, "And you called me here because...?"

He shrugged again and shot me a desperate look. "Ah... I need a second."

"What about Ferdy? Don't tell me he's had the good sense

not to do it?"

"No, Ferdy's a man of honour, too, but he was called away to a family funeral in Northamptonshire last week, and he's not back yet."

"Oh, Lord! But surely you can get out of it. As I said, duelling's illegal. You should be able to opt out on those grounds alone. Or perhaps you could buy the gentleman off. It's not as though you can't afford it."

Charles turned on me an expression of horror. "Of course I can't! Not unless I wish to become a social pariah—which I assure you I don't. You wouldn't want that if it were you, would you?"

"I'm not sure I should care, to be honest with you," I replied. "Not if the alternative were to risk my life in an illegal duel. Not that I'd be such a fool as to commit myself to one in the first place."

"Well, I do care!" Charles tossed off the remainder of his brandy and set the glass down with such force I feared it might shatter. "Will you help me or not, Alex? Either way, I mean to go through with it."

"Then I suppose I must say yes, if only to try to save you from yourself." I ignored his pathetic look of gratitude. "So tell me, what's a second supposed to do?"

"Um, well, you meet my opponent's second and—and arrange the time and the—the place, and—and weapons, and that sort of thing."

"Then I suppose you'd better tell me who your opponent is, and where I can find his second."

Charles's opponent was the Honourable Arthur de Burgh, apparently the son of the local baron, Lord Warrington. He was not one of Charles's social set, and his name was unknown to me, as was that of his second, one Jonathan Wilmington.

"And the young lady?"

"Miss Emsworth, Annabel, a—a sister of Jack Emsworth's. You may remember him from Cambridge."

I did, indeed, remember Jack Emsworth, and if his sister was anything like him, I wasn't surprised at her honour being impugned. I could only suppose she had become Charles's new enthusiasm.

"And what," I asked with a sense of foreboding, "is it about Miss Emsworth that you feel it necessary to uphold her honour in so drastic a fashion?"

Charles looked at me like a puppy caught misbehaving. "De Burgh said any sister of Emsworth's was no lady, and she is, Alex! She's not a bit like Jack, with his ramshackle ways. She's sweet and kind and—and—oh, dash it, Alex, I won't have her insulted by the likes of Arthur de Burgh or—or anyone else!"

"I might have known," I said with a heavy sigh. "Charles, this is not something to fight a duel over, not in this day and age, no matter how much of a saint Miss Emsworth may be. Can't you just settle it with your fists? I'll happily second you in a boxing match."

"No, I offered to fight him, but he insisted on a duel. I gather he fancies himself a bit of a dab hand with a pistol."

"For God's sake, Charles, have you even so much as fired a pistol?"

"Of course I have!"

"When?"

"Um, well, it was some time ago," he admitted with a sheepish look. "And only on a shooting range. To tell you the

70

truth, I didn't like it above half, but I dare say I haven't lost the knack of it."

"I shouldn't have thought you'd had time to acquire the knack," I told him, with more than a touch of asperity, "let alone lose it. In heaven's name, Charles, why did you agree to it?"

Charles's hangdog expression intensified. "Well, I don't suppose I would have, but I was three parts drunk at the time, and—"

"Oh, good God!" I was unable to contain my anger any longer. "You're a fool, Charles. A damned, stupid fool! All right, all right." I put up my hand to stem the impending flood of self-justification. "I'll go and see this Wilmington fellow. With any luck, the two of us can persuade de Burgh to back out."

Charles began to protest the unlikelihood of such an eventuality, besides its being insufficient to uphold the lady's honour, but I cut him short.

"Frankly, Charles, I don't give a damn about Miss Emsworth's honour. My main concern is to bring you out of this mess alive—though I'm sorely tempted to leave you to your fate."

I went for a long, fast walk to calm my temper, and then had one of Charles's horses saddled and rode into Fittleworth, where Jonathan Wilmington lived. I began to have qualms when I called at his home and was redirected to a nearby tavern by a slatternly woman who claimed to be his housekeeper. The moment I set eyes on him, my heart sank.

Mr Jonathan Wilmington was not, as I'd first expected, a young scion of the landed gentry with more money than sense. The man lounging on a bench in the taproom of the

Fox and Hounds, a tankard in one hand and an overripe blonde whose golden tresses owed little or nothing to nature in the other, was fifty if he was a day. And time, or more likely his lifestyle, had not been kind to him. With his broken nose and ruddy, battered visage, he looked like a particularly dissolute ageing prize fighter—as I had little doubt he was. How he came to be known by the son of a baron, much less his second in a duel, I preferred not to speculate. As soon as I introduced myself and stated my business, he sat up, pushing his companion off his lap and sending her off with a slap on her ample rump.

He set his tankard down and wiped a meaty fist across his mouth. "Now then, young gentleman, what can I do for you?"

I briefly explained my mission.

"Your luck's out, there, me young buck," he opined, "for my young gentleman won't cry off, no way, no 'ow, and if your young gentleman weren't wishful to meet him, he oughtn't to've agreed to it in the first place."

Although I could not but concur with this latter sentiment, I inferred from his tone that he probably stood to gain money by the affair. Briefly, I wondered if we might buy him off by Charles offering him a higher price, but this was not a decision I felt able to make without consulting Charles first. I should have to try a different tack.

"I agree wholeheartedly," I said, "that Mr Weston-Greer was foolish to challenge Mr de Burgh in this way. Apart from any other consideration, duelling is illegal." I stressed the word in a manner I hoped Mr Wilmington would find meaningful. "If the Police should happen to get wind of it—"

"I do 'ope you wasn't thinkin' o' tellin' the Peelers, Mr Randall," he interposed, his voice soft, but laden with menace.

"It's surely not likely," I pointed out with as much calm as I could muster, "that no others know of this. Or was the transaction carried out in secret?"

"No, o' course it weren't. It was 'ere in this very room as a matter o' fact."

"I thought as much. And I take it the place was not deserted at the time?"

"O' course not. What are you driving at?"

"Just this," I told him. "Anyone who saw the altercation might well think of informing the Police. Indeed, they may already have done so. It would, after all, be no more than their duty. I don't know what the penalty is for duelling, Mr Wilmington—do you?" As an afterthought I added, "Not to mention aiding and abetting a duellist."

Mr Wilmington fell silent, his stubbled jaw working as though this might somehow help him to think.

"I tell you what," he said at last. "I'll 'ave a talk with young Mr de Burgh, though I doubt if he'll budge."

"Well, see what you can do," I said. "How long do you think it will take?"

This caused him further jaw working, at the end of which he vouchsafed to meet me again in the taproom at six o'clock that evening. I agreed to this, albeit with little enthusiasm. It was already well after half past four, which would not give me time to ride to Compton and back before the meeting, much as I should have liked to speak with Charles on the subject of bribing Mr Wilmington. Fittleworth being but a tiny village, there was little there to hold my interest until the appointed hour. After some thought, I asked the landlord to show me to a private parlour and ordered coffee and an early dinner, since I had had nothing to eat since breakfast. I also managed to acquire writing paper, pen, and ink, and sat down to write a letter to Emmeline.

Wilmington returned as the church clock was chiming six with the unwelcome, though hardly unexpected, news that Mr de Burgh would by no means back out of the engagement. I was uncertain whether this was Mr de Burgh's decision or whether Wilmington had encouraged him. Either way, my only course now was to try to persuade Charles to offer him a sum sufficient to gain his cooperation.

CHAPTER SEVEN

I reached Compton shortly before dusk to find Charles in a state of considerable agitation. He came running to meet me as soon as he heard my horse's hooves on the cobbles of the forecourt.

"Alex, what the deuce took you so long? Did you speak with Wilmington? What did he say?"

It seemed his former determination to duel had deserted him now he had had time alone to reflect on his situation, and I hoped I might yet manage to salvage the situation.

"Come inside, Charles, we can't talk here." I took his arm, and, with some force, led him inside and practically pushed him into an armchair in the parlour before pouring him a large brandy.

When I judged him to be sufficiently calm, I told him of my meeting with Wilmington and its outcome.

"Oh, Lord," he moaned, "I'm done for now!"

"There is one possibility," I told him, "of halting this ludicrous affair."

He raised his head, a pathetic expression of hope suffusing his face.

"It's my belief," I continued, "that Wilmington stands to make money from the duel."

"H-how? What did he tell you?"

"Nothing, but he seems such an unlikely choice for a

75

second that I think it likely de Burgh has offered him money to be his. Have you met Wilmington?"

"N-no. I assumed he was a friend of Arthur's."

I described the man to Charles, adding, "If he's a friend of de Burgh's, I can only assume De Burgh has fallen in with very low company indeed. More likely none of his friends were idiotic enough to agree to second him and he resorted to paying someone."

"For what it's worth," ventured Charles, "I've heard De Burgh keeps some pretty wild company, especially since he came into his inheritance. But how does that help me?"

"If Wilmington has accepted money to be de Burgh's second, then you may be able to prevent it by offering him a higher price for backing out. It's not as though you can't afford it, and you won't be paying off de Burgh himself, in case you're still worried about besmirching yours and Miss Emsworth's honour."

My friend's face lit up at this crumb of hope. "Do you—do you really think that'll work?"

"I haven't the slightest idea, but it must be worth a try. The duel is scheduled for the day after tomorrow, which gives us tomorrow to make the attempt. I'll ride over to Fittleworth in the morning and pay Wilmington another visit. How much do you wish to offer him?"

Charles began to grow agitated once more. "I don't know! How much is de Burgh paying him?"

"I'm afraid Wilmington didn't vouchsafe me that information."

His face reddened, and he clenched and unclenched his fists so that I began to think he would attack me. But all at once he subsided like a deflated balloon. "Oh, God! Just offer him twice whatever de Burgh is paying him. Hopefully that'll do the trick."

"I should think so," I replied, though I was far from hopeful. The success of the ploy depended entirely on the accuracy of my hunch concerning Wilmington, and I had no way of discerning that until I spoke with him again.

* * * *

As soon as I'd breakfasted the following morning, I set out once more for Fittleworth. This time I found Wilmington at home. Rather grudgingly, he invited me into his cottage. The interior was as rundown as the exterior, but clean and tidy enough. Perhaps the woman I'd seen there the previous day really was the housekeeper though, if so, I suspected that was not her only duty. Wilmington offered me a chair by the fireplace—although no fire was lit—himself resuming the one opposite, where he had been in the process of filling a filthy-looking pipe.

"Now," he said, ignoring the pipe and planting his hands on his thighs. "What can I do for you? Don't tell me your fellow's crying off?"

After a moment's thought, I replied, "I'm sure you'll agree with me that a quarrel between two foolish young men is not worth the risk of injury or death—or a term in prison, for that matter."

"Maybe, maybe not, but that's neither here nor there as far as I'm concerned. If your gentleman is fool enough to offer a challenge, and de Burgh wants to accept it, who am I to stand in their way?"

"Especially," I said softly, "if you stand to gain by it." I saw by his expression I had hit the mark. "So, what if Mr Weston-Greer was to offer you more?"

Wilmington's eyes narrowed. "'Ow much more?"

"I've been authorised," I said, "to offer you twice whatever Mr de Burgh has offered."

He whistled softly through his blackened teeth. "Well, now, that's certainly something worth considering."

"I wish you'll consider it quickly, then, so we can bring a halt to the affair."

Wilmington got to his feet and paced about the small room for some minutes, his hands clasped behind his back. Then he turned to me and held out one grimy hand.

"Done!" he exclaimed with what I took to be an attempt at a friendly smile.

"Quite probably," I murmured before ascertaining the sum involved and inviting Wilmington to present himself at Compton at two o'clock that afternoon to receive payment.

I then rode back to Compton to give Charles the good news.

Wilmington arrived as instructed and Charles handed over, in cash, what I considered a ridiculously large sum, but which he appeared to consider well worth it.

"Thank God that's over," I said. "And I sincerely hope you've learnt your lesson."

Charles nodded. "I suppose we'd better lie low for a bit," he said, attempting, but not entirely achieving, a look of contrition. "What do you say to a game or two of piquet after dinner? I've a particularly fine tawny port in my cellar, and this seems a suitable occasion to broach it. What do you say, Alex?"

What could I do but agree? If nothing else, a quiet

evening at home with me would keep him from finding further trouble.

Accordingly, after dining on roast mutton and plum pie, Charles and I repaired to the study and settled down to play cards.

We had just finished our third game of piquet, and were considering whether to play another or to make our way to the games room to play billiards, when a thunderous knocking at the front door startled us. Charles leapt to his feet, scattering playing cards in all directions, and shot me a hunted look before staring about him as though seeking somewhere to hide. But it was too late.

Ward, Charles's butler, entered the room and informed us, "There is a young gentleman wishing to speak with Mr Weston-Greer."

Since Charles seemed incapable, I took it on myself to enquire, "Did the gentleman give his name?"

"Yes, sir, he is the Honourable Augustus Fitzwalter."

I'd expected Charles to show relief that his visitor was not Arthur de Burgh, but instead he cringed back with a look of horror on his face.

"G-Gussie? What does *he* want?"

I managed to stifle my exasperation sufficiently to ask him, "Who, exactly, is the Honourable Augustus Fitzwalter?"

"He's one of Arthur's cronies. And he's a dangerous man to cross, or—or so I've heard."

I sighed. "I can't imagine what possessed you to take up with such people, Charles, but I suppose I can guess his purpose in coming here." I turned to the butler, who had been standing impassively by the door. "Please show Mr Fitzwalter to the small parlour, Ward, and tell him I'll be with him directly."

The Honourable Augustus was a tall, impeccably dressed man of around thirty with a lithe, powerfully muscled body, shrewd grey eyes and a haughty demeanour. "And whom have I the honour of addressing?" he enquired, staring at me down the considerable length of his nose. I half expected him to peer at me through a quizzing glass like some Regency beau.

"Alexander Randall, at your service," I stated in what I hoped was a fair facsimile of his lofty manner. "I take it you've come about the—ah—engagement between Mr de Burgh and Mr Weston-Greer?"

"I have. And what, may I enquire, is *your* part in the affair? I asked to speak to Mr Weston-Greer."

"I've agreed to act as his second. However, I was given to understand the affair is settled, and there will now be no duel."

"Not so, Mr Randall. If Mr Weston-Greer supposes buying off Wilmington has settled the matter, I can assure you he's very much mistaken. Mr de Burgh's honour is at stake, and he is therefore not inclined to withdraw from the engagement."

"Not even if it should land him a prison sentence?"

The expression the Honourable Augustus turned on me left me in no doubt as to his opinion on the likelihood of such an outcome.

"There *will* be a duel," he told me in oppressive tones. "It will take place tomorrow at dawn at The Oaks. Of course, if Mr Weston-Greer lacks the courage of his convictions—"

"Of course I don't!"

I looked round to see Charles standing near the door, his

face like chalk, but with a pugnacious expression on it.

"Gussie, how dare you suggest such a thing?"

"If the cap fits," murmured Fitzwalter with a shrug of his elegant shoulders. "Good night to you, gentlemen. I shall expect to see you at dawn tomorrow."

With that, he turned on his heel and swept from the room. I waited to hear the front door close before rounding on Charles.

"Good God, Charles, have you no sense at all? If you'd left it to me, I'm tolerably sure I could have talked Fitzwalter out of it."

"But—but," stammered Charles, "he called me a coward."

Thoroughly out of temper by now, I threw up my hands. "Oh, I give up! I'm going to bed."

"But Alex, you will come with me tomorrow?"

"Yes, yes, but for God's sake leave me alone until then so I can try and get some sleep. And if you'll take my advice—though I scarcely dare hope you will—you'll do the same."

* * * *

It was still dark when Charles dragged me from a fitful sleep. He looked as though he hadn't bothered to undress, let alone sleep, and his face appeared feverish in the lamplight. In truth, I felt little better than an automaton myself. However, I forced myself from my bed and ordered Charles to wash and change his clothes while I dressed. Neither of us felt up to eating, and I thought it best not to force the issue. The last thing I wanted was for Charles to take ill from eating in his present state of nerves. However, I did pour him a small brandy, which he gulped down in one mouthful, coughing

81

and spluttering as it burned its way down his gullet.

"Now," I asked, "do you have your pistols?"

"Y-yes." Charles went to the hall table and picked up a small black case. It looked rather old, and I suspected it had been his uncle's. I certainly could not imagine his father, an industrious family man, having had any use for a set of duelling pistols.

"Let me have a look."

He handed me the case and I snapped it open to see two pistols of excellent workmanship with ivory-inlaid wooden handles, a small brass powder flask, and two paper rolls of shot. I picked up one of the pistols and opened the breech. It was old, but had clearly been maintained, though not, I imagined, by Charles. Carefully, I replaced the pistol, shut the case, and tucked it under my arm.

"That seems all in order," I said, attempting to sound as though I knew what I was talking about. "I suppose we'd best be on our way now."

Charles's Rolls Royce was standing on the forecourt, its motor purring smoothly, having already been started by one of the servants. Within twenty minutes we reached The Oaks, where the eponymous trees branched over one end of a level stretch of grassland. Beneath their venerable branches, stood de Burgh and Fitzwalter, and another young man, muffled against the cold by a long coat with its collar pulled up, who was presumably there to view the entertainment. I took Charles firmly by the arm, and we went to meet de Burgh and Fitzwalter.

"Good day to you, gentlemen," I greeted them, trying to sound brisk and businesslike.

I shook both of them by the hand and Charles did the

same, making a brave attempt at sanguinity. Both sets of pistols having been inspected by all concerned and pronounced free of defect or tampering, it fell to Fitzwalter and myself to load them with one lead ball each. To my embarrassment, I had to confess I had no idea how to do this, so the combatants agreed they would each load the other's pistol in order to frustrate any temptation to cheat. Fitzwalter, who, unlike me, seemed to have some knowledge of the subject, rehearsed the rules of combat with the opponents before standing them back-to-back, each with a pistol clutched in his right hand. At his order, they walked slowly away from one another for the required number of paces. Fitzwalter, to whom by now I had surrendered the job of masterminding the affair, gave a further order and they turned sideways on to one another to minimise the targets presented by their bodies. Facing each other over their shoulders, they lifted their pistols to take aim. I could see Charles's hand was shaking as he strove to master his nerves. De Burgh, his face pale and tense, seemed scarcely less nervous.

Fitzwalter came to stand beside me. "You can give the signal to fire," he pronounced, as one giving an order to an inferior, and produced from his pocket a clean, white kerchief. "Hold this up so they can see it clearly. When you drop it, they fire. Oh, don't worry," he added, his lip curling in contempt, "I've already explained it all to them."

Not quite knowing how to respond to his peremptory manner, I took the kerchief and went to stand in the appointed place. Making sure both Charles and de Burgh knew what I was doing, I counted slowly to ten and then brought the kerchief down. Almost at once, there were two deafening reports. Instinct had made me clamp my eyes shut as I lowered the kerchief. Now I opened them to find swirling, acrid smoke all but obscuring the two men. As it began to clear, I saw they both lay on the ground. A sick sensation invaded my stomach as I hurried towards Charles. Through the eddying smoke I saw Fitzwalter approach De Burgh.

It took no more than a brief inspection to inform me Charles was badly wounded. He lay unconscious, his face like putty, dark blood welling up from a ragged wound in his chest. I felt at his neck for a pulse. He was still alive, though barely. I knew I should do something to stanch the flow of blood, but what? In desperation, I stripped off my coat, screwed it into a bulky ball, and pressed it hard against the wound, though I had no great hope of its efficacy. When I glanced across at Fitzwalter, he stood staring down at De Burgh, his face a ghastly grey, his throat convulsing as though he were suppressing the urge to vomit. I followed his gaze and saw what had transfixed him. De Burgh lay on the grass, both hands clutched to his stomach. From twenty paces away, I could see the blood soaking his shirt. As I watched, Fitzwalter knelt to place a hand to his neck, as I had with Charles. He looked up, his face tense.

"He's gone," he declared, his voice harsh.

The young man who had accompanied de Burgh and Fitzwalter was hovering nearby, his eyes wide with either horror or excitement—I could not tell which.

"Shall I go for the Police?" he asked.

Fitzwalter fixed him with a withering stare. "Are you insane, Bingham? You'll do nothing, and tell no one, not if you know what's good for you." He turned to me. "I'll take care of Arthur. I'll tell his old man it was a hunting accident. He'll believe me. Arthur is—was—always messing about with guns. But you'd better get Weston-Greer away from here as quickly as possible, and get a doctor to him. Tell him whatever you please, so long as you avoid making him suspicious. You and I know it was an accident, but the coppers mightn't, if they do come to hear of it. Oh, don't worry," he added in response to my gasp of fear, "*I* shan't tell them. After all, I've as much to lose as you or Charles. Though I'm not sure how far I can trust Bingham; I told Arthur not to bring the young fool along. Here, I'll help you get Charles into the car."

I thanked him, and together we carried Charles to the car and managed to haul him onto the back seat. Fitzwalter ordered Bingham to operate the crank handle, presumably considering this a just penalty for his stupidity, and I slid into the driver's seat. How I managed to drive the vehicle I have no idea, but I steered back to Compton at a snail's pace, stopping it by the simple expedient of driving it into the steps at the front of the house, sounding the horn with an urgent blast.

CHAPTER EIGHT

Mrs Trolove, Charles's housekeeper, came running out to meet us, concerned that neither of us had been there for breakfast. I explained Charles had met with a serious accident and she went off to fetch water and bandages.

She must have alerted Ward, who hurried out with one of the stable hands to help me carry Charles inside. With some difficulty, we manhandled him up the stairs and laid him as gently as we could on his bed. His wound appeared to have stopped bleeding, and I heaved a sigh of relief. Perhaps he was not so badly wounded after all. Mrs Trolove bustled into the room just as Ward had finished divesting Charles of his blood-soaked shirt. I forced myself to look at the wound, a ragged gash of dark red against which his skin looked like chalk, surrounded by dried blood and fragments of torn skin. With a supreme effort to control my rebellious stomach, I turned to Ward.

"The—the bleeding seems to have stopped. Is—is that a good sign?"

Without a word, Ward felt at Charles's neck, and then bent over him for a moment, doing something I couldn't see. At length he stood up, his face grim.

"I'm afraid not, sir. I can find no pulse."

"Oh, God! Are you certain?"

"As certain as may be, sir."

I practically shoved him aside in my haste to prove him wrong, but I could find no pulse, either. Mrs Trolove, who had set her towels and jug of hot water down on the bedside table, came to stand beside me.

"Here's Mr Charles's hand mirror," she said, holding it out to me. "Why don't you try that in front of his mouth?"

With a grateful smile, I did as she suggested. No breath clouded the glass.

"I'll send for Doctor Jerrold, sir," said Ward, "but I fear it will be only to write a death certificate."

I nodded. "I think you're right, Ward, but he'll have to be sent for. Can you please let me know when he arrives? I'll be in my room."

In my room, I stripped off my clothes, washed and put on clean ones, and then lay down on my bed to try to compose myself. I felt exhausted, yet I was too tense to rest, let alone sleep. Over and over again I heard those dreadful shots, saw the drifting smoke, saw Charles and Arthur de Burgh lying lifeless on the ground, their white shirts stained with blood. I felt I had—for I blamed myself as much as Charles for being unable to prevent the duel—committed an act so appalling I should be imprisoned by it for the rest of my life, even if, by some miracle, I managed to escape the attention of the police. How could I have let myself become involved? If only I had ignored Charles's telegram and left him to his own fate, I should still have been in London with Emmeline. But of course, I knew I could never have done that. Charles, with all his faults, was a friend.

Tears filled my eyes as I thought of Emmeline. What would she think of me now I was party to the deaths of two men? My tears flowed in earnest at the thought of what I had surely lost.

A soft knock at the door dragged me from the mire of self-reproach into which I had sunk. Wiping my tears away with my towel, I hurried out to find Dr Jerrold climbing the stairs to meet me.

I shook the hand he held out to me. "How do you do, Doctor Jerrold? Thank you for coming so quickly, though I'm afraid it's too—too late to do anything for Charles."

"How do you do, sir? I'm very sorry to hear that. What happened to young Mr Weston-Greer?"

"A—a hunting accident," I temporised, taking a leaf from Fitzwalter's book. "He and Lord Warrington's son were out hunting together. I'm not sure exactly what happened. I—I only heard about it later." I felt almost more appalled by the necessity of lying than by the cause of it, but could think of no other course to take.

The doctor gave a brisk nod, and I ushered him into Charles's room. A few moments sufficed to confirm our own diagnosis, and Jerrold took his leave, tut-tutting over the needless waste of young lives, and promised to send a copy of the death certificate by tomorrow's mail.

After he had gone, I went downstairs and poured myself a very large brandy, at which point I realised I had had nothing to eat that morning, and it was now after eleven o'clock. I rang for Mrs Trolove and requested some tea and toast; I certainly did not feel up to anything more substantial. Having eaten what I could of my belated breakfast, and downed the rest of my brandy, I took myself off for a long, brisk walk, hoping it might induce my brain to function. It seemed to me there must be any number of things I ought to be doing, but my mind would produce nothing but the sight of Charles's cold, white body and the ragged gash in his breast.

Barely had I returned from my walk and set down my hat and gloves when there came a rap at the front door. Ward hurried to answer it, returning a few moments later to announce the Honourable Augustus Fitzwalter.

My heart leaping with fear, I hurried to meet him. "Fitzwalter! Is something wrong?"

"I'm afraid so," Fitzwalter replied, with little trace of his previous haughtiness. He glanced round at Ward, who was still standing by the door.

"You can go thanks, Ward," I said. "Come and sit down, Fitzwalter, and tell me what's to do."

"No, no, I can't stay. I came only to tell you that, although I'd managed to persuade Lord Warrington Arthur's death was an accident, that young fool Bingham has now well and truly set the cat among the pigeons."

"What do you mean?" My voice sounded sharp in my own ears.

"Bingham told his cousin what had happened, and the rattle-pated fool told his father, who's a Justice of the Peace. Now—to come to the nub of the matter—there are warrants out for our arrests. My advice to you, for what you think it worth, is to get as far away from here as you can, as soon as possible, unless you wish to find yourself in prison—or worse. I'm sorry to be so blunt, but there it is. Good day to you, Randall."

"But—but what about you?" I said. "What will you do?"

A faint smile twitched at the corner of Fitzwalter's mouth. "Your concern is admirable, Randall, but I believe I can take

89

care of myself."

"Thank you for the warning," I said, holding out my hand to him. "I—I'm very much in your debt."

"Oh, spare me your gratitude. It's scarcely in my own interest to have you blabbing to the constabulary."

He gave a stiff bow, then turned and strode from the room.

I collapsed onto the nearest chair and put my head in my hands. My heart was racing like an express train, and my head felt as though some fiend were twisting a corkscrew into it just above my eyes. But I had to think—and quickly. My immediate thought was to make for Dover and try to get a passage to France, but for that I should need money, and I had little left of this quarter's allowance, certainly not enough to buy my passage to France and then find somewhere to live there. Then I thought of my father's offer of a Grand Tour. Yes, that was it! I would go home, pretend to be contrite and take him up on his kind offer. If nothing else, that would get me out of immediate danger and give me some breathing space to think of a plan for my future safety.

My relief at coming up with what seemed a viable scheme was palpable, and I hurried to pack my bags. On my way upstairs, I met Mrs Trolove coming down.

"Oh, there you are, Mr Randall. Beg pardon, sir, but I was wondering if you could manage a bite of luncheon, such sad doings as there's been today."

"Yes, yes, all right," I said, my mind so full of my own desperate plans I scarcely took in what she was saying.

"Shall I bring it to your room, or will you have it in the dining room?"

"What? Oh, sorry Mrs Trolove, what did you say?"

"Your luncheon, Mr Randall. Where would you like to eat it?"

I had no real wish to eat, but it occurred to me food might be a good idea if I planned to travel into Bedfordshire.

"Oh, the dining room, thank you."

"Very good. I'll have it ready in twenty minutes."

By the time Mrs Trolove brought me a luncheon of cold mutton, bread, cheese and pickles, with a jug of ale to wash it down, I had my bag packed and sitting in the hallway along with my greatcoat and hat. As I ate—or picked, rather—it occurred to me I should need some mode of transport, and the faster the better. I had no desire to use public transport. It seemed likely to be one of the first places the Police would think of looking for an absconding miscreant. I thought of taking Charles's car, since it would certainly be the fastest transport available, but I soon realised it would be well enough known in the neighbourhood to make it downright dangerous to use, never mind the fact that I was scarcely a competent driver. In the end, I decided to take one of Charles's horses. That way, I could travel cross-country rather than using roads that might be posted with officers of the Police.

I rang for Ward to ask him to have a fast horse saddled for me, then hurried to collect my luggage, thinking how fortunate it was I had brought only a valise sufficient to hold a couple of changes of clothes and my toilet articles—and my journal, of course, since I never went anywhere without that. One day, perhaps, I might turn the present mad escapade into a story—if I came out of it in tolerable safety. By the time Ward came to tell me my horse was ready, I had concocted a story for him about having to return to my ailing father's bedside, though I was pretty certain he did not believe me. However, he wished me good speed with a straight face, adding, "You needn't fear, Mr Randall, we know how to keep our counsel here."

I breathed a sigh of relief and shook his hand. "Good man. I'm sorry for all that's happened."

"Never mind that, sir. Best be on your way, now."

A stable lad was standing by to help me into the saddle and, in a very few moments, with my valise perched before me, I was on my way.

After a cross-country ride that took me through Sussex, Hampshire, Buckinghamshire, and at last into Bedfordshire, I reached Apsley End on the outskirts of Shillington at around five in the afternoon. The ride had stretched both my horse and me to our limits, and we were tired and wind-swept, the poor horse panting and bathed in sweat, and myself not much better. Wary of being seen in such a desperate state, I decided to leave the horse at the *Crown Inn* and make arrangements for it to be returned to Compton later. Delivering it into the hands of the ostler, I made my way into the inn and bespoke a bedroom in which I could wash and render my clothes more presentable before taking tea in the only private parlour the inn possessed. Having eaten nothing since a luncheon to which I had been unable to do justice, I was ravenous, and made short work of my mince pies and plum cake. Afterwards, I felt so weary I decided to rest in my room for an hour or so. In the event, it was dark by the time I awoke. Anxious as I was to reach home and pursue my plan for escape, it seemed counterproductive to wake the household so late in the evening, so I made the best of it and ordered supper and a bed for the night.

The following morning I was up early and, after a hurried breakfast of toast and coffee, set out to walk the short distance from Apsley End to Shillington. The morning was warm and bright, with a light breeze that cooled me as I walked so that, despite my desperate situation, I found myself enjoying the countryside almost as much as I had on my rambles as a boy, recognising such dear, familiar landmarks as the massive horse-chestnut tree beneath which I had joined the village children in gathering chestnuts to thread onto strings to play conkers, and the bramble hedgerow where we had glutted ourselves on fat blackberries, arriving home afterwards with hands and faces stained with their purple juice. Before long, I spied above the trees the tall, brick chimneys of Shillington Hall. My heart began to race as I thought of what I was about to do. Put bluntly, I intended to lie to my father in order to gain his money and unwitting aid in my escape across the Channel to France. In my heart I knew I was nothing more than a fugitive from justice—and a cowardly one at that. But, I told myself, I could not stay to face a situation that was none of my making, yet which, regardless of the outcome, would bring shame on my father. Much as I feared and detested my father's marriage and its issue, I had no wish to do that to the man who, in his own gruff way, had loved and nurtured me all my life. Thus I convinced myself I acted from a nobler motive than merely saving my own skin.

As I walked up the long, gravel driveway, I saw Captain Nuttall striding back from the woods with his gun and a brace of rabbits. He waved at me and called out, "Morning, Mister Alex. London getting a bit hot for you, is it?"

No words could have been better calculated to increase my feelings of guilt, but I forced myself to reply with a cheerfulness I was far from feeling.

Papa greeted me as though I had been the prodigal son, although Captain Nuttall's rabbits—baked into a tasty pie by Mrs Dear—were substituted for the proverbial fatted calf.

That evening, after dinner, I broached the subject of travel as Papa and I sat drinking our port. "Papa, I know I behaved foolishly in rushing off to London as I did, but I've had time to reflect, now, and I—I think—at least I—I'd like to accept your offer of a Grand Tour. I think it would do me a lot of good—that is, if you're still willing—"

"Alex, my boy!" my father exclaimed in his impulsive way. "Of course my offer still stands. I've had time for reflection, too, and I can see I shouldn't have sprung my marriage on you as I did. No doubt I should have written to you first, and introduced you to Mariah, but then, I always was one to act without thinking. Well, well, no use crying over spilt milk, as the saying is. When were you thinking of travelling?"

Steeling myself for the lies I was about to tell, I said, "I'd like to leave as quickly as possible. I'm sorry to rush off again so soon, but some friends of mine are travelling, too, and they've asked me to join them. I'm to meet them at Dover in—in two days' time, if—if that's possible."

The disappointment in my father's face made me cringe with remorse, but all he said was, "Well, well, it seems you've inherited my impulsiveness after all. We'll drive into Luton tomorrow morning and do the business. How does that suit you?"

After a frantic day spent making financial arrangements and

purchasing clothes and other items, I woke early the following morning, devoured a hasty breakfast, and bade farewell to Papa, who had dragged himself from his bed especially to see me off. Mariah and her brat, I was relieved to see, had not joined him, Papa excusing them with the information that Oliver was suffering from some childhood indisposition, and Mariah did not feel able to leave him. I am not ashamed to admit both Papa and I shed tears on parting.

Captain Nuttall drove me to Luton, from where I hired a chaise to carry me and my baggage to Dover. I should have preferred to take the train, but I was wary of using public transport until I was safely out of England. Although I left Luton soon after nine o'clock in the morning, it was almost eight o'clock in the evening by the time I reached Dover. My limbs ached with stiffness, and I could not keep myself from yawning, so I turned in at the first inn I saw, *The Ship's Bell*, and begged a room for the night. Despite the hard bed, I fell almost immediately into a deep sleep from which I was roused only by the clatter of cartwheels in the yard outside early the next morning.

With a mixture of excitement and fear, I washed and dressed and made my way downstairs. I was too nervous to make much of a breakfast, but I managed a couple of slices of toast and a cup of strong coffee, after which I set off to procure my passage to France, leaving my luggage in the care of the landlord of *The Ship's Bell*. To my considerable frustration, there was no ship leaving until the afternoon, 'depending on the tide', as the gentleman in the shipping office told me with maddening calm. This left me with three or four hours to kick my heels waiting. I decided to retrieve my two suitcases from the inn and take them to the embarkation point at Admiralty Pier. The walk proved considerably more interesting than I had anticipated, due to the steam trains puffing their way to and from the pier. These were still something of a novelty to me, and I found myself regretting not having taken the train from Luton. I consoled myself, however, with the thought of the one I should soon be taking from Calais to Paris. Having seen my luggage safely on board *The Empress of India*, the paddle steamer that would convey me across the channel, I strolled off to watch the building taking place to extend the end of the pier. In this way I spent an entertaining couple of hours until the time came to board the steamer.

Only after I was on board did I realise I had had no lunch, and only the sketchiest of breakfasts. As it turned out, this was probably just as well, since the passage, once we were well into the channel, was a rough one, and I pitied the poor seasick passengers who were obliged to spend their voyage on deck in the wind and rain.

At length, I disembarked at Calais, a trifle wan but decidedly hungry. My first action was to enquire after a good, but inexpensive inn. Then, as soon as I had procured my luggage, I hailed a cab to *Le Roquefort*, which proved to be a small, but cosy establishment with an accommodating landlord and an excellent cook and wine cellar. I finished my dinner more than ready for slumber. A maid showed me to a chamber on the first floor. I gazed at its whitewashed plaster walls, the cheerful rug on its scrubbed wooden floor and the narrow bed with its patchwork counterpane, and assured the maid it was most satisfactory. Next morning I rose considerably refreshed. After a hearty breakfast, I made my way to the railway station and bought a ticket for the next train to Paris, which was to leave late that afternoon. I whiled away the day pleasantly enough exploring the ancient town, but was impatient to resume my journey. I had never been on a train before.

I was not disappointed. The swaying of the train, the rhythmic breathing of the coal-fired engine, the clatter of the wheels on the iron rails, all created music excitingly mechanical yet oddly poetic. It was as though some monster out of legend charged headlong through the countryside, a dragon, perhaps, rushing to do battle with Saint George. I sat staring out of the window as the countryside flashed past, mesmerised by glimpses of houses and fields familiar in their generality yet quite alien in their detail. Gradually, the daylight faded, and, half-mesmerised by the music of the train, despite my situation I found myself wondering what this new and unexpected phase in my life might bring.

CHAPTER NINE

The rhythm of the train must have lulled me to sleep, as I was wrenched from a dream of Emmeline's red curls and warm, scented skin by someone speaking my name. I opened eyes still bleary with sleep to see the last person I had ever thought to meet again.

"Henri!" I exclaimed. "What are you doing here?"

I realised the fatuousness of my question, even before he drawled, smiling, "*Enfin*, I suppose anyone may travel on a public train."

"I-I do beg your pardon! I'm just—I didn't expect to see you again."

"Nevertheless, here I am. May I sit with you?"

"Of course. Sorry!" I hastened to remove from the seat next to me the newspaper I had bought to read during the journey. As he sat down, the overhead lamp illuminated Henri's face for a moment, and I saw it was as pale and translucent as when I had first met him, and I wondered yet again whether he was victim to some recurring illness. But of course I could not ask him. Instead, I asked, "Are you travelling to Paris, then?"

"I am," he replied. "Am I to take it that is your destination also?"

"Yes, I'm visiting my cousin and his wife in *Saint-Germain*." I said nothing of my Grand Tour, which was, in any case, nothing more than a ruse to get myself out of England in short order.

"Ah, yes," Henri said, smiling. "A delightful neighbourhood. And is this the first time you've been abroad?"

"It is."

"Then you have a great adventure before you, I think."

"I hope so," I said, feeling a twinge of guilt, yet unable to tell him the true reason for my being in France. "Perhaps I can call on you while I'm in Paris. Do you keep the same hours as you did in London?"

A look I could not quite fathom passed over his features, and a transitory gleam of light kindled in his dark eyes. "I do," he said. "I'm afraid it's one of my little peccadilloes. But even in England, a gentleman is allowed these, *n'est ce pas*?"

"Oh, you mean the traditional eccentric Englishman? Has his fame reached as far as Paris, then?"

"Oh, further, I assure you. You are universally renowned for it, I believe."

I laughed. "Please don't include me in their number. Not being a true aristocrat, I'm sure I'm as dull as ditch water."

He gave a soft, appreciative laugh, his eyes lighting this time with humour. "Ah, but one with an excellent memory. Shall I ever live down my ill-advised remark?"

"I was just funning," I assured him with what I hoped was a suitably contrite look.

He looked puzzled for a moment. "Funning? Ah, you mean you were teasing me? *Touché, M'sieu.* " He inclined his head, raising one arm in salute, like a fencer acknowledging a hit.

Our opening skirmish being over, we conversed as

comfortably as ever, and it was with a feeling akin to disappointment that I realised the train was pulling into the Gare du Nord *in Paris*.

"As always," I told Henri as we made our way between the seats of the train and out onto the platform, "I've enjoyed our conversation tremendously, and I'd very much like to see you again."

I pulled out my pocket book, extracted one of my calling cards, inscribed my cousin's address on the back, and gave it to him. He accepted the card with a few words of thanks, although I noticed he did not return the favour.

"I, too, look forward to renewing our acquaintance," he said. "I'm not entirely sure of my itinerary just yet, but I dare say our paths will cross before very long."

With that, he bowed and left me, vanishing almost immediately into the throng crowding the platform. Once again, I realised I knew almost nothing about him. Somehow, he had managed to avoid being pinned down to any definite arrangements without my realising it until it was too late. Still, I thought, it should be a simple matter to find out more about him. People are always interested in the doings of the nobility. I made up my mind to ask my cousin Jerome about him, and went to retrieve my luggage.

* * * *

Jerome lived in an elegant town house with his French wife, Lucette, and their two young children, Luc and Charlotte. They made me very welcome, filling my waking hours with trips to see the Parisian sights, as well as some further afield. Jerome had taken leave from his accounting practice specifically for this purpose, which gave me an initial twinge of guilt, considering my deception. However, I soon found myself caught up in my cousins' plans for my enjoyment. Several times we went to the theatre and the opera, dining afterwards in one of the cafés and restaurants that seemed never to close. My dear cousins even procured for me an invitation to go with them to a ball being held by Monsieur and Madame de Courcy to celebrate the engagement of their daughter, Antoinette, to the Compte de Vaucluse. The family lived about an hour's drive to the south of Paris.

As our carriage swept up a curving driveway lined with great elm trees, a vast mansion came into view, built in the rococo style favoured in the days before the revolution, and bathed in the light of many lamps.

Inside, the house was also a blaze of light, both gas and candle. Great swathes of gilt and silver flowers and fruit decorated the walls and the balustrade of the curved marble staircase rising from the entrance hall. Our coats and wraps having been taken by one liveried servant, another ushered us up the staircase and into the ballroom. If I had thought the hall brightly lit, the ballroom, a huge gallery with a high, ornately plastered ceiling painted with scenes of Arcadia, would have done justice to the Sun King himself. A row of glittering crystal candelabra hung from the ceiling, while hundreds more candles lined the walls between tall windows swathed in crimson velvet hung with gilded cherubs carrying harps or trumpets or fat bunches of grapes. The room itself was filled with swirling figures. Men in dapper evening dress and women in a rainbow of silks and satins adorned with glittering jewels danced to the music of a full-sized orchestra on a dais at the far end of the ballroom.

The servant announced our arrival, and our hosts moved forward to greet us. Monsieur de Courcy was a tall, courtly gentleman who looked to be in his late forties. His wife, plump and pretty and somewhat younger, wore sky-blue silk trimmed with silver lace, her golden hair piled high and secured with a comb set with sapphires and diamonds. Antoinette, whom I judged to be around eighteen or nineteen, favoured her father, being tall and slender, and handsome rather than fashionably pretty, with dark ringlets tumbling about her face. She was clearly excited by the occasion and looked enchanting in a gown of palest green worn with a simple string of pearls, as befitted her youth and unmarried status. Her betrothed, a handsome young man with black hair and a splendid moustache, looked on fondly as she politely curtsied to us, then moved on with her parents to greet more newly arrived guests.

Jerome and Lucette undertook to introduce me to a number of young ladies, and I had soon added my name to the dance cards of several of them.

I was caught up in a set dance with a pretty redhead called Émilie when I caught a glimpse of a face I could not mistake. Henri de Saint-Clair stood just inside the doorway. Immaculate in evening dress, he was gazing idly about with an expression of tolerant boredom. As soon as the dance was finished, and I had returned Émilie to her parents, I made my way to his side.

"Good evening, Henri! I hadn't thought to see you again quite so soon, but I must say I'm pleased to do so."

Saint-Clair gave a little start, as though his thoughts had been far away, then swiftly recollected himself, smiling as he recognised me. "Alex! I'm enchanted to see you again. Are you a friend of the Courcys?"

"No, I'm here under the auspices of my cousin and his wife. They were kind enough to obtain an invitation for me. Are you a friend of our hosts?"

Saint-Clair inclined his head with a faint, ironic smile. "Not a friend, precisely, but my family and theirs have long been acquainted. Besides, it would never do to miss the ball of the season, and risk becoming a social outcast."

I laughed. "Indeed, that would never do! I shudder to think how close *I* must have come to such a fate. Why, if it hadn't been for my cousins' kindness..."

"A lucky escape indeed!" Saint-Clair's lip twitched in a brief show of humour. "Now, if you'll excuse me, Alex, I must do my social duty and allow you to return to the pleasures of the dance."

Saint-Clair strolled off, bowing in greeting to several guests, but stopping to talk to no one, as far as I could see. Before long, I lost sight of him in the press of dancers. I went to claim my dance with the lady who was next on my dance list, a sweet-faced brunette named Marianne la Page.

I looked for Monsieur de Saint-Clair when supper was served in an adjoining room, but there was no sign of him. Fleetingly, I surmised that, having done his social duty by attending the ball, he'd taken himself off to engage in more congenial pursuits. I was sorry not to have had more conversation with him, but happy enough to escort Mademoiselle la Page in to supper.

* * * *

Over the next few weeks, I had scant time to think of the

elusive Henri de Saint-Clair, so full was my social calendar. Jerome and Lucette included Mademoiselle la Page and one or two of the other young ladies from the ball in a number of our excursions, hoping, I imagined, to attach me to one of them. As much as I enjoyed their company, however, my thoughts were still with Emmeline back in London. The French girls, charming as they were, seemed somehow performing a part compared with Emmeline's genuine sweetness, as though they, and not she, were the true actresses.

One morning at breakfast, Lucette and Jerome made clear their plans for me as I became the butt of my cousin's good-natured teasing.

"I see we did well, my love, in taking young Alex to the ball," he said, with a wink at Lucette.

"*Mais oui, mon cher*," she rejoined, her dark eyes twinkling with mischief. "I believe he may very soon lose his heart. Will it be to Émilie, do you think, or to the sweet Marianne?"

"To one of them, at any event," he said. "As I recall, my love, Alex always was prone to losing things. Why, the number of times I was obliged to cover for him at school when he'd lost his cricket clothes, or his textbooks, or—"

"Now that," I protested, laughing, "is pure character assassination! You were in your final year when I started at Harrow, and far too grand to condescend to the company of a lowly newcomer such as me."

"Now it's you who are falsely maligning *me*! I assure you—" He turned to his wife "—I was always very condescending indeed."

"Ah, *mon cher*, you know I do not always understand the

finer points of the English language, but I am sure you are being very impolite to poor Alex. I shall change the subject." She turned to me with a smile. "Was that Henri de Saint-Clair I saw you talking to at the ball, Alex? How did you come to make his acquaintance?"

"We were introduced by mutual acquaintances in London, and found we had many interests in common. I was sorry when he left London. We'd become good friends. Then we met again by chance on the train to Paris. He's an unusual fellow, but I like him a great deal."

"Do you, indeed?" my cousin interposed. "One must suppose he likes you, too. He puts in an appearance at most of the appropriate social events when he's in Paris, but he's generally considered to be rather standoffish. At any rate, he seems to have few, if any, friends."

"Jerome, you make the man sound like some—what do you say in English?—some social climber. His family is one of the oldest in France. Indeed, the Saint-Clairs are rumoured to be descended from Our Lord himself—or at least from the Holy Mother."

"Nonsense, my dear!" Jerome retorted. "What a ridiculous notion! Put about by his grandfather, I shouldn't wonder. Dreadful reprobate, *he* was, by all accounts—barely had time to produce an heir before he got himself killed. Rumour has it it was in a fight over a dancer in the *Folies Bergères*, if you please." He turned to me, his distaste clear in the curl of his lip. "If you'll take my advice, Alex, you'll have nothing to do with the grandson, either." He excused himself from the table, kissed Lucette, and went to get his coat and hat.

His words of advice failed to have the desired effect. After he'd left for work, I said to Lucette, "I don't suppose you happen to know where Monsieur de Saint-Clair lives?"

"*Mais oui*, Alex, everyone knows the Saint-Clair house! But surely you don't intend to ignore your cousin's good advice?" she added with a mischievous grin.

I gave an answering grin. "I don't see how I'm to know if it *is* good advice without further acquaintance with the gentleman."

"Ah, but by then it may be too late!"

Nevertheless, Lucette wrote out the address on a piece of notepaper. Determining to pay Henri a visit that evening, I folded the note and tucked it into the inside pocket of my coat before setting out to view the splendours of Notre Dame.

That evening, on the pretext of a pre-dinner constitutional, I made my way to Monsieur de Saint-Clair's town house, which was not too far distant from the Rue Saint-Germain. It was in an excellent part of town, and must once have been a very handsome building. Now, it looked rather faded, like a grand old lady who has seen better days. I tugged at the bell rope and heard a hollow clanging somewhere deep within. There appeared to be no one at home, though I thought it strange that no servant came to answer my ring. Just as I turned to leave, the door creaked open and I turned to find myself facing an elderly gentleman whose brown face and sharp, glittering eyes reminded me of a sparrow. I announced myself in my rather halting schoolboy French and begged the honour of a visit with Monsieur de Saint-Clair.

"M'sieu is not available," he informed me bluntly, making

no attempt at the obsequious politeness often affected by English servants. "M'sieu does not receive visitors."

I didn't quite know how to deal with this rebuff and, before I could give him my calling card to let Saint-Clair know of my visit, the old man had shut the door firmly in my face. Amused, despite my disappointment, I made my way back to the Rue Saint-Germain.

After a delightful dinner of *coq au vin* followed by *crème brulée* and fruit, Jerome proposed that he and I attend an evening of card-playing and general male conviviality being hosted by his friend, and Lucette's distant cousin, the Duc d'Embry. Flattered at being considered mature enough to attend a gathering in such exalted company, I was only too happy to accompany him.

I was rather surprised to find the duke's *hôtel*, which lay in the best part of Paris, even more dilapidated than Monsieur de Saint-Clair's.

Seeing my dismay, Jerome grinned at me. "When you're top of the trees, Alex, you've no need to prove it to anyone. Embry comes from one of the oldest families in France. Tradition has it the line goes right back to ancient Rome."

I smiled inwardly to think this was the same man who had scoffed at the rumoured ancestry of Henri de Saint-Clair.

The duke himself went a considerable way towards banishing my first impression. A slender, elegant man I judged to be in his mid-thirties, he was dressed in the height of understated fashion. His dark curls, superbly cut and dressed, reminded me of polished ebony, and smiling eyes the colour of chestnuts softened otherwise severe features. Like the duke, the interior of his *hôtel* bore little resemblance to the exterior. Clearly the abode of a single gentleman, it was as charming a mixture of the antique and the modern as I ever hope to see, with a number of card tables set out for the guests and a large, ornate sideboard laden with refreshments.

Before very long, Jerome and I, with several introductions under our belts, were seated at a card table engaged in a rubber of whist, with a bottle of the duke's excellent burgundy to hand. Although whist was not a game I usually favoured, I had played it before, at Packham's and elsewhere in London, though seldom with such expert players. In spite of myself, I was soon engrossed in the intricacies of the game. This is probably why I failed to notice the arrival of a new guest until I looked up to see him seated at the next table.

It was Henri de Saint-Clair. Dressed in his customary sober black, I fancied he looked less pale than on our previous encounter, the veins beneath the skin of his face less noticeable, and the skin itself less like alabaster. His demeanour seemed less grave, almost animated, as he sipped his wine and gazed about him, nodding pleasantly to acquaintances. As soon as my game was over, I went to join him.

"Ah, Alex," he said, looking up at my approach, "did I not tell you we'd meet again soon? I trust you're well?"

"Indeed I am, thank you, and pleased to see you again. Are you a friend of the duke's?"

Saint-Clair smiled. "The Saint-Clairs and the Embrys are both ancient families."

I noticed he did not really answer my question, but felt it would be impolite to press the point. "May I join you?" I asked instead.

"Certainly. Would you care for a glass of our host's delightful burgundy?"

"Thank you." I disposed myself opposite him as he poured wine for both of us. "Do you not care to play cards, Henri?" I asked, thinking back to our conversation at Packham's.

"Only with those I dislike," he replied, the hint of a sardonic smile on his lips. "With you, I should much rather converse. I trust you're enjoying your stay in the City of Light?"

"Oh yes!" I exclaimed, and began to regale him with my adventures.

To my gratification, Saint-Clair listened with every appearance of enjoyment, even looking wistful at times, as though such simple pleasures were somehow denied him. He seemed to have an encyclopaedic knowledge of Paris and its history, and so engrossed did we become in our conversation that when it was time to leave I was surprised at how quickly the evening had passed.

"I hope I may have the pleasure of calling on you soon," I said. "I called earlier this evening, but your man said you weren't available."

Saint-Clair gave a slight smile. "I'm afraid I'm rarely at home to visitors."

If I'd hoped for an invitation, it seemed I was to remain disappointed.

CHAPTER TEN

A few days later, two letters arrived from England: one for me and one for Jerome, both addressed in my father's heavy hand. Mine was quite short, although cordial in tone, hoping I'd arrived safely in Paris and urging me to write and let Papa know how I was going on. As I was refolding it, Jerome looked up from his own letter.

"You didn't mention Uncle John had remarried," he said, and I found myself bridling at the hint of accusation I detected in his voice. "Nor that he and his wife had had a son."

"He didn't think to inform me, either." My attempt to suppress my still smouldering resentment was less than successful. "He only bothered to tell me after it was a *fait accompli*."

Jerome glanced again at the page he still held. "To be fair," he said gently, "your Papa gives the impression it was a rather impulsive decision on his part, and had only just taken place when you arrived home from Cambridge."

"Nevertheless, he might have seen fit to invite me, his only son. At least I was," I added in bitter tones, "until the new Lady Randall produced her brat."

"Alex!" exclaimed Lucette reproachfully. "How can you speak so of a darling, innocent little baby?" She turned her doting gaze on young Luc and Charlotte as though to emphasise her point.

"He's not a darling," I retorted. "He's a red-faced, squalling brat, and although *he* may be innocent, I'm convinced his mother is not. It's my belief she's under orders from her brother." I explained how Mariah's brother owned the neighbouring estate, and my suspicions about his designs on my father's estate, but I could tell my words fell on deaf ears, as Jerome and Lucette continued to exclaim over my father's good fortune, and what joy the latest addition to his household must have brought him.

"I'm going for a walk," I announced at last, getting up from the table.

That neither of them seemed to have heard me added fuel to the rapidly rising flames of my anger. Striding out to the foyer, I shrugged myself into my coat, jammed my hat onto my head and left the house, barely managing to resist slamming the door behind me.

How could Jerome, of all people, be so blind to my distress? I thought as I strode along the street, oblivious alike of the warm sunshine and the signs of spring burgeoning all around me. How could he and Lucette find joy in a situation that had already robbed me of my only remaining parent, and stood to rob me of my birthright as well? If they thought I was going to sit meekly by and listen to their sickening sentimentality, they had another thing coming.

It must have taken a full hour for my seething anger to cool to mere sullenness. By that time I was exhausted, and hot, and very thirsty. I cast my gaze about me and spied a small café that would have been lost amongst the larger shops surrounding it were it not for the tables and chairs on the pavement outside. Pulling off my coat and draping it over my arm, I made my way towards it. Only once I was inside did I realise that, unlike English coffee houses, French cafés sold alcoholic beverages as well. Such was my mood that I instantly ordered a bottle of burgundy. Rather than sitting at one of the pavement tables in the sun, I took a seat at a small table in a corner of the tiny establishment. It was not a conscious decision, but I suppose the dark panelling, subdued lighting, and general air of being down-at-heel suited my mood.

The wine helped me feel more in charity with the world, or, if not quite in charity, at least numb to its more painful devices of torture. Some time later, more than a little befuddled, I left the café and made my way to the bank of the River Seine, where I sat on a bench under some trees for I know not how long, staring at the water, and the boats and barges travelling slowly to and fro beneath the graceful arches of its bridges. Before too long, the wine and the slow rhythms of the river sent me into a doze, from which I awoke, chilled by a cool breeze that had sprung up, to find the afternoon well advanced. With a sigh, I donned my coat and, since I had nowhere else to go, began to make my way back to the *Rue Saint-Germain*.

As soon as one of the servants had let me into the house, Lucette flew to meet me.

"Alex, where have you been for so long? I was so worried that you had become lost, or—or worse. There are some very bad people out on the streets, you know."

During my walk home, I had determined to curb my feelings as well as I could, for the sake of harmony if nothing else, so I gave a reassuring smile and said, "I'm sorry to have worried you, Lucette. I've been out walking, and watching the boats on the Seine, and I'm afraid I fell asleep in the sunshine. I do hope I may not have contracted sunburn." I said nothing about my visit to the café, thinking my cousins would be bound to disapprove of my imbibing strong drink in the middle of the day.

"Well," she said, "at least now you are home safe. Shall we have a cup of tea? Jerome has instructed Marie how to make it in the English style."

"Thank you," I said, and indeed, a cup of tea was exactly what I needed to chase the last of the wine fumes from my head.

Lucette took my arm, drew me into her cosy little parlour, and rang for the maid. Before she sat down in her accustomed chair under the window, I noticed she removed a ball of white wool and knitting needles and placed them on the low table beside her. Seeing my glance, she lifted the bundle and said,

"See, I am knitting a coat for the little Oliver."

Inwardly, I gritted my teeth, but managed—if only just— to hold my tongue and smile.

Over the following weeks, however, I found it increasingly difficult to keep my feelings concealed. At every turn, or so it seemed, my cousins persisted in rubbing my nose in the fact that I now had a rival for my father's affections.

How I regretted becoming embroiled in Charles's affairs. If only I had had the sense to follow my first inclination when he asked me to be his second, I told myself, I should still be in London with Emmeline instead of being obliged to listen to my cousins going into raptures over the mewling baby I was convinced would supplant me in the home I loved—and that should rightfully have been mine one day. I was so filled with bitterness I completely ignored the fact that, even had I not agreed to act for Charles, even if that fateful duel had never taken place, I should still be estranged from my father.

Nevertheless, my regret over leaving Emmeline was genuine. I'd written to her a couple of times to let her know I was alive and safe, since I knew she would have heard about Charles's death, but I dared not give her my address in case the Police should somehow come to learn of my whereabouts, and so I had not even the consolation of reading her letters.

Once or twice I caught sight of Henri, always at night, and always at a distance. Perhaps, I mused, I could have borne my situation with some equanimity if I'd only had the company of someone as compatible as Henri. But I knew no one else in Paris. No wonder, I persuaded myself, I was forced to seek solace in the bottle.

One night, as I was setting out for my favourite café near the river, I heard someone call my name. I whirled, my heart racing, thinking it must be Henri. Instead I saw a raw-boned giant of a man with a shock of ginger hair and clothes that seemed a size too small for him striding towards me like a steam engine ploughing through a snowdrift.

"Hello there, Randall," he cried, his booming English voice slicing through the air like a hot knife through butter.

"Fancy meeting you here!"

It was Giles Barnaby, a friend of Charles's and mine at Cambridge. He seemed even taller and larger than when I had last seen him, although his high top hat and pale fawn coat might have contributed to that impression.

"Hello, Barnaby," I said. "What are you doing in Paris?"

He took my proffered hand and wrung it in his outsized one with such force it was as much as I could do not to wince in pain. "I might ask you the same question, old chap. I'm staying with my Uncle Gerry—Gervase Barnaby, you know, the painter." I hadn't the faintest idea who Gervase Barnaby was, but I had the wit not to say so, since it was obvious Giles held his uncle in great esteem. "So what brings you to the continent?"

If only you knew, I thought, considering it best to favour him with the same mendacious tale I had told Papa and Jerome. "I'm starting off my Grand Tour by staying in Paris for a few weeks with my cousin and his family."

"Capital! Uncle Gerry's a great gun, but it'll be good to have someone my own age to knock about with. Where are you off to now?"

"Just off for a drink at a little café down by the river— *Café Tournai*. Do you know it?"

"Can't say I do, but I'll go with you. Always happy to find a new café, and we can't have you drinking alone, can we?"

"Certainly—as long as you have no other engagement."

"No, no, just doing a bit of exploring. Uncle Gerry's—um— busy this evening, and wanted me out of the way for a bit."

It took little imagination to guess what Uncle Gerry's 'business' might be, but I was happy enough to have Giles's company. I had no real wish to drink alone. By the time our evening concluded, we had consumed three bottles of wine between us, as well as omelettes with ham and mushrooms and a selection of *patisseries*, and were very merry indeed.

It was rather late by the time I arrived back at the *Rue Saint-Germain*, but Jerome was up waiting for me, wearing a mulberry-coloured brocade dressing gown and an angry frown.

"Ah, Alex," he said, his voice as cold as a lake in winter, "you've finally decided to grace us with your presence. When you didn't come home for your dinner, Lucette and I were extremely worried."

His words made me feel like a recalcitrant schoolboy—not a good tactic in the state of mind I was in. "Well, you needn't have been," I told him. "I met an old friend, that's all. Someone I knew at Cambridge."

Jerome narrowed his lips. "Alex," he said, "when Uncle John wrote and asked us to take care of you while you were in Paris, I'm tolerably certain he did not mean it to include allowing you to stay out until all hours getting drunk." He held up a hand to forestall my protestation. "Oh, yes, I'm perfectly aware you've been drinking far more than is good for any man."

"You don't know that," I said.

"How can I not, when you come home smelling like a wine vat? I'm no killjoy, Alex, but this is the outside of enough. And I'll not have you worrying Lucette."

"I'm sorry," I muttered, though with a very ill grace.

Jerome nodded. "All right, then. Have you eaten?" I nodded. "Good, at least you have that much sense. I'll bid you goodnight, now, Alex, I've work in the morning. And I suggest you get some rest yourself."

After he'd gone upstairs, I sat for a while mulling over my troubles—or at least what I perceived to be my troubles. It seemed to me then that everything had gone wrong since Papa remarried. In my mind, his act of foolishness had all but ruined my life. If he hadn't married Mariah Wenley, they wouldn't have had a son, and if that hadn't happened, I'd never have gone to London and become mixed up in Charles's dubious affairs and had to escape to France, where I knew no one except cousins who had nothing better to do than to go into raptures at every opportunity over my father's stupidity and its consequences, with no thought at all for how it had affected me. No, wait! I did know one other person in Paris. I dug my hands in my pockets and pulled out the card Giles had given me. Turning it over in my hand, I saw it was, in fact, his uncle's card. It bore his name, and an address in Montmartre. This, I knew, was a district of Paris frequented by artists, writers and bohemians. To my maudlin mind, it seemed the epitome of romance. I made up my mind to go there and visit Giles.

The following morning after breakfast, having borrowed a map of Paris from Jerome's library, I set off to walk to Montmartre. After Jerome's words to me the previous night, I was careful to let Lucette know I was going to visit an old friend I had met, and that I might well be gone for the best part of the day. It was a fine morning, with just a few clouds like puffballs blowing across the sky, and the sun already warm on my shoulders at ten o'clock in the morning. I enjoyed the walk to the eastern end of the Rue Saint-Germain and across the river at the eastern tip of the Île Saint-Louis by the Pont de Sully, where I stopped for some minutes to gaze at the Seine flowing beneath me. Having reached the right bank, I proceeded along the Boulevard Henri IV, which I discovered led to the Place de la Bastille with its high *Colonne de Juillet*. I could not resist stopping to read that the people of Paris had erected the plaques adorning it, from which I gathered the column celebrated the storming of the Bastille prison in July 1830. How strange it seemed to me. It seemed impossible to imagine our staid English folk doing anything so dramatic, although some part of me could not help wishing they would, from time to time.

Consulting my map, I struck out in a direction that seemed to lead in the right direction for Montmartre, but it was not long before I realised I was hopelessly lost, and I was beginning to feel Montmartre was a great deal further away than I had first thought. Of course, I now admitted ruefully, I should have asked Lucette's advice on the best way to get there, but my pride had prevented me. Besides, I had rather relished the idea of a secret adventure. Now, however, I was hot and tired, and had no idea where I was, much less where I should be going. Feeling thoroughly demoralised, I sat down on a low stone wall, wondering what to do next. Just as I was contemplating admitting defeat and retracing my footsteps, I spied a couple of *voitures*, the Parisian equivalent to the English hansom cab. Leaping to my feet, I waved a frantic arm, and to my relief one of them pulled in to the kerb in front of me.

Pulling Giles's card from my pocket, I showed it to the driver.

He nodded. "Ah, oui M'sieu. Entrez, s'il vous plait."

I climbed into the carriage and, with a crack of the driver's whip, we were off.

After a dizzying tour of Paris streets, of which I remembered nothing, the cab turned into a street named Rue Saint-Georges, and drew to a halt outside a café whose colourful sign pronounced it to be the *Cafe Cherbourg*. After paying the driver what seemed to me an exorbitant fare, I alighted from the cab. A buzz of conversation assailed my ears, mingled with the cheerful wheezing of an accordion. An assortment of men and women of varied ages and types occupied the tables and chairs set out on the pavement. A group of young ladies in gaudy dress, whom I thought might have been actresses or dancers, sat chattering at one table while, at another, two elderly, bearded gentlemen were engrossed in a game of chess, their glasses of wine all but forgotten at their elbows. Adjacent to the door of the café, I saw a rather battered green wooden door bearing a roughly painted number forty-five. Consulting Giles's card once more, I saw I had reached my destination. There being no door knocker, I used my cane to rap loudly on the door.

A window above the café opened, and a large, bearded head crowned by a tousled mop of greying ginger hair poked out and said, in a grumpy voice, "*Oui*?"

Hoping, after all my trouble in getting there, I was not in for a repeat of my visit to Henri de Saint-Clair's house, I summoned up my meagre store of French and explained who I was and the reason for my visit.

"Ah, you must be the chap Giles told me about. Just a sec."

The head—which I gathered belonged to Gervase Barnaby—disappeared, and I heard Giles's name being bellowed, followed, a few seconds later, by a loud thumping on the interior stairs. Then the green door flew open to reveal Giles himself, a huge grin on his face.

"Alex! Good to see you again! Come on up." He stood aside to reveal a narrow wooden staircase ascending into darkness, and waved me in. "Uncle Gerry has an apartment above *Le Cherbourg*," he explained as he led me up to a tiny

119

landing and threw open a door leading off it. "Here we are," he announced. "Welcome *chez* Barnaby!"

CHAPTER ELEVEN

The room into which Barnaby led me was considerably larger than I had expected, long and low ceilinged with wide windows overlooking the street. Two lacquered screens of vaguely oriental provenance divided the room into two areas, the part that was visible being furnished with a couple of low divans and a mahogany table and chairs. The polished wooden floors were strewn with threadbare oriental rugs and a litter of large cushions. A massive mahogany bookcase against the end wall held not only a jumble of books and magazines, but also several statuettes in bronze and alabaster, two wooden boxes inlaid with ivory, and a crystal ball on a wooden stand. A door beside this assortment apparently led to a kitchen, as I could see through its open door a wooden bench with plates and glasses on it.

As I stood surveying the room's somewhat faded charm, Gervase Barnaby emerged from behind the screens, wiping paint from his hands with a grubby cloth. It was immediately obvious he and Giles were related. Although he lacked the former's height, and was of a stockier build, he had the same untamed ginger hair, albeit liberally flecked with grey. A beard of a startling deep auburn straggled across his chin and upper lip. He wore a dressing gown of faded purple brocade over paint-stained trousers and a white shirt, and had a pair of paint-spattered leather slippers on his feet. A cigarette drooped from his lip, bobbing up and down as he spoke *at* me rather than to me in a voice as cavernous as his nephew's.

"Welcome, welcome! Gervase Barnaby, at your service. Any friend of young Giles's is always welcome here, though you'll have to take us as you find us—which is to say perennially short of funds." He gave a great guffaw at this, as though it were a prize jest. "But we can always find meat and drink for friends. Speaking of which—" He turned to his nephew "—Giles, run downstairs and see if Gaston will let us have something for our luncheon, and a couple of bottles of *rouge* if you can persuade him to part with them. Tell him I'll settle up as soon as I'm paid for that painting I sold last week."

With a nod, Giles took himself off downstairs, leaving me alone with my host.

As I stood there wondering what to do next, a distinctly feminine voice with a French accent and a plaintive tone emanated from behind the screens.

"Gervase, *mon cher*, have you finished with me yet? I am frozen like ice and I should like to dress now, *s'il vous plait*."

Gervase gave a start and clapped a hand to his brow. "Ah, *ma petite*, a thousand pardons! I quite forgot you were there. Pop some clothes on and come and meet our guest."

I heard a rustling, mingled with some muttering in French, and a few moments later a very young woman emerged, still pinning up her dark hair. With her olive skin and huge, dark eyes, she looked like a startled fawn. Gervase went to her, wrapping his arm about her and imparting a kiss to her succulent lips before drawing her over to where I stood.

"This is Alouette," he said to me. "She's been sitting for me." He turned to the girl with an affectionate smile. "And this, *chérie*,' is Alex, a friend of Giles's."

"I am happy to meet you," the girl said, holding out her hand. "My name is not truly Alouette, however. It is Antoinette, but Gervase says I am like a lark. Do you think I am like a lark, Alex?"

Rather taken aback by her question, I managed, I thought, quite a creditable reply. "Mademoiselle, your voice is as sweet as your face, so I must agree with him."

She clapped her hands delightedly. "Oh, bravo! I like you, Alex! You must please call me Alouette also."

"You mean you like compliments," laughed Gervase, giving her waist a squeeze.

"*Mais oui, mon cher.* Does not everyone?"

Gervase kissed her again, saying, "Out of the mouths, etcetera, etcetera, eh, Alex?"

At that moment, there came a clattering on the stairs and Giles burst into the room bearing a string of smoked sausages draped over one arm, a bowl of salad vegetables, a small round cheese, a baguette at least a yard long, and two bottles of red wine stuffed into his coat pockets. While he deposited these treasures on the table, pushing aside a bowl of somewhat desiccated fruit and a heavy brass ashtray, Alouette went to the kitchen, bringing back plates and glasses and a small bowl of olive oil. Seated with the others chattering in a mixture of French and English, and eating such fare, I felt very far from England, and somehow very much alone, despite the congenial company.

Our meal being finished, Gervase and Alouette elected to return the salad bowl to the café, declaring they would leave

Giles and me to become reacquainted. Giles went to the bookcase and brought back one of the wooden boxes I had seen earlier, and which turned out to be a cigarette case. He took a cigarette and offered the box to me, which I declined. Giles struck a wax Vesta and lit his cigarette, inhaling deeply and breathing a stream of smoke towards the ceiling.

"So," he said, gazing at me through a haze of bluish smoke. "You're here visiting your cousin? Have you managed to see much of Paris yet?"

"Oh, a little," I replied. "What brings you here—apart from visiting your uncle, I mean? I'm surprised your father isn't after you to join the family firm."

"Why do you think I'm here?" grinned Giles. "Pa doesn't know it, but I've no intention of becoming a manufacturer of footwear, even if he cuts me off without a penny—which he's already threatened to do, by the way."

"So what *are* you going to do?"

"Already doing it, old chap. I'm a poet." This was the last thing I could have imagined Giles doing, but of course I refrained from saying so. "I've already had a couple published," Giles told me, a note of pride in his voice. "Uncle Gerry's friend Monty says I show promise, and he's a published writer."

Out of politeness more than anything, I asked to see some of his poems. He jumped up and went to the bookcase, returning with a fat manila folder tied with a length of red ribbon and depositing it in front of me.

"You know, these are not bad at all," I told him after reading a few. "You've a very nice turn of phrase, Giles, and an excellent sense of metre."

A grin of pleasure suffused his face. "Thank you, Alex.

Coming from a bookworm and fellow scribbler like you, that's high praise indeed!" He leaned back against the pillows, puffing on his cigarette and gazing up at the ceiling. "So," he drawled, "what are you planning to do after your Grand Tour? Helping your Pa on the estate, I suppose?"

I had not intended telling Giles anything of my miserable affairs, but reading his poetry seemed to have created a bond between us, so that I felt us to be, in some sense, kindred spirits. Whether it was that, or the wine I had drunk with luncheon, after a short silence in which thoughts and feelings tumbled over one another in my head like a house of cards, its precarious balance overthrown, I found myself confessing the entire sorry saga, from my unwelcome discovery of my father's remarriage to my quarrel with Jerome the previous night.

"Charles is dead!" Giles exclaimed when I'd talked myself out. "Good Lord! Still, you're the one who has my sympathy, Alex, old chap. If you ask me, Charles completely lost his head when his uncle left him all that money. Even before I left London he was lording it around the town as though it gave him *carte blanche* for every bit of foolishness that took his fancy. But to involve you in his sorry affairs, on my word, that was very badly done. So now you're on the run from the Police? I take it your cousin doesn't know?"

"No, and neither does Papa, and I don't want them to, either. But it does mean I can't go back to England for the foreseeable future. Not that I want to, with the new wife and her ghastly brat ensconced at Shillington Hall..."

"No, I can see that," Giles said. "But she can't really steal your inheritance, can she?"

I shrugged. "I don't know, but I have a terrible feeling she plans to try—her and that brother of hers. The thing is, Giles, I'm completely stumped. Even if I could return to England, I couldn't stand to see the two of them worming their way even further into Papa's affections. It was bad enough before I left, and now my cousins are at it, too, forever going into raptures over the new baby, and expecting me to join them. The fact is, Giles, I just don't know what to do. I don't feel welcome anywhere, now."

"Look," said Giles, "why don't you stay and have dinner with us? Uncle Gerry won't mind, and if things get too tricky with your cousin, you can stay here until you're ready to leave on your travels. I'll be only too happy to show you the sights—including a few your cousin probably wouldn't show you."

"Thank you, Giles, I'll be very happy to stay to dinner, but I don't want to impose on you any further than that."

"Nonsense! No trouble at all," Giles assured me, apparently speaking for his uncle as well as himself.

Around dusk, Gervase and Alouette returned, both slightly tipsy, bringing with them several small pies, a loaf of bread, some fresh fruit, and a couple more bottles of red wine.

"Ah, you still here?" said Gervase, nodding in my direction.

"I've invited Alex for dinner," Giles said, not asking permission so much as stating a fait accompli.

Gervase, busy depositing food on the table, gave a nod and a grunt that I supposed might be interpreted as approval. Alouette had gathered up our luncheon dishes and gone out to the kitchen, from where I heard water being boiled and crockery being washed. Gervase drifted out to join her. Some time later the two of them returned with plates, glasses, and cutlery. Giles, who had opened one of the bottles of claret, poured us a glass each. It seemed to me neither Gervase nor Alouette stood in need of more wine, but this did not seem to be their own view, and Gervase, in particular, downed several glasses more with quite alarming rapidity, his loudness and animation increasing with each glass.

After dinner, Alouette brewed coffee for us, pouring it, thick and dark, into small porcelain cups. Giles fetched two well-used decks of cards from one of the boxes on the bookshelves, and we commenced a series of hilarious games of chance, played for coloured counters rather than money. Gervase, despite his inebriation, managed to amass a considerable pile of them.

At length, however, he yawned and stretched, announcing, "I'm for my bed," and he and Alouette disappeared through a door at the far end of the room.

Glancing at my pocket watch, I realised it was far too late to attempt to find my way back to the Rue Saint-Germain.

"Never mind," Giles said. "You can stay here. There's a spare bed in my room."

"I really should have let Jerome and Lucette know I'd be out late," I said.

"But you didn't know you would be, did you?" With this statement of inexorable logic, Giles got up and went to open a door I had supposed led to another room, but which was, in fact, a large cupboard. He pulled out sheets and quilts, and a fat feather pillow, and led the way to another door near the one through which Gervase and Alouette had disappeared. The room it opened onto was quite small, and furnished with two more divans and an ornate mahogany dressing table and mirror. "That's where I sleep," he told me, pointing to the one of the divans, made up, rather haphazardly, as a bed. He threw his armful of bedding onto the other divan, saying, "Just take what bedding you need. I'll put the rest away tomorrow."

While Giles went to put out the lamps in the living room, I gathered up quilts and cushions and made myself as comfortable a bed as I could. Divesting myself of my boots and outer clothing, I climbed between the quilts. Despite the unfamiliar surroundings and the strange bed, I was asleep in minutes.

The following morning I woke early—before anyone else judging by the snores rattling through the wall from Gervase's room. My head throbbed and my mouth felt like one of Gervase's paint rags. Throwing back the pile of coverlets that had wound themselves about me, I hauled myself to my feet and staggered to the kitchen, where I rinsed out a glass and filled it with water, downing it in one draught. Then I poured a second and returned and sat down on the divan under the window to drink it more slowly. Presently, I began to feel a little better, although my head felt as though it were being pounded with a rather large hammer. The apartment reeked of stale alcohol, cigarette smoke, and linseed oil. Deciding this probably was not helping my head, I got up to open one of the windows. As I was wrestling with the latch, which seemed not to have been used in decades, I heard a drowsy voice behind me.

"Alex, what on earth are you doing?"

"Trying to get some fresh air."

"Well, you won't do it that way," Giles told me through a cavernous yawn. "The latch is stuck on that one. What time is it?"

I retrieved my jacket from where I had cast it the previous night and consulted my pocket watch. "Almost ten past eight."

"Oh, God!" Giles said with a groan. "No wonder I feel like death warmed up. Go back to bed, Alex."

"I can't, my head's hurting too much."

Giles squinted up at me, shading his eyes with one hand. "What you need is a hair of the dog. There must be something left from last night. If not, I think there might be some brandy in that cupboard under the bookcase."

It was my turn to groan. "Don't, Giles! After last night, I swear I'm taking the pledge."

"Hah!" was Giles's succinct comment. After a few moments, he added, "You could try dousing your head in cold water. That usually works for me."

The bathroom on the landing was tiled in a sickly shade of green, and boasted a stained, claw-footed bath, an equally stained basin, and a water closet whose bowl was painted with primroses and violets. The mirror hanging on the wall above the basin was set in an incongruously opulent gilt frame. Dousing my face and head with as liberal a quantity as the tap's meagre flow would permit, I dried myself with the grubby towel hanging from a hook on the wall. I returned to the apartment to find Giles dressed, and in the process of opening one of the windows.

"I don't suppose I could borrow a razor?" I asked. "And some soap?"

Giles turned round. "Bathroom cupboard. Shall I put the

kettle on, or shall we have coffee downstairs?"

Keen to escape the still clinging fumes of paint and cigarettes, I opted for the café. Ten minutes later, having performed a perfunctory shave and run a comb through my damp hair, I set off down the stairs with Giles, who had eschewed both of these options, and consequently resembled a haystack.

The café was quite busy, even at this hour of the morning. Even before we entered, a buzz of conversation reached our ears. The tables and chairs set out on the pavement were almost all occupied. Giles seemed to know many of the patrons, calling cheerful greetings to them in French as he led me into the dimly lit interior. I bought us both *café-au-lait* and *croissants*, which we carried to one of the inside tables, since we both found ourselves rather sensitive to the garish sunlight. I would have preferred the more substantial breakfast fare I was used to at home, but Giles informed me, as an old hand instructing a neophyte, that this was what was eaten for breakfast in France. I did, however, manage to procure some cheese, and a jar of strawberry conserve for the *croissants*.

"Mmm, this is the ticket," observed Giles through a mouthful of *croissant*. "What shall we do today?"

"I know what I *ought* to do," I replied. "I should go and beg my cousins' pardon for staying out for so long without telling them. I imagine they'll be all but frantic by now, and Jerome was so angry with me the other night I should think it'll take a fair amount of begging to get back into his good graces."

"I'll go with you if you like," offered Giles.

Perhaps the sinking of my heart at the prospect of

confronting Jerome again had shown in my face. However, much as the idea of having support in this enterprise appealed, I was by no means certain the outsize presence of Giles, with his dishevelled appearance and his booming voice, would help matters.

"To tell you the truth," I admitted at length, "I'm not sure I want to go back there at all, not if they're going to keep going on and on about the dratted baby. Still, if it comes to it, I can always leave early for Italy," I added, sticking to the story I had concocted for my father's benefit. "Though I should like to have seen more of Paris first."

"Then why don't you come and stay with me and Uncle Gerry? You can stay as long as you like, and I can show you around Paris."

"But won't your uncle...? I mean shouldn't we ask him first?"

Giles waved a dismissive hand. "Oh, he won't mind. I've had people stay before, and 'the more the merrier' is all he says. As long as no one bothers him while he's painting, he doesn't care who comes and goes."

And so, despite my misgivings, I found myself agreeing to stay with Giles and his uncle. That afternoon, Giles and I hired a *voiture*— or, rather, I did, since I paid the fare—and went to pick up my belongings from my cousins' house. I had decided Lucette would be easier to face than Jerome, but nevertheless, my guilt made me dread having to tell her I was leaving. In the event, I was spared facing either of them. The door was opened by Paul, my cousins' manservant. When I asked after them, he informed me neither *M'sieu* nor *Madame* were at home. To my shame, my heart leapt at this news. I hurried upstairs, Giles at my heels, and hastily threw clothes, shaving, gear and other accoutrements into one of my suitcases. Tossing my precious journal, pens, and ink on top of the rest, I fastened the suitcase and asked Giles to carry it down to the waiting *voiture* while I penned a hasty note for my cousins, leaving it on the hall table with their other mail.

CHAPTER TWELVE

We arrived back at Gervase's apartment to find him and Alouette lounging on one of the divans, smoking and conversing animatedly in French. They looked up as I entered.

"Giles! Alex!" Alouette leapt up and came to embrace us both. "Gervase has received payment for his painting and we are going out to celebrate! You will come too, *n'est ce pas*?"

"My felicitations," I said, bowing in Gervase's direction.

Gervase acknowledged my good wishes with a nod of his shaggy head. "Yes," he trumpeted, "celebrations are definitely in order, so I'm taking us all to *Le Mirliton*. That's Aristide Bruant's *café concert*, you know, and he's bound to be singing."

"At the risk of sounding ignorant," I replied, "who is Aristide Bruant, and what's a *café concert*?"

"Bruant? Only one of the most famous singers in all Paris." Giles grinned. "He used to perform at *Le Chat Noir* until he grew wealthy enough to open his own café. You'll like him, Alex, I'm sure. His songs are very affecting."

At that moment, I could happily have consigned Monsieur Bruant and all his works to the devil; a sense of melancholy— no doubt born of guilt—had settled over me since visiting my cousins' house. Having, as I supposed, cut my ties with them as well as with family and friends in England, I felt like

Wagner's Flying Dutchman, doomed to remain forever an outsider, no matter where I might roam, and never able to return to my home. However, I could scarcely spurn my host's offer of entertainment, so I went to wash and dress for the occasion.

Le Mirliton was not in the least what I had expected. Unlike the *Café Cherbourg*, which was small and intimate, it was huge, more a hall than a café. Under its brilliant lights, a mass of people from all stations of life, or so it seemed, mingled together cheek by jowl in apparent amity. The entire crowd seemed to be in constant motion, presenting a veritable kaleidoscope of changing colours. At one end of the café was a sort of raised dais on which stood an imposing gentleman in a black coat, a red scarf and a black hat with a large brim that shaded his eyes. This, I presumed, was Aristide Bruant. He appeared to be bantering with the crowd, and I wished my French were better so I might have understood what was causing such amusement. With consummate skill, he quietened the crowd and readied them for the next performer, a dark, exotic-looking lady in a gold satin gown that revealed almost as much as it concealed, who sang a romantic ballad in a voice hinting of hot nights in some sultry clime far from Europe. The audience seemed to be paying scant attention to the *chanteuse*, but constantly drifted about fetching drinks or food, or greeting friends. A number of couples were dancing in front of the stage. The entire scene was like nothing I had seen before. It was less raucous than the music halls, but utterly unlike a theatre. Neither was it like a café, at least not as I had hitherto understood the term.

I felt a tap on my shoulder and turned to see Giles moving

off with Gervase and Alouette. Not wishing to become lost in the throng, I made after them, pushing my way through the crowd, as everyone else seemed to be doing. Gervase found us a table quite close to the stage, and beckoned a waitress to take our order. Not having dined yet, we were all famished, so Gervase ordered us food and wine. I had little idea what he had ordered, nor did I much care. I was too busy taking in the scene. In the event, we dined on a very tasty tart concocted of ham and tomatoes and eggs, washed down with the seemingly inevitable red wine, and followed by some sort of cake with rum in it, which I found utterly delicious. As we settled down to take in the performance, Gervase once more hailed a waitress.

"A bottle of *Pernod*, if you please, and a jug of iced water," he boomed, then, turning to Giles and me, said, "You can't come to Montmartre and not try *absinthe*."

The waitress returned a short time later with a tray containing the emerald-green *Pernod*, a jug of water, a small bowl of sugar cubes, half a dozen small glasses of an unusual, bulbous shape, and an even stranger-looking silver slotted spoon.

Gervase, having thanked her and paid her a handsome tip, commenced to pour a small measure of the liquor into each glass, then to add water. Fascinated, I watched the green spirit begin to turn cloudy as the water spread through it.

"There you are," said Gervase, pushing a glass across to me. "See how you like it. If you find it too bitter, you can add sugar."

He eschewed the addition of sweetener, so I decided to try mine in the same manner. It was strongly alcoholic, tasting of aniseed and something rather bitter that I could not identify. Giles, I noticed, added sugar to his glass, but I found I rather liked the faintly medicinal flavour of the unsweetened liquor. I sipped some more and felt the tension begin to drain from my mind and body. Before long, I began to feel positively relaxed, and settled back to enjoy the singing of Aristide Bruant, who had once more taken the stage and was singing about, as far as I could tell, the lives of those who must live on the streets of Paris. This seemed to me a strange subject for a song, as though an English music-hall singer were to extol the virtues of the life of a tramp or a prostitute. As I ruminated on this, my thoughts, such as they were by this stage, began to take on a definite flavour of aniseed, and I found myself feeling very much at home in my surroundings. Indeed, had you asked me just then, I should have professed the ability to feel at home in any surroundings whatsoever.

I was, therefore, considerably taken aback when I stood up and collided with a young man negotiating his way through the throng. Before I could prevent it, he was lying sprawled on the floor, and only by clutching at the table was I able to prevent myself from falling on top of him. As he got to his feet, I began apologising in my rudimentary French, acutely aware that my tongue seemed incapable of functioning correctly, yet somehow unable to do anything about it.

As I stood there swaying, he clapped me on the shoulder and proclaimed, "Ah, you are English, *n'est ce pas*? Permit me to introduce myself. Roland Mercier, *a votre service.*"

At this point, Giles, who was sitting next to me, pushed me back into my chair and Gervase offered Monsieur

Mercier a glass of *absinthe*. We all introduced ourselves and, as Mercier sipped his absinthe, I was able to observe him more closely. His skin had a dark olive hue, and he had thick, springy black hair and hawkish features that reminded me a little of Henri de Saint-Clair. He was even thinner than Henri, however, his worn clothes hanging on his meagre frame like those of a scarecrow. Yet, for all his apparent lack of substance, there was something arresting about his almost luminous eyes and his air of restlessness, as though he were aquiver with some inner energy.

It was the early hours of the morning before we left *Le Mirliton* and wound our way home, conversing raucously and singing snatches of songs we had heard that evening.

Not surprisingly, I woke later that morning with a thundering headache that made me feel positively ill. With a low moan, I pulled the quilt about me and rolled over, hoping to return to blessed unconsciousness. It was then I saw Roland Mercier. He was sleeping on the floor rolled up in a quilt, his head on a red velvet cushion. I had no memory of his accompanying us back from *Le Mirliton*. On reflection, however, I found I could recall very little beyond the point when I began drinking *absinthe*.

Well, I told myself, that was one essential Paris experience I was not anxious to repeat. However pleasant it might have felt at the time, the aftermath was simply not worth it.

Abandoning all hope of further sleep, I rolled off my bed and staggered to the kitchen to fetch a glass of water. I almost abandoned the exercise when I saw the state of the kitchen. The wooden bench top was littered with what seemed like dozens of glasses, empty wine bottles, cups, and plates bearing the remains of yesterday's meals. Almost retching at the sight, I quickly rinsed out a glass, filled it with water from the tap and drank it in one draught. Then I refilled it and returned to the bedroom, where the semi-gloom was kinder to my burning eyes. Mercier was sitting up, still wrapped in his quilt, yawning and stretching. When he saw me, he broke off this activity, and gave me a cheerful grin.

"*Bonjour*, Alex," he greeted me. "I hope you will excuse my intrusion, *mais vraiment*, I think I could not have found my way home for the trying. It is the *absinthe*, you know; it—ah—it carries away the mind."

"It certainly does," I concurred with feeling. "I can't help wishing it had taken my head as well."

"*Ah, oui, moi aussi.* " He grinned. "Ah, please excuse, Alex. I must try to speak English for you, *n'est ce pas?*"

"Not if you find it difficult. I think this is not a morning for trying anything that requires effort."

"You are right, *mon ami*. Shall we visit the café below for coffee? Perhaps it will help both our heads and our minds."

I was only too happy to agree to this.

There were very few patrons in the café, for which I was grateful. We ordered strong black coffee and took it to a table on the pavement. There had been rain during the night, rendering the air very clear and bright, and steam rose from the pavement and the windowsills as the sun warmed their surfaces. I leaned back in my chair and, eyes closed, turned my face to the sun as I had done when I was a child sitting on the old wooden bench beside the kitchen door at Shillington Hall. For a moment, I was back there once more, feeling the weathered wood and the soft, warm fur of Phoebe, the little grey tabby cat that had performed such sterling service in reducing the mouse population in the house and stables. Tears started in my eyes at the memory of a time when life had seemed so simple and pure. I shook my head to clear the memory, and then groaned as the steam-hammer once more began to pound against my temples.

I opened my eyes to see Roland regarding me with an expression of sympathy.

"*Oui, absinthe* takes one to heaven at the time, but sends one to hell afterwards, *n'est ce pas?*" he remarked with a grin.

I returned a rueful smile. "Oh, it's not just the *absinthe*. I'm rapidly coming to believe I'm not cut out for carousing."

"Ah, Alex, *mon ami*, we all think so on the morning after. But the moment, ah, that is what matters, is it not? That fleeting moment of beauty, of truth—of life!"

I shook my head. "Forgive me, Roland, but my head hurts far too much for philosophy just now."

"Then we shall have more coffee—and a little something to help the head, *non?*"

"Oh, not the hair of the dog, I beg of you!"

A puzzled frown creased his brow. "The hair of the dog? Is this some English medicine? It sounds very unpleasant."

I laughed, and then grimaced as sudden pain flared behind my eyes. "I'm sorry. I must try to speak more plainly. It's an English expression. It means curing the ailment by taking more of what caused it, in this case, *absinthe.*"

"Ah, I see. No, it is not *absinthe*, it is this."

Roland pulled a small brown bottle from his pocket.

"What is it?" I asked, curious. "Is it some kind of medicine?"

"*Oui*, it is medicine to—ah—heal the pain. But first, the coffee, *non*?" He turned and beckoned to the waiter. "*Deux cafés* noirs, s'il vous plait."

When our coffee arrived, Roland uncorked the brown bottle and carefully poured a little of its liquid into each cup.

"What is it?" I asked again. I had no wish to drink any substance without knowing what it was, especially after the previous night's experience.

"It is called *parégorique*. What it is in English, I do not know."

"Paregoric," I told him. "Well, I suppose that's not so bad. I remember being given it when I had tonsillitis as a boy."

I drank my coffee, and quite soon the pain began to subside, and a feeling of well being crept over me. Roland pulled a battered tobacco tin and a box of matches from the pocket of his jacket. He rolled one for himself, then offered me the tin. Being a non-smoker, I declined. He shrugged and struck a match on the sole of his well-worn boot, sheltering the fragile flame with his hand as he lit his cigarette. He drew deeply on it, and then leaned back with a sigh of contentment.

"To live in the moment," he murmured, "that is the essence of happiness."

I found myself leaning forward and asking him to explain what he meant, and we were soon engaged in an intense discussion of the meaning of reality, truth, and other such imponderables. I quoted Keats's 'Ode on a Grecian Urn': 'Beauty is truth, truth beauty, that is all ye know on earth, and all ye need to know'.

Roland replied by quoting some French poets with whose work I was unfamiliar, though I found their ideas intriguing.

He also referred to the Buddhist religion of the Orient, and for the first time I learned of the concept of *maya*, the belief that the entire world in which we live is an illusion. I must confess it made little sense to me, but I was fascinated to hear of beliefs so alien to the ones I had been taught and which, indeed, formed the basis of the entire society into which I had been born. I found myself speculating on how different my life might have been were it not for a mere accident of birth.

For how long we sat talking I cannot tell, but it was past noon before I suddenly realised I had had nothing since waking besides strong, black coffee, and that my stomach was aching for food. I beckoned the waiter and ordered bread and the spicy sausage that appeared to be a speciality of the café, along with the Camembert cheese Roland recommended and a bottle of *vin ordinaire* that we drank with water in the French style. Conversation ceased as we addressed ourselves to this simple, but appetising fare. At the end of our meal, Roland declared he must go, as he had promised to meet some friends that afternoon. He invited me to go with him, which I would have liked to do, since I was enjoying the company of this scarecrow of a man exceedingly. But I had begun to feel very weary, so I reluctantly declined.

"Then you must please come to visit me on another day," he declared, pushing his unruly curls back from his forehead.

"Thank you," I replied, "I should like that very much. Where do you live?"

"At the *Hotel Rimini*. It is not far from here, near the *Sacré Coeur*."

"Then I shall certainly visit you soon."

"*A bientot*, then, Alex!"

He sauntered off, leaving me to climb the stairs to discover who might have invaded Gervase's apartment in my absence.

CHAPTER THIRTEEN

A few days later, I found my way to the *Hotel Rimini*. It was not a hotel in the English sense, but rather one of those imposing Parisian dwellings originally built as town houses for the well to do. A stone building of Herculean proportions in the neo-classical style that became popular in France after the Revolution, it rose some five storeys from the pavement. Its door was set into a tall archway flanked by statues of what I supposed were intended to be Grecian or Roman deities, although they were so grimy and damaged it was difficult to tell. Indeed, the entire building was little more than a ruin, its windows cracked and broken and draped with cobwebs, and the massive door looking as though some madman had attacked it with an axe. I found it difficult to imagine its being home to anyone, yet this was the address Roland Mercier had given me.

With considerable trepidation, being in fear of the entire structure collapsing on top of me, I pushed open the front door to reveal a square, stone-flagged foyer with a marble staircase curving upwards at one side. Both floor and staircase were littered with dirt and a variety of detritus, including, as if to confirm my fears, chunks of stone and plaster as well as fragments of old paper, wine bottles, cigarette butts, broken crockery and the rusting skeleton of an umbrella. Several battered doors led off the foyer, but there was no indication as to who, if anyone, lived in the rooms behind them. From somewhere far up in the building drifted the strains of a violin playing a Chopin waltz badly. Encouraged by this sign of life, I began to trudge up the stairs.

I had reached the top floor, a cramped space directly under the roof of the building, before I located the source of the execrable music and knocked on the door. The playing screeched to a halt and moments later the door opened a crack to reveal the face of a young man whose mahogany features and crimped black hair indicated African ancestry.

"I'm looking for M'sieu Roland Mercier," I said in the best French I could muster. "I believe he lives in this building."

"Fourth floor, next to the stairs," the young man replied, his French sounding as though spoken through a mouthful of treacle.

I was about to thank him when he withdrew and shut the door. As I made my way back down the stairs, the violin resumed its excruciating recital. On the fourth-floor landing I quickly found the door closest to the stairs, and knocked on it. I heard the sound of footsteps, then the door edged open and Roland's rather startled countenance appeared in the narrow opening.

As soon as he recognised me, his face lit up in a smile of welcome.

"Alex! *Bonjour*! How it is good to see you! *Entrez, mon ami, entrez!*" He threw wide the door with an extravagant gesture and ushered me inside.

What I saw was, in a word, appalling. The room was meagre, possibly part of the original servants' quarters, with bare, unpolished wooden floors and one narrow window that admitted little more than a sliver of light through its dust-encrusted glass. Dominating the room was a fireplace with a marble surround all grimed with soot and a hearth littered with bits of wood and paper. In the fireplace sat a cast-iron pot, presumably used for cooking or boiling water, and on the hearth a few chipped pottery bowls and a small jug. The mantelpiece held a large, white china jug, the stub of a candle in a tarnished and pockmarked silver candlestick, and a pile of books. A number of unframed canvases were attached to the walls by means of large thumbtacks. They seemed to be the only thing preventing the wallpaper from falling off the crumbling plaster. In a corner near the window lay a stained mattress with a couple of tattered blankets, a grubby patchwork quilt and a pillow with no pillowcase. The entire distressing scene was completed by a wooden chair with a broken back and a litter of papers on its seat, and a wooden crate beside the bed bearing a candle in a chipped enamel candlestick, a couple of dirty wine glasses of cheap manufacture and a partially consumed bottle of brandy. All about the room, leaning against the walls, were lengths of timber, looking as though some building project had been abandoned, but which I guessed had been brought in to provide firewood.

Roland hurriedly scooped up the papers from the chair and deposited them on the floor. "Please sit, Alex. It is very good to see you. Would you like brandy?"

"No thank you, not this early in the day," I said, thinking mainly of the filthy glasses and the fact that the room evidenced no means of washing them.

He shrugged his thin shoulders, pulled his tobacco tin from his pocket and rolled a cigarette. I longed to ask him why on earth he consented to live in such squalor, but of course to do so would have been unpardonably discourteous. Instead, I pointed to the open book beside his bed and asked, "What are you reading, Roland?"

"Baudelaire, *Les Fleurs de Mal*. Do you know it?"

"I've heard of Baudelaire, yes, but I've not read him. Is he good?"

Roland's sharp features became animated, almost feverish in his sudden enthusiasm. "*Mais oui*, he is one of France's greatest modern poets, one of our greatest thinkers, *en effet*! Look, I will show you." He seized the book and leafed through its pages until he found the passage he wanted. "*Ici, lisez ceci.*"

I took the book and read the passage. It was, of course, in French, but I translated it to read thus:

'If poison, arson, sex, narcotics, knives
Have not yet ruined us and stitched their quick,
Loud patterns on the canvas of our lives,
It is because our souls are still too sick.'

I was considerably taken aback by its frankness, and I must confess I found its sentiments confusing, if not downright dubious. Was the poet saying we ought to embrace such evils, or that they form a sort of trial by fire with which we strengthen ourselves? I asked Roland.

"He is saying, I think, that we must embrace all that life offers, the bad and the good, or we are not fully human."

"That's surely a rather dangerous creed?"

"*Mais oui*, life is dangerous, *n'est ce pas?*"

I recalled the past few months of my life and found I was inclined to agree with him. "Do you embrace danger, then?" I

146

asked.

He shrugged in his expressive way. "*Mais oui*, I am a disciple of Baudelaire, and of Rimbaud and Verlaine also."

He scrabbled amongst one of his piles of books until he found the two he wanted and handed them to me. I read in silence for a short while, saying, at length, "This is very beautiful work, but I'm not sure I can agree with its sentiments."

"You are not French," he said, "so you do not understand."

Of course I could not let this pass without asking for an explanation and, for the next hour or so, Roland expounded, in his halting English, on the French Revolution and the Paris Commune of 1871, when the workers of Paris had organised a rebellion against its occupation by the German Army during the Franco-Prussian War. Although I had read of this as part of my studies, I had never heard it described with such passion, nor from the viewpoint of the class of persons from which it arose. As Roland went on to speak of how these events had created a spirit of revolution and a distrust of authority among the poor people of Paris, I began to understand the sentiment behind the songs of Aristide Bruant. Monsieur Bruant was a champion of the poor and the dispossessed, those, indeed, who lived as Roland himself lived, in poverty and squalor.

The two of us were still deep in conversation when dusk fell and I remembered I had promised Giles to accompany him to the *Folies Bergères* that evening. Of course I invited Roland to join us.

"Ah, my apologies, but I cannot," he said, turning down the corners of his mouth in a comic grimace of disappointment. "Tonight I am meeting a young lady."

"I see," I replied, smiling. "Then of course that must take priority."

"*Bien sur.*" His grin implied that a thorough embracing of the principles of Monsieur Baudelaire might well be on the agenda.

I took my leave, feeling unexpectedly uplifted by Roland's enthusiasm. Indeed, it seemed to me he positively embraced the life fate had given him, determined to live it to the full despite his material circumstances. Somehow, it made the social conventions under which I had been nurtured seem petty and self-indulgent. I recalled what he had said during our conversation in the *Café Cherbourg*: 'To live in the moment, that is the essence of happiness'. Perhaps he was right. Perhaps I should think less of what might or might not be and more of what was. Pondering thus, I made my way back to the Rue Saint-Georges.

* * * *

Over the following weeks, my friendship with Roland Mercier grew. I visited him often, and sometimes he visited me at Gervase's apartment, or accompanied me and Giles to various entertainments about the city. As I came to know Roland better, I became correspondingly disenchanted with Giles's shallow outlook on life, and his penchant for the *Folies Bergères* and the girls who worked there. This is not to imply that I did not enjoy their company—what young man could fail to enjoy the company of attractive young ladies? But it often seemed to me Giles's only real interest in them lay in the fact that many of them were happy to accommodate his amorous desires. I dare say I could also have taken advantage of their easy ways, but I found the rapaciousness of Giles and other young men like him abhorrent; besides, my thoughts were still of Emmeline back in London. I still found myself, in idle moments, thinking of her with great fondness. In my mind, I heard her throaty laugh, saw her red curls and smiling eyes, smelled her sweet perfume. For all I knew our affair had not been a love match, and that it could never have prospered if it had been, my affection for Emmeline had been genuine. She had taught me how to be with a woman, and the thought of never seeing her again was melancholy indeed, especially given the uncertainties of my current situation.

Grateful as I must be to Giles and his uncle for giving me shelter, the longer I lived with them, the more I felt like a fish out of water. What with Giles's amorous adventures—which he inevitably recounted to me later in embarrassing detail—and Gervase's mood swings according to the fortunes of his art, and his cavalier treatment of Alouette, his mistress and supposed muse, I began to wonder whether I might not have been wiser to remain with my cousins, despite their embracing of my father's folly. At least there I could have found a little of the tranquillity my soul increasingly craved.

Late one afternoon, after a longish walk in the *Parc Monceau*, I returned to find Alouette alone and in tears. I hurried to where she was sitting hunched on one of the divans.

"Alouette! What is it?"

She raised her tearstained face at my approach, and I thought I saw a hint of fear in her eyes. "Ah, Alex, it is you. Please forgive me. It is nothing."

I sat down beside her and took her hand in mine. "But you're crying. Something has upset you. Have you had bad news?"

"No, it is not that," she replied, wiping her eyes with her sleeve and sniffing.

I pulled out my handkerchief and gave it to her, and she dabbed at her eyes again and blew her nose.

I had seen Alouette happy, and I had seen her angry, but never like this. "Is there anything I can do to help?" I asked.

She looked up at me again, fresh tears trickling from her swollen eyes. "You are very kind, Alex, but I don't think so. It is just—just..."

"Come," I said, taking the handkerchief and gently wiping her eyes. "Tell me what's distressing you. Perhaps, after all, I can help."

She shook her head, but said, in halting tones, "It is Gervase. He tells me he loves me, but he becomes so angry with me, although I do my best to please him."

Once started, it was as though a floodgate had opened, and out poured a distressing tale that confirmed what I already half suspected: Gervase had been using his supposed love for Alouette—and her emotional dependency on him—to obtain not only the obvious benefits, but also money from her meagre inheritance from her father, promising to pay it back when he sold his work, but largely failing to do so, despite her being the subject of many of his successful paintings. In brief, he was taking advantage of her in the most despicable way. In addition, she was beginning to suspect him of being unfaithful. Earlier that day, she had summoned the courage to tackle him on these subjects. The result had been a shouting match that had ended in Gervase striking her and then storming out of the apartment.

At the end of such a poignant tale, what else could I do but put my arms around her and attempt to soothe her while she laid her head on my shoulder and sobbed out her misery?

As we sat thus, hurried footsteps sounded on the stairs. Alouette started back with a gasp, just as the door flew open to reveal Gervase, clearly the worse for drink. He stared at us for a moment, his mouth gaping, and then strode towards us while loosing a volley of oaths.

"What the hell do you think you're doing?" he thundered, thrusting me aside with such force that I fell to the floor. He began to shout at poor Alouette in such rapid French I could barely understand a word, while she cowered back, shielding her face with her hands as though expecting him to strike her again. I leapt to my feet and grabbed him by the arm, pulling at him with all my strength.

"Leave her alone!" I had to shout to gain his attention. "Haven't you upset her enough already?"

He turned on me, his face reddened and distorted by fury, his breath reeking of alcohol. "Ah, the snake in the grass! I welcome you into my home, and what do you do but try to seduce my Alouette the moment my back's turned? If you want a woman, have one of Giles's cast-offs, but keep your damned, filthy hands off mine."

Of course, I should have said nothing, but my own anger was by now aroused, as well as my sense of injustice. "Don't be so ridiculous!" I cried. "I found the poor girl badly upset— by *you*, sir, I might add—and was merely trying to comfort her. If you had any sense of what's right, you'd be doing it yourself, not shouting the odds at her."

"How dare you!" Gervase lurched towards me, his fists swinging. Without thinking, I put up my own. My intent was to fend him off, but some automatic reflex came into effect—no doubt a relic of the boxing training I had had while at Cambridge—and before I knew it, I had landed a very handy right to his chin. He staggered back, falling against the divan, half stunned. Alouette shrieked, struggling out of the way of his falling body.

Giles arrived just in time to witness the unedifying tableau of Gervase sprawled across the divan clutching at his injured face, Alouette huddled against the wall, sobbing, and me standing looking horrified, and rubbing my right fist.

"Good Lord!" he exclaimed. "What on earth's going on?"

"He hit me," Gervase muttered from the divan, glowering in my direction.

"Alex? Alex hit you? But—why?"

"I caught him out with Alouette, and when I tried to remonstrate with him, he hit me."

"Caught him out...? Alex?" Giles turned to Alouette. "Is this true?"

"It is true that Alex hit Gervase," Alouette said, sitting up. "But he was not—"

"He damned well was!" Gervase insisted, nursing his bruised chin in a melodramatic way. "I saw him with my own eyes."

"It wasn't what it might have seemed," I said, keeping as firm a rein on my own anger as I could manage. "I found Alouette crying, and I was trying to comfort her, that's all."

Ignoring Gervase's spluttering protestations, Giles addressed Alouette once more. "Is that how it was?"

Alouette shot a nervous glance at Gervase, who glared

back at her as though daring her to disagree with him. "I—I..." she began, but I could see she was torn between admitting the truth and self-preservation.

"It's all right," I told her. "You needn't say anything. No doubt Gervase will believe what he wants, regardless."

"I know what I damned well saw!" Gervase roared, staggering to his feet. "And I won't have any damned interloper trying to usurp my place in my own home." He pointed at the open door in the exaggerated manner of an actor in a melodrama. "There's the door, sir! Use it, before I give you what you deserve."

Without a word, I turned on my heel, and, with what dignity I could muster, marched out of the room and down the stairs. Giles came hurrying after me, catching up with me on the pavement, where I stood leaning against the wall, unsure whether to give vent to tears or hysterical laughter.

"Don't mind Uncle Gerry," Giles said, clapping me on the shoulder. "I dare say he's a trifle under the weather just now. He'll come about before too long, I promise you."

"I'm not sure I care any more," I replied, and told him what Alouette had confessed to me.

If I had expected Giles to be as horrified as I had been, I was to be disappointed.

"Oh, well, as to that," he said, with a dismissive wave of his arm, "it's just the way they are together. You mustn't mind it. Come and have drink with me. We'll come back later, when they've kissed and made up."

"But Giles, surely you can't condone Gervase's treating Alouette like that. He's using her—making money from her as his model, and, instead of paying her for it, he's taking her money for his own use."

Giles shrugged. "She can always leave if she doesn't like it. That's what the last one did."

"My God, Giles! You disappoint me. I always thought you were a decent sort of chap, but now I see you're no better than—" I'd been about to say 'no better than Charles', but managed, just in time, to stop myself. "Well, no better than you ought to be," I amended.

"Oh, pooh!" Giles retorted. "Don't be so damned stuffy. If I'd known you were going to be such a wet blanket, I'd never have invited you to stay. I'm going for a drink. Come with me or stay here. It's up to you."

He marched off, but I stayed where I was. At that moment, I could happily have consigned both Giles and his wretched uncle to the innermost circle of hell. I entered the *Café Cherbourg* and ordered *café noir,* strong, seating myself at the most out-of-the-way table I could find. I needed time to allow my nerves to settle. After a time, I came to the sobering realisation that I had managed to quarrel with the two people in Paris who afforded me shelter. I could scarcely return to my cousins after my underhanded manner of leaving them, and I was tolerably sure that, even if Gervase consented to accept me back into the fold, it was unlikely Giles would. Besides, I had become increasingly uncomfortable with their ramshackle way of life. I still felt my criticism of Gervase was just, but, I chided myself, why could I not have kept my thoughts to myself, at least until I had a few more friends in Paris to whom I might turn for help or advice? As things stood, I had managed to alienate those few I did know, and, being unwilling to access what funds my father forwarded to Jerome's bank on my behalf for fear of alerting the authorities to my presence in Paris, I now had insufficient funds to rent a room of my own.

Then it occurred to me that I might, perhaps, call on Henri's goodwill. I knew he liked me, but it seemed probable he valued his privacy more. I was still a little in awe of his air of self-possession and his sometimes mordant wit, and was loath to alienate him by presuming too much on his goodwill, even assuming his manservant would give me the *entrée* to his home. Henri himself had already told me he was rarely at home to visitors, and, since leaving my cousins, I had not had the ability to attend any social occasion where I might have seen him.

I glanced out of the café windows and realised it was almost dark. Whatever I was going to do, I thought, I had best do it without delay. As I walked along the pavement, I remembered, with a sinking sensation, that Henri's town house was on the other side of the city. I felt unable to justify a cab fare to *Saint-Germain*, and I had no desire to walk that far at night. I had spent long enough in Paris to realise it could be just as dangerous at night as London for a lone pedestrian, especially one unfamiliar with its streets.

In the end, I decided to call on Roland Mercier. If nothing else, perhaps he could advise me what to do. My talks with him had led me to believe he was a man of considerable good sense and insight, despite his extraordinary lifestyle. Indeed, I had come to feel he was the closest friend I had in Paris, since Henri was so elusive as to make further friendship difficult. I had never made friends with any great ease, perhaps due to my solitary life as a child, but with Roland I felt I could speak my mind, and that I could expect the same from him. And if there was anything I needed at that moment, it was someone with whom I could share my confused feelings, and perhaps unravel them sufficiently to see a clear path ahead.

CHAPTER FOURTEEN

I reached the *Hotel Rimini* only to discover Roland was not at home. His door was unlocked, however, so I decided to let myself in and wait for him. Since it was by now dark, I lit a candle and began to search through the various piles of his books. I had read quite a number of them already, but I came across one I had not seen before that purported to be a treatise on Kabbalistic magic, and lay down on Roland's bed to read it. However, although my French was much improved since my arrival in Paris, I found it difficult, and therefore tedious, to read, and before long I fell asleep.

It was quite late when I awoke to find Roland shaking me by the shoulder. As I opened my eyes, he sat down on the bed beside me, a concerned look on his face. He had lit both candles, and eerie shadows leapt about the room as draughts of air blew at their flames.

"Alex, are you all right?"

"No, not really."

"Do you wish to talk about it? Sometimes it helps, *oui*?"

I sat up, drawing my knees up to my chin and wrapping my arms about them. "To tell you the truth, Roland, I'm not entirely sure what I want to do. Look, I haven't had any dinner. Do you know where I can buy some food?"

"But of course. There are many restaurants and cafés nearby."

"Good, then I'll take you to supper."

From his enthusiastic grin, I surmised he might not have eaten, either. Together we descended the stairs, and before long were ensconced in a small café, quiet at this time of night, supping on chicken casserole and braised artichokes. Roland made no further mention of my unexpected arrival, and I was in no mood for inconsequential chat, so we ate our meal in silence, returning to the *Hotel Rimini* afterwards.

"We shall have brandy," Roland announced as he lit the candles.

To my immense relief, he took the two glasses and went to wash them in what I assumed must be a bathroom on one of the lower floors.

"You wish to stay here?" he enquired as we sipped our brandy.

"I think I'd better, if you don't mind, at least for tonight."

I sat biting my lip for a few moments, thinking I ought to offer some sort of explanation for my odd behaviour, then, before I quite knew what I was about, I found myself pouring out the entire story, beginning with the events that had forced me to leave England. Roland listened sympathetically, offering neither advice nor comment, until I had finished. Then he laid his hand on my shoulder.

"*Mon ami*, you have been greatly wronged, I think. This Charles must have been a very stupid person, and Giles and his uncle have treated you not well. I cannot mend your affairs, Alex, but I welcome you here for as long as you wish to stay."

I clasped his hands in mine. "Thank you, Roland! You're very kind. I'll stay tonight, but I can't possibly impose on you for any longer. Tomorrow I'll find myself a room in a hotel—

if I can find one I can afford."

His lips curved in a quizzical smile. "But here is an hotel, Alex! There are rooms empty here." My face must have shown something of my feelings, for he said, "*Certainement*, it is less beautiful than other hotels, but it is free."

"It is?" I asked, surprised. "Why?"

"One day, *Le Rimini* will be, what is it, destroyed? Yes, destroyed, for a new building to be made, but until that day, we who have no money live here. When it goes, so shall we. Tomorrow I will show you the empty rooms, *n'est ce pas?*"

"Thank you, you're very kind."

He shrugged his shoulders, saying simply, "You are my friend. I help you, *c'est ainsi.*"

* * * *

I awoke the following morning feeling stiff and cold, which reinforced my determination to find myself more comfortable accommodation. Roland must have woken earlier than me, as he was nowhere to be seen. Stretching my limbs and straightening my clothes as best I could, I ventured out on to the landing to see if I could find a bathroom, although, due to my precipitate departure from the apartment in the *Rue Saint-Georges*, I had not so much as a comb about my person, and my ablutions must, perforce, be rudimentary. As I descended the stairs, however, I spied Roland on his way up, carrying newspapers, a baguette and a jug that emitted steam and the aroma of coffee.

"*Bonjour*, Alex," he called up the stairwell. "I have breakfast for us, and today's *gazette.*"

We ate breakfast sitting on the mattress in Roland's room, dipping chunks of the freshly baked bread into the hot, milky coffee Roland poured into two of the pottery bowls from the hearth, and scanning the newspaper he had brought.

As soon as we had finished breakfast, Roland jumped to his feet. "Come, I show you the rooms."

"It's very kind of you," I replied, "but I've been thinking I really might be better suited at a hotel. You see, I'm quite dreadfully *bourgeois*, and I like to be comfortable."

He laughed at my self-definition. "I will show you, then you can choose whether to stay or to go."

My tour of the hotel was extensive, revealing many empty rooms, most in a state of disrepair surpassing even that of Roland's quarters. Along the way, I met a number of the other tenants, all of whom seemed to be artists of one kind or another. Curious as to the nature of Roland's art or craft, I made so bold as to ask him. He threw back his head and laughed heartily.

"I am *un philosophe*, Alex. I read much and I think much. Perhaps one day I shall write a book, *oui*?"

"I'm sure you will," I said politely. "And are you a follower of any particular philosopher?"

"*Mais oui*, I have told you, I follow Charles Baudelaire."

"I thought he was a poet, not a philosopher."

"He is both, I think. Have you read his latest book, *Mon Coeur Mis a Nu?*"

"My Heart Laid Bare," I translated. "No, I must confess I haven't."

"Then you must read it! It is there that he says 'There can be no progress (real, that is, moral) except in the individual and by the individual himself.' This is what I believe, Alex. It is what *le Bouddhisme* teaches, also, n'est ce pas?"

"I'm afraid I know very little about Buddhism. It wasn't part of the curriculum at Cambridge."

Roland laughed again, in his quick, keen way. "These universities exist only to produce those who will follow the tenets of society. The only true education, I think, is life."

"You may well be right," I said, echoing his laughter. "In which case you're undoubtedly an educated man and I am an ignoramus."

"Oh, no, I am not a wise man. It is Baudelaire who has the wisdom of life. I am merely a student."

"At any rate," I told him, "I'm sure you're wiser in the ways of the world than I am."

I meant this as little more than a pleasantry, but it evidently pleased him, as he clasped me in a sudden embrace and kissed me on both cheeks. A little embarrassed by this display of affection, I walked on in silence, thinking what a mass of contradictions my new friend seemed to be, yet finding I liked him no less for it.

My tour of the *Hotel Rimini* completed, Roland suggested we visit a nearby café where he intended to introduce me to some friends he expected to be there. We strolled to the *Café Coqueliquot*, a rustic-looking establishment with outdoor tables and wooden bench seats set on a brick-floored terrace beneath two trees, and with vine-covered, trellised archways leading past pots of geraniums to a minuscule indoor area with room for only three tables in addition to its counter. It was in this indoor area we found half a dozen or so of Roland's friends drinking wine and filling the place with pungent smoke from their cigarettes and pipes, whilst carrying on what sounded like a very robust discussion.

Somewhat to my surprise, the company included three women, two of whom were of about our own age, but the third a handsome woman of at least forty years of age, whose dress was an idiosyncratic blend of high fashion and the exotic, and who, to my amazement, was smoking a pipe. They broke off their discussion to greet Roland, pulling up chairs so the two of us could join their circle.

"And who is your friend, Roland?" asked the older woman. "Introduce us, if you please."

"*Oui, Madame*, this is Alex Randall. He is English. Alex, this is Madame Aurore le Compte, who is famous for her beauty and intelligence."

Madame inclined her head in acknowledgement of what I suspected she considered a just description rather than a compliment, and held out her hand for me to kiss, saying in excellent English, "Good day, Alex, it's a pleasure to make your acquaintance."

"The pleasure is mine, Madame," I replied, receiving a flirtatious smile from the lady.

Roland proceeded to introduce me to the rest of the circle. A young man by the name of Etienne poured wine for us and in minutes the discussion had resumed. My French was still fairly rudimentary, so I found it difficult to follow the intricacies of what seemed to be a rather rambling discussion of the relative merits of the republic and the monarchy. Naturally, since England still retained a monarchy, my views were sought on the latter, which I gave to the best of my ability, although I was forced to admit it was not a subject to which I had given much thought. This earned a scandalised raising of the eyebrows from Madame le Compte.

"But you must think about it, Alex! The manner in which

a society is ruled determines the degree to which it progresses, does it not?"

"I'm not sure that it does," I replied, and gave Roland's quotation from Baudelaire in support of my contention.

Madame exclaimed, "Ah, you have read Baudelaire! It is a very cultured Englishman, is it not?"

I chose not to disillusion her, and Roland gave me a grin and a wink behind her back.

It was several hours later that the company finally began to disband when Madame le Compte made to leave, accompanied by Sophie and Marie, the two young ladies, whom I supposed must be her acolytes. As Madame knocked out her pipe into the overflowing ashtray, she spoke to the others in French, adding for my benefit, "Alex, I should like to invite you to my *soirée* this evening. Roland knows where I live, so you can come with him."

"Why, thank you, Madame, I should be honoured to attend."

Again, she bowed her head in acknowledgement, confident of her own worth, yet without the least trace of arrogance. As Roland and I strolled back to the *Hotel Rimini*, I asked him about Madame le Compte, and what I might expect at her *soirée*.

"Ah, Madame's *soirées* are a legend!"

"In what way? Are they like the Paris *salons* of which I've read?"

"Not exactly," was his cryptic reply. "This evening, you will find out."

* * * *

Madame le Compte lived on the ground floor of a large building not unlike the *Hotel Rimini*, with the difference that it was built of brick and had been very well maintained. Sophie, one of Madame's *protégées* whom I'd met at the *Café Coqueliquot*, answered our knock, looking very charming in a multi-coloured outfit that gave her the appearance of a gipsy girl. She bade us welcome and led us into a large, high-ceilinged room. Decorated in a warm terracotta hue and hung with green plush curtains, it was furnished with a pleasantly eclectic collection of furniture and plants, and paintings and ornaments veering wildly from classical portraits and landscapes to a collection of masks I thought might have come from Africa, and brass ornaments that reminded me of the ones my Uncle William had brought back from his travels in the Orient, although his were considerably more chaste. I was not surprised to see an entire wall given over to books both old and new. In a corner near the window, a string quartet was playing Schubert *lieder*.

On a green chaise longue reclined Madame le Compte, all done out in Arabian style in a coat of pink-and-gold brocade draped with silk scarves and long ropes of pearls, very full trousers of gold satin and her feet shod in pink embroidered slippers with turned-up toes. Her head was swathed in a striped silk turban decorated with pink feathers, from which a few curls of dark hair had been allowed artfully to escape. One elegant hand held a glass of champagne, the other a long-stemmed ebony pipe, with which she beckoned Roland and me to her side.

"Ah, my friends, welcome *chez moi*! Marie, *ma petite*, run and get our guests some champagne, there's a good girl." She raised herself to a sitting position and patted the chaise longue invitingly. "Alex, come and sit with me. I should like us to become better acquainted. Roland, I'm afraid you must use a cushion."

So saying, she plucked one from the couch and tossed it onto the floor beside him. Roland deposited himself on it and accepted a glass of champagne from Marie.

"*A la liberté!*" he exclaimed, raising his glass.

I said, "What a charming room you have, Madame, and such interesting *objets d'arts*."

"Why, thank you, Alex. My Papa collected them. He travelled quite widely, as you can see."

"Indeed, Madame."

"But," she said with a smile, "I want to know about you, Alex. It's not often I play host to an English gentleman. So, *mon cher*, what is it that brings you to Paris?"

Since I had no wish to acquaint Madame with the true reason for my flight from England, I told her the same tale I had concocted for my father and cousin. For some reason I felt less comfortable lying to Madame le Comte than to my own family—or perhaps I was simply tiring of feeling like a fraud. Fortunately, the arrival of more guests allowed me to escape further scrutiny and, with Roland, to commence a tour of the room.

As the evening progressed, it became clear to me this *soirée* was not in the least like the intellectual Paris salons of which I had read. The room positively overflowed with the most incredible variety of people I had ever encountered in one place, ranging, it seemed, from tramps to academics, and from street girls to elegant ladies, all mixing together in great amity. As the sedate classical music was superseded by

165

more modern styles, I observed a rather elderly cleric dancing with a young woman wearing a bizarre assortment of ragged clothes, and Albert, a tall young man I had met earlier in the day, wrapped in the lithe arms of a young black woman as they swayed together in time to the music. Others were playing cards or dice, or debating in animated style. A plump, middle-aged gentleman lay fast asleep in an armchair, a white scrap of a dog snoozing on his lap. I was rather scandalised to see Madame le Compte engaged in kissing and caressing Marie, who appeared to be responding to her attentions with enthusiasm. Just what kind of ' *protégées'* were she and Sophie? I wondered.

Over the entire scene hung a cloud of smoke redolent of tobacco and an odour I did not quite recognise, mingled with those of perfume and warm human bodies, both clean and unwashed.

Amidst the crush, Roland and I came across Pierre and Etienne, to whom Roland had introduced me at *Le Coquelicot*. They were smoking from a pipe, sharing it between them, and I recognised the unknown odour I had sensed before.

"What is that?" I asked Roland.

"It is a journey to Paradise." He smiled. Reaching for the pipe, he offered it to me. "Here, try it."

I was much inclined to demur, but, as if to show I need have no fears, Roland took a deep draught before offering the pipe to me again. This time, though I cannot tell why, since I was a non-smoker, I accepted it and breathed deeply of the thick, sweetish smoke, feeling its warmth flow down my gullet and into my lungs—at which point I was suddenly racked by a fit of violent coughing.

"Ah, poor Alex," said Roland, slapping me on the back and informing our companions, as an aside, that I was unaccustomed to smoking. "But do not worry, *mon ami*, you will soon become used to it. Here, drink some champagne."

He took the pipe from my hands, replacing it with a glass of champagne from a tray one of the servants was carrying about the room. I sipped it gratefully. Through it, I could still taste the hot, sweetish, almost viscous smoke I had inhaled. I thought of enquiring once more what it was, but Roland gave me the pipe again, and after a second lungful of smoke I began to find I no longer cared. Indeed, all worldly cares vanished before the sensation of extreme pleasure that spread through my being. It was akin to what I had experienced with Emmeline, but of an intensity surpassing even that exquisite delight. Every inch of me, body, mind and soul, seemed more joyously alive than ever before. As I listened to the music, it seemed a living embodiment of sound, moving within me and around me, as sensuous as an oriental dancer. Everything on which I turned my gaze seemed an archetype of itself, so sharp and clear did it appear. My very thoughts became infused with an ecstasy bordering on the divine. In short, I felt myself to be in a state of grace, at peace with myself and at one with the world.

I looked at Roland, who was leaning against the chair occupied by Pierre, and his smile and dreamy eyes told me he felt as I did. As my gaze rested on him, I experienced such a depth of love for him it ought to have shocked me. Instead, it seemed to me it was a pure love such as God might feel for His creation. And I knew, with absolute certainty, that Roland felt the same for me. How I knew this I could not conceive, and cannot to this day, except for the effects of the contents of that miraculous pipe. The closest I have come to an explanation is that Roland and I, and the others in the room, and indeed all creation, seemed inextricably connected by some subtle, yet powerful force that, in my normal state, I could not perceive. How long I remained in this delightful condition I know not, although it was still with me as Roland and I walked home in the early hours of the morning through streets made darkly beautiful by the divine breath we had ingested.

The following morning I awoke to a feeling of lassitude that yet retained an echo of the previous night's sensations. When Roland roused himself, the two of us went to a nearby café for a breakfast of hot *café au lait* and bread rolls.

"Roland," I asked as we sat at one of the outdoor tables soaking up the sunshine. "What was in that pipe we smoked last night?"

"Opium," he replied through a mouthful of bread.

"Good Lord! Isn't that dangerous?" I asked, thinking of descriptions I had read of opium dens full of derelicts.

He swallowed some coffee and hitched his shoulders in a characteristic shrug. "Yes, if one takes too much or too often, but it is the same with most things, *n'est ce pas?*"

"I suppose so. I've heard of it being used medicinally, but I had no idea it had such a salutary effect."

Roland grinned. "*C'est merveilleux, n'est ce pas?*"

"It most certainly is!"

CHAPTER FIFTEEN

The strong bond I now felt between myself and Roland meant I did not, after all, move out of the *Hotel Rimini*, taking up residence in a room on the third floor that was in a somewhat less parlous condition than most of the others I had seen. In a fit of enthusiasm—and considerable wonder at how I was choosing to live—I cleared out the room thoroughly, installing rugs—very threadbare and faded, but still serviceable—a proper bed and an old table and chairs, all of which I bought for next to nothing at a street market and carried home with the help of Roland, Etienne, and Pierre. I wanted to purchase a bookcase as well, but my friends baulked at this, since the proposed item was both large and heavy and, as Roland reminded me, I had no books. I assured him I should soon remedy this, but then realised just how low my funds had sunk—and I had no means of accessing more without putting myself in danger of arrest.

Being thus unable to purchase clothes, I swallowed my pride and returned to Gervase's rooms, taking Roland as a sort of bulwark against any unpleasantness. As luck would have it, however, neither he nor Giles was at home, and I was able to collect my belongings, including my precious journal, telling myself I should take up my writing again immediately on reaching my new home.

The immense pleasure I derived from writing of my

experiences is difficult to describe. All I can say is that it was, as it always had been, my refuge, my means of self-expression, and a way of understanding the experiences life threw in my way.

* * * *

One morning, about a fortnight after Madame le Compte's *soirée*, Roland and I were sitting outside our usual breakfast café when Albert appeared with the black girl, whom he introduced as Amélie. He was giving a recital that evening, he informed us, at *Le Chat Noir*, which we were invited to attend. Of course I asked Roland about *Le Chat Noir*. I had heard of it from Gervase as the place where Aristide Bruant had performed before purchasing his own café, but knew nothing more about it.

"It is," he informed me, "one of the first and the most famous of the Paris *cafés concerts*. It is a very splendid place. You will like it, I think."

My first sight of *Le Chat Noir* was disappointing. A squat structure set between two taller buildings, it was timbered on the outside in the Tudor manner, making it seem rather homely. Its interior, however, was unexpectedly eccentric, the curved ceiling imparting the appearance of an outsize railway carriage, and its walls covered with a profusion of posters and pictures. Along the side walls wooden seats were set with tables in front of them, so that the patrons sat facing one another across a sort of gangway. The waiters passed along this, as did the patrons. When I commented on the rather splendid attire of the waiters, Roland told me it was the uniform of the French Academy, a group of august persons whose task it was to regulate the French language. Precisely why the café's proprietor felt this to be suitable dress for waiters, however, he was unable to tell me, merely shrugging his shoulders and pulling down the corners of his mouth when I asked him.

We found Albert, along with Amélie and the apparently inseparable Etienne and Pierre, seated at a table near the stage. I had half expected Madame le Compte to be there, along with her two young ladies, but it seemed they were engaged elsewhere that evening. There were, however, two couples I had not seen before. A striking young woman with jet-black hair, skin as pale as milk, and luminous, dark eyes Albert introduced as his cousin, Josephine. She was accompanied by her husband, Jean, an elegant young gentleman training to be a doctor. The other couple, of more prosaic appearance, proved to be Albert's brother, Jacques, and his wife, Marthe, who owned a café on the Left Bank near the Sorbonne University. Jean had provided our company with several bottles of good wine, which he insisted on pouring for us himself. I noticed Albert was not drinking, and supposed this was because he was performing that evening. Having heard the musical efforts of Charles and Ferdy when in their cups, I could only feel this was a wise policy on his part.

After a comedian, two different versions of the seemingly mandatory sultry female *chanteuse,* and a rather *risqué* dance performed by six ladies clad in little besides a few ostrich-feather fans, it was Albert's turn to entertain us with a virtuoso pianoforte performance of what Roland informed me was the new jazz music from America. I enjoyed this exceedingly. With its intricate and exciting rhythms, arresting changes of tempo and tone, and exhilarating sense of immediacy, it was like nothing I had heard before.

Albert's guests departed soon after his performance, leaving the rest of us to finish off the wine. As soon as they had gone, Albert pulled what looked like a brown medicine bottle from his jacket pocket and set it on the table.

"A little supplement for the wine," he explained with a wink.

Pierre seized on it with alacrity, removing its stopper and pouring a few drops into his and Etienne's wine glasses before passing the bottle back to Albert. Albert, like a generous host, insisted on serving Roland and me before himself. I had already realised this must be laudanum, a tincture of opium used medicinally to allay pain and calm the nerves. A thrill of excitement ran through me at the prospect of repeating my experience at Madame le Compte's *soirée*. I did not expect to be able to match that first divine sensation, but I discovered soon enough I was wrong. If my experience that night lacked the novelty of the first occasion, it more than made up for it in other ways. The music and the sounds of laughter and conversation combined to create a vast symphony that washed all about me, and I found that if I concentrated on any one thing it acquired a clarity and depth bordering on the sublime, as though it were haloed with an aura of bright, electric energy, even, in some mysterious way, sound and touch. I thought of Roland's references to Buddhism and wondered whether its adherents achieved such heightened awareness by their meditation. But why meditate, when the contents of a bottle obtainable at any apothecary's shop for no more than a few *sous* could produce the same effect in a fraction of the time and with no effort?

* * * *

It was no more than a week later that I bought a bottle of laudanum myself. Under its influence, Roland and I saw plays, heard concerts, or simply strolled the streets of Paris, our enjoyment made magical by its benign effect—or so I thought at the time. It kept at bay the harshness of our living conditions and engendered in our long discussions of literature, art and philosophy a rare and gratifying insight. I could even think of Emmeline and not feel her loss under the kindly influence of Madame Laudanum. Even when I realised I could no longer live comfortably without Madame, I was not concerned. After all, the expenditure of a few *sous* would bring me her delightful company once more.

And I wrote. Hour after hour I would scribble in my journal, oblivious to all but the melding of thought and word and the satisfying scratch of pen on paper as I began to write stories based on my life in Paris. I continued to write to Emmeline, too, even though I could not have the pleasure of reading whatever she might have replied. What need had I for letters, I consoled myself when, with the help of a small brown bottle, I could obtain her company as often as I wished? Little by little, then, Emmeline became little more than a beautiful dream. My real lover was now Madame Laudanum.

Gradually, as the months passed, my available funds grew smaller and smaller until at last they were almost gone. This sent me into a panic. How should I procure more laudanum without money? However, with the help of Madame le Compte, who was exceptionally well connected and saw herself as, in some sort, a patroness of impoverished artists, I was able to have some of my stories published in English-language magazines, which kept complete penury at bay, albeit sporadically. It was at this time, too, that I learned exactly how Roland acquired his books, along with such other necessities as food and drink. Not to put too fine a point on the matter, he stole them, assuaging his conscience with the philosophy that, if society were run as it ought to be, such things would be free to all who wanted them, and there would be no need of money at all. Somewhere in the increasingly hazy recesses of my mind I sensed there was a flaw in this logic, but the need to keep hunger at bay on a regular basis, not to mention the inexorable demands of my sweet Madame, formed a powerful argument in its favour, and I became a willing pupil to Roland's expert teacher. And so summer became autumn, and my affair with Madame Laudanum consumed ever more of my being.

One cool, but sunny morning, Roland and I sallied forth from the *Hotel Rimini* to procure our breakfast in the usual fashion, which is to say by stealing food from the market stalls and devoting what little cash we possessed to purchasing hot coffee and, in my case, more laudanum. Unlike me, Roland was not a regular imbiber. After breakfast, we set off for the *Café Coquelicot,* where there was to be a poetry reading attended, or so we had heard, by a couple of well-known Parisian poets. In the event, none of the poets in attendance were at all well known to either of us, but Madame le Compte was there with Sophie and Marie, as well as Albert and several friends of his, one of whom, a scholar of English literature, had read one of my stories and expressed a gratifying degree of praise for it. The poetry reading over, Madame le Compte treated our party to lunch, and so we contrived to pass a most enjoyable day.

As the afternoon shadows lengthened, the others began to leave, and Roland and I set off home, carrying what food we had managed to secrete about our persons, intending it for our supper. Since I had become almost as adept as Roland at the art of pilfering, this promised to be rather more festive than usual, as the bottle of burgundy hidden under my jacket would serve to complement it. Had my mind not been affected by Madame Laudanum's ministrations, I should have been horrified by what I had become. As it was, I accepted it, if not with equanimity, as least with resignation.

After supper, Roland went to meet his young lady while I took myself off to my room and spent the remainder of the evening in the company of my muse until I began to feel that sweet lassitude that always followed the hours of divine inspiration afforded by laudanum. With a sigh of pure pleasure, I curled up on my bed to sleep, little realising what the morrow would bring.

* * * *

I dreamt I was back at Shillington Hall. I was eight years old and Papa had just given me my very own pony, a chestnut filly called Russet. Filled with pride, I set off to accompany Captain Nuttall on his survey of the estate, on a day of perfect blue skies and warm sunshine, the air filled with birdsong, the woods awash with bluebells, and the lake as calm as a millpond and reflecting the cobalt blue of the sky. Together we rode into the wood beneath oak trees that remembered a time before the Normans conquered England.

As Captain Nuttall turned towards me, a sudden terror stabbed at me. His face had transformed into that of a black panther that opened its mouth and began to roar. I could see its needle-sharp teeth, its rough tongue dripping saliva, its throat belching flames and smoke as it roared, and roared, and roared... All at once I was awake, my heart pounding like a piston, my breath thickening in my throat. I heard footsteps outside my room and someone calling my name urgently.

The door burst open and Roland stood there, his eyes wide with fear and his bedclothes in his arms.

"Alex! Make haste, we must leave!"

I shook my head to clear away the cotton wool that seemed to fill it. "Roland, what is it? What's wrong?"

"The hotel, it is on fire!"

As he spoke, there came a great crashing from below and the acrid stench of smoke assailed my nostrils. Galvanised into action, I leapt from my bed and reached beneath it for my overnight bag. Most of my few clothes were already in it, since I had nowhere else to put them, leaving only a few necessary items to be added: my journal and writing implements, and my precious bottle of laudanum.

With Roland urging me to hurry, I hoisted my bag onto my shoulder and we raced for the stairs. As we half ran, half stumbled down them, the entire staircase began to quake beneath our feet and chunks of plaster from the ceiling to fall on our heads. That we reached the pavement with nothing worse than a few scratches and a liberal coating of plaster dust was little short of a miracle. Amongst the small crowd standing forlorn in the narrow street I recognised several other residents of the hotel, but I took little heed of them, nor of the *gendarmes* who were attempting to herd them away from danger. Roland and I ran until we were well clear of both crowd and hotel, leaning against a wall to catch our breath as we watched the leaping flames and saw the building collapse slowly to the ground, sending great plumes of black smoke and showers of sparks up into the dawn sky.

After a time, Roland spoke in tones of resignation, as though no blow fate could deal him had the power to surprise him. "Well, we must find another home, I think. But first, we must eat."

He began to walk along the street and I followed him, still dazed by the sudden turn of events and the after-effects of the previous night's laudanum. Realising I was not quite myself, Roland sat me down on a low stone wall and bade me stay there while he went to procure us some food, returning perhaps a quarter of an hour later bearing a small loaf of bread, two cooked sausages and a chunk of cheese. Fortified by these, I dug in my pocket for a few coins to purchase coffee at a nearby café. We sat at one of the pavement tables, our meagre possessions at our feet, endeavouring to conjure up a solution to our predicament. All of a sudden, tears welled up in Roland's eyes and began to roll down his cheeks.

"My books!" he cried in great distress. "All of my books— gone!"

There was nothing I could say to comfort him, but I laid my hand on his arm to show I felt for him, as indeed I did, knowing how precious to him was his treasure trove of stolen books.

"You are my true friend," he told me, and in that moment it was only my ingrained English reserve that kept my own tears at bay.

After a time, we left the café and began to walk again, barely noticing, much less caring, where we went. Whether by chance or design, we eventually found ourselves outside the *Café Coqueliquot*. Seeing no one we knew amongst those sitting at the outside tables, we made our way across the brick terrace and through the trellised archway into the tiny indoor area. Roland's eyes brightened immediately on seeing two young ladies seated in a corner devouring a luncheon of ham, cheese and bread rolls as though they had eaten nothing for days, as, judging by their appearance, might well have been the case, for beneath their bright clothes and makeup they were both painfully thin.

"*Ah, Lisette, chérie,*" cried Roland, hurrying to kiss the darker of the two. "*Comme j'heureux suis de tu voir!*" He bent and kissed each of the girls on both cheeks, then spoke to them in rapid French before turning to me. "Alex, come and meet Lisette and Mimi. They are sisters, and very dear friends of mine."

I bade the young women good day in French, as it seemed they spoke no English, and they looked up at me from under their painted lashes and smiled at me with their painted lips. They looked like two undernourished porcelain dolls. I wanted to ask Roland who on earth they were, but felt they would find me sadly lacking in manners if I did so in French, while to speak in front of them in English would be equally ill bred of me. So when Roland sat down at their table, I followed suit, contenting myself with conversation on such common place topics as my French permitted. Roland seemed particularly friendly with Lisette, so it was no surprise when he leaned towards me and murmured that she was the young lady he visited so frequently. It seemed she and Mimi worked at a nearby tavern.

"Let me speak with them again," he said. "We may find somewhere to live."

I fervently hoped this would not require me to take up with Mimi as he had with Lisette. She was far too haggard for me to find her attractive, and in any case she looked so unwell I should have feared becoming infected. Of course, I must have looked even more unappetising to her, having neither washed nor shaved for days, nor eaten properly for even longer, but at the time I had no conception of how far I was under Madame Laudanum's influence.

Whatever Roland said to the sisters, the upshot was they pronounced themselves willing to share their accommodation with us until we were able to find something else. They rented two tiny rooms with an enclosed balcony on the upper floor of a boarding house near their work, and told us we could use the balcony area to sleep in, but we must be discreet, since their landlord would charge extra if he knew they had guests. Before long, they left to return to work, saying we could call at their rooms after eight o'clock that evening.

Sharing quarters with Lisette and Mimi seemed almost luxurious by comparison with the *Hotel Rimini*, despite being dreadfully cramped. Unlike our former abode, it had lights and taps that worked, and a small gas stove so that we could heat water for washing, all of which afforded us some respite from our immediate difficulties.

During this time, however, Madame Laudanum underwent a transformation. She ceased being my delightful lover, becoming instead a demanding mistress who would visit terrible punishments on me if I failed to satisfy her increasingly merciless demands. Whereas previously a small dose of laudanum would provide me with hours of delight, followed by sweet dreams, I now found I needed increasing quantities at shorter intervals to achieve anything approaching pleasure, and my dreams became ever more feverish and bizarre. Quite often, I dreamed of Henri, but when I did his face seemed distorted until it resembled the livid countenance of some Oriental demon, leering at me with lolling tongue or piercing me through with huge, black eyes. Or I would dream of blood, great cataracts and gushers of it that threatened to drown me or to wash me away in its glutinous torrent. At other times, I seemed lost in a vast waste swirling with vile creatures that swarmed about and over me, clinging to me with slimy, viscid limbs, or tearing at me with claws like meat hooks. And when, as often happened now, I failed to meet Madame's demands, she visited on me such horrors as to render me unfit for my own company, let alone that of others. One minute I would burn with fever, the next I was shivering with cold. My limbs would ache until I wept from the pain, or I felt as though insects were crawling over my body; and I felt sick almost all of the time. There was only one thing that could ease my distress, and even that was providing diminishing returns. Indeed, I could barely perform the basic physical functions unless aided by my callous mistress.

One day, Roland asked me to walk out with him, and I agreed, since I needed to find more laudanum. As we walked, he began to speak to me in tones of great anxiety.

"Alex, *mon ami*, you are making yourself ill with

laudanum. It is not good to take it so much or so often. I beg of you, please stop before it is too late."

"I can't," I told him, "since I can't be in the least degree comfortable without it."

"But you must, Alex, you must, otherwise it will kill you."

"How can that be?" I cried in accusing tones. "You told me yourself it wasn't dangerous. Did you lie to me, then?"

He sighed, and took my arm. "Alex, I said it was safe if you did not take too much or too often. It is not possible to take it as often as you do without becoming ill. I fear you are already very ill, *mon ami*, and so I beg you to stop now, before the damage is irretrievable."

"Why didn't you warn me, then? What kind of friend are you to let me endanger myself without so much as a word of warning?"

"Alex, please, I didn't realise until we were sharing a room how bad it was with you, but I will help you to stop if you'll let me. It will not be easy, I think, but I swear to you I'll do all I can."

I flung myself from him, filled with a sudden fury that I had been so hardly used by one I had trusted. When he tried to take my arm again, to my undying shame I struck him. His hand flew to his face, but his eyes betrayed a hurt far worse than any physical pain. Then he drew himself up and spoke to me with a quiet dignity that must surely have pierced any heart not in thrall to addiction.

"Alex, I perceive you will not accept my help, and I cannot bear to see you so ill and in pain. I am sorry, Alex, but I do not wish any more to share quarters with you. When you decide to let yourself be healed, go to Lisette and Mimi at the *Auberge Valois* and they will tell you where to find me. Until then— *au revoir, mon cher ami.* I wish you the best of luck in your life, for you will surely need it."

After he had gone, I wept bitter tears of frustration and self-pity. It was long before I could accept that it was I, and not Roland, who was to blame for my enslavement to opium. Certainly, he had introduced me to it, but it was I, and I alone, who had courted it with such devotion. At the time, however, I saw nothing beyond what my mind and my body craved, and I hated Roland for so much as suggesting I should give it up.

With no money left, and my dread hunger to assuage, I took to stealing laudanum as well as food, living on the streets and sleeping in shop doorways or church porches. There were times when I begged for money, but for the most part I found it impossible to stay in one place for long enough, feeling compelled to be constantly on the move, as though I might somehow outrun the pain and nausea, and the itching of the skin that were now my constant companions. No longer did I take laudanum to attain pleasure. I needed it to escape the worst horrors of the nightmare into which I had fallen. As winter drew on, my case became ever more desperate. No matter how much laudanum I was able to procure—and I had by now acquired a sort of low cunning in such matters—it was never enough. And from sleeping outside for so many months, I had developed a cough that racked my body constantly. I was little more than a skeleton covered with skin, and that skin a sickly greyish hue from grime and illness. If I caught my reflection in a shop window, I would start back from the grim apparition I beheld, unable to believe it was me, and not some ghoul that had taken possession of my body. Yet in truth I was possessed, by the grimmest of spectres, opium.

One morning, as I sat leaning against a wall near the *Sacré Coeur* attempting to warm myself in the thin winter sunshine, I saw Giles out walking with a young lady. As he glanced in my direction, I raised a hand in greeting, but he turned back to his companion. He had not even seen me. So debased had I become that I was beneath the notice even of such as Giles. Tears filled my eyes and I dashed them away in anger. I reached into my pocket for my laudanum bottle and flung it from me, only to scrabble after it again as the awful reality struck me that it was all I had left now. So I sat there clutching to my breast the thing I had come to hate, and yet desired more than anything else on earth.

On another day, I happened to pass by the spot where the *Hotel Rimini* had stood, and stopped to gaze on its blackened corpse. As I stared, unable to drag my eyes away, I noticed part of the ground floor was still standing. On closer inspection, I discovered stone steps leading down to a basement of whose existence I had previously been unaware. Very slowly, I picked my way down the stairs until I found myself standing in a cavernous underground cellar. It was almost dark, even during the daytime, and smelled strongly of mould and burnt wood, but it would afford shelter from the worst of the winter weather, and I should not have shopkeepers or churchwardens hounding me away from their premises. So I spent the rest of the winter entombed in the ruins of the *Hotel Rimini*, venturing out only to steal food or laudanum.

CHAPTER SIXTEEN

Winter passed, and the days began to grow longer, yet to me the entire world seemed made of ice, since I was by now so thin my body could not create warmth. Occasionally, the employees of the café across the street from the *Rimini* would take pity on me and give me hot coffee, or perhaps some bread or cake that was too stale to serve to customers. Because of this, I never attempted to steal from its proprietors, but I scavenged anywhere else I could, even taking scraps of food left by café customers, or swallowing the dregs of their wine. I think my mind had all but ceased to function save in a basic animal fashion, yet, like an animal, I retained the instinct to cling to life and the cunning to achieve this, however tenuous might be my grasp.

One afternoon I ventured from my lair, prompted, as always, by my craving for laudanum. I had, of course, no money with which to purchase it, but I had some vague notion of begging for a few *sous* outside the nearby *Sacré Coeur*. Perhaps I thought the sanctity of its shadow would render those who passed by more charitable. Whatever might have been my distorted reasoning, by the time the shops were beginning to close I was no better off than when I had started, and my skin was crawling with the need for laudanum. Cursing the miserliness of the citizens of Paris, I began to shuffle back towards the *Hotel Rimini*, my limbs twitching as though attempting to shake off the agony that gnawed at them like a starving rat. My mind knew only one thing: I must, by whatever means, give Madame Laudanum what she craved and gain respite from her cruel torture, at least for a time.

I passed by the *Café Coquelicot*, but did not go in. I dreaded the thought of my old friends seeing me, and besides, what I needed could not be found there. Some little way beyond the cafe, however, I found what I sought. In a small side street, the proprietor of an apothecary's shop was locking up for the night. Desperation lending me speed, I stole up behind him, glancing around to be sure the street was clear of people. Having ascertained this, I closed on the man, launched myself at him from behind and knocked him to the ground. Crying out in surprise and pain, he began to struggle to his feet. I scrambled up and struck at him with my foot, knocking him down again. My one thought was to get hold of his keys so I could gain access to the shop, and I kicked him again and again, oblivious alike of his cries of distress and of the pain to my own ill-shod feet, until he lay still. Then I snatched up the keys he had dropped and began to try them in the lock, glancing down every few seconds to make sure my victim was still unconscious. After what seemed an aeon, I found the key I needed, fumbled it into the lock and, with a grunt of satisfaction, turned it and pushed open the door.

The shop was in darkness, but I dared not draw attention to myself by lighting a lamp, and so I slipped behind the counter and began peering at the shelves in the gloom, pulling bottles and jars off and flinging them aside until I found what I wanted. I snatched up a bottle, tugged off the stopper, and poured some of the contents down my throat. With a sigh of relief, even though the laudanum had not yet taken effect, I stuffed the bottle into my jacket pocket, following it with as many more as my pockets would hold. So intent was I on my task I failed to notice that the proprietor, still lying on the pavement, had regained consciousness. As I left the shop he lunged out and gave my ankle a sharp wrench, sending me sprawling. Terrified, I scrambled to my feet, ignoring my grazed hands and shins, and ran as fast as my weakened limbs would carry me, neither knowing nor caring where I went, so long as I might escape retribution.

I ran until my legs simply buckled under me, and then collapsed onto the pavement, gasping for breath. Each breath I took seemed to engender a paroxysm of coughing that racked my chest with such excruciating agony I was convinced I was about to die. At length, however, my breathing eased a little and I was able to look around me. I had no idea where I was, but I saw I was close to a small park. Inch by inch, I dragged myself off the pavement and onto the grass. This took considerable effort since, now my concentration was not fully taken up with the mere act of breathing, I began to feel the pain of my injuries. I reached into my jacket pocket for the laudanum bottles I had stolen. My fingers encountered only broken glass and soaking wet fabric. The bottles must have smashed when I fell. Weeping bitter tears of frustration, I began to pick out the pieces of glass and throw them away. The foolishness of this was brought home to me in no uncertain fashion when I gashed my hand on a shard. With a low moan of desperation, I sank to the grass and lay there clutching my bleeding hand, convinced I should not survive until morning.

How long I lay there I cannot tell, for if I was not unconscious, I was as close to it as made no difference. But at some point I became aware I was no longer alone. Terror seized me, as I knew I could no more prevail against an attacker than could a kitten. Some instinct bade me lie still and pretend I was dead, but it seemed my assailant saw through this feeble ruse as I sensed rather than saw or felt him crouch down beside me. I must have been lying on my stomach, as I felt strong hands roll me over onto my back and begin to tug open the collar of my shirt, exposing my neck and chest to the freezing night air. My throat constricted with dread and I dared not open my eyes, certain I was about to be strangled. Then it seemed my attacker drew back, and I heard a low exclamation.

"*Mon Dieu!* Alex, is it you?"

My eyes opened wide in amazement, for I recognised that voice. It was Henri de Saint-Clair.

I tried to speak, but could make no sound other than a hoarse moan.

Henri spoke again. "Alex, what in God's name has happened to you? But no, don't try to speak. There'll be time for that later. I must get you to safety."

He lifted me up as easily as though I had been a child. I think I must have fainted from the sudden movement because, when I came to my senses again, I was lying on a couch in a room I had never seen before. In a chair beside me sat Henri, regarding me gravely. When he saw my eyes open, he leaned forward, smiling.

"Ah, you're awake. That's good. I've done what I can for your hand, Alex, and I believe it will heal quite quickly." My curiosity aroused, I looked at my injured hand. The wound was still an angry red, but it was no longer bleeding, and already showed signs of beginning to heal. I raised incredulous eyes to Henri's, but his grey eyes forestalled me. "We can talk later, Alex. I'm afraid I must go out now. There's some urgent business I must complete. I'll return as soon as I can. Please rest here until then. I'll have Fournier bring you some food and wine."

So saying, he went to the bell cord and tugged on it. Seconds later, the elderly man who had opened the door to me all those months ago hobbled into the room. Henri must have brought me to his home. He issued swift instructions to Fournier and strode from the room. I heard the front door open and close. Fournier also left, returning some minutes later bearing a tray, and I smelled the appetising aroma of chicken soup.

He came to stand beside me. "Are you able to sit up, M'sieu?"

I nodded. "I think so."

My voice emerged as a feeble croak, but with some effort I was able to drag myself to a sitting position and to balance the tray on my knees. As I had thought, it contained a bowl of chicken broth, accompanied by a thick chunk of bread. Between fits of shivering and coughing, I managed to drink the soup and to eat some of the bread. Given how long it had been since I had eaten, I was surprised at how poor a job I made of it, but supposed this to be due to the after effects of the laudanum I had taken earlier. While I was dealing with the soup and bread, Fournier fetched me a glass of red wine. He had mixed it with water, as was the French custom with meals, but to me it might have been the very nectar of the gods. Having eaten, I began to feel exceedingly tired, so

Fournier helped me to lie down again with a cushion beneath my head, pulled a rug over me, and bore away my tray, leaving me to sleep.

I think it was only an hour or two before the sound of the front door opening woke me, and Henri came into the room. He smiled when he saw I was awake, and came to sit beside me. As I looked up at him, it seemed to me some deep fire, or perhaps only its embers, burned in the depths of his grey eyes, but my enfeebled mind could make nothing of this.

"Are you feeling a little better now?" he enquired in a gentle voice.

I nodded. "Yes. Thank you for your kindness, though I don't deserve it."

"Perhaps not, but I must admit that, apart from the parlous state you were in, I was very pleased to see you again. I had been hoping for some time that we might renew our friendship. I'd missed our discussions. But let's not think of that just now. The main thing is to restore you to health. What on earth has happened to you, Alex, to bring you to this parlous state? I had supposed you still to be living with your cousin, although I confess I thought it odd that you seemed no longer to accompany him to social events."

"It's a long story," I began, but was immediately overcome by a fit of coughing. Henri went to a sideboard and poured me some brandy, holding the glass to my lips so I could take it in small sips. As I tried to speak again, he shook his head.

"No, no, you must rest. You're not at all well, Alex. Quite apart from your injuries, you have a bad case of bronchitis— and you've developed an addiction to opium, *n'est ce pas*?"

I gasped, "How—how did you know that?"

"Apart from the physical signs, with which I'm familiar,

189

your clothes reek of laudanum. Indeed, you appear to have been bathing in the stuff."

I couldn't help laughing at this, and was punished with another coughing fit.

"My apologies," Henri said. "I shall try not to make you laugh any more until that cough has gone. Speaking of which, I have some skill in the healing arts, and I believe I can help you if you are willing to put your trust in me."

"But of course," I said. "How can you doubt it? But truly, Henri, I don't deserve such kindness."

"I dare say you're right," he replied, "but I happen to have a fondness for you, Alex, and I have no wish to see you suffer, no matter how foolish or wicked you may have been. Call it your punishment if you like that, instead of affording you the blessed oblivion of death, I shall heal you so you may face your troubles and defeat them, if you will, or otherwise suffer the torments of a guilty soul. Though it's my belief your only sin has been ignorance, and experience is an excellent cure for that if you take heed of its lessons. Now, will you let me help you?"

"Gladly."

"Good. I'll arrange for a bath to be drawn for you. I assure you I have no wish to lay hands on you in your present condition."

Once again he rang for Fournier and, before very long, the old gentleman was helping me up the stairs to the bathroom. To my surprise, Henri himself helped me to undress, kicking my filthy clothes into a corner of the room to be disposed of later, and assisting me to climb in. He sent Fournier off for towels and a nightshirt, staying with me himself to make sure I did not slide into the water from sheer exhaustion, and drown. As I lay in the steaming water, for the first time in many months I began to feel warm, and I could happily have gone to sleep with the water caressing my body. So utterly weary did I feel, and so relaxed, it was an effort simply to wash my body and my lank and matted hair. But at last I was done, and Henri helped me out of the bath and wrapped me in a towel as though I were a small child. I half expected him to dry me as well, but he left me to perform that office for myself, merely handing me the nightshirt when I had done.

"Come now," he said, "I'll show you to your room. I've had a fire made up there, which should help you to stay warm. Fournier will bring you breakfast in the morning, and you may then sleep or read, as you wish. I shan't see you again until the evening. I keep to my rooms until then."

The chamber to which he showed me seemed, to my grateful eyes, like a room in Paradise, with its great bed bathed in golden lamplight and the fire crackling in the grate. Henri waited only until I had settled myself between the sheets before bidding me goodnight, assuring me I might ring for Fournier if I needed anything.

* * * *

I awoke the following morning with an intense craving for laudanum. When Fournier brought my breakfast, I was sitting on the bed in agony, my arms clasped about my knees, rocking back and forth in an attempt to control the violent twitching of my body. Fournier came to me quickly, a concerned look on his face.

"What troubles you, M'sieu? Are you ill?"

I nodded dumbly, not trusting myself to speak without

anger, since my fearful mistress was tormenting me like the devil.

"What is it you need, M'sieu? I will get it for you if I can."

"Laudanum," I whispered. "I hurt, Fournier, I hurt all over."

"And you have a fever, I think," he said, placing his gnarled hand on my brow. "Excuse me, M'sieu, I shall return directly."

He was as good as his word, bringing with him a bottle and a small glass. As he made to pour me a dose, I snatched the bottle from his hands and administered a large dose of its contents directly into my mouth. If Fournier was surprised at this, he did not show it, nor did he try to stop me. When he reached out for the bottle after I had finished, I pulled it away, clutching it to me as though he had tried to steal my most treasured possession—as indeed he had, in my eyes. This time his eyes widened in surprise. I thought he was going to remonstrate with me, and prepared myself for a fight—to the death if need be—but he merely shrugged, then bowed and left the room.

Once the laudanum had begun to take effect, I was able to eat my breakfast of bread rolls with honey and *café au lait*, then I pulled the coverlet over myself and slept for the rest of the day, a sleep mercifully devoid of the dreams I had come to dread.

Darkness had fallen by the time Henri came to see me. I had taken more laudanum, so the worst of my pain had abated, although the coughing fits had worsened. I looked up when he entered the room, but I was unable to hold his gaze, which seemed to pierce right through me.

He picked up the laudanum bottle. "There will be no more

of this," he told me in stern tones.

"But—but—I need it!" I cried in horror. "I assure you I can't go on without it."

He raised one eyebrow. "And I assure you it's the very last thing you need. If you keep taking this, you will die."

"Please, Henri! I swear I shall die without it!"

"No you won't, not if you'll let me help you. Now, will you trust me to do that?"

"I will if you'll let me have that," I said, pointing to the bottle in his hand. "It'll be the last time, I swear to you."

He laughed. "Oh, very good, Alex, but your little tricks won't work with me. Believe me, I've seen them all. Now, look at me."

Glowering, I deliberately turned my head away, but he took my chin firmly in his hand and forced me to hold his gaze.

"That's better. It's no use, Alex. I've dealt with obstacles far more difficult than a petulant young man in the throes of addiction. You want me to heal you, don't you? Then you must look into my eyes so I can assess your situation and see what must be done."

What he was saying made no sense to me but, once my eyes were fixed on his, I found it impossible to turn them away. As his eyes bored into mine, he continued to talk to me in a soothing way, but within seconds I had ceased to hear his words. All I could hear was a gentle wash of sound breaking softly against my ears like waves on the seashore. Then that, too, ceased and I was aware of nothing but his gaze, like a beam of light penetrating to my very soul. I had the extraordinary sensation that he was somehow moving within my mind, reordering my thoughts like a librarian arranging books on a shelf. I was terrified, then, but he spoke to me without words, reassuring me that all he was doing was restoring my mind to its true nature, undoing the distortions created by the opium. Had I been fully awake, I am sure I should never have believed him. All I can say is that at the time it made perfect sense to me, and so I let him do his will.

At some point, I am uncertain how much later, I felt his mind receding from mine, and then I was looking into his grey eyes, which, as when he had found me in the park, seemed to flicker with fire in their depths. Gradually, the flames faded away, and I was able to look away from him.

"What did you do?" I asked in wonder. "Was it some kind of mesmerism?"

He smiled. "Something like that. I think you'll find you'll have no further need of laudanum. Now, let me see that injured hand of yours." I held it out to him. "Ah, good, it's progressing well."

"It's almost healed!" I exclaimed, staring at it in astonishment. "How did you do that, Henri? It seems like sorcery to me."

"No, it's not sorcery, though I dare say you would think it so."

"Then tell me. I should like to understand."

"Perhaps I shall, one day, but not just now. Shall I have Fournier bring your dinner here, or do you feel well enough to join me downstairs?"

"I'd like that," I replied, "but I have no clothes, and I don't think I should go to dinner in my nightshirt."

"Oh, dear, how remiss of me. Tomorrow I'll have Fournier buy you some clothes. You'd be swamped in mine, so in the meantime I'm afraid you'll have to make do with a dressing gown. I'll ask him to bring you one."

A short time later I joined Henri in the dining room, wearing a luxurious silk-brocade dressing gown the colour of rich, ruby wine, albeit one a couple of sizes too large for me. Henri kept me company while I dined on roast chicken and vegetables, although he ate nothing, assuring me he had eaten earlier. If it seemed somewhat strange that he had not waited so we could dine together, such thoughts soon became lost in the pleasure of his conversation. Indeed, the only thing spoiling my enjoyment of the evening was the incessant coughing that still plagued me.

As we sat in the parlour after dinner sipping brandy, Henri looked at me in a considering way and said, "Your cuts and bruises will soon heal, but that cough is altogether more serious. We shall have to do something about it."

"I dare say it'll go, in time."

"Perhaps, but bronchitis can easily become a chronic condition, especially in one who has become as thin and as sickly as you have. If it's left, you might well develop pneumonia. No, I think we should not leave it to chance."

"But what can you do? I thought it was usually treated with laudanum, and you say I can't have that."

"Many conditions are treated with laudanum," he said with a dismissive gesture, "but it merely treats the symptoms. It's not a cure, as your own condition attests."

"Well, then, what do you suggest?"

Henri got to his feet. "Wait here," he said, and strode from the room.

Perhaps ten minutes later he returned, bearing a small crystal tumbler filled with a dark red liquid, saying, "Drink

195

this. I think it will help."

I eyed the glass with suspicion. "What is it?"

"Just a restorative wine. I assure you it will do you no harm."

I took the glass and stared at its contents, recalling the revolting witch's brews I had been made to drink as a child. I gave it a cautious sniff; it smelled a little like port wine.

Henri smiled at my hesitation. "I could have sworn you said you'd trust me," he murmured.

Thus chided, I took a deep breath and downed the liquid in one gulp. Its taste was not quite like port wine, or, indeed, any other wine I had ever drunk, but I found it pleasant enough.

"There," said Henri, "was that so bad?"

I grinned. "You sound just like my nanny when I was a child."

"And a most recalcitrant child, too, I dare swear. Now, would you like to play cards, or shall we converse?"

"I rather think I could manage both."

"Excellent! I do believe you're on the road to recovery already."

CHAPTER SEVENTEEN

Henri was as good as his word, and the following morning Fournier brought to my room two sets of clothes he had purchased for me, as well as a razor, a brush and comb, and various other articles I needed to make myself presentable. How he—or Henri—had correctly gauged my size, I had no idea; perhaps Fournier's experience as a valet had given him the ability. At any rate, my new clothes fitted me admirably, and had clearly been selected to suit me both in style and colouring. For the first time in many months, I began to feel human again. My body's need for opium had abated, and I no longer ached, apart from the injuries I had sustained in my fall, and the strain to my body caused by my coughing fits. From time to time, my mind still called for the drug's solace, especially during the lonely hours of daylight, when I had no company and Henri's extensive library had ceased to engage my interest.

I was exceedingly curious as to why it was that Henri kept to his room during the day, but when I asked Fournier, all he would say was, "It is not for me to question the habits of my master." My curiosity piqued even further by this unsatisfactory reply, I determined to ask Henri myself when next I saw him. For some reason, however, once I became engrossed in conversation with him, the subject invariably left my mind, to resurface only during the day when I was unable to broach it with him.

I found I had no desire to leave the house. The bronchitis left me exhausted much of the time but, more than that, I feared to put myself in the way of temptation, as it seemed the addiction of the mind was even stronger than that of the body. So that I might not feel quite cut off from the world outside, Fournier undertook to bring me one or more of the Paris newspapers each morning. Since I tired easily, and my powers of concentration were still rather haphazard, I found the short articles easier to read than Henri's books. The subject matter was certainly more sensational. I discovered, for example, that over one hundred people had died during a film screening at the Charity Bazaar after a curtain caught on fire from the ether used to fuel the projector lamp. And, during the months I had been in thrall to laudanum, a series of unexplained deaths had occurred in Paris. The body of the most recent of these, a young man thought to have been on his way home from a performance of *La Sorcière* at the recently opened *Grand-Guignol* theatre, had been discovered only the previous day in an alleyway near the theatre.

When I mentioned these to Henri, he showed a proper sympathy, but commented that such occurrences were by no means rare in any large city, citing the horrific Whitechapel murders in London as an example.

"Yes, I know," I told him. "I'm just amazed I could have been so estranged from reality as to be completely unaware of them. Indeed, when I think how I was living, I might well have become a victim myself."

"Very true," he replied, "but thankfully you did not, and now you're well on your way to being able to rejoin society."

Indeed, under Henri's care my body had already begun to repair itself. My cuts and bruises soon healed and, with regular, nourishing meals, I began to regain the weight I had lost. Henri's restorative wine became a regular evening ritual. Try as I might, I could not induce him to tell me what was in it but, whatever it was, it invariably left me feeling revitalised both in body and spirit. Indeed, it produced in me such a feeling of elevation I suspected Henri of simply replacing one drug with another, although he assured me this was not the case. Nevertheless, I became possessed of an increasing desire to discover what it was that induced in me such a marked state of wellbeing.

One evening, therefore, soon after he had left to get my restorative, I crept after him. I was well aware of the need for stealth, since Henri seemed to possess an uncanny awareness of what was happening in his vicinity, even when it was beyond his sight. Indeed, had I believed in such things, I would have suspected him of being a mind reader. So, staying well beyond his line of vision, and keeping a wary eye out for Fournier, I followed him out to the hall and up the stairs, where I saw him enter his room, closing the door after him. I tiptoed to the room next to his and carefully opened the door a little, thus providing myself with swift access to a hiding place should this become necessary. Then, feeling both foolish and more than a little guilty, yet overcome by curiosity, I tiptoed to Henri's door, knelt down, and peered through the keyhole.

I saw him go to a cabinet and take from it a small glass tumbler and a wine bottle. It was impossible to see what variety of wine it was but, when he poured it into the glass, it glowed like garnets in the soft lamplight. Expecting him to leave the room then, I retreated into the empty bedroom. When he failed to emerge, however, I risked returning to my post at the keyhole. He had unfastened the left cuff of his shirt and pushed the sleeve back a little way, exposing his wrist. What I saw next I could scarcely believe, for he raised his wrist and applied his mouth to it. What on earth could he be doing? Unable to take my eyes off him, I watched him hold his wrist over the glass. I saw drops of dark, viscous liquid drip into the glass and realised, with a sickening jolt, it was his own blood he was decanting into the wine. When, presumably, he judged he had added a sufficient quantity, he raised his wrist and licked at the spot he had pierced with his own teeth. Incapable of dragging away my horrified gaze, I watched as the two wounds in his skin simply vanished before my eyes. Overwhelmed by the implications of what I was seeing, I fled back downstairs.

When Henri returned to the parlour, I was sitting by the fire trying my best to look composed. He gave me a sharp look, but said nothing, merely placed the glass on the small table beside my chair and invited me to drink. But my stomach revolted and my throat constricted at the thought. How could I drink its contents, knowing what they contained?

He gave me another sharp look. "You seem reluctant to drink, Alex. Can it be that you feel yourself already restored to health?" As if to answer him, I was overcome by another coughing fit. "Hmm," he remarked, "clearly not. Then what is it? Do you doubt its power to cure you?"

"No—no—I don't—I can't..."

One minute he was leaning against the mantel, the next he was beside me, bending over me so that sheer instinct made me draw back in dread.

"Tell me what you saw." His voice was little more than a murmur, yet it so chilled my heart that when I tried to speak no sound came. "Tell me, Alex," he repeated, this time more gently.

"I—I think—you put blood—your own blood—into the wine." I gulped convulsively. "But—but—my God, Henri, why? What are you doing to me?"

He rose to his feet and heaved a sigh of resignation. "I had hoped to be able to avoid this discussion but, since you've allowed your curiosity to overcome your manners, I see some explanation is required. To put it very simply, Alex, my blood—indeed, all my bodily fluids—contain that which has the power to heal. I really can't explain it further, so I beg you will not ask me."

"But—your *blood*...?"

He gave me a quizzical look. "You'd have preferred me to spit into the wine, perhaps?"

I chuckled at this, despite myself. "No, I would not! But truly, Henri, I can't bring myself to drink it, knowing what's in it. It's—monstrous!"

"As you wish," he said with a shrug. "I merely observe, however, that you've not been so squeamish about eating meat, which of course contains blood."

"Yes, but animal blood, not that of people."

"Are people not also animals?"

"I dare say that depends on whether one believes in the Bible or follows Charles Darwin."

"You know, Alex, I had rather expected you to have an opinion of your own."

"I'm sorry if I disappoint you," I said, my horror turning

201

to anger at what I saw as his condescending manner. "But it's not a subject to which I've had occasion to give much thought, until now."

"And your conclusion?" he enquired in a more conciliatory tone.

"On the whole, I think I'm with Mr Darwin. If we are above the animals, I've seen precious little evidence of it these past months. But still, drinking human blood—surely that's cannibalism?"

Henri smiled. "Whatever you choose to call it, you surely can't deny that it's benefited your health?"

"No," I admitted, "that I can't. I suppose it's more the thought of it than anything."

"*Vraiment*, Alex, I wish you hadn't seen—what you saw—but you did, and I can't undo that. But please believe my only thought was for your welfare. I hope, with all sincerity, you can bring yourself to accept my gift, for the sake of the friendship I bear you if not for that of your health. But if you can't..." He broke off with a shrug and returned to lean against the mantelpiece.

I felt almost certain I was being manipulated, yet I could not doubt the sincerity of Henri's friendship. He had gone out of his way to help me, even bringing me into his own home to take care of me. For some time I sat weighing up the opposing demands of friendship and my desire to be healthy again, and the powerful prohibition instilled in me by society. Then I burst out laughing. How could I who, for almost a year now, had kept myself alive by stealing, and had courted death by my constant use of laudanum, talk of morality to a man who had done nothing but show me kindness and caring?

Fighting back my revulsion, I took a deep breath, picked up the glass, and drained its contents.

* * * *

Within a very few weeks, I felt quite well again. My cough was gone, I had almost regained the weight I had lost while living on the streets, and no longer did my mind importune me for laudanum. With my improving health, however, came restlessness, especially during the daytime when I had little to do but read, since even that pleasure at length began to pall. A number of times, I attempted to resume my writing, but my concentration was still too fragmented. One evening as Henri and I sat chatting after dinner—although not once since I had been in his house had I seen him eat—I told him of my feelings.

"But Alex," he pointed out, "you're not a prisoner here. You can go out whenever you wish. I know you've felt wary of rejoining society, and I understand why. An addiction is a very frightening thing. It robs one of one's willpower and distorts one's view of reality. But you're healed now, and you've learned your lesson, *n'est ce pas?*"

"I—I think so, but..."

He nodded. "I understand. However, I do think it's time you resumed a more—normal life. How would you like to go to the theatre one evening? There are some excellent plays being presented at the moment."

"Oh, I should like that of all things! It seems years since I last went to the theatre—the proper theatre, I mean, not the *cafés concerts.*"

"Quite. When Fournier brings you your newspapers

tomorrow, you must tell me if anything advertised there appeals to you."

"Perhaps," I suggested, "I could go out and buy the papers myself."

"An excellent idea! I'm sure it will do you the world of good to go about in the fresh air, especially now the days are growing warmer."

It was on the tip of my tongue to ask him how he could know this, since he never left his rooms until the sun had set. But of course that would have been unpardonably ill bred of me. The look he gave me, however, made me wonder if he had guessed my thought.

The following morning, as soon as I had breakfasted and was up and dressed, I was eager to be about my errand. I had no sooner set my hat on my head, however, than I remembered I had no money. Shuddering at the mere thought of resorting once more to theft, I rang for Fournier and rather shamefacedly explained my predicament.

"Ah," he responded in his usual grave manner, "with your kind permission, M'sieu, I shall give you some money."

"Lend," I insisted. "I promise I'll repay you as soon as I can."

"No, no, M'sieu. M'sieu Saint-Clair has already told me he will take care of everything."

I was much inclined to demur, as it seemed to me it had been an over-dependence on the generosity of others that had led me astray in the first place. However, I swallowed my pride, promising myself I should find employment as soon as possible, perhaps at one of the English-language newspapers or magazines, or even as an English tutor, although that held little appeal. Slipping the coins Fournier had given me into my pocket, and with a certain degree of trepidation, I stepped out onto the pavement.

The sun shone brightly in a lapis sky, and on the branches of the trees lining the street, pink and white blossoms danced, their skirts fluttering in the light breeze, complementing the vivid colours of the awnings shading the shop fronts. During my recuperation, spring had come to Paris! Breathing in the sweet air, I set off along the pavement. Although I had been to Henri's house only once before, it was not long before I began to recognise features I had seen during my early days in Paris: a milliner's shop to which I had accompanied Lucette; the smart little café where we had refreshed ourselves afterwards with tea and *madeleines*; an elderly gentleman selling matches. I was so glad to be out and about again, and feeling better than I could recall ever having felt before that, after I had bought the papers, I walked to a nearby park and took a brisk turn around its gardens before returning to Henri's house. I thought of visiting Lucette, as she and Jerome lived not far away, but guilt over the shabby way I had repaid their kindness prevented me from doing so.

I spent much of the day happily perusing the newspapers and wrestling with my French to complete the crosswords some of them carried. When Henri made his appearance that evening—although he must already have been out, I realised, since I heard Fournier open the door to him immediately before he came into the parlour—I was eager to discuss with him my ideas for our entertainment. Like me, he seemed in uncommonly good form, with more colour in his cheeks than I recalled having seen before. Perhaps, like me, he had been for a constitutional walk in the fresh air.

As we sat before the fire sipping port wine, I told Henri I should like to visit *La Comédie Francaise*, which was currently showing a play by Molière.

"An excellent choice," he approved, "especially since it's the plays of Molière for which the theatre is famous. I'll have Fournier purchase tickets for us tomorrow." I was about to say I should be happy to do this myself when he added, "One does not purchase one's own tickets, Alex; that's what servants are for."

Once more I was struck by his apparent—and somewhat unsettling—prescience but, as he chose that moment to fetch the chess set, I was distracted from quizzing him about it.

Two evenings later, Henri and I set out for *La Comédie Francaise*, he in his customary sombre black, me in the evening clothes Fournier had purchased for me: the black trousers and evening jacket all gentlemen wore, but with an embroidered waistcoat and a blue silk tie pinned with a diamond pin, this last being borrowed from Henri's own collection. I felt very splendid as we alighted from our taxi outside the theatre. The theatre itself was huge, at least four storeys high, and built of a pale pinkish stone in a severe classical style with pillars along its front forming a sort of cloister topped by a wrought-iron *balcony*. *The play*, The Doctor in Spite of Himself— *Le Médecin Malgré Lui* to give it its French title—was, of course, in French, but with its broad humour and the excellent acting I found it easy enough to follow, and enjoyed it enormously. I could scarcely remember when I had laughed so much.

Afterwards, Henri treated me to a splendid supper before hailing a *voiture* to take us home, although, as on previous occasions, he ate nothing himself, merely sipping a little wine.

"Henri," I enquired as the taxi bore us through the darkened streets, "I don't wish to seem impolite, but I can't recall ever seeing you eat, and I can't help wondering why."

"I keep to a very particular diet," he replied smoothly. "I have no need for other food, and so I don't eat it."

Once again I had the distinct impression I was being fobbed off, but I said nothing more on the subject, feeling I had perhaps already overstepped the mark of courtesy. I was unable to stop thinking about it, however and, by the time we reached home, I had formed the firm intention of discovering the truth, although I had no idea how.

CHAPTER EIGHTEEN

In pursuance of my as yet half-formed scheme, I took to observing when Henri left and returned to the house, and soon discovered a pattern. Just after sunset, Fournier would go to him, presumably to help him dress as, not long afterwards, he would emerge from his room and leave the house without giving me any indication he was up and about. Typically, he would return a couple of hours or so later—sometimes more, sometimes less—at which point he would join me in the parlour, either to converse with me as I ate my dinner, or a little later for a post-prandial drink. When he returned, he would be in excellent spirits, which I thought strange, since he invariably seemed pale and drawn when he left the house, with an intensity about his features that I found vaguely disturbing. I could find neither rhyme nor reason for this odd behaviour, which, of course, made me even more eager to discover one if I could, although I knew it would not be easy, given Henri's almost preternatural ability to discern my very thoughts. Besides, I did not yet know just how I might proceed.

In the meantime, encouraged by my successful visit to the theatre, I began to go out more during the day, enjoying frequent walks in the park or along the Left Bank, since Henri's house was not far from the Seine. Visiting the Louvre Museum, the Notre Dame, the Eiffel Tower, and various other places of note that were within walking distance, I found myself amazed at how I had managed to live in Paris for so long without seeing these famous sights. On one occasion, I thought I spied Lucette out walking with the children, and found myself altering my route to avoid them. I still felt too embarrassed to risk an encounter.

There was also the matter of the restorative. I knew I should stop taking it now my health was recovered, but found myself unwilling to forego a substance that produced in me such a tremendous sense of wellbeing. Its influence seemed to extend far beyond mere bodily health. I felt fitter and stronger than ever before, my mind clearer, my very senses more acute.

I began to write again, not just keeping my journal, but writing stories and poems in abundance, my pen barely able to keep pace with the ideas and images that flooded my mind. At times, as I went about the neighbourhood, I could almost have sworn I sensed what people were thinking and feeling. All these I could only attribute to my drinking Henri's blood. I could think of nothing else to account for them. After my dire experience with opium, I formed the worrying suspicion that there might be something in Henri's blood that was addictive—or worse, that I had simply become prone to addiction.

With considerable trepidation, I broached the subject with him one evening. Once again, his reaction surprised me. I had expected him to dismiss my fears, having already assured me I could come to no harm from his unusual treatment. Instead, his expression grew serious.

"Hmm," he said, tapping a forefinger on the arm of his chair, "reactions such as yours don't usually take place so quickly, especially with the small amount you've been taking. I can only assume the cause is its following so closely on your opium addiction and subsequent illness."

"Yes, I suppose that must be it. But what is it about your blood that makes it addictive, and why does it produce such changes in my perceptions?"

"As for the first," said Henri, "I don't believe it is an addiction any more than normal eating or drinking. I think perhaps the answer lies in your second question. Who wouldn't wish to continue taking a substance that improves his wellbeing and enhances his senses? As for the reason it has this effect, why, who's to say? I must confess, however, to some concern over these changes in perception you mention. We can discontinue the treatment if you feel you're completely well now, or perhaps reduce its frequency to start with."

"I think the latter might be the best course," I replied.

The truth was, of course, I simply did not want to give up something that induced in me such vitality; and, to be quite honest, I was enjoying my new sensitivity far too much to forego it, although I was unable to admit this at the time, even to myself. I must have done an excellent job of duping myself, since even Henri failed to see through me, and my 'treatment' continued, albeit less often.

For a time, I felt no abatement either in my creativity or my sensitivity. I continued writing at a furious pace, and began to entertain serious thoughts of submitting some pieces to magazines and publishers. Henri read some of my work and pronounced this an excellent idea, so I began to prepare a manuscript, often sitting up far into the night, since my vitality seemed greater then. This, of course, meant

I began sleeping late into the morning, often not rising before lunchtime. However, I found I was less inclined to activity during the day, preferring to take my outings in the evening, usually before dinner so I could keep Henri company when he returned. I put this change down to my altered sleeping pattern. After several weeks on my new regime, I began to feel strangely bereft if I must go for more than a few days without my restorative dose, experiencing a sense of having lost something necessary to my contentment of mind. I even thought I noticed a physical change in myself at these times, my features seeming paler and more haggard, as though my illness were returning. However, since my next dose would restore my strength and wellbeing, it was easy to convince myself this was nothing more than my system adjusting to the new regime.

It was at about this time, also, that I revived my interest in discovering where Henri went on his nightly outings, since I could not help feeling it might somehow be connected with the qualities peculiar to his blood. I had no real reason for suspecting this other than some vague notion that his clandestine behaviour must have a cause, and that the unusual properties of his blood must have a cause also. Just why my mind connected the two, I could not articulate. However, I fancied some notion of a connection lay at the back of my mind, one I could not quite grasp, and so I determined to follow Henri and see if I could discover where he went.

One night, therefore, as soon as I heard the door close behind him, I waited only for Fournier to return to wherever he went when his services were not required before slipping out of the house.

Henri was moving at a terrific pace, but there were few people about so I had little difficulty keeping him in my sights as he strode towards the park I had been wont to visit on fine days. His pace was such I could only assume he had urgent business somewhere, so I was more than a little surprised when he turned in at the park gate. I followed suit, but, to my disappointment, could see no sign of him. However, my ears caught the faint crunch of boots on a gravel pathway, and I hurried in the direction of the sound, grateful for my enhanced senses. Before long I was gratified to glimpse him through the trees. He was making for a secluded grass area in the midst of a cluster of trees and bushes, where I had often seen families picnicking during the day. It was furnished with several wrought-iron bench seats, and on one of these lay a figure swathed in a large coat, or perhaps a blanket. I shuddered as I recalled the times I had been forced to sleep in just such a manner. Henri raised his head, looking about him as a cat would do when hunting, and I hastened to conceal myself behind some bushes. Crouching down and peering through the branches as best I could, I watched as he approached the prone figure, wondering what on earth he was about. He could not, surely, be proposing to steal from the person. What could a vagrant possibly have that a man of Henri's standing might covet? When he reached the figure, he bent over it but, to my chagrin, he had his back to me and I could see nothing of what he was doing. The figure on the bench seemed to stir a little, giving a low moan before relaxing back onto the seat. I could not, for the life of me, imagine what was going on. It did cross my mind it might be something of a sexual nature. Henri would scarcely be the first man of rank to indulge himself in a similar manner, although it seemed to me a very strange way to go about it when the city was provided with an abundance of low taverns and gaming houses. I was still grappling with this conundrum when I saw Henri stand up and move swiftly away through the trees, heading for home, judging from his direction.

I knew I must wait before retracing my own footsteps. Although Henri was now accustomed to my going out at night, I dared not let him know I had followed him. As I waited behind the bushes, my curiosity increased. The figure on the bench had not stirred for some time. When I was sure Henri was no longer near, I crept across the grass to what I now saw was a middle-aged man, although worn down by his precarious existence, as I had been whilst in thrall to laudanum. His face was a ghastly grey colour in the moonlight, and I wondered if perhaps Henri had been checking to see how he fared; this would certainly be of a piece with his treatment of me. For all I knew, his nightly outings might even be missions of mercy to the poor and dispossessed of the city. As I moved closer, I half expected to find some coins had been left with the man, or perhaps food. What I saw, however, produced in me such a feeling of revulsion it was all I could do to prevent myself from vomiting. The man's filthy shirt collar was covered in blood, though none seemed to be flowing from any wound. In horrid fascination, I bent over him to discern the source of the blood, and saw on his neck two ragged puncture wounds, quite close together, about where, from my limited understanding, I judged his jugular vein would be.

My mind flew back to the wounds I had seen on Henri's wrist. These seemed to have been made in the same way, but

I could make little of the similarity. It seemed impossible that Henri, my friend and saviour, should commit such a foul and depraved act, unless... Charles's joking comment on reading of those strange deaths in London came back to me, but I rejected it. The very thought was insane. Henri must, surely, simply have noticed the man lying wounded and gone to see if he could help.

Although it does me no credit to have to admit it, I removed myself from the park with as much speed as I could muster. I had no wish to be implicated in the vagrant's death—and I felt almost certain he was dead, although I could not bring myself to take steps to ascertain it for certain. For some considerable time, I continued walking in an effort to calm my mind, taking a different route back to Henri's house, one that did not pass by the park.

When I arrived home, I found Henri sitting in the parlour smoking a cheroot and sipping port wine. As after his previous outings, he looked markedly healthier than when he had left. I was almost loath to join him, afraid of betraying my feelings. However, he merely looked up when he saw me, greeting me with a friendly smile.

"I trust you've had a pleasant walk?"

"I have, thank you," I replied, doing my best to sound more composed than I felt. "I've devoted so much time to my writing lately, I thought it would do me good to stretch my legs and get some fresh air."

He stubbed out his cheroot in the silver ashtray on the table beside him. "Ah, yes, and how is the writing coming along? Have you submitted anything yet?"

"Not yet. I've been reviewing my poems, and I think I may have the makings of a collection."

"Excellent! If you'd like a second opinion, I'll be happy to look them over for you."

"Oh, thank you! I can get them now if you like."

"By all means, please do. I'll pour you a glass of port while you're gone."

I raced up the stairs to my room, where I splashed cold water on my face, staring into the mirror, anxious to see if I could discern any trace of the turmoil I was feeling. Having schooled my features into what I hoped was impassivity, I gathered up my sheaf of papers and returned to the parlour. My glass of port was waiting for me, and I sipped it while Henri read my poems, grateful for its calming effect. As soon as I could, however, I excused myself, pleading a desire to do some more writing now my walk and the port had refreshed me. Henri made no demur, saying he would return the poems with his comments once he'd finished reading them.

Feeling as though I had escaped I knew not what, I retired to my room to try to make sense of the evening's events.

* * * *

Despite my best efforts over the following days, I could neither explain away what I had seen, nor understand it. Furthermore, the dreams featuring Henri had resumed their nightly visits, assuming a character still more sinister and fearful than before. I had no explanation for this, either. I thought of mentioning them to him, but found myself wary of doing so, even though my curiosity now verged on obsession. I waited for almost a week, which was as long as I could bear, and then set out once again to follow Henri, hoping to determine once and for all whether my friend was a man or a monster. What I intended to do with such knowledge I scarcely knew, but I was certain I could not rest until I possessed it, whatever it might turn out to be.

This time, Henri set off in the same direction as before, but passed by the park. He walked swiftly, pausing occasionally to look about him in a way that reminded me of my father's hunting dogs scenting a fox. As I followed him, it seemed to me that, as often as not, he would change direction slightly after pausing, and I began to wonder whether he knew I was there and was attempting to confuse me. If so, his ploy worked. Before very long, I had not the slightest idea where I was—until I recognised the Romanesque dome of the *Panteon* looming out of the darkness. We passed this by, veering a little to the right and continuing until we reached a park, a sign by its gate informing me it was the *Parc Montsouris*. Although I was unfamiliar with it, I recognised the name from the map of Paris I had borrowed from Jerome while I was staying with him and Lucette. I knew we must have travelled some distance to the south.

Henri passed through the imposing gateway, turning off the path and through a wooded area that bordered one side of an artificial lake. As I sought to keep him within my sights, I found myself thinking, with a sick feeling in the pit of my stomach, that he must be seeking another vagrant such as the one in the park near his home. Then I heard a woman's laughter drifting across the night air. Henri was instantly alert. I could almost have sworn I saw him sniff the air like a hunting animal before moving with silent tread in the direction of the sound. Rounding the end of the lake, he set off across an area of parkland and gardens towards the shadowy bulk of a large, domed building. With a mixture of dread and excitement, I followed him.

Then I saw the object of his silent pursuit.

Sitting on the steps of the building were two young women sharing a bottle of wine and chatting and laughing together. From their shabby, yet gaudy dress I guessed them to be street girls, either prostitutes or two of the many poor people to be seen living and begging on the streets of Paris— and London, Rome, and Vienna for that matter, since poverty is no respecter of nations. Unwilling to risk either Henri or the girls seeing me, I hid behind a large tree where I could watch without being seen. Somewhat to my surprise, Henri did not approach the girls directly, but flitted in swift silence through the deep shadows in the lee of the building's wall, stopping where he was just out of their sight. He stayed there, immobile, for what seemed to me an agonisingly long time, although it was probably no more than five or six minutes. As I watched him, it seemed to me there was an air of alert intensity about him, again reminding me of a hunting animal. Then one of the girls stood up and spoke briefly to her companion before moving away. The other girl watched her leave, and then picked up the wine bottle and drained the remainder of its contents.

All of a sudden, she raised her head and gazed about her as though she had heard a sound and was wondering whence it had come. Then she got to her feet. With mounting horror, I realised she was walking in a slow, trancelike way towards the spot where Henri waited in the shadows. I wanted to cry out, to warn her, but a sick terror gripped me by the throat, rendering me speechless. She rounded the corner of the building and Henri moved swiftly to meet her, smiling as he drew her back into the darkness. I peered into the gloom, but could see nothing but a dark shape against the stone wall. Feeling half horror, half fascination, I crept closer, crawling on my belly from tree trunk to tree trunk until I could see the two of them. Henri had gripped her by the shoulders and was staring into her eyes. She seemed to swoon or faint, and he slid one arm about her waist to hold her up, pulling and tearing at the collar of her dress with his other hand. As he did so, his face took on the expression of a ravenous beast and his eyes glowed like coals in a fire. My flesh began to crawl and my breath clotted in my throat. What manner of creature was he, this man I called my friend? Unable to drag my eyes away, I saw him raise his head, saw two fang-like teeth flash for a moment in the darkness before he fell on the poor girl's neck. She gave a little cry that might have been either of pain or pleasure, which was cut short at the same moment I heard a sound as of flesh tearing. Then she was silent. All I could hear was a soft, fleshy sound I could not identify until I recalled the puncture marks in the vagrant's neck and the blood on his shirt collar. When I finally realised what it was I was hearing, I turned and fled, stumbling over the roots of trees, heedless of branches tearing at my clothes, intent only on putting as much distance as possible between me and the appalling sight I had just witnessed.

CHAPTER NINETEEN

The *Parc Montsouris* was a great deal larger than I had realised, and so full of hills and dales, and paths that seemed to lead nowhere, that I was soon thoroughly lost. Panting heavily, I leaned against a tree and stared about me. I felt as though I were in the midst of a bad dream, one of those where every effort seems doomed to frustration. Then it occurred to me, even if I managed to get myself out of the park and find my way through the unfamiliar streets, I could hardly return to Henri's house. How could I face him again with anything approaching equanimity, having seen what I had just seen? Indeed, how could I ever erase the sight from my mind? I wanted to scream to heaven for mercy—or to curse God for persecuting me so. It seemed to me then that everything that had happened to me, from Papa's marriage to this present horror, had been sent to punish me. But for what? Did my repudiation of my father's remarriage truly merit such treatment?

As I was thus castigating the powers that be, my ears caught a faint sound nearby, perhaps the cracking of a twig, or the rustling of leaves underfoot. Before I had had time to look about me for the cause, two arms wrapped about me in a grip like bands of iron, so I could neither turn nor raise my own arms to fend them off. Frantic with terror, I strained against my bonds, kicking out at my captor, my breath coming in strangled gasps.

"You might as well stop struggling, Alex. It will do you no good." It was Henri's voice that spoke in my ear in soft, yet compelling tones. "I have no wish to hurt you, but if I must, be assured that I can—and will." He kept hold of me until, despite myself, I had calmed down a little. "That's better. Now, if I loosen my hold on you, will you swear not to attempt to escape me again?" I nodded. "Good. Not that you could," he added in a soft and dangerous tone.

As he released me, I felt my body sag and tears of despair fill my eyes. "For God's sake, Henri, why don't you just kill me now and be done with it?"

"Kill you? What makes you think I want to do that?"

"You seem to have no compunction about killing others," I gasped, "so why not me?"

"Is that what you think I was doing?"

"What else can I think, when I saw you with my own eyes?"

"Sometimes, Alex, the eyes can deceive one. I think you and I must talk, but not here. Come."

He took my arm and began to steer me along a path through the trees.

When we reached his house he took me, not to the parlour, but to his library, telling Fournier we were not to be disturbed. Like a perfect host, he offered me brandy. I was half minded to refuse his hospitality, but thought better of it, having had a glimpse of what he could do if he chose. I flinched instinctively as he came towards me bearing the brandy glass.

"Oh, for the love of God, Alex," he said, "if I'd wanted to hurt you, do you not think I would have done so before now?"

"I no longer know what to think," I said, his tone stirring in me a flash of anger.

"No, I suppose not," he responded in a more kindly tone, once again surprising me with his reaction. "Then I suppose I'd better try to explain." He pulled up a chair and sat down opposite me. "First, let me assure you the young woman with whom you saw me is not dead. She'll feel faint for a time, but will fully recover."

"What about the vagrant in the park? He looked pretty dead when I saw him."

"Yes, he was perhaps not an ideal choice, being in poor health to begin with, but beggars can't be choosers, as you English say."

"How dare you use such a cavalier manner?" I retorted, my anger lending me courage. "He may have been just a poor, sick vagrant, but he was a person! What kind of monster are you, to treat people with such scant regard?"

Henri gave a faint sigh. "Ah, now we come to the nub of the matter. I do what I do, Alex, not because I want to, but because I must. I assure you I have precious little choice in the matter."

"Please don't toy with me, Henri," I said, my voice stiff with affront. "Tell me plainly what you mean."

"Unfortunately, that's not as simple as it sounds. I shall, however, try my best."

He went to one of the bookcases that lined the walls of the room, rapidly scanning the shelves before pulling out a small volume bound in green leather and bringing it to where I sat. On its cover I read: *Dissertation sur les Revenants en Corps, les Excommuniés, Les Oupirs ou Vampires, Brucolaques, etc.*

"What is this?" My voice was sharp with fear and anger. "Didn't I ask you not to toy with me?"

"Believe me, Alex, I'm in deadly earnest. The author himself professed to be sceptical on the subject, yet his research and most of his findings are above reproach."

"For God's sake, Henri, what on earth are you talking about? What is this vampire nonsense? Everyone knows they don't exist."

"Read it, Alex, I beg of you. I can't blame you for disbelieving. Indeed, I'd have done so myself, had my own experience not taught me otherwise."

I stared at him in astonishment. "You're not saying...? You're not trying to tell me...?"

"Yes, Alex, that's precisely what I'm trying to tell you. Unbelievable as it must seem, what I am is a vampire, and that is why I must hunt humans and drink their blood. As I told you, I do it because I must, not because I want to. If there were another way, believe me, I'd take it."

"You're insane!" I cried. "You must be!"

Henri shrugged, his mouth twisting in a wry smile. "If I am, then I'm an insane vampire."

I shook my head in sheer disbelief. "So—let me get this right—you're expecting me to believe you're some blood-drinking monster like Bram Stoker's Count Dracula?"

"Not entirely like Mr Stoker's creation, no. I can't walk on walls or dissolve into mist, or, indeed, turn into a wolf or a bat, though I've sometimes thought such abilities would be interesting, not to mention useful. On the other hand, I have the advantage of the Count in that I'm not restricted to sleeping on the soil of my homeland, which certainly renders travel a great deal less onerous. And I'd like to think I'm no monster, although I can quite see that my means of sustenance must seem monstrous to you. But please, read the treatise. I believe it will help you to understand my kind."

"Your *kind*? Do you mean to tell me there are others who—who...?"

"Indeed, there are, though I believe our numbers are not great. It's quite some time since I met another such as myself."

"Then we must be thankful for small mercies, I suppose," I retorted with a laugh verging on the hysterical.

He smiled at my words, though I hadn't intended them to please him. "Alex, I shall leave you now. I presume you've not dined this evening, so I'll have Fournier bring you something to eat. When you've read the treatise, we can talk further."

"How can you expect me to eat, after what I've seen tonight?"

"No, of course not. I forget, sometimes, the particular sensitivities of humans. If you change your mind, however, you can ring for Fournier. I've already instructed him to regard your requests as though they were my own. Oh, and please make yourself free of the brandy—or anything else you care to drink."

With that, he bowed and left the room.

I sat staring at the book for a long time, feeling rather as though I were having one of my bizarre opium dreams. Indeed, it seemed to me Henri's explanation might, in some way, account for the dreams that had haunted my sleep since my first meeting him. Perhaps, even then, naïve as I undoubtedly was, I had sensed something of what he was, and my dreams had been my mind's attempt to explain it to myself.

With a sigh, I poured myself a large brandy and opened the book's cover. It was with some surprise I saw the treatise had originally been published over one hundred years previously, and by no less a person than a Dominican monk, one Dom Augustin Calmet, OSB. The thought of a monk writing an apparently serious treatise on vampires and the undead so appealed to my sense of the ridiculous that, despite my natural scepticism—not to mention revulsion—I began to read. Although I was by now quite fluent in everyday French, the style of writing was rather formal and old-fashioned, so this was no easy task, but I soon became so fascinated by the good brother's collection of folklore, anecdotes, and supposedly true accounts that in the end I took both book and brandy up to my room, finally falling asleep in the early hours of the morning.

Since I was unable to speak about it with Henri until the following evening, I spent much of that day plundering his library for further tomes. I had become enthralled by the subject of revenants and vampires, and was determined to learn more. Henri's library contained a great many books on this and similar topics, far too many for me to read in a day— or even a year—so I contented myself with dipping into his collection more or less at random, and perusing the contents to the best of my ability.

When Henri came to find me in the library that evening, I was sprawled in a chair surrounded by books, attempting to decipher a treatise in Latin by John Christian Stock.

"Good evening, Alex, I see you've been spending your day profitably," he said on seeing me.

"Well, it is a fascinating subject," I acknowledged, "though I'm not sure I'm any closer to accepting the reality of such creatures."

He smiled, and shrugged in his expressive way. "It is a lot to take in. Fournier informs me your dinner will be served directly but, after that, I'm entirely at your disposal. I imagine you must have a number of questions for me, and I'll do my best to answer them."

As soon as I had finished my dinner, I repaired to the parlour, where Henri was reading the evening newspapers and smoking one of his habitual cheroots. I felt a strange excitement tinged with panic, as though a sacred mystery was about to be revealed to me.

"Ah, Alex," said Henri, looking up at my entrance. "I trust your dinner was enjoyable?"

"Yes, thank you, although I could hardly eat for the questions chasing each other around my head."

Henri put down his newspaper and stood up. "Then please sit down and perhaps I can begin to answer them. Would you care for some port—or brandy, perhaps?"

"Brandy, if you please."

Henri went to the sideboard and poured brandy for me and port for himself.

"Now—" He smiled, once we were both settled "—what would you like to know?"

I drew in a breath and expelled it again. "I scarcely know where to begin but, if I understand what I've read aright, and assuming it's not all moonshine and superstition, or that you're insane, I must assume you have died and risen again."

Henri pursed his lips and drummed his fingers on the arm of his chair for a moment as though thinking how best to reply. "If you mean in the sense of dying and being buried, that's certainly not how *I* became a vampire. You see, vampires are, if you'll pardon the blasphemy, made and not begotten. As far as I'm aware, no one has ever been born a vampire, nor, for that matter, have I heard of vampires producing offspring."

"Then how are they 'made', if not by dying?"

"It is, I suppose, as close to dying as one might come without actually doing so. It's done by an exchange of blood between a vampire and a human. The vampire all but drains the human of blood, and then the human must drink of the vampire's blood. There is then a period during which, to all appearances, the person is dead. Indeed, there have been those who have been buried during this phase in the belief that they were dead, which is probably what gave rise to the tales of vampires rising from the grave or sleeping in their coffins. In fact, once the candidate for vampirism, if I may put it that way, has drunk the vampire's blood, it only needs for his body to produce enough of it for him to revive again as a vampire, and to continue thus, provided he can procure a reasonably regular supply of human blood, for this is what keeps him viable."

"Are vampires immortal, then, as the books say?"

"We can be killed, of course, as can any creature if enough of its body is destroyed, which is why such remedies as beheading and burning are recommended in some books on the subject. However, I've not heard of silver bullets being efficacious in this regard, except, I suppose, if enough of them were to enter the body to prevent its healing. Vampires are prodigiously fast to heal, you know."

"Is that how you've been able to heal me with your

blood?"

"It is, and it imparts other qualities, too, as you've noticed."

I nodded. "Yes, in some ways, its effect is not unlike that of opium—at least in the early stages of addiction—which is why I supposed it might be addictive."

Henri nodded. "I thought it must be something of the sort."

"A number of the books I've read have suggested it's possible to kill a vampire by driving a wooden stake through its heart," I said.

"Ah, yes, I think we have Mr Stoker to thank for promulgating that particular theory, although, as you've no doubt read, it also exists in folklore. Well, my dear Alex, I imagine a stake driven through the heart would kill anyone, don't you? And I may as well dispense with the garlic and the cross while I'm about it. The idea that garlic will keep vampires at bay is, I assure you, pure fantasy and, as for the Christian cross, I can only assume we're thought to be harmed by it because vampires are believed to be evil."

"And you're not?" I asked, unable to suppress a note of antagonism as I thought of what I had so recently witnessed.

Henri gave a sigh. "In terms of the beliefs of human society, of course what we must do to gain sustenance appears evil, especially when, as sometimes happens, a person is killed in the process. From our point of view, however, it's really no different from, say, eating meat, which invariably involves a creature's death."

"Yes but, as I said previously, those are animals, not people."

"I'm not sure how much difference that makes to the

animal," he pointed out, "or, come to that, to those of the Buddhist faith, to whom all life is sacred, for which reason they eschew the consumption of meat. But does that make you, a meat eater, more evil than them?"

"I hope not," I replied, unable to keep a smile from my lips. "If it does, I must become a vegetarian forthwith."

"What, and kill defenceless vegetables? Are they not also forms of life?"

I laughed outright at that. "All right, you've trumped me there. So you need human blood to sustain you. Is that what makes you immortal, then?"

"I believe so, barring the events I've already mentioned. I, myself, have been a vampire for three hundred years, more or less, but I've known vampires who were considerably older than that."

I shook my head in bewilderment. "Henri, unless I'm to pronounce you a liar, then I suppose I must believe what you've told me, but I must confess the very idea of creatures that feed on human blood and live forever seems completely fantastical to me."

"Yes, I can see how it would. As I told you last night, I should never have believed it myself until it happened to me."

"Will you tell me how it happened?" I asked, fascinated in spite of myself.

"Why, certainly, since we've come this far, but first, shall I pour you another brandy?"

"If you please."

He brought it to me, and then began to pace about the room as though trying to marshal his thoughts.

"I was," he began, turning to face me, "a younger son of

the Saint-Clair family, a very old French family, as I dare say you've heard."

I nodded. "I gather some believe them to be descended from Our Lord himself."

"Ah, yes," he said, with a soft chuckle. "I've also encountered that belief, according to which He did not die on the cross, but survived, later travelling to our land. Supposedly, Mary Magdalene was His wife, and came with Him, and their children were the progenitors of the Merovingian dynasty of Frankish kings, from whom the Saint-Clairs are said to be descended."

"And is it true?"

"I haven't the slightest idea." He gave a dismissive wave of his hand. "And frankly—if you'll forgive the rather feeble pun—I care even less. At any rate, as a younger son I could inherit nothing of my father's considerable estate, my only options being a career in the church or the military, or marriage to a woman of wealth and property—or at least to an heiress. Being of an adventurous nature, I opted for the military. This was at about the time Henri the Fourth, the first of the Bourbon kings, came to the throne. Henri was a Protestant, and his claim to the throne was immediately contested by the Catholic League, backed by the King of Spain, and I saw as much action in the king's service as even the most adventurous young man could have sought. Eventually, as you may have read, Henri became a Catholic, making his wars a complete waste of time, not to mention money and lives. However, that's another story entirely. I turned out to be a good soldier, so I prospered in the army, rising to the rank of Brigade Captain. But once France settled down following King Henri's conversion, I began to find army life boring and restrictive. As a soldier of rank who had served in the wars, I was entitled to a pretty decent pension, and so I left the military and set out to travel Europe in search of other adventures."

"Like a sort of Grand Tour," I interposed, thinking, not without a twinge of guilt, of how I had deceived my family and friends.

Henri nodded. "Just so. I shan't bore you with the detail of my travels but, a year or so after I set out, I was living in Venice, where I met a most beautiful and enticing young lady, with whom I promptly fell head over heels in love. Her name was Angelina, and to me she seemed, indeed, an angel. She had the colouring and features of a woman in a Botticelli painting, and I adored her. She reciprocated my feelings, and I was on the point of asking her father for her hand in marriage when she became very ill. Her father hired the best physicians he could find, but none could determine the cause of her sickness, nor find a cure for it. It began with her becoming very easily tired and occasionally feverish, but as time went on she became increasingly weak and pale, and was unable to bear sunlight, so that the curtains in her room must be drawn at all times. At length, she seemed to be at death's door, and the doctors were joined by priests, who prayed for her day and night, but to no avail.

"Naturally, I was devastated by the thought of losing my beloved Angelina. I visited her as often as her father would allow, sitting at her bedside under the watchful eye of her devoted nurse, holding her hand that had become so cold and pale. Then one night as I sat in my rooms, reading in a futile attempt to banish my melancholy thoughts, there came a knock at my door and I opened it to see Angelina, appearing miraculously restored to health. I was so overjoyed to see her that it didn't occur to me to think how strange it was that she, a young, unmarried woman, should visit me alone in my rooms at night."

I must have looked shocked, as Henri smiled, saying,

"Indeed, such behaviour would be considered shameful today; back then it was unheard of, and would certainly have ruined her character—and her chance of a good marriage—should anyone have come to hear of it. But, as I said, that was the furthest thing from my mind at the time, and so, with a joyful heart, I invited her in.

"As I looked at her, she seemed to me more beautiful than ever. Her skin was still as pale as a linen sheet, yet it seemed to glow with an unearthly translucence like snow in the moonlight, and her eyes shone with a radiance unlike anything I'd seen before. Yet when I took her hand and kissed her lips they were both as cold as ice. I couldn't understand this, and it frightened me a little. I suppose the passion she showed towards me should have frightened me, too, for she was normally as circumspect as any other well-bred young lady. But man is ever a slave to his desires, and so I responded as any man would. As we were making love, a change came over her. Her eyes began to glow like embers in a fire. She leaned close to me and I felt a sharp pain as something pierced my neck.

"Yes, I see you've already guessed, Alex, she had done to me what you saw me do to that young woman last night. My beloved Angelina had become a vampire, though of course I had no inkling of this at the time. My initial reaction was one of terror, since I had no idea what she was doing to me, or why, unless she had taken to consuming human flesh.

Then—and this was almost more terrible than that dread thought—as she began to suck blood from the vein she had pierced I was overcome by a delicious sensuality. I was, quite literally, entranced. When she finally ceased taking blood I was so weak I was practically dead. It was only afterwards, when she told me what she'd done, that I knew she had pierced a vein in her own wrist and squeezed her blood into my mouth, inducing me to swallow it.

"I woke to find Angelina beside me on the bed, her sweet mouth still rimmed with my blood, watching me as a mother might watch a beloved child, as indeed I was, in vampire terms, since she had made me."

"But how," I asked, perplexed, "did she come to be a vampire?"

Henri gave a bitter laugh. "It was her new father confessor who made her. The old priest had died, and the one who took his place was a vampire who took the notion of conversion rather more literally than is usual. I believe he made a number of 'converts' among his flock before complaints were made about his strange behaviour and he was defrocked. Not, I imagine, that anyone realised what he was really doing."

"But why did Angelina want you to become a vampire?"

"Because she loved me. Her father apparently didn't see a mere younger son as a suitable match for his only daughter, and I imagine that would have been the end of the matter had she not fallen foul of this priest. But once she was a vampire, she saw how she could use it to thwart her father and bring us together—forever."

"And yet you didn't remain together?"

Henri gave a weary smile. "Perhaps, after all, her father

was right. But vampires are immortal, Alex, or as near as makes no difference, and forever is a very long time. Besides, the life of a vampire is essentially a solitary one. We're hunters, and we hunt people, so we need to be able to blend in with them. One or two vampires may well pass among humans, even with such strange habits as not going about in daylight, and be thought nothing worse than eccentric."

I thought of my London friends' amused acceptance of his odd habit, and nodded.

"It can be almost unbearably lonely at times, but a sizeable group of us would be bound to draw unwelcome—and dangerous—attention to ourselves."

"Yes, I can see that. But why can't you go out during the day? Those books of yours say it's because vampires are evil and therefore can't abide the light of day, but I must say that seems a trifle unlikely to me."

"Quite. People are very fond of condemning as evil what they don't understand, but I really have no idea why light is inimical to us. I only know that it's so. If I were forced to give a reason, I should say it probably has something to do with our being hunters, rather like cats, which spend the day sleeping and hunt by night. Either that or the simple necessity for secrecy has, over time, become an ingrained habit that has become impossible to break. At any rate, our senses are markedly inferior during the hours of daylight, and the desire for sleep overwhelming. Speaking of which, Alex, I must leave you soon. Dawn is not far away. Before I go, however, I must have your solemn promise that you'll repeat nothing of what I've told you to anyone, now or in the future. I can, if necessary, make you forget it, but I should infinitely prefer your willing agreement. I feel sure I can trust you in this, or I wouldn't have told you, but I promise you if you prove me wrong, it will not go well with you."

A tremor of fear ran through me at his words, yet I found my regard for him was in no way lessened by what he had told me, and so I gave him my promise.

CHAPTER TWENTY

That evening, Henri seemed somehow more at ease, as though speaking about his vampirism had afforded him some release, as confession is said to do. This in turn gave me the confidence to broach the subject further, since I was by now thoroughly intrigued.

"Henri," I asked as we partook of our customary after-dinner drink. "Can you describe what it's like to be a vampire, if you please, as I'm not finding it easy to imagine."

"Why," he replied, "it's both beautiful and terrible. It's beautiful because we're so much more attuned than others, both to ourselves and the world around us. Our senses are more acute, so we see and feel with greater depth, rendering our appreciation of art, of music, of nature, keener and more affecting than any human could ever imagine, or, indeed, bear. Everything is suffused with such an aura of intensity as would be unbearable to most mortals, although I've sometimes wondered if some of the saints and seers throughout history might not have had similar experiences."

"You know," I said, "what I felt when I first took opium was very much of that nature, and I wondered if religious meditation might produce the same effect."

"Then imagine, if you can, being constantly in that state, but without the horrors of addiction."

"That sounds like pure Paradise to me!" I exclaimed with

a grin.

Henri laughed. "Ah, but how well would you cope with the fact that, to maintain it, one must indulge in an act seen by the entire world as evil—and, indeed, by oneself prior to becoming a vampire? All human societies condemn the taking of the life force of another human being, and the superstition that surrounds the very notion of the vampire means we must be constantly on our guard, which, believe me, becomes more than a little wearing after a century or so. Add to this that our extreme sensitivity to sunlight makes it impossible for us to live a normal life in any case, and that we must continue thus for all time, and you can, perhaps, understand why I say it's a terrible condition as well as beautiful."

"But surely you can simply stop taking blood and die that way, if you find the life so dreadful."

"My dear Alex, have you ever tried starving yourself to death? I assure you it takes a great deal more willpower than *I* possess."

I thought of how I had resorted to theft, and even violence, in order to keep my hold on life, even when that life had become one of misery. "Yes, I take your point. But it seems odd to regard something for which practically everyone craves as a terrible thing."

"Indeed, entire religions have been fabricated on that very craving. All I can say to you, Alex, is that those who long for eternal life have not had to endure it."

"Do you truly hate it so much, then?"

"Perhaps hate is not the right word, but I have often, down the years, resented the gift Angelina gave me, despite its undeniable glories. I've seen so much, Alex, that I'm weary of experience, yet the instinct to live is so strong in me I find it impossible to deny, but must go on forever, in the world yet not of it, my very nature making me an object of universal vilification, and unable to reveal myself for fear of the consequences."

"Except to me."

"Yes, and you may consider yourself greatly honoured. In over three hundred years, the number of those I've felt able to trust with my secret can be counted on the fingers of one hand."

"I'm flattered. I suppose Fournier is one of those in the know?"

"He is. I could never manage with a valet who was not privy to my—ah—habits. How could I trust such a person not to betray me, even if unintentionally? Members of the Fournier family have served me ever since I saved one of them from certain death over two hundred years ago. We have what you might call a symbiotic relationship, in that as long as one or another of them serves my interests, I see to it the family is well provided for."

"Is that why you told me? Because you wish me to serve you in some capacity?"

Henri laughed. "Not at all! I've no need of an amanuensis. But my life is, at times, immensely lonely. I have all I need in life—wealth, independence, the ability to go where and when I desire—everything, in fact, but lasting friendship. I happen to like you, Alex," he went on, "and I've learned to value true friendship, however fleeting it may prove to be." He gave me a quizzical look. "Besides, I had to find some way to curb that curiosity of yours. Did no one ever warn you how dangerous it can be?"

I grinned. "Oh, constantly but, as you see, their warnings fell on deaf ears."

Henri gave his quick, rather wolfish smile. "Now why does that not surprise me? Oh, by the way, I've finished reading your poems, Alex, and I think you should have no trouble finding a publisher for them. In fact, with your permission, I should like to send them to a gentleman I know in the publishing business."

"Oh, thank you!" I exclaimed. "I should like that of all things."

"Very well, I'll write a letter to M'sieu Lefebvre and have Fournier deliver it in the morning."

We spent the rest of the night conversing in the most comfortable way imaginable on poetry, and a variety of other topics—although I noticed Henri deflected any attempt to advert to his vampirism—until the approach of dawn sent both of us to our beds. As I lay in bed waiting for sleep to overcome me, I could not help reflecting, with a shiver of something between horror and excitement, on the strangeness of whatever fate had decreed that the one who would become the closest friend I had in the world should be a creature out of legend.

* * * *

Henri was as good as his word. Within a little over a month, I made my way, in a state of considerable trepidation, to the offices of Lefebvre et Fils to sign a publishing contract for my poems. Not wishing to risk publishing under my own name, I chose as a *nom de plume* the name William Martin, culled from a couple of advertisements I had seen in one of the

English-language newspapers. I called my collection of poems *Verses from Exile*, as that was how I thought of myself since my flight from England. It was almost midsummer before the book was released and I was able to view copies of my poems, bound in maroon leather with gilt lettering, displayed in the windows of several bookshops. Notices were sent to a number of the English-language papers and magazines that served the expatriate English community of Paris and, before long, I had received several favourable reviews, and found, to my immense gratification, my book was beginning to sell. To help encourage further sales, Monsieur Lefebvre placed advertisements in the papers for an evening at which I should read some of my poems.

With the onset of summer, Paris had become almost unbearably hot, and the night of my readings was no exception. Nevertheless, I dressed myself in my best and set off with Henri for *Chez Chartier*, a fashionable restaurant in the Latin Quarter that Monsieur Lefebvre had booked for the occasion. By the time we arrived, I was almost ill with nervousness, and afraid I should be unable to read my poems, much less speak to the assembled crowd, which seemed to contain a large portion of the English *émigré* population of Paris. I half expected to see Jerome and Lucette in attendance but, to my considerable relief, I saw no sign of them, or anyone else I recognised.

As I took my place with Monsieur Lefebvre before the assembled patrons, I saw Henri sitting at the back of the room, unobtrusively, as was his wont. When I glanced in his direction, he nodded and gave me an encouraging smile. After Monsieur Lefebvre had introduced me, flattering me by referring to me as 'one of the best new voices in Paris letters', it was my turn to perform. Despite my nervousness, I thought I managed to acquit myself quite well, thanking my publisher and editor, and then proceeding to read some of my verse. I was sorry to be unable to express my thanks to Henri, who had shown such faith in both my writing and me, but he had, of course, insisted on remaining anonymous. Although, as the sole remaining descendant of one of France's oldest families, he was very well known, and appeared at all the appropriate social occasions, given what he had disclosed to me, I was unsurprised by his aversion to being singled out.

After my reading, Monsieur Lefebvre had arranged for supper and drinks to be served. Henri sought me out and begged to be excused from the festivities.

"I'm not particularly fond of company. I find it rather... distracting. However, please don't feel you must curtail your enjoyment on my account. Either Fournier or I will let you in whenever you choose to come home. Enjoy yourself, Alex, and my heartiest congratulations on your success."

"I'm sure I couldn't have done it without you," I said, but he waved my words aside.

"And I'm equally sure you could. You're an excellent writer, Alex, and I've played no part in that. Goodnight. Enjoy your evening."

With that, he bowed and was gone.

Someone gave me a glass of champagne and I stood with it in my hand, feeling rather lost as I watched a crowd of complete strangers swirling about me. Many of them appeared to know one another, and I supposed they had banded together for mutual support, as outsiders will do in a foreign environment. Whether because of the strange life I had been leading, or from some other cause, I felt very much out of place in the assembled company, as though I belonged to an entirely different world and spoke a different language from the rest of them, even though most of them seemed to be native English speakers. As I stood there, exchanging pleasantries with those who spoke to me, I began to feel a terrible longing, as though there were something for which I hungered, something I must have or I should go mad. At first I thought it was my old hunger for opium, but I soon realised that was not it. Indeed, the very thought of it almost nauseated me. It was not alcohol, either; the glass of champagne I held remained untouched. Little by little, as I looked about me, it was borne in on me that the chattering voices had grown faint, like the distant roar of the sea, overridden by another sound I could not at first identify, a sort of rhythmic pulsing I sensed, rather than heard. Then, as though a sudden flash of lightning had illuminated my mind, I knew what it was.

I was listening, with some sense other than normal hearing, to the beating of hearts, and the rhythmic pulsing of blood through thousands and thousands of veins. A feeling of panic swept through me as I realised its import, and I fled from the room.

Outside the café, I stood irresolute, my own blood pounding in my ears, listening to the hubbub inside and thanking God I could no longer sense that alluring yet terrifying rhythm. I knew it must be from drinking Henri's blood, but I was shocked to realise how powerful was the effect of a few drops diluted with wine. I knew I should go back inside, but I equally knew I could not. I was terrified of what might happen to me, of what that dreaded longing might engender in me.

Feeling like an ill-bred coward, yet unable to help myself, I took to my heels.

* * * *

Henri looked up from his book in surprise when I walked into his parlour some three-quarters of an hour later.

"*Mon Dieu*, Alex! Don't tell me the evening is over already."

I shook my head. "I—I had to leave. I'll have to make my excuses to M'sieu Lefebvre tomorrow, but—I just couldn't stay any longer."

"Why, what is it? I know you were nervous to start with, but—"

"It wasn't that, it was—it was..."

I took a deep breath, feeling as though I were gasping for air, then told him what had happened to me, my words tumbling out as though anxious to leave me before I lost my nerve. As I spoke, Henri's face became grave, and he leapt to his feet and paced about the room.

"Ah, *Mon Dieu*! The effect is much stronger than I had imagined. Please forgive me for frightening you. If I had had any idea..."

"But you must have known, surely," I blurted out, my voice betraying both anger and fear. "In all the time you've been alive, can you honestly tell me nothing like this has happened before?"

"I swear to you, Alex, if it has, I've not heard of it. I can only assume that for some reason you're particularly susceptible, and I apologise most profoundly. If I'd known, I should never have sought to help you as I did."

"Well," I said, "I have to admit I've found the heightened senses a source of considerable pleasure, and even being able to read people's thoughts—although I must say most of them are excruciatingly banal—but the hunger tonight, and the way everything sank into nothingness apart from the beating of hearts and the pulsing of blood, and the smell of it, that was just plain terrifying! Please tell me how to get rid of it, because I assure you I can't go on like this."

"I'm sorry, but I think you may have to, at least for a while. You must, of course, stop taking my blood. It will leave your system completely in time. Your body is constantly creating new blood, which will gradually dilute the vampire blood until none remains in your system. What I cannot tell you, however, is the length of time this will take, though I feel confident it will be a matter of weeks, at most."

I sank, dejected, into a chair, and Henri came and laid his hand on my shoulder.

"I'm truly sorry, Alex. Please believe I should never have visited this on you had I known."

I sighed and looked up at him. "I know you meant well, Henri. It's just... Is it like that for you all the time? If so, I can see what you meant when you told me it was terrible being a vampire."

"Not all the time, no, and after a while it becomes little different from the pangs of hunger you, yourself, might experience. I dare say what frightened you was the thought that you might be becoming a vampire yourself, but you won't, you can rest assured on that score."

While I was not happy with the picture Henri had drawn

of the next few weeks of my life, now I knew there was nothing I could do about it, so I determined to endure it as best I might, hoping my book would prove successful enough to distract me from the battle raging within me.

CHAPTER TWENTY-ONE

Determined to do my best to ensure the success of my book, and to assure Monsieur Lefebvre I was not usually so ill-mannered, I presented myself at his offices the following day and proffered my apologies, along with the best excuse I could think of that would not sound like an outright lie.

His response was gratifying. "There's no need to apologise, M'sieu Randall. Many new authors experience nervousness at first. The answer, I think, is for you to become more used to public appearances. I shall arrange some more poetry readings for you, smaller ones, perhaps in the Montmartre area, since there are many cafes there that patronise the arts, and many English *émigrés* who patronise the cafes."

My heart gave a warning lurch when he mentioned Montmartre but, after my behaviour the previous evening, I was loath to disappoint him, and so I gave my assent. I was relieved when, a week later, a letter arrived informing me I was to give a reading of my poems at a café with which I was not familiar, *Le Merle*, not far from the *Gare du Nord*. Since this was where I'd first arrived in Paris, it seemed fitting, somehow, that I should have come full circle, although I could not help hoping no one from my former life would turn up there.

On my way home, I stopped at a newsstand to purchase

copies of several newspapers, hoping to see reviews of my book, or perhaps reports of my poetry reading. When Fournier let me into Henri's house, I asked him to bring a pot of tea to me in the library. This duly arrived, and I settled down to read my papers, starting with *Le Temps*, which happened to be on top of my small pile. Before I had even opened it, a front-page headline caught my eye: 'Woman's body found in *Bois de Boulogne*'. Being as susceptible as most people to sensational headlines, I began to skim the article. It seemed the body—that of a young prostitute—had been found the previous morning by a gentleman out for an early-morning stroll. A preliminary examination of the body had found no obvious signs of injury, but the woman appeared to have been suffering from some kind of wasting sickness. The article suggested the death might be linked to several other recent deaths in the city, and I thought back to the articles I had read a few weeks before. Further information was promised once an autopsy had been completed. This was certainly intriguing but, with no more information available for the time being, I soon returned to my original purpose, leafing through the rest of the paper to find a brief, but gratifyingly positive, mention of my poetry reading. *Le Figaro* yielded a review of *Verses from Exile*, which, while not precisely bursting with enthusiasm, pronounced the work to be 'promising'. I found these mentions flattering enough to make up my mind to resume buying the newspapers on a regular basis.

* * * *

On the evening appointed for my next poetry reading,

Monsieur Lefebvre himself came for me in his automobile, a De Dion Bouton, which, he told me with more than a little pride, he had purchased only that week. It was considerably smaller than Charles's Rolls Royce, being capable of seating only two but, with its crimson and gold paintwork, it was considerably jauntier. Henri had already excused himself from the earlier part of the evening, for what purpose I could easily guess at. Knowing what he was had not lessened my liking for him, my admiration, even, especially given the means by which he had become a vampire and his own views on the matter. Yet the thought of what he must do for sustenance filled me with a feeling I preferred not to examine too closely, and so I did my best to put it from my mind.

The café was bursting with patrons, which both Monsieur Lefebvre and I interpreted as a good omen. The evening went much as the previous one had, although it was a little less nerve-wracking for me. Nevertheless, I left as soon as I could afterwards. Despite having stopped taking Henri's 'restorative', I dreaded another onset of what I had experienced at *Chez Chartier*.

I arrived home to find Henri smoking one of his cheroots, a glass of port on the small table by his chair. The newspaper he had been reading had fallen to the floor, and he gazed ahead of him with unseeing eyes. He looked up at my entrance, and I had the feeling he was forcing himself to return from somewhere far, far away. His eyes looked even darker than usual. However, he spoke to me with his usual calm urbanity.

"Good evening, Alex. You're home early. I trust you've had no recurrence of your—ah—problem?"

"No, but I left before I could put it to the test."

"Does it worry you so very much?" he asked, an expression in his eyes I could not interpret.

"It frightens me," I said, "because I can't seem to control it. It reminds me of my addiction to opium—and then there's the thought of what it might lead to..."

Henri shook his head, smiling. "It won't come to that."

I had the feeling he had been about to say more, but he merely stubbed out the remains of his cheroot and stared into the fireplace. At length, he looked up at me.

"Please sit down, Alex. I have some news you may not quite like." I sat in the chair he indicated, and he looked at me with sad eyes. "I'm obliged to go abroad for a while, and since Fournier will be coming with me, my house will be closed while I'm away."

I felt a stab of fear at the thought of being cast adrift from one I had come to depend on, but I did my best not to show it. "You're not in any trouble, I hope?"

Henri smiled. "No, no, nothing of that kind. I have some business interests that require my attention."

"I'm pleased to hear that," I said. "But I'll miss you, you know. I've so much enjoyed our discussions."

"As, indeed, have I. As I've already told you, Alex, the life of a vampire can be intensely lonely, and a friendship such as ours is a pearl beyond price. For the first time in many, many years, I find myself reluctant to relinquish it."

He fell silent, and returned to staring into the fire. But it seemed to me I could sense within him a great longing to speak further, as though he yearned to express something, but dared not do so. For myself, I was reluctant to lose Henri's friendship, not just because I was so grateful for his help and kindness, but because I, too, felt I should be losing a rare treasure. Vampire he might be, but it seemed to me our minds were in harmony to a degree I had not yet found among my fellow humans. The thought of returning to loneliness filled me with dismay. Even the excitement of becoming a published author seemed somehow less thrilling when I thought of being unable to discuss it with Henri. But I felt hesitant to express my feelings, so I, too, remained silent.

* * * *

The next few days brought more flattering reviews of my poetry, but when Monsieur Lefebvre reported that my book was selling better than expected for an unknown author, and that an English-language literary magazine wanted to interview me for an article, I found myself unable to enjoy his good news as I should. The truth was I was dreading Henri's departure. Part of my anxiety centred on my doubts concerning my ability to manage alone in Paris, for I still knew very few people there. But the greater part of my unhappiness arose from the loss of my friend whom, for all I knew, I might never see again.

One evening, just after Fournier had taken away my dinner tray, Henri said, "Why so pensive, Alex? Surely a successful author should be brimming with happiness."

Unable to confess my true feelings, I took an oblique approach. "Of course I'm happy, just perhaps a little tired. How long do you expect to be gone from Paris, Henri?"

"I'm afraid I can't say, at this stage." He shot me a keen glance. "I'm sure you'll manage very well without me, Alex. After all, you're quite well again, now."

"It's not that," I told him, "at least not entirely."

"What is it, then?" He fixed his grey eyes on me, and seemed to be looking into my soul. "Come, Alex, you need have no qualms about speaking your mind to me. I thought we were better friends than that, and close friends need have no secrets, surely?"

For a long moment I said nothing—trying to muster my courage, I suppose. Then I blurted out, "I wish you weren't going away, Henri, or—or that I could go with you. I feel as though I was lonely all my life until I met you."

"Thank you, Alex, I appreciate your words, the more so because I know you found it difficult to say them—your English reserve, I dare say. For my part, I shall feel your loss deeply. I should very much like to take you with me, but I'm afraid it would be impractical."

"But why?" I demanded. "Where are you going? Or is it because you're a vampire and I'm human? It hasn't been a problem these last few months, so why should it be in future?"

A slight frown creased Henri's brow. "I don't know how long I must be away from Paris—it could be months, it could be years—and it would be unfair of me to drag you away from your new-found success. Besides, there are many difficulties inherent in vampire-human alliances. By our very nature, we vampires must do things you would find repugnant in the extreme."

"More repugnant than I've seen you do already?"

"Oh, yes. You see, Alex, although I care for *you* a great deal, it's no longer in my nature to care for humans in general. To me they're primarily a food source. I do try to harm them as little as possible but, to be quite blunt, that's

250

because it's in my own interest, not out of any fellow feeling or compassion. For all that I was once human, I've been a vampire now for three centuries and more, and most of my humanity has long since died away."

"But that's not true!" I protested. "You've shown me every kindness these past months. You've been kinder than most humans I've known."

He smiled. "That, my dear Alex, was because it was you. However, I really am a shockingly selfish creature. It's my vampiric nature. I've cared for you because—well, because I craved your companionship. I only wish there was a way to have your company on my travels. It would mean a great deal to me, more than you can imagine. But my life when I'm travelling is much harder than here in Paris, and it can be dangerous as well. It would be unfair of me to subject you to it."

I longed to argue the point with him, but I knew I should merely sound like a petulant child—scarcely the right approach to convince him I was a fit companion for his travels. I was also possessed of a strong curiosity to know more about his life as a vampire. However, when I broached the subject, he smiled, but refused to indulge me.

* * * *

Over the following days, the newspapers were full of news of a mysterious wasting sickness afflicting a number of people in the city, which medical investigators seemed to feel might be the cause of the recent deaths. For some reason I could not quite comprehend, this news served to deepen my sense of anxiety.

Henri seemed to go out of his way to cheer me up, taking me to the theatre or the ballet, and even to the cinema, which I enjoyed a great deal, despite a lurking fear that the projection equipment might explode and asphyxiate us. Whether it was these amusements or a natural balance reasserting itself, I found my melancholy abating, and made up my mind to enjoy what was left to me of Henri's company.

Monsieur Lefebvre arranged a further poetry reading for me, this time at his own home near the *Bois de Boulogne*. At my earnest request, Henri agreed to accompany me. Our host lived in a modest but smart dwelling built in the classical style so beloved of Parisians. Henri and I were greeted at the door by a middle-aged servant and ushered into a sizeable room hung with a rather oppressive burgundy-coloured wallpaper that was scarcely relieved by a quantity of mustard-coloured plush curtains and several crimson Turkey rugs. Monsieur Lefebvre had invited a number of people well known in the Paris literary scene, whom he thought would be useful contacts for me. I allowed myself to be led around the room and introduced, although I felt very much out of my depth in such—to me, at least— exalted company. It was comforting to know Henri was there, although, as usual, he remained in the background. He seemed to have a knack for making himself unobtrusive, despite his striking appearance.

I read some of my poems, and answered a number of questions about my writing and my life, although I took care to be circumspect about my reasons for leaving England and my time as a derelict living on the Paris streets. No doubt it would have enhanced my *cachet* as an artist, but the entire episode still embarrassed me so much I had no desire to share it with the world. At length, however, Monsieur Lefebvre thanked me and told the assembled guests where they might buy copies of my work, and I accepted a glass of champagne from a valet hovering nearby.

Now I was less preoccupied, I began to notice a certain quality of intensity in the sounds and odours of the room. To my dismay, I began to hear the rhythm of hearts beating, as I had at *Le Merle*, and another sound, like waves breaking on the shore, which I could not identify although it seemed oddly familiar. And worst of all, a scent filled my nostrils, sweet and metallic, and overwhelmingly alluring even as I felt a twinge of pain from my stomach contracting in response to it. A wave of nausea, tinged with a terrible excitement, rushed over me as I recognised the scent of human blood. Panic overwhelmed me, constricting my throat so I could barely take my next breath. This should not still be happening. I scanned the room until I saw Henri, and hurried to his side.

"Well done, Alex," he murmured, smiling. He lightly touched my arm with his hand, then recoiled slightly. "Something is troubling you. What is it?"

I took a deep breath and let it out slowly in an attempt to quell my panic. "I need to speak to you, Henri, but not in here."

"Certainly. Come." He led the way out of the noisy room and into the spacious hallway. As he closed the door behind us, the hubbub faded and I began to feel a little calmer. "Now," Henri said, "what is it that's troubling you?" I thought I saw something in his eyes that made me wonder if he already knew, but in a fraction of a second it was gone.

"Henri," I began, "ought I still to be feeling that heightening of the senses I felt at *Le Merle*?"

"Perhaps," he replied, looking thoughtful. "As I told you, it will take some time for my blood to work itself out of your system. There's really no set time for these things. It depends very much on your own metabolism. It's not too unpleasant for you, I hope?"

"No, quite the reverse. That's what I found so frightening."

Henri smiled. "There's no need, I assure you. If anything were wrong, I'd know it and, after all, it may be little more than the perfectly natural exhilaration of the occasion. I suggest you simply enjoy it."

He put his hand on my shoulder and gazed into my eyes, and at once I felt calmer. I passed the rest of the evening in a pleasant state of exhilaration, no longer troubled by the allurements borne to me on my senses. When the evening drew to a close, I thanked Monsieur Lefebvre and his wife for their hospitality, gave my card to several gentlemen who expressed a desire to stay in touch, and joined Henri, who stood by the door waiting for me.

"It's such a delightful night," he said as we made our way down the steps to the pavement. "Why don't we walk home?"

The gas streetlights bathed the quiet streets in a warm, golden glow, and the sweet, heady scent of lilac came to my nostrils from some nearby garden.

"Ah, lilac," said Henri, breathing in the aroma. "It reminds me of a garden I knew once, in Istanbul I think it was, or perhaps it was Athens."

"You must have travelled a great deal," I said. "I feel so ignorant by comparison."

"Not ignorant," he replied, and I could sense, rather than see, the fond smile on his lips, "just inexperienced. You have many years ahead of you in which to see the world."

"But I'll never see as much as you have. Oh, Henri, how I wish I could go where you've been—see what you've seen!"

"But you can, Alex. Did you not tell me yourself that Paris is but the beginning of your travels?"

I sighed, reflecting on the lie I had propagated. "But to see it all through your eyes, to feel it as you have, that would really be something! For me, the stars will never shine as they do tonight, the lilacs will never smell as sweet, because soon my senses will become merely human again."

"But isn't that what you want?" Henri stared at me, a look of puzzlement on his ashen face.

"I know," I said. "But tonight everything seems different, somehow. I'm not sure what I want any more."

Henri linked his arm in mine, and we walked on in silence. It seemed to me I could feel the chill of his skin, even through his clothing, and a shiver ran through me. I glanced at his face, gilded by the gleam of the streetlamp under which we passed, and saw on his features an intense sadness almost bordering on pain, as though some great heaviness oppressed him. I wished I could find some words of comfort to say to him, but nothing seemed adequate to address three centuries of existence.

We arrived home a little after midnight. Fournier let us in, took our coats and hats, and then vanished into the nether regions of the house. There was a fire lit in the drawing room, and candles, which seemed to lift Henri's mood of melancholy, and mine as well. Henri poured wine for us.

"I can call for Fournier if you'd like something to eat," he said, handing me my glass.

I shook my head. "No need to bother him. I'm not hungry."

Henri took his usual seat by the fire, although I knew by now he did not need its warmth. I took the seat opposite him. As we sipped our wine in companionable silence, I found myself acutely aware of the sounds of the room: the ponderous ticking of a grandfather clock, the crackling of the fire, the slight shifting of floorboards, even the minute sounds of the flickering candle flames. I leaned back in my chair and let the feel of the room wash over me in all its intensity, no longer frightening, but as familiar and soothing as the beat of my own heart. Somewhere in the far recesses of my mind, I wondered what was happening to me; my enhanced senses no longer seemed alien, but as natural— almost as natural—as though they belonged to me. Some part of me, I realised with a thrill of excitement, *wanted* them to be mine—wanted them to be *mine*—forever...

"Henri," I murmured, my voice pensive and dreamy. "Tell me what it's really like to be a vampire."

"Not just now," he replied. "It's almost dawn. But soon, Alex," his voice seemed to take on an almost hypnotic quality, "before I leave Paris, I promise you you'll know everything."

CHAPTER TWENTY-TWO

Consumed by curiosity about Henri's vampirism, I broached the subject again two nights later. I had dined earlier, while Henri was out finding his own sustenance, and he returned to find me devouring the latest news concerning the mysterious wasting sickness and yet another death ascribed to its malign influence. 'Even the leading doctors of Paris,' claimed the article, 'are mystified as to its cause. This newspaper's own research has discovered a number of similar outbreaks reaching back as far as the Middle Ages, not only in Paris, but throughout France and elsewhere in Europe, but no satisfactory explanation for them has ever been found outside the realms of myth and fantasy. Investigations are currently focussing on the possibility of an infection transmitted by some human or other agent.'

"What's that you're reading?" asked Henri on entering the drawing room. I showed him the article. "Ah, yes," he said. "These stories must be doing wonders for the circulation of the daily newspapers."

"I wonder what it can be?" I said.

"If the best doctors in Paris can find no answer," he observed, "then I see no point in applying our lesser understanding to such a conundrum."

"Still," I said, "I should like to know."

Henri had strolled across to the sideboard and picked up

the port-wine decanter. Now he turned to me and smiled. "Would you care for some port, Alex?" I assented, and he poured out two glasses and brought one to me. "This has become quite a little ritual with us, has it not?"

"One more thing for me to miss when you're gone," I said. "When do you leave Paris, Henri?"

Soon," he replied. "I'm afraid I cannot remain here for much longer." As his eyes met mine, I sensed a deep melancholy within him, which chimed with my own feelings. He seemed to be aware of this as he smiled and raised his glass. As the candlelight caught the ruby liquid, the facets of cut crystal seemed to shed droplets of blood. "I propose a toast, Alex, to friendship."

"To friendship," I echoed, raising my own glass, and drank deeply of the rich, warm wine as though this might nourish the longing I felt in my depths. "To lasting friendship."

"Indeed," said Henri, sipping his wine. "May it last forever."

"If only it could," I murmured with a sigh. "If only it could."

"And if it could? Is that what you truly want?"

I sighed again. "Of course I know it isn't possible. Everything comes to an end, doesn't it? Love, friendship, lives—nothing lasts forever."

"Some things do," Henri said, his voice a gentle murmur.

I stared at him, not comprehending at first. "Oh, you mean your own life," I said at length, "and of those like you."

"I do," he averred, "and where life is everlasting, may not friendship be also?"

"It didn't last with you and Angelina," I countered.

"True, but that was the love of a young man for a young woman, and based on physical attraction. Such a love must always be more fragile than a friendship based on the meeting of minds, *n'est ce pas?*"

"I suppose so," I said. "At least, I'd like to think so. But you've been alive for three hundred years, Henri, and from what you've told me, you haven't had such a friendship."

"Then you've misunderstood me, Alex. Granted, such instances have been rare, but they have occurred. To find such a friend is like discovering a shining vein of gold hidden in the drab ore of the world at large."

I nodded, smiling, and drank the last of my wine. "A fitting metaphor, Henri, yet I gather they haven't lasted, either?"

"But that was due to human frailty."

"You mean they died?"

"Yes. Or, rather, they lacked the courage to live."

It took me some moments to digest Henri's words. The realisation, when it came, made me gasp. My heart began to pound like a piston as a sensation compounded of equal parts fear and exhilaration took possession of me.

"Just so." Henri smiled, but in his eyes I still saw sadness lurking. Then his face cleared and he got up from his chair and came to stand in front of me. "Shall I pour us some more wine?"

I agreed, hoping it might have a calming effect on my racing heart. Somewhat to my surprise, Henri did not return to his customary chair, but pulled up a stool to sit close beside me.

"Another toast," he said. "To you, Alex—and to courage." Noticing my puzzled frown, he added, "I meant to *your* courage, of course."

"I can't drink to that," I said, lowering my eyes in embarrassment. "What I am today I owe to you, not to any courage on my part, far from it. But I'll gladly drink to you, Henri, and to your great kindness, without which I'm sure I'd be dead by now."

Henri demurred, shaking his head, but I raised my glass to him and drank deeply. Almost at once, a mood of elevation spread through me, so strong it was as I might have imagined religious ecstasy to be, or the enlightened state to which Buddhists aspire, about which Roland had told me what now seemed a lifetime ago. As I gazed around the room, everything on which my eyes rested seemed preternaturally intense: colours were like dark jewels glinting with an inner fire, the light from the candles shimmered like phosphorescence, and everything seemed drenched in a sort of visual perfume, as sharp and sweet as the lilacs I had smelled a few nights ago, but of an intensity that made all my previous experience seem drab by comparison.

"Magnificent, is it not?" murmured Henri, laying his hand on my arm and smiling.

"What is it?" I gasped.

"You see, Alex," he murmured, "I kept my promise to you."

I frowned, unable to make sense of his words. I must be drunk, I thought.

Henri said, "Not drunk with wine, Alex, but with the beauty *I* see every night, and will do forever. I told you I should show you my world, and I've kept my promise."

"But—how...?"

He gazed into my eyes and in their dark depths I glimpsed something that sent my heart racing like an express train.

"How doesn't matter, Alex." His voice was soft and soothing, and I seemed to be drowning in the power of his gaze. Just for a moment, I struggled against it, then gave a long sigh and relaxed into it. Through a cocoon of bliss, I heard him speak: "Alex, if there were a way for you to come with me on my travels, would you do it?"

"Yes." My voice seemed to be floating somewhere above me, like a disembodied spirit. "I've already told you it's what I want, but you said it was impractical."

"There is a way—a way for us to be together as equals—if you have the courage."

"The courage...?"

"Yes, if you have the courage not to fail me as others have. Can you do that for the sake of our friendship, Alex? Can you?"

"What is it you're asking of me, Henri? I don't understand."

"Then let me be plain. Your friendship is very dear to me, Alex, as I believe mine is to you." I nodded, half lost in a vision of eternal companionship. "I've been lonely for so long, Alex, and now I've found your friendship I don't want it to end. Don't you feel the same?"

"You know I do."

"Then—will you come with me, into my world? Can you dare to do it?"

He leaned towards me, and his gaze seemed to reach into to my very soul. I realised, with a sense of coming home, it was all I had ever wanted.

"Yes," I breathed.

"Thank you." I sensed rather than heard his words. His face was very close to mine, and the chill of his skin felt soothing against my hot cheeks. His breath, which smelled faintly metallic, was like a cooling breeze. He grasped my shoulders and pulled me against him in a strong embrace. Before I had time to wonder what he was doing, let alone to react, I felt something sharp pierce the skin at the side of my neck, and pain shot through me like a red-hot skewer. I cried out in terror, and tried to pull away, but Henri held me in a grip so tight I could scarcely move. I closed my eyes as though that might somehow stop what was happening to me, and felt Henri's lips against my neck, icy cold, and unexpectedly soft, moving rhythmically against my flesh with tiny suckling sounds, like a baby at its mother's breast. In moments, the pain eased and a feeling flooded through me akin to sexual pleasure or opium delirium, but magnificently, terrifyingly more intense. Every part of my being tingled with delight. That was when I knew I was feeling what Henri had felt with Angelina—and when I knew he was doing to me what she had done to him. I was powerless to stop him, and, a thousand times worse, I no longer even wanted to do so. For what seemed an eternity, I felt his lips against my neck, drawing out my life force. At last he raised his head and I caught a glimpse of his eyes glowing like burning coals, his mouth smeared with blood— my blood!—that trickled down his chin in slow, crimson rivulets. Then I felt myself sinking into unconsciousness. I was certain I was about to die.

When I first regained some awareness of myself, it seemed my body was an empty shell lying on some desolate beach.

As I lay inert on the sand, energy and light began to pulse through me, at first almost indiscernible, then growing and spreading until I throbbed with light and power that shone out of me as though I were a sun. I opened my eyes to see Henri gazing down at me, and realised I was no longer in the drawing room, but was lying on my bed. Then it was borne in on me that, although the room was in complete darkness, I could see as clearly as though it were day. What had happened to me? Why did I feel so strange? There was a faint throbbing at the side of my neck, and when I put my fingers to it I felt two swollen welts, perhaps an inch apart. With that touch, the memories came flooding back.

I pulled myself upright and glared at Henri, seething with fury. "How dared you?" I hissed through clenched teeth.

A look of bewildered hurt showed on his pale countenance. "But why are you so angry, Alex? I did what you wanted. Now we can travel as equals. Our friendship can last forever."

"What I wanted?" I cried. "What the devil made you think that?"

"You told me so. Don't you remember? I should never have done it without your consent."

I cast my mind back over the events of the evening, and all at once grasped what must have happened. Without my knowing it, Henri had begun giving me his blood again. No wonder my mood had lifted so miraculously over the past week or so. And tonight, he must have given me even more, creating the state of ecstasy in which I had unwittingly agreed to his subtly worded suggestions.

"Of course I wanted our friendship to last," I spat at him, "but not like this." In despair, I waved my hands in front of him. They were as white as chalk. "Never like this!"

Henri sat down on the bed and made to take my hand. I flinched and drew back, and the look of desolation on his face gave me a savage satisfaction.

"You deceived me, Henri." My voice was as cold as my undead flesh. "You drugged me with your blood, and then asked me questions in such a way as to obtain the answer you wanted. Are those the acts of a friend?"

He turned away from me, but not before I saw the bleakness in his face. "I've been so lonely," he whispered, "for so very long. I see now I was mistaken, but I swear to you, Alex, my intention was never to hurt you. Yes, I gave you my blood again, but only because I couldn't bear to see you so unhappy. I could see you were distressed because I must leave, but I have no choice in that. It would be dangerous for me to stay here much longer; you've read the newspaper reports. So you see if I took you with me as a human, you'd be in constant danger from those who don't understand us, and therefore see us as evil. I was not prepared to expose you to this, so what else was left to me but to bring you across? Oh, Alex, you cannot imagine my joy when you agreed to join me! After centuries of loneliness, I was to have the companion my heart would have chosen."

"Did it not occur to you I was in no state to make a proper decision?" I flung at him. "Surely you must have known I was under the spell of your blood?"

"But I wanted so much for you to come with me, Alex. I thought it was what you wanted, too."

A snarl of fury that was not quite human erupted from my mouth. "Oh, God!" I moaned. "Look what you've done to me, you—you monster!"

"Is that truly what you think I am?"

"What else should I call someone who drugs me, and then tricks me into agreeing to something I could never have agreed to in my right mind?"

Cold tears of rage started from my eyes and I began to pummel him with my fists. Almost faster than even my enhanced eyes could see, he turned and grasped my forearms in an iron grip.

He spoke to me almost as though I were a naughty child. "No, Alex, you can't hurt me. You're not strong enough. It will be some time before you attain your full powers. Soon the hunger will take hold of you and you'll need to feed. You'll need my help with it at first, whether you like it or not."

I wrenched myself out of his grasp with a snarl and leapt off the bed. "You've done more than enough for me already, don't you think? I want nothing more from you, you *fiend*, not now, not ever. Just leave me alone!"

I made a dash for the door, marvelling, in spite of myself, at my new strength and speed. But Henri was quicker. He gained the door before me and stood barring the way. The expression on his face shocked me into immobility. I had never before seen him look so cold, so—inhuman.

"Alex," he said, his voice like frozen steel, "do you think I went to such lengths only to lose you again?"

"You intend to keep me prisoner?" I demanded, trying to make my voice as frigid as his.

He stared at me, fires of anger blazing in the depths of his eyes. "You may think it so if you wish, but I assure you you'll have everything you need—including blood, which, believe me, you'll need before long. I'd have preferred to offer you a more natural hunting ground, but if you persist in this foolish obduracy, I have no choice but to keep you here until you see reason."

"So much for friendship," I spat at him, and knew, somehow, that answering fires flamed in my own eyes.

I turned on my heel and began to pace the room. Instinct told me I could not yet hope to outmatch Henri in strength or cunning; after all, he had a three-hundred-year advantage. Yet I was determined to escape him somehow, and began to rack my brain for at least the beginnings of a plan. In the midst of my furious pacing, my entire body was suddenly racked by spasms of such agony as I had never before experienced. I sank to the floor, clutching my arms about me and rocking back and forth in an effort to control the pain, which was akin to what I had experienced during my withdrawal from opium, but more powerful—and more frightening since I had no idea what was causing it. Then a different sensation assailed me, at first mingled with the pain, but gradually superseding it until I realised what I was experiencing was hunger, but of an intensity beyond anything I could have imagined as a mere human being. I knew, then, the reason for the terrifying longing I had felt that night at *Le Merle*. Henri was right; I was going to have to feed, to find some hapless victim and attack him for his blood. The very thought filled me with revulsion, yet I knew I had no choice. Forcing myself to my feet, I turned to face him.

"Very well," I said through gritted teeth. "You win—for now."

"*Bien*," he said, stepping forward to take my arm. "That's sufficient—for now."

As soon as I was in the open air, I began to realise the extent of the changes that had taken place within me. With the instinct of a hunting creature, I began to scent the air, amazed by what I was now able to perceive. The air itself, the pavements, the trees, everything about me gave up its secrets to my newly honed senses. With Henri's strong grip guiding me, I began to walk towards the nearby *Jardin de Luxembourg*, searching for I knew not what. Until, that is, I finally sensed it. Wafting on the night air came a scent I could not quite identify, yet knew with every atom of my being was what I sought, what I *must* have to assuage my terrible hunger. I began to follow it, a strange excitement mounting within me until I became aware of a rhythmic pulsing I felt rather than heard, and all at once I recalled where I had felt it before. It was blood. Blood pulsing through the veins of a living human being. Now I was not just horrified, I was jubilant as well. I wanted to cry out like my father's hounds when they scented a fox, but some instinct prevented me from doing so.

It was not long before I caught sight of my quarry. A few yards to my left, beneath a massive elm tree, a ragged figure lay sprawled fast asleep, beside him an empty wine bottle. With Henri's hand on my arm now all but forgotten, I crept towards him on silent feet. Crouching down beside him, I pulled back the grubby shirt from his equally grubby neck. In fascination, I stared at the veins throbbing there just beneath his skin, and willed him not to waken. Just for a moment, I was sickened by what I was about to do, but then Henri pushed my head down towards him and instinct took over. Swiftly pinning him to the ground with hands stronger than I had ever known them, I bent over his neck. As I did so, I felt a peculiar, throbbing sensation in my gums—my eye teeth were elongating, growing into pointed fangs like those of a carnivorous animal. My lips drew back in something akin to a snarl and I sank my fangs into the man's neck, piercing his jugular vein. Lifting my head, I stared, mesmerised, as his blood welled up dark and viscous, and began to spread out across his skin in crimson streams. How enticing it looked!

"Drink!" Henri urged, and pushed my head down again.

I felt my fangs retract as I bent over the unconscious man and began to lap up his blood like a cat, and then to suck at the wounds my teeth had made. Thick, warm blood flowed into my mouth and slid over my tongue, metallic and salty with a faint tang of alcohol. As I drank, I felt life flooding into me, bringing with it a sense of well being, of strength—of ecstasy. No longer did I feel pain. I was drunk on the very elixir of life!

When there was nothing left to drink, I sat back and simply revelled in the life that filled my being, knowing the blood I had just drunk was even now imbuing me with energy and power far above those of mere mortals.

I looked down at the man still grasped in my arms. In my blood lust, I had failed to notice, but his eyes were wide open in an expression of terror, staring up at me from his bloodless visage as though, with some part of his being, he knew what I had done and cursed me for it. Within this dead man's gaze I realised that, for all I had gained, I had lost something as well. Beneath my euphoria, guilt made its insistent murmur, but there was no longer enough human left in me to weep. I knew then that thousands of faces yet to come would haunt me as this man's did, yet none would ever draw a tear from my eyes. And I mourned—mourned for the nameless man whose life I had consumed, mourned for the sunrises I should never see but, above all, I mourned for the loss of my humanity. In that moment I began to comprehend the true price of the gift Henri had conferred on me.

It was only when Henri tugged at my arm that I realised the man I still held in my arms was dead. Enough of the human remained in me to render me acutely aware of the possible consequences of what I had done. I glanced up at Henri, who crouched beside me, his hand still grasping my arm.

"Come," he whispered. "We must leave, quickly."

"But what if someone saw me?" I whispered back, casting furtive eyes about me. "Shall I have to kill them as well?"

Henri shook his head. "Not if we leave right now. The body will almost certainly be found in the morning, but the death of one more drunken vagrant is unlikely to create any great excitement amongst the local *gendarmerie*."

"But shouldn't we hide him—it—the body?"

"Of course not," Henri said, a note of impatience in his voice. "That would be bound to arouse the suspicion of whoever came on it. All we need do is leave here without further delay."

He emphasised the urgency of his words by shoving the inanimate body out of my arms and onto the ground. With Henri all but propelling me in front of him, we hurried away across the park.

We did not go home straight away. Henri insisted I take some time to explore my new nature, so, with my arm clasped firmly in his lest I try to abscond, we wandered the streets of *Saint-Germain*. Nothing I had experienced before came close to the sheer ecstasy imparted by the warm blood now coursing in my veins. It enhanced my senses to a degree that would have been unbearable before. The night was like daylight to my newly awakened eyes, except that everything was painted with a darker, richer palette. Overhead, I heard the beating hearts of birds roosting in the trees, all around me the fluttering footsteps of tiny creatures in the undergrowth. On the breeze I smelled the green, slightly acrid scent of leaves, wood smoke from fires, even wax from the votive candles in a church somewhere nearby, mingled with the sensual sweetness of incense. In the delirium of fresh blood, I was filled with delight in the new world Henri had opened up to me.

As the first rays of dawn began to light the sky, however, an immense weariness crept over me. I had been so engrossed in discovering and exploring my new nature I had all but forgotten Henri's presence (and he had remained unobtrusive, as he well knew how), let alone the practical ramifications of my transformation. But now my entire being cried out for sleep.

Henri said, "Come, we both need to sleep."

By the time we reached Henri's house, I felt as though I could not walk another step, and the lightening sky was beginning to engender in me a sense of acute unease.

"Yes," Henri told me, his voice as gentle as my old nanny soothing me to sleep when I was a boy. "It's the same for all of us. We must make haste now."

Fournier let us into the house and locked and barred the door carefully behind us. When did he manage to sleep? I wondered.

"Well, Alex," Henri said as we climbed the stairs. "Have I not given you a beautiful gift?"

With the need for sleep overwhelming me, my former elation had deserted me. "And terrible," I reminded him. "You said so yourself, remember?"

"*Eh bien*," he said with one of his eloquent shrugs. "If you wish it, we can speak further of that tonight. But now you must sleep, and so must I."

We were now just inside the door of my bedroom. I noticed my bed had been remade in my absence, presumably by the redoubtable Fournier, and lay pristine and inviting. Henri remained as I undressed, pulled on my nightgown, and pulled back the sheets. Only when I was sinking into oblivion did he leave.

CHAPTER TWENTY-THREE

Not long after sunset, I was awakened by pangs of hunger gnawing at my gut. The elation of the previous night was gone, and I felt more animal than superhuman. I quickly washed and donned clean clothes and went to the door of my room. It was locked. But before I had had time to decide whether to bang on the wooden panels and demand my release or await Henri's pleasure with stoicism, I heard the key turn in the lock and Henri opened the door.

"Good evening, Alex. I trust you slept well?"

"Oh, indeed," I said. "Like the dead, you might say. But of course I am dead, now, aren't I? You've seen to that."

Henri gave a sigh expressing both chagrin and a kind of weary patience. "I can see you're having some difficulty adjusting to your new state, so I shan't take offence at your sarcasm. I expect you're feeling famished. I've already fed, however, so I can accompany you. Last night's feast was perfectly understandable for a new vampire, but you can't afford to take so much blood as to kill everyone from whom you feed, and I can help you to learn something of this skill."

"You mean as you did with that tramp," I said. The words had no sooner left my lips than my mind flew back to the newspaper articles I had read—the unexplained deaths, the mysterious wasting sickness. "My God!" I exclaimed. "It was you! No wonder you need to leave Paris in such a hurry. And

I suppose that was you in London, too?"

"Even an experienced vampire is not completely immune from error," Henri replied with a shrug. "That's why we must try to choose people who won't be missed, such as vagrants and whores. It makes life a little less dangerous for us, at least."

The enormity of his words left me speechless. As I attempted to find words adequate to express my revulsion at his callousness, I felt sharp pangs of hunger clutch at me. Henri must have sensed it, too, as he came forward to usher me from the room. But I drove him with all my strength against the corner of the dressing table, throwing him off balance. He was swift to recover, but I had already rushed past him and down the stairs. As I reached the front door, I heard him close behind me. I twisted the door handle and yanked open the door, shouting as I did so, "I don't want you or your so-called help, Henri. I'll make my way through hell alone!"

Then I fled.

To my astonishment, when I finally slowed my pace a little I found Henri had not followed me. Perhaps, I thought, he had judged it best to leave me until I came to my senses, as he would see it. I strode along the empty street, determined not to bend to his will. Before very long, however, the hunger became overwhelming, and I knew I could not put off feeding for much longer.

This time, I eschewed the *Jardin de Luxembourg* in favour of somewhere further afield. Even an animal knows better than to draw undue attention to itself in a hostile environment, and I had no need of Henri to remind me the world would be hostile to such as I now was. Moving with all speed, I crossed the Seine and made my way towards the *Champs Élysées*, though I scarcely expected to find suitable prey there. Plenty of people would still be about at this time of night, drawn by its fashionable cafés and theatres, but it was too open and too well lit for my purpose. I crossed the broad avenue of the *Champs Élysées*, ignoring the people strolling there despite the demands of my hunger, and soon reached the vast, empty space where the *Tuileries* Palace had stood until only a few years before. Roland had told me it was once the residence of French royalty, but had been so badly burned by the *Communards* during the 1871 uprising the authorities had decided to demolish it, although they had left the formal gardens created in earlier, happier times. A popular family picnic venue during the hours of daylight, at night they were favoured as a trysting place by lovers, and it was amongst these, in some secluded spot, that I hoped to find what I sought.

As I entered the gardens, a terrible excitement grew within me. My gums and teeth began to tingle, the very thought of fresh blood causing the transformation that had so shocked me the previous night. It seemed I was already becoming a creature of instinct. I found this both exhilarating and profoundly disturbing, as though the two aspects of my nature were engaged in a monstrous battle and I was by no means certain which would win. My philosophical musings were cut short when I caught the warm, enticing scent of blood. Pausing only to determine the direction in which I must proceed, I slipped into the shadows of a large, wooded area to my left and crept through the trees, led on by my newly enhanced senses. Before long I saw a young lady wrapped in a dark blue *pelisse* sitting on a wooden bench under an elm tree, looking about her as though expecting someone. I hid myself in the shadows, uncertain what to do next. I could not afford to risk frightening her by approaching her directly, but I had no idea what else I should do. Then I recalled Henri looking deeply into my eyes and his mind moving within mine, and I suddenly knew this was something I could also do.

I stepped out from the shadows.

At the sound of my footfall the girl turned towards me, her mouth opening in a gasp of surprise as she saw me. She was very pretty, with golden curls escaping from the hood of her *pelisse*, soft pink cheeks, and eyes the colour of summer skies. Although I hated myself for it, I forced myself to ignore her youth and vulnerability, to see her only as a source of sustenance. I fixed my eyes on hers and drew her towards me. How I was able to do this I had no idea. It was done by pure instinct. As soon as she was close enough, I slid my left arm about her waist and held her fast. Keeping my eyes fixed on hers, I pulled her into the shadows. With my right hand I pushed back her hood, and her hair with it, to expose her neck, so delectably smooth and pink. I gazed at it, noting the faint line of her jugular vein, and felt my teeth transform into fangs. She screamed as they penetrated her neck, and I clamped my hand over her mouth to silence her. Her blood, compared with my feast of the previous night, was like fresh Beaujolais compared with the cheapest *vin ordinaire*; it was like drinking in the essence of springtime. Before long, she relaxed in my embrace and gave a soft sigh, and I knew she was feeling the sensual pleasure I had felt with Henri. A similar pleasure burned within me so that, in drinking from this young stranger, I might as well have been making love to her.

Fear gripped me then, and I lifted my lips from her neck to make sure I had not killed her. But no, she was still breathing, though all but unconscious. Like a cat, I lapped up the blood still seeping from the wounds I had made, and was gratified to see it cease flowing. I caught her up in my arms and swiftly returned her to the rustic bench on which I had found her, pulling her hood over her head and propping her up against the trunk of the tree, alert for signs of anyone approaching. Then I slipped away through the trees towards the *Champs Elysées*.

When I came to the river, I sat down on the grass beneath a tree to watch the dancing of the lights on the ink-dark water and to listen to its gentle lapping against the banks. But the fresh blood racing in my veins made me restless, so I got up again and began to stride along the bank, not caring in which direction I went, so long as it was away from Henri's town house.

As I walked, thoughts of Shillington Hall crept into my mind. Despite my bitter comments to Charles in the depths of my despair following my mother's death and my father's remarriage, I *was* his eldest son, and ought, therefore, to inherit his estate when he died, regardless of any second wife and child. I began to wish with all my heart I had been less hasty in my actions. For all that I could not, even yet, bring myself to accept his succumbing to the blandishments of Mariah Wenley so soon after Mama's death, I had never stopped loving my father. Still, what did any of this matter when it was impossible for me return to England for fear of the law? I was determined not to return to Henri, however. Despite all his protestations of friendship, he had taken my very life from me by deception, just to ameliorate his loneliness, and that I could not forgive. Not yet. Perhaps not ever. Somehow, I must find a way to prevent his finding me until I could be certain he had left Paris.

Yet what sort of life could I expect in Paris, alone and friendless, with precious little money, and unable to go abroad by day? True, there might, by now, be money due to me from the sale of my books, but how should I explain to the likes of Monsieur Lefebvre my suddenly becoming a creature who went abroad only at night, and who never ate? Even if they knew the truth, at best they would believe me insane, at worst they might seek to kill me, and, I told myself, I had not clawed my way back from my wretched, laudanum-soaked existence on the streets of *Montmartre* only to give up on myself now, no matter how abhorrent I found my present state. Somehow, I would find a way to make my life bearable.

The imminent approach of dawn made me realise my first act must be to find somewhere to sleep through the coming day. Casting my gaze about me, I realised I was quite close to the Eiffel tower, and therefore to the *Passy* cemetery, which Jerome had pointed out to me when I first came to Paris, explaining it was where the aristocracy of the city were interred. Perhaps I might find there some family mausoleum where I could conceal myself until nightfall—a fitting resting place for a vampire, I thought with a bitter laugh.

As I had hoped, there were a number of such sepulchres dotted about amongst tombstones gleaming white as teeth in the moonlight. I soon found one whose uncared-for state led me to hope it was no longer in use. It was built of corpse-pale marble, and styled like a small Romanesque temple with a

277

pillared portico and a cupola crowned with a cross. Climbing the narrow stone steps, I gave the black-painted door an experimental shove. Much to my relief, it opened readily, albeit with a shriek of rusted metal hinges. If it had ever been locked, the mechanism must long since have rusted away. I slipped inside and carefully closed the door. Casting my gaze around the gloom, I saw the interior was like a tiny chapel, with an altar at one side still covered by a decayed and faded blue altar cloth edged with the remains of gold fringing. A tarnished silver crucifix and two candlesticks—one lying on its side—stood on the altar, sad remnants of former devotion. Most likely, I thought, the family it commemorated were now all dead—so much the better for my purpose. Two dilapidated kneeling stools lay before the altar on a floor laid with flagstones, now uneven and grimed with the dust of years.

Towards the centre of the room I noticed one larger stone set into the floor. Scuffing away the dirt with my boot sole, I saw it had a metal ring set into a recess at its centre. This must, I thought, open into an underground vault housing the coffins of the deceased. But the thought of viewing coffins repulsed me, and in any case I was by now too weary to investigate. Indeed, my body seemed scarcely able to do my bidding as I dragged myself across the tiny chamber to the far side of the altar, where I hoped I might be less visible if anyone happened to enter the crypt. Brushing away the worst of the dust, I lay down with my head on my arm and allowed myself to sink into a deathlike sleep.

* * * *

The second I awoke, before I had even opened my eyes, I sensed something different about my place of rest. I was no longer alone. My immediate thought was that I should not be obliged to hunt to appease the hunger that already gnawed at my gut. Then it occurred to me that some mourner must have found me out, and I should be forced to commit murder to preserve my secrecy. Leaping to my feet, my body taut with the expectation of both sustenance and battle, I peered through the gloom. The sight that greeted me filled me with dismay.

Just inside the doorway, leaning against the doorjamb, stood Henri, looking more than usually severe.

To say I was dumbfounded is to underestimate the feelings that tumbled through me. Had Henri tracked me down to punish me for spurning his offer of eternal friendship? Was he going to try to force me to be his companion, and what means might he use to accomplish this? I was all too aware of his superior knowledge of the methods a vampire might have at his disposal to enforce his will. Or would he kill me outright? Would he grant me this mercy—if mercy it were? And how had he managed to find me?

"That was not in the least difficult, my dear Alex." Henri spoke softly, but there was steel in his voice. "You share my blood, and that creates a link between us—and always will. As for your fears, I have no intention of killing you. It would be like severing part of myself."

I gasped, "You can read my thoughts, then?"

"*Mais oui*, of course I can. We share the same blood. You can read mine, too—unless I withhold them from you, of course."

A rush of fury overrode my other emotions. "How dare you?" I cried. "How dare you violate me like that?"

"I'm sorry," Henri said with an elegant shrug. "But when you left me, I sensed your confusion, and was concerned for your welfare—and with good reason, if this is the best you could do for a bed." He looked about him with distaste. "If you wish it, I can teach you how to block me."

"I want nothing from you," I hissed at him. "You've taken everything from me—stolen it without my consent—and I'd rather sleep in a gutter than submit to your will."

"My dear Alex—"

"Don't call me that! You have no right."

Henri sighed. "But you are dear to me. I've already told you that. However, I do understand your anger, especially if, as you claim, you misunderstood my motives."

"Misunderstood? You deceived me, Henri, and well you know it."

"Please, Alex, let's not quarrel over details. What's done is done, and we must make the best of it. And the best could be very good indeed, if you'd just rid yourself of your bitterness."

Henri pushed himself away from the wall and moved towards me, his hands outstretched. From instinct, I retreated, snarling, behind the end of the altar. A wave of anger swept across his face, but he quelled it almost immediately.

"You have no need to fear me, Alex," he said. "I give you my word."

"And that's worth so much," I replied, my lip curled in derision.

At that, Henri crossed the floor in a stride and grasped me

280

by the arms, his eyes blazing. "*Mon Dieu*, Alex, but you try my patience! In over three centuries, I've made only one other vampire, and he was taken from me by the ignorance of humans. You can have no idea of the pain of that loss, and the loneliness I've endured since. How could you, young as you are? Do you truly hate me so much you would have me suffer it again?"

I struggled in his grip, but he held me fast.

"You talk of suffering," I jeered. "How dare you when, in one fell swoop, you've deprived me of friends and family and condemned me to an eternity of blood hunger!"

Henri's lips drew back in a snarl. I flinched, expecting him to attack me but, with a visible effort to control himself, he released me, almost flinging me from him so that I fell backwards, grasping at the edge of the altar to keep myself upright. Part of the decayed altar cloth came away in my hands, sending the crucifix and one of the candlesticks flying. They fell to the flagstones with a dull clang like a cracked bell. Henri gave a brief start at the sound, then his hands fell to his sides and the fire slowly faded from his eyes.

"Do you indeed hate me, Alex?" he asked again, his voice now gentle. "Can you not forgive me for the wrong you perceive me to have done you?"

"Yes! No!" I threw up my hands and shook my head, frowning. "I don't know, Henri. But what I do know is that I hate what you've made of me. I dare say, as you've told me, there are wonderful aspects to being a vampire, but it sets me apart from my fellow men, and I never wanted that. How can I hope to make peace with my father, or take up my inheritance, being what I am? How can I face my cousins, my friends, knowing it could be their blood for which I hunger?

You've healed me of one addiction only to plunge me into another, and for all eternity, if what I've heard and read is true. How can you expect me to forgive you for that?"

"But you need not be denied all those things," Henri told me. "I had already been a vampire for some decades when I inherited the Chateau Saint-Clair after the deaths of my elder brothers' descendants. And before you ask, Alex, no, they did not die by my hand. They succumbed to a plague that was ravaging Europe at the time. Friends and family are considerably more problematic, I admit, but the blood hunger can be managed, with practice. As your maker, it's my duty to teach you these things, and I'm only too willing to do so—if you'll let me."

In an agony of confused emotions, I began to stride about the room, knowing my eyes were blazing fire as Henri's had.

"And the worst of it is," I said, turning to him at length, "when I'm hunting, when I'm drinking the lifeblood of some innocent victim, it fills me with an ecstasy that would be divine, if it weren't so vile, and I hate myself for taking pleasure in so degraded an act. Tell me, Henri, how can I trust someone who did that to me? And how can I forgive without trust?"

Henri held out his hands to me as though in supplication. "Alex, had I realised your true feelings, I swear I wouldn't have brought you across. But let me at least make some amends by teaching you all I know, to help make your new life easier. Will you not stay with me for that long?"

I shook my head, resisting the temptation of his offer with all the might of my injured feelings. "No. I wanted your friendship, Henri, not your control. Every day I spent with you, every minute, would remind me of what I've lost—of what *you've* stolen from me. If I stay with you, I'll grow to detest you, and I don't want that. Since I must now live a stranger to the world I knew, let me do it alone, with only myself to blame if I make a mull of it."

Sparks of fire flashed in Henri's eyes. His lips drew back from his teeth, his fangs emerging, needle sharp, and he snarled like a wild cat. "You can't leave me," he hissed. "I won't let you!"

I felt my gums tingle as my own fangs began to grow in response to his. An answering snarl left my lips, and my fingers curled like claws as I readied myself to counter his attack. With a roar of fury that made me flinch in terror, Henri turned abruptly and began to pound on the door with his fists, shattering the heavy timber as though it were old cardboard. My instinct—that of a vampire, I realised with mounting horror, not that of the principled human I had been—was to attack him while his back was turned. As I stood there, hands clenched, torn between the vampire and the man, Henri turned to face me, his injured hands dripping blood onto the dusty flagstones. His grey eyes glowed, but with something other than the fire of anger. My heart, beating with our shared blood, echoed a feeling of cold despair.

"No," he said, his voice almost inaudible, as though he were thinking aloud, "you are blood of my blood. I cannot harm you. Since you choose to reject my friendship, I must leave Paris alone. But remember this, Alex, you and I are blood kin. Wherever in the world we may be, that tie remains, and no amount of rejection can break it, until one of us—or both—meets the true death."

With these words, he gave me a slight, formal bow. Then

283

he turned, wrenched open what remained of the door, and rushed out into the night without glancing back.

I stared after him, too stunned to think of following. When I finally came to myself, he was nowhere to be seen, and I could sense no trace of him.

As I stood in the graveyard bathed in the cold light of the waning moon, I became acutely aware of the hunger raging within me. With a sigh of resignation, I set off in search of sustenance. Striding between the tombstones and mausoleums of the desolate cemetery, it occurred to me I might never see Henri again. Knowing I wanted nothing more to do with him, he would be even more anxious to leave Paris, and I had no idea where he might go. Despite my resentment towards him, the realisation that I was now truly alone in the world pierced my heart like a shard of ice.

* * * *

In the days—or, rather, nights—that followed, I learned a great deal more about being a vampire. I realised, through a somewhat brutal process of trial and error, that I could manage quite comfortably by drinking small amounts of blood from several people, thus avoiding inadvertently killing anyone. At first, I found it difficult to avoid being carried away on a tide of blood hunger and being unable to stop in time, and, in spite of myself, I began to appreciate Henri's difficulty. It was easy enough, however, to find two or three—I still found myself thinking of them as victims—in a night, since my vampiric senses were far more finely honed than those of the unsuspecting humans, and my newfound ability to mesmerise meant I could not only induce them to come to me willingly, but afterwards I could wipe from their minds all memory of what I had done to them. Despite the undeniable pleasure I took in hunting and feeding, I found myself living in an almost constant state of apprehension lest I be caught about my dreadful business, for I could not rid myself of a sense of disgust at what I must do for sustenance. I both feared and detested the relentlessness of the blood hunger, yet, like Henri, I was unable to resist it.

Despite my fine words to Henri, I now found myself living much as I had after the destruction of the *Hotel Rimini*. I slept in a deserted building, and my craving for laudanum had been replaced by an even more terrible yearning. It was impossible to keep myself clean, and I hovered in a constant state between dread and boredom. Since leaving Henri, I had been unable to pursue my writing, having no pen or paper and no way of acquiring them. During the hours of darkness, my mind was such a ferment of new sensations I found it impossible to concentrate, while during the day I was simply too fatigued. Once or twice I tried visiting a café or theatre, but I would very soon become overwhelmed by the confusion of thoughts, feelings and other sensations I picked up from those around me—not to mention the blood coursing in their veins, and the rhythmic pounding of their human hearts— and my rudimentary attempts to shut them out were less than successful. However, I could not bear to stay in my dreary mausoleum except for sleeping, so most of the night I wandered the streets, lonely, bored, and restless.

One evening, having satisfied my hunger with a couple of vagrants I found in the *Bois de Boulogne*, I became so exasperated with my own company I decided to go for a long walk. If nothing else, it would serve to while away the time until dawn drew me back to my dusty resting place. I made my way through the *Arc de Triomphe* and towards the *Champs Élysées,* and then turned back towards the Seine. For some time I wandered along the riverbank, making a deliberate effort to ignore any signs of human life, concentrating, instead, on the river itself and the shifting lights reflected in its pitch-dark water. Crossing by a bridge near the *Place de la Concorde,* I walked towards the looming bulk of the *Louvre* Museum. As my senses drank in the myriad aromas and sounds carried on the chill night air, my mind became calmer, the rhythm of walking acting as a sedative. From time to time, thoughts, or fragments of thoughts, would rise to the surface of my mind, but I avoided focusing on them, finding it more restful to bathe in the kaleidoscope of sensations wafting about me and through me like a multi-hued and ever-changing cloud.

I scarcely knew how far I had walked when a single sound arose from the generality, a word—my name, in fact— repeated in urgent tones. I stopped and stared about me, terrified lest Henri had come, after all, to punish me. As my name was called once again, I realised with a sigh of relief it was not Henri. Yet it was a voice I knew well. I felt a hand on my shoulder and spun round, only just managing to suppress an instinctive snarl, to find myself staring into the concerned face of my cousin Jerome.

"Good God! Alex! I thought you must have left Paris long since."

"N-no," I stammered, "n-not yet." I made a supreme effort to pull myself together, adding, in what I hoped was a suitably cheerful tone, "Anyway, what are you doing out at this time of night?"

"I might ask you the same question, young Alex. As it happens, I've been at a card party. Had I known where to find you, I might have invited you along, although, on reflection, not in your present state. You look as though you've been sleeping in ditches. Where *are* you staying, by the way?" He took me by the arm. "Look, you must come home with me. I know Lucette will be pleased to see you, and besides, I want to know what you've been up to since leaving us the way you did, with barely so much as a word. Come along now, you shall regale us with the tale of your adventures."

He had been urging me in the direction of the *Boulevard Saint-Germain* as we spoke, and I felt I had no choice but to go with him. In truth, I was pleased to see him, if only to relieve the intensity of my loneliness, although I quailed at the thought of being subjected to a quizzing, no matter how well meant, and the lies I should have to concoct to keep myself safe. In no more than a few minutes, we reached Jerome's house. Lucette came to greet him, and gave a cry of surprise as she saw me. She came running to embrace me and kiss my cheeks.

"Alex! *Bonsoir*! How happy I am to see you safe and well. Jerome and I have been so worried about you. But you are cold, my dear cousin. Come into the parlour and I'll have Hortense make up a fire."

Feeling as though I were sinking beneath waves of hospitality, I followed Lucette into the parlour, where I was soon ensconced in a chair by the fire with a glass of brandy in my hand. The heat was an affront to my vampiric sensibilities, but at least it was too late in the evening for me to be offered food. Jerome settled Lucette in the chair opposite mine and fetched a chair for himself.

"Now," he said, "you must tell me what on earth you've been doing all these months. As far as any of us knew, you simply dropped off the face of the earth when you walked out of here—which you needn't have done, you know. I know I took you to task over your drinking, but that didn't mean I was giving you your marching orders. After you left, I quite thought you'd left Paris to continue your travels, but apparently not—unless you've been and come back again."

"I'm sorry about the way I left," I said, "but I was very confused and angry at the time about Papa remarrying, and the new baby, and I'm afraid I just couldn't bear to hear you and Lucette talking about how wonderful it all was, when to me it meant not only an insult to Mama's memory, but also the loss of my home—the place where I was born and grew up."

"But what on earth made you think you'd lost your home? I'm sure Uncle John had no such thought in his mind."

I felt anger surge within me, leaping up like a flame when a fire is stirred to life. With an effort, I pushed it down. "Perhaps not," I admitted with reluctance, "but Mariah's such an encroaching sort of woman I felt sure she was planning to cut me off from Papa and put her own brat in my place. In fact, I'm still not convinced that isn't the case."

"But she couldn't have done that, Alex. As Uncle John's eldest son, the inheritance was—indeed, is—yours by right. If you'd only consulted Mr Jennings, you'd have known that."

"Yes, but Mariah's brother is also a lawyer, and he's bound to exert himself on behalf of his sister and her child when it comes to it. They've plenty to gain, you know, given that her brother owns the neighbouring estate. It's quite a bit smaller than Shillington, but if they could join the two together..."

To my chagrin, Jerome burst out laughing. "Oh, Alex, you've been reading too many penny dreadfuls. The only way Mariah and her son could gain your birthright is by your death, and you surely don't mean to tell me you think her capable of that?"

I laughed, in spite of myself. "No, I don't think that—though I'm not sure I'd put much else past her. Oh, I don't know, Jerome, I was just so furious with them I couldn't bear to be at Shillington any longer, so when Charles wrote inviting me to stay with him in London..."

"Charles? Do I know him? Was he at Harrow with you?"

"No, I met him at Cambridge, Charles Weston-Greer."

"Ah, I think I knew his cousin Cedric many years ago. Nice enough chap, if a trifle insubstantial."

"I think it must run in the family," I said with a grin. "That describes Charles to a T. But he'd always been good company, and his invitation offered an escape from circumstances I found intolerable. It turned out he'd inherited a vast fortune from some rich uncle, so I was assured of an excellent time."

"No doubt." My cousin's tone was as dry as the dust in my sepulchre.

"Yes, well, it didn't quite turn out like that." I endeavoured to explain what I could of the events that had led to my coming to Paris, and Jerome and Lucette listened with apparent sympathy.

"That was certainly a dreadful position you found yourself in," Jerome said at length. "Charles behaved like an irresponsible idiot, though, if I may say so without seeming callous, it seems he got his just deserts. And frankly, I should have thought the Honourable Augustus to have had more sense by now."

"You know him?"

"Oh, yes, Gussie and I are old acquaintances—though hardly friends. He was a regular rakehell when we were at Cambridge, though I'd expect him to have settled down a bit by now."

"I thought him pretty high-handed," I said, "but to do him justice he behaved perfectly honourably under the circumstances, and he had the decency to warn me the police were on my trail."

"Oh, they are all, all honourable men, these sons of the aristocracy—though with scarcely a brain between the lot of 'em, for the most part. But I do wish you'd told us about it when you first arrived in Paris. I might have been able to help you in some way. I'm not entirely without contacts, you know, despite being a lowly accountant."

"I wanted to, believe me, but I'd been implicated in the deaths of two men, and the police were hunting me. How could I have visited such shame on you and your family? I just couldn't do it, Jerome."

My cousin nodded, and said with a sigh, "I wish you had, though. And I wish you'd kept in touch with us, even if you felt unable to stay here any more. Mr Jennings has been trying to locate you these past six months. I'm very sorry to have to tell you, Alex, that Uncle John died of pneumonia last June."

To say this news left me speechless is to understate its impact. For some time I could do nothing but stare down at my hands clasping and unclasping the stem of my brandy glass as though they had become independent of the rest of my body. When Jerome offered me more brandy, I gulped it down, welcoming its fierce burning as a distraction from the grief I could not articulate. I desperately wanted to cry, but, as I had already discovered, no tears would come.

At last I whispered, "I'm sorry," and found, once started, I was unable stop myself from repeating the inadequate words over and over again.

Jerome laid his hand on my shoulder, saying, "Alex, I know, as I'm sure Uncle John did, that you would have wished to be with him at his passing, but none of us can know the hour or the manner of our departing. When he remarried, your Papa did so, I'm certain, from the best of motives, and he couldn't have foreseen how much it would upset you. If he had, who knows, perhaps he might have acted differently. But he did what he did, and you did what you did as a consequence. You must try not to blame him for remarrying, and you mustn't blame yourself for being absent from his deathbed. I understand his death was quite sudden, and even had you heard he was ill, it's unlikely you could have reached him in time. What you need now is some time to come to terms with the news. You must stay here tonight, Alex. I'll have Hortense warm your bed and light a fire in your room."

He patted my shoulder. "You see, Alex, we still think of it as your room, and you'll always be welcome to use it whenever you wish. If you'll give your clothes to Hortense, we'll see what can be done to render them less disreputable. Tomorrow, when you're rested, we can begin to sort out your affairs."

Panic struck me at these kindly words, for fear I should be

unable to stay without inadvertently revealing myself to my cousins. "But—but..." I stammered, my brain working hard to think of some excuse. Nothing came to mind.

Lucette came and put her arms around me, rocking me as though I had been a distressed child. "Alex, *mon cher*, you must stay. You shouldn't be alone at such a moment."

She continued to rock me thus until I was calmer, and I agreed to stay because I could think of no way to avoid it without seeming ungrateful. I could only be thankful I had already fed. When Jerome and Lucette went to bed, I climbed the stairs to my room and spent much of the night staring out of the window at the clouds drifting like wisps of gauze as the stars performed their nightly wheeling dance through the heavens, trying to take in my cousin's news. I had no clear idea of what it might mean for me. All I knew was that I was desperately sorry I had not made my peace with Papa while it was still possible.

CHAPTER TWENTY-FOUR

As the first pale rays of dawn began to dust the sky with pink, I forced myself, despite my desperate weariness, to dress in the cleaned and brushed clothes the maid had returned to my room, and crept down the stairs and out of the house, leaving a note for my cousins claiming I had remembered an important meeting first thing in the morning, but would return that evening. I then hurried back to my mausoleum to sleep through the day.

As soon as I awoke that evening, I hastened out to hunt, choosing the nearby *Bois de Boulogne* because it was large enough to enable me to find several people from whom to feed without any of them being aware of the others. Having drunk from a prostitute setting out to ply her trade on the streets near the *Champs Élysées*, and a young man lying drunk under a tree, I cleaned myself up as best I could, making use of a small fountain I had noticed earlier, and set off for my cousins' house. My visit required careful timing, since I must arrive late enough to avoid any offers of food— and the awkward explanations my refusal would entail—yet early enough not to appear impolite.

The previous night, Jerome had promised to see what he could do to facilitate my safe return to England, since it was quite plain to him I must now go. It was considerably less plain to me, since I did not relish the all too likely prospect of having to oust Mariah and her brat from my own home. However, I told myself, it couldn't hurt to gain some idea of how the land lay.

A feathery, light snow had begun to fall, dusting the ground like icing sugar on a cake. I hoped it would not become heavier, not because I felt the cold any longer, but because it would make it difficult for me to refuse the inevitable offer of a bed for the night with my cousins. I strode through the dark streets musing on the obstacles being a vampire put in the way of normal social intercourse. How Henri had managed for three centuries, I could not imagine. I was already exhausted by the necessity of concealing my nature from those in whom I should most wish to confide. However, the importance of discovering the state of my affairs was not lost on me, since inheriting my father's estate would provide me with a safe *pied-à-terre*, and Jerome could help me in this. Besides, I could not deny my pleasure at having his and Lucette's company once more. With them, I could almost feel human—at least for a short while.

When I arrived just before nine o'clock, Lucette came running from the parlour to greet me.

"*Bonsoir*, Alex! You should have come earlier, you know, then we could have given you dinner."

"Thank you," I said, smiling. "But I had a dinner engagement elsewhere." The dark irony of my statement sent an involuntary shudder through me.

Lucette, interpreting this as due to the freezing weather, drew me into the parlour where a fire crackled in the grate and Jerome was already pouring wine for us. He looked up, smiling, at our entrance.

"Alex, my boy, good to see you again! You'll take some wine?"

"Just a little, thank you," I replied. Although I had often seen Henri drink wine or spirits, I had not done so myself since becoming a vampire, and had no wish to bring on myself some effect that would reveal the transformation I had undergone, or worse, put my cousins in danger. The novelist Henry Fielding wrote that strong drink reveals a man's true nature, and I dared not risk testing the truth of his statement.

"Now," said Jerome once we were all seated. "I've made a start on looking into your affairs in England, Alex. I've written to Mr Jennings, but I've been obliged to ask him to write to you here, since you neglected to give me your address. When you write to him you can easily remedy that, of course, but we'd like to have it, too. You never know, we might just take it into our heads to visit you."

A bolt of panic shot through me. Feeling guilty for deceiving them, I gave my cousins a false address, since it would have seemed suspicious in the extreme to refuse their request. I could only hope they would not make good their proposal to visit me.

"I've also written to Captain Nuttall," Jerome continued, "to find out how things stand at Shillington Hall, you know, whether Mariah and her son still live there, that sort of thing. Uncle John may well have made some such provision in his will."

"Oh, undoubtedly," I said, unable to keep the bitterness from my voice. "He was completely besotted with the woman, and their brat."

Jerome gave me a disapproving look. "Alex, I wish you'd

295

try not to be so ungracious about your father's remarriage. It will eat away at you if you let it."

I shrugged. "In any case, I'm not sure I'd wish to live there. I've grown used to city life."

"Well, we'll see," said Jerome. "I imagine it'll be some weeks before we hear back from either Jennings or Nuttall."

And so it proved. It was over a month before word came back from them. I was disappointed, though hardly surprised, to learn Mariah and her son were still living at Shillington Hall. However, although I should have preferred to be relieved of the necessity, I thought I would have few qualms about ousting the two of them. After all, Mariah could always return to living with her brother, and take her mewling brat with her. As for the matter of the police warrant issued against me, the news was even less gratifying. It seemed I should be obliged to await the results of further enquiries by the diligent Mr Jennings.

In the meantime, I had realised I could not go on living in a mausoleum, regardless of its safety from prying eyes, not if I wanted to avoid attracting the wrong kind of attention. However, despite their kind offers, living with my cousins presented problems I felt inadequate to overcome. By dint of investigating some of the more modest boarding houses in the area of my favourite hunting ground, the *Bois de Boulogne*, I managed to find myself lodgings on the top floor of a large, somewhat rundown house presided over by a landlady of similar description with the implausible name of Bellerose, who seemed not to mind how or when I came and went as long as the rent was paid on time. I promised to pay for a month in advance, with a little extra for Madame Bellerose's promise to leave me undisturbed. To avoid arousing her suspicion, I told her I was a writer and needed complete peace and quiet in order to carry out my work. In the course of my wanderings, I also discovered the existence of public bathhouses, so I was able to keep myself clean. However, I still needed more shirts in order to be able to have laundered the one I had been wearing for far too long. But how to acquire these was a conundrum. I had already decided I must risk withdrawing money from my bank account if I were to have any sort of bearable life, but how could I do this when, as a vampire, I could not go about by day?

Or could I?

If Henri was right in thinking the vampire's repugnance for daylight was related to his being a hunter, rather than to some systemic cause, then perhaps it might be possible, after all, to go out during the day, even if only for short periods of time. I resolved to put myself to the test the following morning.

As soon as the sun was up, I made my cautious way down the stairs. It was still very early, and, to my considerable relief, no one in the building was abroad yet. Reaching the ground floor, I tiptoed across the foyer and opened the door, taking care to leave it a little ajar in case I needed to beat a hasty retreat, and stepped out into the dawn light. The first reaction I became aware of was a profound sense of unease. My very soul revolted against what I was doing, as though I were about to commit some horrendous crime—as if anything could outdo what I had already accomplished. As I stood on the pavement, a sweltering heat began to spread through my body. I felt I was being consumed by a raging fever, yet when I felt my brow it was icy cold. Determined to test myself to the limit, I fought down these feelings and stood my ground. A survey of the exposed areas of my skin revealed no sign of burning, in spite of the sharp, prickling sensation I felt, and so I came to the tentative conclusion that, although daylight would almost certainly cause me acute mental and physical unease, it would probably do me no physical harm. If I could master my feelings sufficiently, I should be able to manage simple tasks like visiting the bank and shopping—or so I hoped.

My first self-imposed task was to visit the shops near the *Champs Élysées*, where I spent what little money I had left in purchasing shirts, collars, and a tie, some basic toiletries, and a clothes brush. One of the few benefits I had discovered in being a vampire was that my beard appeared to have stopped growing or, if it did, it was at such a slow pace as to be unnoticeable. Next, I needed to visit the bank where Monsieur Lefebvre had arranged to pay any royalties for my book into an account in my name. However, going abroad in daylight for the first time had been such an ordeal I was only too happy to scurry back to my garret and spend the rest of the day in my narrow bed with the heavy curtains drawn tightly across the one small, dingy window.

That night, I set off on my nightly hunt soon after sunset. This time, I decided not to use the *Bois de Boulogne*, but crossed over the Seine, continuing along the riverbank past the *Quai d'Orsay* until I came to the Church of *Notre Dame de Paris*. There I turned right into a street I recalled from that fateful night when I had followed Henri and discovered his secret. Before long, I found myself outside the park known as the *Jardin de Luxembourg*. By now, my stomach felt as though it were being devoured from the inside, so I hurried into the park and through the deep shadows of the trees.

It was not long before I scented prey, and moments later came on a young woman wandering along one of the pathways, looking very tired and dejected. Her appearance, as well as my vampiric senses, told me she was a prostitute, and one having a particularly bad night. On silent feet I moved so as to emerge from the shadows slightly ahead of her.

With a smile, I bowed before her. "Good evening, Mademoiselle. What business brings you here by night?"

She looked at me with dull, kohl-ringed eyes and forced an answering smile. "Why, M'sieu, what business would you have me engage in?"

"Just this, Mademoiselle," and I put my arms about her and drew her to me.

"Then we must agree terms," she said, attempting to pull back from me.

But I held her fast and stared into her eyes until I could see she was mesmerised, then pulled her back into the deepest shadows. I felt rather sorry for her, so I took great care not to harm her beyond the wounds my fangs made in her neck—which would heal soon enough—and a temporary weakness from loss of blood. When I was done, I sat her down against a tree, pulled a couple of coins from my pocket and thrust them into the neck of her gown where she might find them when she woke. The Luxembourg Gardens afforded me two further small meals, one also a prostitute, the other a well-dressed young man who appeared to be sleeping off the effects of overindulgence in alcohol. Then I set off again towards the *Champs Élysées*, feeling replete, yet oddly unsatisfied.

It was, I thought morosely, like sexual congress without love or affection. The body might respond, yet the emotions and the soul were left unengaged, so that the experience was ultimately hollow. In my melancholy, I had visions of spending an eternity performing, night after night, an act whose very pleasures were abhorrent to me, each vile iteration serving not only to remind of me of what I had become, but also of what I had done. Should I, I wondered, one day become incapable of love? Indeed, was that already my fate? Although Henri had been kind to me, I had no real evidence that this arose from any ability to love, despite his protestations of friendship. Might it not just as easily stem from his need for self-preservation, a way of disarming those who would seek to harm him if they knew the truth? The likely answer to this was frighteningly clear. Had I not presented myself that very night to two unsuspecting prostitutes in the guise of an innocuous customer in order to serve my own needs? Had I, even so soon after my transformation, sunk to the very depths I despised in my creator?

Filled with self-loathing, I wandered for some time without noticing where I was going, until a deep weariness descended on me like fog, signalling the approach of dawn.

I remembered, then, I had promised myself a trip to the bank first thing in the morning. A glance down at myself made me realise that, if I went to the bank looking as I did, I should probably be refused entry, so I turned my steps back towards the *Champs Élysées*. I had noticed a public bathhouse in the area during my previous wanderings. With any luck, it might be open by now.

For once, my luck was in, and I was able to perform some much-needed ablutions. Back in my room, I set about brushing the dust from my coat and trousers before donning them again, along with one of my new shirts. I was not looking forward to braving the day again so soon. Try as I might, I seemed unable to shake off an overwhelming sense of disquiet during the hours of daylight. However, I knew it must be done, and so I steeled myself and set off again towards the city.

The walk to the bank took a great deal longer than felt at all comfortable, but it was worth it to find Monsieur Lefebvre had deposited into my bank account a sum of money that was gratifying both in size and as a testament to my book's popularity. I decided to withdraw it all to obviate further such unpleasant excursions, secreted it in an inner pocket of my coat, and hurried home, pausing only to buy a copy of *Le Figaro*, telling myself that, for all I might be a vampire for eternity, I could at least make the attempt to retain some small vestiges of humanity along the way.

* * * *

It was not until the following night that I thought of reading my newspaper. Immediately on reaching my room, I had lain down and sunk into vampiric slumber, and, on waking again after sunset, hunger drove me out to hunt. Much later, I returned home and saw the newspaper lying on the floor by the bed. I picked it up and spread it out on the counterpane. Even with my vampiric sight, I found the print difficult to read in the dark, so I felt in my pockets for matches, finally discovering a box that still had a few unspent. I leaned across and lit the candle on my bedside table. As soon as I sat back on the bed, the front-page headline leapt out at me: 'Unusual occurrence in *Parc Monceau*'. My heart thumping, I read began to read the article.

'A curious discovery was made late last night, when a young woman was found unconscious in the *Parc Monceau* by two gentlemen returning home from a visit to the theatre. While one gentleman attempted to resuscitate the young woman, the other fetched the *gendarmerie*. When later questioned, the young lady, who gave her name as Marie Blanc, said she did not know what had happened to her, but that she had woken from what she assumed was a faint to find herself seated on the ground leaning against a tree. She then got up to return home, but was overcome by another fainting fit, collapsing again near the park gates. Doctor André Roux, the doctor who examined her, told *Le Figaro* that Mademoiselle Blanc did not appear to be suffering from any illness, and was physically unharmed apart from two unusual puncture marks on her neck. What these were, he refused to speculate, however Police Inspector Jean Rousseau, who is in charge of the case, states the investigation of the incident is ongoing.'

Tossing the newspaper aside, I leapt to my feet and began to pace the room. I seemed to be in an impossible position. I had taken considerable care not to cause any lasting harm to the girl, Marie Blanc, yet still she had managed to attract the attention of the authorities. Of course, a young woman leading the precarious life of a prostitute might well already have been unwell, so perhaps I had merely exacerbated some existing weakness. Nevertheless, her injury, slight as it was, was of such a peculiar nature it must arouse suspicion, particularly if others with similar marks came to the notice of the police. Yet what choice had I but to continue risking discovery since, like Henri, I was incapable of resisting the onslaughts of that appalling hunger?

Then a possible solution came to me. Like Henri, I must remove myself from Paris, at least for a time. But where could I go? For some time I pondered on this as I paced, until all at once I recalled Jerome had made enquiries concerning my possible return to England. It was several weeks since I had seen him, so he might well have heard from Mr Jenkins by now, and if not, I could write to him myself, impressing on him the urgency of my case, since a return to England seemed to me by far the best solution. It would afford me safe, rent-free accommodation in London, as well as a country retreat should I need it. Failing this, I supposed I must remove myself to another area of France, or to some other country on the Continent, although this prospect was considerably less appealing. I did not relish the prospect of being obliged to become a sort of eternal gipsy in an attempt to avoid discovery. I began to appreciate anew the difficulties of life as a vampire, and to admit my grudging admiration for Henri for coping with so little apparent anxiety.

Having discovered a possible escape route, I became impatient to put it in train. Would it be too late to visit Jerome and Lucette tonight? I consulted my pocket watch and thought it would not, since it was not yet ten o'clock. Back home at Shillington Hall, everyone would be in bed by now, but city folk tended to keep later hours. No doubt my cousins would be surprised to see me, but I could always tell them I had been visiting someone in the area. Feeling a great deal more positive, I set off for the *Boulevard Saint-Germain* at a swift pace, and before very long I was knocking on their front door. My cousins' butler answered my knock. If my visiting at such an hour surprised him, he showed no sign, but ushered me inside and went to fetch Jerome. Moments later, my cousin appeared, wrapped in an unexpectedly flamboyant pink-brocade dressing gown, closely followed by Lucette, similarly attired in lavender silk embroidered with pale-pink roses.

"Alex!" exclaimed Jerome, looking concerned. "What brings you here so unexpectedly? Is something amiss?"

"No, no, it's nothing of that kind. I'm sorry to call on you at such an unsociable hour, but I was visiting in the area and I recalled I'd meant to find out whether you'd heard anything further from Mr Jennings."

"No need to apologise, my dear boy, it's always a pleasure to see you, and it's not really so late. As it happens, I have heard from Jennings. I was going to call on you tomorrow. Come into the parlour and I'll fetch his letter."

He went off to do this and I followed Lucette to the parlour, giving silent thanks that Jerome had not attempted to call on me at the spurious address I had given him.

"Would you like some tea, Alex, or perhaps some hot chocolate?" Lucette enquired. "Hortense has gone to bed, but I can easily make you something myself."

"Thank you, Lucette, but please don't go to any trouble on my account. I really don't need anything, and this is only a short visit. I mustn't keep you from your bed."

She smiled and nodded. "But you must pay us a longer visit soon, perhaps during the day when the children can see you. They dearly love to have visitors, and they've seen all too little of you since you've been in Paris."

I assured her I should visit soon, feeling like a miserable wretch for lying to her.

Jerome came into the room carrying a long manila envelope. "Here you are, Alex. I think you'll find it good news."

I practically tore the letter from its envelope, unfolded it and read:

'My Dear Mr Randall,

I have made the enquiries you requested, and am pleased to be able to inform you that the police case against your cousin, Mr Alexander John Travers Randall, was dropped some time ago, since the original informant retracted his statement on discovering that the victims of the affair, the Honourable Arthur de Burgh and Mr Charles Weston-Greer, died as a result of their being engaged in an illegal activity, namely duelling, and police enquiries had, in any case, determined that Mr Randall was an unwilling participant, and had done his best to prevent the affair.

You may therefore inform Mr Randall that it will be perfectly safe for him to return to England, and I shall be only too happy to continue to act in his interests should he require my services.

Yours faithfully,

Richard E. Q. Jennings.'

Unable to suppress a broad grin, I raised my eyes to Jerome's. "I must thank you, cousin! It's a huge relief to know I can return to England and take up my inheritance. I really can't tell you how grateful I am for your help!" I seized his hand and shook it with enthusiasm.

"No gratitude needed, I assure you," he demurred. "I was

only too happy to help. I could see you haven't been happy here in Paris."

"It's a very beautiful city," I said, "but I think the circumstances of my coming here have rather taken the edge off my enjoyment of it. It's a very sobering thing to imagine oneself a permanent outcast from one's homeland."

"Indeed, it must be," said Lucette in heartfelt tones. "We shall miss you, *cher* Alex, but I'm very happy you no longer need fear being arrested, for I cannot believe you could ever have committed such a vile act as murder."

"Thank you, Lucette," I replied, kissing her on the cheek, noticing, as I did so, her slight, unconscious shiver at the coldness of my touch. "I shall miss you, too, both of you. You've been so good to me." I felt shame, knowing how unfounded was my dear cousins' faith in me, but I pushed it aside, saying, "I think I'd better go, now. I'm keeping you up. I expect I'll return to England as soon as I can arrange it, but I promise I'll come and see you before I leave."

I walked back to my lodgings carrying the letter from Mr Jennings against my breast like a talisman, and feeling happier than I had in months. As I watched the full moon glide serenely across the velvety darkness of the night sky, I reflected on how I should soon echo its voyage with one of my own.

CHAPTER TWENTY-FIVE

Having bought my boat ticket, packed my bags, and said my few goodbyes, some few days later I took the evening train from Paris to Calais, arriving about an hour before midnight. I had hoped to be able to take the ferry to Dover the same night, but discovered the only crossings took place during the day. I decided I had best take the early ferry. It would mean reaching Dover in the middle of the day, but at least I could find a room somewhere in which to sleep until nightfall. I dared not risk going to sleep before the ferry left, for fear of being unable to wake again until sunset.

On reaching Calais, I retrieved my one suitcase and set out to find somewhere to leave it until the ferry sailed, since I needed to hunt, and could hardly do so with a suitcase in one hand. I decided on *Le Roquefort*, the inn at which I had stayed on first arriving in France—how long ago that now seemed—since it was only a short walk from the ferry terminal. I bespoke a room for the night, left my suitcase there, and then set out to hunt.

The back streets of Calais proved a fruitful hunting ground. It appeared a ship had recently berthed, as the narrow thoroughfares almost thronged with seamen winding their way in and out of the abundant taverns, and with the women who made a living by satisfying their animal passions.

My senses on the alert, I strolled the streets until I spotted a wiry sailor with a grizzled beard leaving a tavern whose tattered sign, bearing the name *La Reine de la Mer*, ill accorded with its begrimed appearance. The sailor had clearly partaken well of the inn's wares, swaying on his filthy bare feet as though wondering where to go next. It took only a moment to lure him into a dark alleyway and set about my work. I left him hunched against a brick wall, almost unconscious, a few *sous* clenched in one grimy hand to assuage the guilt that still lurked behind the delirious pleasure of his hot blood, tinged with alcohol, pulsing into my eager mouth. My next target was a young prostitute I found wandering alone through the shadows of a narrow lane. As I presented myself before her, her tired eyes took on a rapacious gleam, and her reddened mouth curved in a travesty of a welcoming smile. I fixed my eyes on hers, wondering for a brief moment whether mine held the same predatory glow, and held her gaze until I was sure I had her enthralled, then, taking her arm, I guided her into the deepest shadows. Having eased my hunger with the sailor, I took the time to savour the blood of my youthful victim. Like his, it tasted faintly of alcohol, but it was rich with a youth that had not yet been ravaged by her trade, so that it was all I could do to restrain myself from draining her dry. As her young blood coursed over my tongue, I felt a strange kinship with her, for both of us had been turned by circumstance into hunters of human flesh. I was gentle as I lowered her to the ground and leaned her quiescent body against a wall, and I left her with several francs with which to buy herself some solace.

My hunger was now sated, yet I felt an emptiness inside

that I suspected would never be wholly satisfied. When Henri had taken my blood, he had taken something even more precious—my humanity. As I wandered the dark streets, taking in the myriad scents and sounds of the seaport, I reflected, with a fair degree of bitterness, on the problems of being a vampire in a world built and ordered for humans. Had Henri become so out of touch with his humanity, I wondered, that he had forgotten how difficult he would be making my life by 'bringing me across', to use his quaint phrase? Or did he simply not care? But then, I remembered, he had supposed I should be under his aegis. I found it more than a little disheartening to think a vampire of Henri's age, with all his enhanced abilities, should still be capable of such self-delusion.

Back at *Le Roquefort*, after repairing to my room to cleanse myself and don a fresh shirt, I took a seat near the window in the parlour and set myself to reading newspapers until the time came for me to catch the Dover ferry, hoping the occasional comings and goings in the street outside—for the inn's other residents were all long since in their beds— would keep me awake until it was time to board the ferry.

At eight o'clock in the morning, having dosed myself with copious amounts of strong coffee at *Le Roquefort*, I boarded the ferry. The voyage across the Channel, although uneventful, was slow torture to my vampiric sensibilities. It was not difficult to find a spot out of direct sunlight, but the ferry was so crowded with passengers I was bombarded by a welter of sounds and sensations for the entire three hours it took to reach Dover. The only positive effect of all this was that it kept me awake, if only from a constant desire to pounce on some hapless passenger and help myself to his blood. When, at long last, I stepped onto English soil for the first time in over two years, I was shaking from head to toe from the sensory onslaught and the need for sleep. I booked myself into a small hotel in a quiet street, gave orders that I was not to be disturbed under any circumstances, and gave myself up to blessed slumber.

That evening, after paying for my room—with a little extra thrown in for the landlord to take care of my suitcase—I set off once more to satisfy my relentless hunger. My hotel, The County Inn, lay on Townwall Street. I wandered along this thoroughfare, letting my vampiric senses guide me, until I came to Woolcomber Street. Here I picked up what I was seeking—a blood scent that filled me with a sudden excitement. Wondering, not for the first time, at the way my vampiric senses would single out one scent among many for my undivided attention, I followed it to just past where Woolcomber Street became Maison Dieu Road, and turned into a narrow lane, my gums tingling with anticipation. My quarry was now very close. Then I saw what I was seeking. A woman wrapped up in a drab cloak against the night chill was sitting on the steps of a long, brick building that looked like a warehouse. She had a clay pipe clenched between her teeth and a gin bottle beside her on the step. Taking advantage of my new ability to travel at supernatural speed, I moved to stand in front of her. Surprised, she looked up, her clay pipe falling from her mouth to reveal stained and blackened teeth. The stench of decay was almost overpowering. Quick as thought, I fixed my gaze on her bloodshot eyes. In seconds, she was under my power. I sat down beside her and grasped her shoulders, turning her to face me. As I stared at her slack mouth, her skin yellowed by years of smoke and dirt, I realised that, ravenous as I was, I could not bear to come nearer to that raddled visage and noisome mouth. Instead, I lifted her arm, pushing back the sleeve of her gown, and sank my fangs into a vein in her wrist. With her warm blood pulsing into my eager mouth, my disgust was soon conquered by the pleasure of ingesting her life force.

I pressed a few coins into her fist and left her slumped unconscious against the steps. As I walked back to Maison Dieu Road, I felt disgust of a different kind creep over me like a chilling mist—the now familiar self-loathing at what I must do to sustain myself. I cursed Henri then, with all my heart, even as my body revelled in the strength and heightened senses imparted by a worn-out woman's unwitting gift.

Revulsion did not, however, prevent me from feeding again—this time from a much younger woman whose face bore the shrewd, yet defeated expression I had come to associate with those forced to earn their living on the streets—before returning to the County Inn to collect my suitcase, and walking to the Admiralty Pier railway station to see if I could catch a train that would carry me to London before daybreak. I had no wish to spend another day in Dover if I could help it.

My luck was in, and I was in time to take the last train to London, and even to find an empty compartment, since, as I supposed, most of those who might have taken the train had opted to stay overnight at one of the grand hotels built near the harbour for the convenience of travellers. Two hours later, I was standing on the platform at Charing Cross Station.

I had made up my mind during the journey to call on Mr Jennings first thing that morning to set about claiming my inheritance, even though it meant once again braving that all-pervading sense of unease and aching weariness with which I was now familiar. Soon enough, the first pale rays of light signalled the approach of dawn, but it would be some hours yet before I could present myself to Mr Jennings, so I bought an early edition of *The Times*, took it to a nearby café and read it over a cup of possibly the most abysmal coffee it had ever been my misfortune to drink.

The offices of Wyllie, Palter & Jennings, Barristers and Solicitors, stood in Carey Street near Lincoln's Inn, not very far from The Strand, and, as soon as I judged the office would be open, I left the café and hailed a cab. Early as I was, however, Mr Jennings was already engaged with a client, and so I was obliged to kick my heels in extreme discomfort in a rather Spartan waiting room until he could see me. However, within a little over an hour thereafter, all the necessary papers had been signed and I was not only the legal possessor of a town house in a terrace at Holland Park in Kensington, of Shillington Hall and its estates in Bedfordshire, and of a fortune sufficient to allow me to live comfortably off its income for the foreseeable future, but also a baronet. I was dismayed to discover I should be unable to see Mariah and her son off my estate at Shillington after all, since the terms of my father's will gave them the right to live there until Mariah's death or remarriage, whichever occurred first. In my imagination, I was sorely tempted to hasten the former. Since becoming a vampire, my attitude towards life and death had, perforce, undergone some change, but I trusted I was not yet so depraved as to kill a member of my own family, however detested she might be. In any event, for now all I wanted was to sleep. On reaching Chancery Lane, I hailed a cab and asked the driver to take me to 37 Holland Park.

The house had clearly been unused for quite some time. Its walls looked sadly faded, its furniture was hidden beneath dust covers, and its air smelled musty and stale. I should need to arrange for it to be thoroughly aired and cleaned, and for gas and electricity to be connected, since I might as well live in comfort now I had the means to do so. But for the time being, I wanted nothing more than to climb the stairs and take possession of the first bed I came to, pausing only to throw off the dust cover before settling down to sleep.

That night, after finding sustenance in the leafy environs of Holland Park, I returned home and began pulling the dust covers off all the furniture. With each new revelation of a memory from my past, I felt more and more at home. Some memories brought sadness, but many more recalled happy times from my youth. As I uncovered the great four-poster bed and walnut dressing table in my parents' bedroom, memories flooded back of the times we had spent the Season in town. In my mind, I saw again my mother seated at the dressing table with its large, oval mirror as Betsy, her maid, put the finishing touches to her hair or jewellery before she and my father left for some grand occasion. How lovely she had looked, with her flaxen hair piled up in shining curls, and her silken gowns—cornflower blue had been her favourite colour as it matched her eyes—and her jewels. Had I still been able, I would have shed a tear, then, for the loss of the mother I had loved so dearly.

I spent most of the night roaming through the house

reacquainting myself with its every detail, from the paintings of my ancestors adorning the walls to the plain wooden table and benches in the kitchen, where I had often sat as a boy, chatting with Mrs Rushton the cook and the other servants as they went about their work, and begging tasty morsels from Sally the kitchen maid, who was more soft hearted than Mrs Rushton, and thus more likely to capitulate.

Seating myself on one of the kitchen chairs and leaning my elbows on the table, I closed my eyes, breathed in the faint scents of spices, herbs, and fruit my vampiric senses could still perceive, and gave myself up to memories. So clear were they I half expected Mrs Dear to come in and remonstrate with me for wasting Mrs Rushton's time, and to bustle me off to some pursuit she deemed more appropriate. Eventually, however, I returned to the present and went in search of clean linen for my bed. I had decided to sleep in my old room, in my old, familiar bed, fearing that if I slept in the master bed I should be haunted by the spectres of my parents. I was not yet ready to lay those particular ghosts.

Having made my bed to the best of my inadequate ability, and unpacked the few belongings I had brought with me from France, I fetched pen, paper, and ink from Papa's old study and took them to my desk beneath the window in my room. There I set myself to making a list of the things I deemed necessary to be done to the house, including not only cleaning and refurbishing, but also the installation of a telephone, since it had occurred to me this modern convenience would provide an ideal way of communicating my needs to the outside world without having to go abroad by day. It was an easy enough matter to determine what needed to be done, but quite another to accomplish the

314

practical details; I could scarcely expect workmen to carry out their tasks by night. In the end, I decided to write to Mr Jennings and ask him to arrange matters, the work to be paid for out of my estate. While this was in progress, I would stay at Shillington Hall. I dreaded having to confront Mariah—and quite possibly her brother as well—but I wrote to Captain Nuttall, advising him of my return to England and letting him know my plans. Finding some stamps in my mother's bureau, I affixed them to my letters and went out immediately to post them, breathing in the scents of mown grass and earth, tree bark and leaves, chimney smoke and animal droppings carried on the cool night air as I strolled across the dew-covered grass of Holland Park. How relieved I was to be home again, and breathing England's air!

At the approach of dawn, I slipped between the clean sheets of my childhood bed and slept, as a child should, soundly and without troubling dreams.

* * * *

I awoke soon after sunset with a feeling somewhere between excitement and fear mingled with the usual aching hunger. At first, I wondered why, but then I remembered I was to travel to Shillington to deal with Mariah. But first things first. I quickly dressed and set off to hunt, this time crossing Uxbridge Street to the north of Holland Park, and on to the Ladbroke Grove area, where I recalled there were several areas of trees where I might find not only sustenance, but also cover in which to enjoy it undisturbed. Despite the sense of urgency that always accompanied my hunger, I forced myself to walk at a pace suggesting to any observer that I was merely taking an evening stroll. Soon enough, I picked up a scent. Reaching a treed area, I increased my pace until I had my quarry in my sights: a middle-aged man whose gait suggested he was more than a little tipsy—so much the better for my purposes. I waited until he was well into the trees and shrubs before closing on him. It took only a few seconds to induce in him a state of quiescence; brandy had already done half my work for me. I backed him into the darkest shadows beneath a massive oak tree, bared his throat to my fangs, and drank in the warmth and life-force that would satisfy my blood hunger—at least for the time being.

Hurrying back to Holland Park, I washed, changed my clothes, packed what I thought I should need into a valise I found in the cupboard under the stairs, and set off to find a cab to take me to St Pancras Station. I had stopped on my way home from seeing Mr Jennings to purchase a timetable of trains travelling into the East Midlands, and was pleased to discover several trains each day travelling to Luton and beyond. From Luton, I should have to make other arrangements, but I foresaw no difficulty in that regard, since the Randalls were well known in the area, and well regarded. By the time I reached St Pancras, it was after eight o'clock, but I was just in time to climb aboard a train before it departed, with much screeching and clanking, in a cloud of acrid coal smoke and steam. In a little over an hour, I had reached Luton.

The town was almost deserted at that time of night, but at an inn near the railway station I was able to hire a decent horse to carry me the short distance to Shillington Hall. Once we cleared the town, we set off at a steady canter along the country lanes. The light from the waning moon was more than sufficient for my vampiric eyes to see the direction ahead, and the horse seemed to know the roads and lanes, so I was able to enjoy to the full the fresh country air, and a sky so crowded with stars it seemed they must have been breeding in my absence. As my horse's hooves sped over the ground, the breeze blowing past me seemed to carry with it a regeneration of my battered spirits. Perhaps, even yet, I had a chance of redemption.

In less than an hour, I saw the familiar sight of Shillington Hall's tall chimneys and roof ridge rising above the trees. My heart leapt at the familiar sight of my childhood home—until I thought of what I might meet there. It was in a somewhat chastened mood I rode between the high, wrought-iron gates and up the long, curved driveway flanked by chestnut trees hundreds of years old, but pride surged through me as I came at last to the dear, remembered sight of the elegant Georgian brick manor house. Drawing my mount to a halt before the wide steps leading up to the front door, I allowed myself to gaze at the house for some minutes before dismounting and leading the horse to the stables that were the sole remainder of the original Tudor house. A stable lad whom I had not seen before came out, rubbing the sleep from his eyes, and took the horse away to give it a rub down and to water and feed it before stabling it for the night.

I strolled up to the house and rang the bell. Several minutes later, I heard hurried footsteps and muttering, and then the door opened to reveal Barrett, my father's butler, with many more wrinkles than when I had last seen him, and his head now almost bald, but his bearing still as straight as a yard rule. As soon as he saw me, his disgruntled expression turned to a smile of welcome.

"Mr Alex!" he exclaimed. "You've come home! I knew you would, one day, despite what *some* said contrariwise." He peered behind him as though my detractors might, even now, be waiting to gainsay him. "But come in, Mr Alex, come in. I'll get one of the maids to fetch you a hot drink and a bite to eat; you must be famished, as well as frozen to the bone."

"No, no," I said. "Please don't go to any trouble on my account. I—ah—ate on my way here."

At that moment, Mrs Dear, a little more stooped and shrunken than before, but still a substantial woman, came into the hallway, wiping her hands on her apron. "Mr Alex! I thought I heard your voice. I'd recognise it anywhere, even after so long. Oh, why didn't you write to let us know you were coming, so I could have had your room made ready?" She trotted off again, calling for one of the maids to help her get the Master's bed made up and warmed, and a fire lit in his room.

I was gratified to hear myself referred to as 'the Master', although I wondered what Mariah would think of this. As though reading my thoughts, Barrett said, lowering his voice to a conspiratorial murmur, "Lady Randall is abed this hour since, Mr—sir, but I can send her maid up to wake her—if you wish it."

I smiled. "No, no, Barrett, there's no need to disturb her. I'll meet her soon enough, I dare say."

With the faintest complicit twitch of his lip, Barrett said, "Very good, sir. Can I take your coat and hat, then?"

I was very happy to allow him to perform this office for me, adjuring him to take himself off to his bed before mounting the stairs to inspect the room—my old room, I was pleased to see—that was being prepared for me. An hour later, I was able to bid Mrs Dear and the maid, Mary, a good night, advising them not to wake me in the morning.

Mrs Dear nodded and smiled at this. "Of course, Mr Alex, you'll be weary from travelling, I dare say."

I returned her smile. "That, and the fact I've picked up a few bad habits while on the Continent."

Mrs Dear nodded again, her expression suggesting nothing those foreigners might do would surprise her in the least, and steered Mary—who was inclined to gawp at me as though I were prize exhibit in a museum of oddities—out of the room.

It was now approaching midnight, so there were a little over six and a half hours until dawn. Since becoming a vampire, I had developed an acute awareness of the sun's diurnal journeying. Left to my own devices, my choice would have been to spend the intervening hours rediscovering my boyhood home, but I had no desire to risk rousing the woman I had come to view as my nemesis. That confrontation could wait until I was rested and had an entire night to devote to it—should this prove necessary.

CHAPTER TWENTY-SIX

Late the following afternoon, I was dragged from my deathlike slumber by raised voices in the corridor outside my room. With a snarl of exasperation, I hauled myself to a sitting position, my head swirling with the remnants of dreams, to hear a strident female voice that could only be the fair Mariah.

"Why didn't someone tell me as soon as he arrived?"

Barrett's gentle voice attempted conciliation. "The Master was so good as to request me not to disturb your sleep, My Lady, and I..."

"The Master, indeed!" Mariah interrupted in dismissive tones. "And what, I should like to know, is he doing still abed at this time of day? Such foreign habits will not do for us here at Shillington, I assure you. Barrett, I order you to stand aside!"

I had barely time to digest the idea of poor Barrett attempting to bar the door against the shrill-voiced termagant when the door flew open and the woman in question stormed into the room, followed by Barrett, who cast an apologetic glance in my direction.

"It's all right, Barrett, you can go," I said, and the poor man, his expression a mixture of relief and outrage, made good his escape.

While Mariah was still raging about my late rising, her not

being informed of my arrival, and any other grievance she could think of on the spur of the moment, I mustered what dignity I could, being clad only in my nightgown, and glared at her until her tirade spluttered to a halt. With my eyes fixed on hers, I waited until she lowered them.

"Thank you, Madam," I said in my frostiest voice. "And what, might I enquire, is the meaning of this unseemly behaviour?"

She raised her eyes again, not quite daring to hold my gaze, and repeating, in a sulky tone, "I should have been told of your arrival."

"And so you would have been," I replied, "in due course. Clearly, you were anxious to meet me, but this hardly justifies your bursting in on me in my own room without so much as a by your leave."

My sarcasm was not lost on her. Her breast, encased in black bombazine, heaved, and her face flushed with wounded dignity. "If you had had the decency to rise from your bed at a civil hour, I should not have been forced to such a measure."

"Excuse me, Madam," I returned in a voice like ice, "but it is not for you to attempt to order my habits in my own home. Have the goodness to leave, and I'll come to you when I'm ready."

Her mouth opened in astonishment, and she appeared to have been struck dumb. Unfortunately, this state of affairs soon passed. "Your own home?" she shrilled. "And where were you when your poor, dear Papa passed away, I should like to know? Not so much as a word have we heard from you this past two years, leaving me, his grieving widow, to manage as best I might, and you speak of *your* home?"

In fairness, I should have acknowledged this as a home hit, but I was not inclined to be fair to a shrieking harpy. "Nevertheless," I told her, "it *is* my home, and you'd better reconcile yourself to that fact if you'd continue to live here."

She drew herself up to her full height, a look of triumph on her face. "I have as much right to live here as you do. For your information, it is written into my late husband's will that Oliver and I may continue to do so until—"

"Yes, yes," I interrupted with an impatient wave of my hand. By now, the hunger was beginning to gnaw at me, and I was by no means certain I could prevent myself from attacking her if she continued to anger me. "I'm quite aware of the terms of my father's will, thank you. They also state that I am owner of the Randall estate. You, my dear Madam, are here only by virtue of your marriage to my father— *I* am here by right of birth. I advise you to keep that in mind. And now will you please quit my chamber, or must I dress in front of you?"

With a final gasp of outrage, she turned on her heel and stalked from the room, slamming the door behind her.

By sheer force of will, I managed to dress myself without tearing the room asunder in my rage, and rushed down the stairs and out of the house. Where I might find the blood for which I hungered I had no clear idea, but, by sheer instinct, I set off at a furious pace towards the village of Shillington, some three-quarters of a mile distant. My fury with Mariah had already led my fangs to emerge, and I was quite certain my eyes were smouldering like pits of fire as I reached the outskirts of the village. There I halted and forced myself into a calmer state before proceeding. The last thing I needed was to appear to the villagers as the monster I truly was. When I was satisfied of presenting a reasonable appearance, I began to walk along the High Street, attracted by the warm light issuing from the windows of the *Crown Inn.* I remembered it quite well, and wondered if the landlord, Josiah Pimm, still dispensed hospitality there. However, I knew better than to expose myself by entering, instead skirting the yard and secreting myself in the shadows cast by the stables, listening to the breathing and shuffling of the horses and the snoring of a couple of stable boys within its weathered walls.

As I stood there, every sense alert, contemplating whether to lure one of the boys out to me, I heard a peal of feminine laughter. The back door of the inn swung open and in a flare of golden light a young woman came out. From the apron she wore over her plain gown, I supposed her to be one of the serving girls. Keeping to the shadows, I reached my mind out to hers, which was filled with thoughts of a young man with red hair, whom she hoped would propose to her before the year was out. I soon emptied it, however, and filled it with a burning desire to come to me instead. Dropping the pail she was carrying, she walked towards me, her eyes wide and staring. My gums tingled and I licked my lips at the thought of what was to come. As she reached me, and I drew her into the shadows, a feeling flooded over me composed of equal parts blood longing and my still smouldering anger towards Mariah. The girl's low-cut gown made my task easy. Grasping her by her plump arms, I pulled her against me and, without preamble, tugged her head to one side by her hair and sank my fangs into the vein thus exposed. Her shriek of pain I extinguished by thrusting my arm across her mouth and pressing hard, so that her head thudded against the stable wall. With the taste of her blood, a great savagery had arisen within me. At that moment, my humanity was all but extinguished by blood lust and fury, as though in hurting her I was also hurting the detested Mariah.

Sated at last, I dropped the girl and fled, neither knowing nor caring whether she was alive or dead. It was only later, in the solitude of my own room, that guilt washed over me like a bitter tide, leaving me limp and breathless with regret that I had allowed my baser self to override what remained of my humanity.

The following evening, I went downstairs to find Mariah and her brother in the drawing room, their heads together in close conclave. As I entered the room, they looked up, startled to see me. Their thoughts were hidden before I could catch them, but I was certain they had been discussing me, and in no flattering terms.

"Oh, good evening, Alex," said Mariah, feigning a politeness I could sense she was far from feeling. "I trust you've rested well. I do hope you don't mind, but I've invited dear Joseph to dine with us."

I made a slight, formal bow in their direction. "Good evening Lady Randall, Mr Fordham," I replied, determined to match Mariah in feigned politeness, and to outdo her in formality. "Of course Mr Fordham is welcome to dine here, but I'm afraid I'll be dining out this evening." Some change seemed to have occurred within me since Mariah's intrusion the previous day, and I took a vicious pleasure in the secret meaning of my statement.

An expression of annoyance came over Mariah's features, but she quickly stifled it and said, with a counterfeit smile, "Oh, what a pity. But perhaps, soon, we can have a real family dinner together. May I ask where you'll be dining?"

Fixing a smile on my own face, I replied, "I'm dining in Shillington with—ah—with friends."

"I advise you to be careful, then," Fordham said. "There appears to be a murderer loose in the area—and a vicious one, by all accounts."

"Really?"

"Oh, yes," Mariah said, with that avidity that overcomes so many otherwise genteel people at the mention of violence. "A constable from the village came this morning—while you were still asleep, Alex." Her barb hit home, but I forced myself to conceal my anger. "He came to enquire whether we'd seen any strangers about recently, as one of the servants at the *Crown Inn*, a young woman, was found dead last night with her throat all torn and bloody."

"Good heavens!" I exclaimed, and my horror was genuine enough as I recalled my needlessly savage treatment of the girl. "But surely such a wound suggests attack by an animal. Should the police not be looking for a rabid dog or some such?" I cringed inwardly at the need for these disingenuous words.

Fordham shrugged his thin shoulders. "Perhaps, but the police seem convinced the girl was murdered."

"In that case," I said, "I shall certainly take care, but I doubt I'll come to harm at a friend's house."

"Let us hope not, indeed," said Mariah, her pious expression belying what I sensed in her thoughts, and inducing in me a great desire to slap her deceitful face, even as I grudgingly recognised my own duplicity.

Not wishing to risk going to Shillington again so soon, I passed it by and made my way north. If I had hoped the walk would serve to work off my anger, I was mistaken. By the time I reached the village of Gravenhurst, I was in a towering rage with both Mariah and her mealy-mouthed brother. For all I had not managed to glean what they had been talking about when I came on their little *tête-a-tête*, I was convinced they conspired against me in some way. It was clear to me from our altercation the previous day that Mariah had come to think of Shillington as hers in all but name, and resented my return to puncture her fantasy of being lady of the manor. Well, I thought with a snarl of fury, I'd soon show her and her 'dear Joseph' who was master of Shillington Hall. For all my father had proved a besotted fool at the last, I was damned if I'd allow anyone to deprive me of what was mine by right, least of all the grasping woman who had played on his loneliness to her advantage.

When I came on a farmer's lad wending his way home to one of the outlying farms, as well as sating my hunger, I vented my anger on him as though I had, indeed, been a ravening beast, leaving him lying at the roadside without so much as a second thought.

* * * *

The next few weeks grew to be a living nightmare for me. Mariah became ever more strident in her demands that I keep 'decent' hours, so that I was rarely able to have as much sleep as I needed. As a consequence, I became increasingly short tempered, finding myself snapping at the servants as well as at Mariah and her son. Under different circumstances, I think I should have liked the child—even at his young age, he was intelligent and engaging, with a sharp eye and an impish smile—but in my increasingly disordered mind, he seemed yet another proof of my father's disloyalty and Mariah's perfidy, and so I shunned him as much as I could, despite Mariah's protestations. She had taken to ordering the household, including going over the accounts and other papers with Captain Nuttall. I suppose I should have expected this. After all, someone had had to do it in my absence. But I could only see it as an attempt to take over my rightful role. In addition to these trials, I was becoming ever more aware of the difficulties imposed by my being a vampire. How could I, after all, run my estate as I should wish to when, to all intents and purposes, I could go abroad only by night? Had it not been for Mariah and her damned interference, I told myself, I could have left everything to Captain Nuttall. It was not as though he was not up to the job, and, after all, plenty of estates were run perfectly well in the absence of their owners. But I was damned if I was going to hand it over, by default, to Mariah and her darling son.

Torn asunder by these conflicting feelings, I became so filled with rage that I all but abandoned my vow to retain my humanity. The countryside for miles around became my hunting ground, and each new report of violent death, described in the most lurid terms by newspapers as far away as London, served to spur me to greater depredations. And the more I disgusted myself, the less human I became, as though some demon were driving me to become the very thing I had dreaded.

In my vampiric cunning, I took great care to let no hint of my activities enter Mariah's mind—a simple enough task, in truth, since she seemed interested in little beyond what concerned her and her precious family—and such a limited mind was simple to manipulate. As far as she was concerned, my behaviour in staying out all night and sleeping all day was merely a continuation of profligate habits I had acquired on the Continent, and proof of my unfitness to be my father's heir. My euphoria after drinking blood she took for drunkenness, and it served my purposes to allow her to think this—or so I believed.

CHAPTER TWENTY-SEVEN

One night, after sating my blood hunger with the unconscious driver of a cart I found overturned in a ditch, I returned to Shillington Hall intending to spend the remaining hours of darkness reading a copy of Wilkie Collins's novel *The Moonstone*, which I had discovered in my father's library. To my surprise, instead of Barrett, it was Mariah who opened the door to me.

"Mariah!" I exclaimed, in my surprise forgetting my determination to be formal with her. "It's not like you to stay up so late. Is Barrett ill?"

"No," she replied. "I've sent the servants to bed. There's something I wish to discuss with you, Alex, which is why I'm not yet in my own bed. Come into the drawing room, if you please."

I was not the slightest bit pleased at the prospect of another dressing down but, with a sigh, I followed her.

"Well, Mariah, what is it? I shouldn't wish to keep you up so long past your bedtime."

She gave me a hard look. "It is *your* bedtime I wish to discuss, Alex."

"I beg your pardon, but I can't conceive what that has to do with you."

"Can you not, when you're out carousing until all hours of the night—and womanising, too, I shouldn't wonder—

coming home drunk and looking like a tramp, and then wanting to sleep all day? I cannot imagine what your poor, dear father would have thought of you, never mind the example you're setting dear little Oliver. Do you care nothing for the welfare of your little brother?"

"Half brother," I corrected her. "And why on earth should I want to set him any kind of example? I didn't ask to have him foisted on me any more than I did you."

"Alex, you can't mean that!" she cried in melodramatic tones, raising a hand to her brow like Mrs Siddons depicting the tragic muse. "How can you be so unfeeling?"

"Quite easily, I assure you, where you and your brat are concerned, and if you don't like it, you're quite at liberty to leave this house just as soon as you like."

"Your poor, dear father wished us to stay," she said, glaring at me so the veins stood out on her forehead. "And that is what we shall do. This is our home, whether you like it or not, and as long as it is, I'll thank you to conduct yourself in a more seemly manner, for Oliver's sake, if not for mine."

Until now, I had managed to preserve an appearance of icy calm, although it was far from what I was feeling. Now, however, I could hold back no longer. "This is *my* home," I hissed at her, "and I'll do what I damned well please in it! You're here only because you seduced my father into marrying you. And if you thought giving him your brat of a son would establish you as mistress of Shillington Hall, let me tell you you're damned well mistaken."

Her face reddened with outrage. "How dare you use such language to a lady?"

"I wasn't aware I was speaking to a lady," I snapped, only just managing to keep from baring my teeth in a snarl.

"How dare you!" She took a step towards me, her hand raised as though to slap me for my insolence.

That one step, that one gesture, seemed to cross some divide. Without conscious impulse, I flung myself at her, my hands reaching out for her, the fingers curved into talons. She tried to step backwards, but caught her foot in the hem of her gown and tumbled to the floor. I stood over her, hissing and snarling and baring my teeth, my gums prickling as my fangs began to emerge. Her eyes widened in terror, and I knew my own must be glowing red with fury. Through her fear, I saw a sudden comprehension light her eyes.

"It was you," she whispered, clambering to her feet and backing away from me, one outstretched hand pointing at me in accusation. "All those deaths—it was you! In God's name, Alex, what have you become? What kind of—of monster are you?"

She had seen me in my true light, and I knew I must prevent her from betraying me. I must control her mind and erase all knowledge of what she had seen. As quick as the thought, I was at her side. Despite her shock—or perhaps because of it—she had continued flinging her accusations at me, demanding, in a voice hoarse with dread, to know what evil influence I had succumbed to. My hands shot out to grasp her neck and choke off that condemning voice while I took control of her mind. I was still unused to my vampiric strength, however, and before I quite realised what I was about, I heard her gurgle in her throat, and her flailing hands fell to her sides as her body went limp. As I moved to prevent her fall, I saw the marks of my fingers white on her plump, pink neck, and the faint blue line of a vein, not pulsing, but ominously still. For a long moment I gazed, fascinated, then

I wrenched her body hard against mine. My fangs had emerged in response to the sight of that vein. Now, with an inhuman snarl of triumph, I sank them deep into it, drawing her blood into my mouth and swallowing it in great gulps, all the while tearing at her soft flesh like a fox with a chicken. After some time I realised her blood was no longer flowing. Heedless of the crimson rivulets running down my chin, staining my shirt and dripping onto her breast, I raised my head and stared at her ashen face and glazed eyes.

I realised she was dead.

With a gasp, I dropped her lifeless body, staring in disbelief as it fell to the floor, as limp as a rag doll. Panic gripped me. I darted my eyes about the room as though I expected some spy to be hiding behind the curtains or the sofa. But I was alone—alone with the corpse of the woman whose life I had sucked out with her blood, which was even now coursing through my veins, as intoxicating as wine. A great shudder racked my body as I grasped the enormity of what I had done. My immediate instinct was to flee. With a moment's reflection, however, I recognised the foolishness of this. Indeed, nothing could be more calculated to indicate my guilt. What I must do was to make it seem the act of the murderer everyone already believed to be in the neighbourhood. But how best to achieve this? I began to pace the room, cudgelling my brain for an answer. I glanced at her again and saw the carpet was stained with her blood. If I moved her, I should have to clean up the blood, and I could not do that without going to the kitchen for water and cloths, and even if these implements escaped notice, the carpet would still be wet when the servants got up, which, I then realised, would be quite soon, since dawn was not far off. The situation was becoming more complicated by the minute.

Then I recalled Henri's advice when I had accidentally killed the first man I had drunk from in the *Jardin de Luxembourg* in Paris. If I tried to hide Mariah—and where could I hide her, anyway?—it would arouse more suspicion than if I left her where she was, the apparent victim of the supposed murderer. But how would the killer have gained entrance to the house? I was stumped. Already I was beginning to feel the bone-chilling weariness that signalled the approach of dawn, yet I must find some solution before I could risk going to my bed. Once again, I stared around the room. I thought of opening a window to make it seem this was how the killer had gained entrance, but the windows opened only from the inside, and why would anyone have opened one on such a chilly night, let alone have left it open? My next thought was the front door. Could it, perhaps, have been left unlocked? Unlikely, but it seemed the best option I could conjure up at short notice. When asked, I could say Mariah had let me in—which was true, after all, and she was scarcely in a position to deny it—and I had then gone straight up to my room. All I had to do then was to evince sufficient shock and horror at her death, and I saw a disturbing lack of difficulty in that.

As I had expected, I was called from my bed long before I had achieved my fill of sleep. I had had the good sense to clean myself and don my nightshirt before collapsing onto my bed, but I felt little better than a corpse myself when I staggered down the stairs to view what Mary the maid had found on going to clean out the grate and set the fire for the day. The girl was still in hysterics when I entered the drawing room, supported by Mrs Dear, who was trying her best to soothe her and to administer the contents of a vinaigrette. I ordered one of the scullery maids, who stood sniffing into a handkerchief, to fetch Mary some brandy, and turned to Barrett who, though clearly shaken, was managing to preserve much of his usual decorum.

"Barrett," I said, taking him aside from the group staring at Mariah's body. "Can you tell me what's happened here?"

He cleared his throat. "It's as you see, sir. Mary found the—Lady Randall—this morning. No one knows when she died, sir, but the—the blood has all but dried, so I should say it was some hours ago."

"Yes, I see," I said, in the unforgiving light of day hating myself for deceiving him. "Has anyone gone for the Police?"

"Oh, yes, sir, I sent Jarvis off to fetch the Constable and Doctor Phillips as soon as we—as soon as Lady Randall..."

I nodded. "Thank you, Barrett. I think you'd better have some brandy, too—and make it a large one."

"Thank you, sir. Very much appreciated."

Since Shillington did not boast a Police officer, Jarvis, the head groom, had been obliged to ride to Shefford, and it was afternoon by the time Constable Perkins arrived, travelling on a bicycle muddied by the dirt roads he had travelled. Doctor Phillips, who had been out on his rounds when Jarvis called, was not far behind him. I had spent the intervening time in my room, although I dared not risk falling asleep, despite the fact that my entire being ached for it. But the thought of remaining in the vicinity of my grisly handiwork was more than even I could bear, and so I sat on my bed with my head in my hands trying to come to grips with the depths to which I had sunk in my ungoverned resentment of my father's new wife. I could scarcely believe what I had done, not just to Mariah, but to all those other innocent victims of my rage. Once again I cursed Henri. How could he, who had claimed to love me as a friend, have visited on me his vile curse of vampirism from which I might never escape? Must I now shun all human company in case some hapless person should arouse my anger? Over and over again, I told myself I hated him for it. In my heart, however, I knew it was myself I truly hated.

By the time Barrett knocked on my door to tell me the Constable had arrived, I had decided I had only one honourable course left to me. But first I must steel myself to deal with Constable Perkins.

In the event, this was not such an ordeal as I had feared. When I arrived in the drawing room, Doctor Phillips had already signed the death certificate, satisfied that Mariah had died from blood loss following an attack by person or persons unknown, and Constable Perkins was interviewing the staff one by one in the library. When my turn arrived, the Constable was apologetic, but I waved this aside.

"You've your duty to do," I said. "I understand that." I told him the tale I had settled on, and he believed it, seeing no reason not to do so. As soon as he had left, I returned to my room and, despite my mood of self-loathing, fell into a corpselike sleep until after sunset.

That night, I did not allow myself to feed. After such an orgy of evil, I asked myself, how could I ever again trust myself to keep a check on my baser self? If only Henri had warned me. If only he had taught me how to control my instincts as he seemed able to do. But the principles of honesty in which I had been raised asserted themselves at last, forcing me to admit that I, and I alone, had allowed my resentment of Mariah—and of my father for marrying her— to rule my feelings when I should have exerted control over them. I had no one to blame but myself for the evil I had caused. And there was only one way to ensure no one else would die at my hands. Somehow, I must contrive to take my own life.

How I might achieve this was not at all clear, since it seemed vampires were all but impossible to kill. The most certain methods—if what I had heard and read were true— were destruction by fire or beheading, and I was a loss to see how I could succeed in inflicting either of these on myself. Henri had not believed silver bullets to be harmful, although I supposed enough of any kind of bullet might well do the job. But how, I asked myself, could I shoot my body with enough bullets? Even with a repeating pistol, I imagined I should be rendered unconscious before I reached this point. And how many bullets would it take, anyway? I set myself to remember the other methods of which I had read in Henri's books. A wooden stake through the heart seemed to be the most commonly accepted method, but it would be difficult in the extreme to apply this to myself. Still, I had read of Roman soldiers falling on their swords, so perhaps I could achieve something similar. There were a couple of swords in the munitions room, and any number of other sharp objects about the house. Since the killing blow seemed to consist of piercing the vampire's heart, perhaps one of these would have the same effect. I decided not to make this my first recourse, however, since the results if I should fail were almost too horrific to contemplate. The last thing I wanted was to inflict yet another bloody body on my household.

Besides, if I survived it would be clear to all that I was guilty of Mariah's murder. How long, I wondered with a shudder, would it take to be 'hanged by the neck until dead'? I remembered Henri had also told me vampires were not susceptible to garlic or crosses and, in any case, from what I had read they were tools for protection against vampires rather than for killing them. Despite this, however, I was determined to try all possible avenues, and to lose no time in doing so lest I lose my nerve, miserable creature that I was.

As soon as I knew all the servants were safely in bed, I crept downstairs, grateful that Doctor Phillips had arranged for Mariah's body to be removed from the house. Of course, I could still sense the residue of her presence, and smell the lingering tang of her blood, despite the servants' best efforts to clean it up, but at least it was now more bearable. In the kitchen, I made straight for the larder, needing no vampiric sense of smell to lead me to where ropes of onions and garlic hung from hooks in the ceiling. I tore down a string of garlic and crammed the cloves into my mouth. Only when my stomach began to revolt did I remember Henri telling me vampires could not process food. I spat out the semi-masticated cloves in disgust. However, apart from making me feel nauseated, they appeared to have done me no harm. So much, I thought with a grimace, for the efficacy of garlic.

I was, however, determined not to give up. If anything, this first defeat made me more determined to find some way to end my existence. My mouth still tasting disgustingly of garlic, I crept back up the stairs but, instead of returning to my own room, I went to Mama's old room, hoping to find there some silver object amongst her jewellery. In a drawer of her dressing table, I found a silver cross on a chain, which

I had vague memories of her wearing when I was a small boy. As I picked it up, I saw the chain was broken, no doubt the reason she had stopped wearing it. At any rate, it did me no harm whatsoever—another disappointment.

I began to despair of ever finding a non-violent way of ending my life. Without access to Henri's library of esoterica, there was only one more remedy I could think of, but it would have to wait until the following night since I could already sense the approach of dawn.

The next evening, after once more waiting until the household was abed, I crept out of the front door and into the star-sprinkled night. Having denied myself the previous night, the hunger was tearing at my insides like a wild animal, rendering me almost incapable of coherent thought. It was not long before I reached Shillington village, where instinct—and my prodigious hunger—had me scenting the air for blood. But I vowed this would be the last time I should feed, telling myself I was only doing it because I needed a clear head for my main object in coming to the village. I could only pray it would serve me as I hoped.

I dared not return to the *Crown Inn*, but a little way to the south of the village I came to another inn called the *Musgrave Arms*, and secreted myself in the shadows of a stand of trees at the edge of its yard. The scents of those making merry within were so tantalising as to be all but unbearable, so I reached out with my mind to see what I might find there. At first, such a welter of thoughts and emotions, heartbeats and pulsing blood overwhelmed me that I wanted to leave forthwith. However, my tearing need kept me there, and after a time I was able to single out one person from amongst the confusion—a young man just out of boyhood, by the feel of him—and to draw him out to where I waited. It was the work of but a few moments to get him under my control and to tear off the red, spotted kerchief knotted about his neck. As my fangs emerged and I bit into his flesh, with its faint taste of sweat and soap, I felt the familiar elation rise within me. His blood, young and sweet and warm, flowed across my tongue and down my throat so that I could do nothing but exalt in my vampirism, in the joy of drinking in his youth and vitality. It was all I could do to prevent myself from using him up entirely, as I had all those others, but somehow I managed to stop myself while his heart was still beating. I lowered him to the ground and left him propped up against the trunk of a great oak tree to recover.

I was far from replete, but at least I could think clearly again, and I sought to alleviate my guilt with the reflection that I had not, after all, killed the lad, and besides, he was to be the last of my victims.

With that thought, I set out for my next destination.

CHAPTER TWENTY-EIGHT

The Church of All Saints stood some way north of the *Musgrave Arms*, on Church Street, off the High Road that passed through Shillington village. Within a few minutes, I stood gazing at the neat stone building set back from the street on a low hill, taking in its row of Gothic windows and the square tower at one end, all familiar to me since I had accompanied my parents there every Sunday from my earliest youth. I shuddered to think of the use to which I would soon put the loved landmark. But I was desperate to quit what Henri had left to me of my life, and desperate situations require desperate measures—or so I reassured myself.

Not yet quite trusting my vampiric senses to warn me of danger, I cast furtive glances about me before making my way past the tombstones dotting the grassy hill, and up to the church doors. I was relieved to find these unlocked—not that I could not have wrenched them open with ease, but what was left of my humanity shrank from the idea of doing so—and slipped through into the cool, dark church, breathing in the spicy aroma of incense I recalled so well. My heart thudded like the hooves of a galloping horse as I gazed about me at the solid wooden pews, the well-worn, frieze-covered hassocks, the leadlight windows depicting the apostles, and the carved lectern on its marble plinth. For some time I was lost in a reverie of times past, hearing in my mind the voices of both choir and congregation raised in song, smelling the sweet tang of communion wine mingled with the spicy incense. Then, recalling just why I was there, I banished these dear remembrances and looked to my left where, just inside the church entrance, stood the carved wooden plinth that held the font. Standing in front of it, I took a deep breath to steel myself for my intended blasphemy, then leaned down and scooped some of the sanctified water into my mouth. Nothing happened. In desperation, I ladled up more and more of it in my hands, heedless of the water splashing onto my clothes and trickling onto the floor.

Nothing.

Covering my eyes with my dripping hands, I sank to the floor and sobbed out my misery in great, shuddering gasps. A creaking sound made me look up, terrified someone had found me out, my tearless sobs turning to relief when my senses revealed nothing more than the shifting of beams in the old church's framework. Nevertheless, I fled from the church and back down the path, passing through the wrought-iron gate with a sigh of gratitude that no one had seen me.

As I sped home through the darkness, I felt caught between two powerful forces that threatened to tear me asunder. The past weeks had led me to believe myself all but incapable of controlling my hunger for blood, and by the time I reached Shillington Hall, I had come to the conclusion there was now only one course open to me. The mere thought of it filled me with dread, and I had no idea if it would even work, but I was certain I could not go on as I was. I could only hope I had the courage to carry it out.

Much to my relief, Shillington Hall was in darkness. As I crept through the door and into the high-ceilinged hall, it seemed to me the entire house breathed in slumber. On silent feet, I made my way to the kitchen and took a sharp knife from one of the drawers, then set about scanning the fireplace for a stick suitable for carving into a pointed stake. I found nothing. Cursing under my breath, I padded across the room, across the hall and into the drawing room, but a search of the fireplace there yielded nothing smaller than thick tree branches cut into short lengths. Panic struck at me, mingled with a fear so strong I knew if I hesitated much longer I should be incapable of accomplishing my aim. Forcing down my dread, I hurried up the stairs and into my room. I saw the maid had lit the fire for me earlier, but it had long since burned itself out, leaving only a few charred remains. Groaning in despair, I threw myself onto my bed and began to pound it, for all the world like a child in a tantrum. As soon as I realised what I was doing, my mood turned to disgust. What sort of pathetic creature was I that could destroy others, but lacked the resolve to kill myself?

All at once I saw that, while I had been beating my hopeless fists on the bed, the knife I still held in my hand had carved great shreds out of the counterpane, its white lining reminding me sickeningly of the fat beneath the skin on a side of mutton. I turned the knife over in my hand. The faint moonlight shining through the gaps in the curtains glinted along its sharp blade, worn thin by years of honing, and it came to me that here was my solution. If I could only stab myself through the heart, it would surely no longer be capable of pumping blood—the blood I must steal from

342

others—through my body. In my own hand lay my last chance to end my wretched existence.

I tore open my shirt, then, holding the knife before me like Shakespeare's Mark Antony about to fall on his sword, I knelt on the counterpane, positioning myself—or so I hoped—so that when I fell I should plunge the knife further into my breast. My heart racing, and my mouth dry with terror, I raised the knife in my two hands and closed my eyes lest I see the blade and lose courage at the last moment. The blade had just touched my bare breast when a high, thin wail pierced the carapace of my intent. Sheer instinct made me stop and listen. I realised it was Oliver, Mariah's infant son.

I flung the knife from me, barely noticing as it clattered against the dressing table and fell to the floor with a dull thud, appalled at what I had become—a creature obsessed with my own feelings, with nurturing my sense of ill usage until it became the maelstrom of hatred that had driven me to kill Mariah without sparing so much as a single thought for the innocent child she left behind. It came to me then, like a bolt of lightning illuminating the night sky: the true monster was not just the vampire I had become, but the selfish, immature and shallow *human* I had already been when Henri brought me across. To think I had contemplated ending my own perceived troubles at the expense of a child who was, after all, my own flesh and blood filled me anew with self-loathing. How could I even have thought of denying him the parental love I had, myself, received in such full measure?

After a few moments I heard footsteps, and then Mrs Dear's voice murmuring in soothing tones, and before long the crying stopped.

I leapt from my bed and paced the length of the room like a caged tiger. It was clear to me I owed it to my father's memory, if nothing else, to ensure his son had the best care and education I could give him. It was equally clear that Mrs Dear, who had grown old in service to the Randall family, should not have to cope alone with the care of a growing child. However, I knew I could not stay on at Shillington Hall after the horrors I had committed. Not only would I be in danger of discovery as a murderer, I was terrified of what my vampiric nature might lead me to do to the very folk it was my duty to protect. And how could I be sure I would not, in time, harm even my own half brother? No, I would have to leave—and as soon as possible. But where could I go? My intention had been to live in the house at Holland Park, but this no longer seemed viable. Even London was too close to the scene of crimes—and one, in particular—that might yet be connected with me. In London, too, there was the risk of running into old acquaintances, or that Oliver would wish to visit me, and for my brother's safety I was determined he should not see me again until he was a grown man and able to determine the course of his own life, by which time I should have developed a greater degree of self restraint—or so I hoped.

As I paced my room, striving to reach some resolution of my situation, I felt the familiar weariness lay its hand on me, and knew I could make no further plans until I had slept.

My last thought before sleep overcame me was of the bitter irony that it was my own actions that would force me from the very home I had been so afraid of losing.

* * * *

When the dying rays of the sun brought me once more to consciousness, it was as though I had made up my mind in my sleep. I knew just what I must do. All that remained was to set my plans in motion. After washing and dressing, I went straight to the drawing room and rang for Mrs Dear, who hurried in looking rather flustered.

"Ah, Mrs Dear," I began, "I do hope I've not called you away from anything important."

"No, no, Mr Alex, I was just making sure Jane hadn't forgotten about young Master Oliver's tea."

I nodded. "Good. In fact, that's what I want to talk to you about—Oliver, I mean. I'm obliged to go away again soon, and it could be for quite some time. Of course I'll make provisions for Oliver's care, but I'm inclined to feel he should perhaps have someone younger as his nurse. Not," I hastened to add, "that I don't think you'll apply yourself to his interests with as much care as you gave to me, but—"

"Begging your pardon, Master Alex," she broke in, "but I can't but agree with you. I'm getting much too old and creaky to be running after such a sprightly lad as Master Oliver is growing to be."

"Well, I didn't mean..." I began, feeling more than a little discomfited.

She cocked her head on one side like a sparrow, a twinkle in her grey eyes. "Well, there's no denying the truth of it, Master Alex, so I'll not make the attempt."

I smiled, reaching out to pat her black-clad arm. "In that case, perhaps you can recommend someone to take on the boy's care. I'd rather it was someone local than a complete stranger."

"As it happens," she said, "I think I know the very person. My niece's eldest girl, Alice, is as kind and sensible a girl as you'll find in a month of Sundays. She's had plenty of experience caring for her own younger brothers and sisters, and it so happens she's looking for employment in the neighbourhood. If you want a reference for her, I'm sure the Reverend and Mrs Paull will be only too happy to oblige, as she's been cleaning the vicarage on a regular basis these past two years, as well as helping at the Sunday school."

I suppressed a shudder at the memory of my recent nefarious activities in the reverend gentleman's church, assured Mrs Dear her own recommendation would be sufficient, and told her I'd write to Mr Cox, the girl's father. Dismissing her go about her business, I asked her tell Barrett I'd like to see him.

My business with Barrett was soon concluded, consisting only of advising him of my imminent departure, and authorising him to take on an assistant if he felt it needful. I didn't insult him by telling him so, but I felt he, too, was becoming a trifle 'old and creaky', and deserved some respite from his duties.

Having thus made a beginning to my plans, I took myself off to hunt while it was still early enough for people to be about. Returning home a couple of hours later, I saw the light still on in the cottage behind the stables, in which Captain Nuttall lived, and hurried into the house to wash and put on clean clothes before paying him a visit.

He answered my knock in his shirtsleeves, with his pipe in one hand. "Good evening, sir. Please come in, if you'll pardon my clutter. I've been running through the last quarter's accounts, so you've come at a good time if you'd like to look them over."

"Oh, I don't think so," I said, taking in the stacks of bills and ledgers covering the table. "So long as there's nothing in particular you want me to see, I'm sure I can leave everything in your more than capable hands."

"Thank you, sir, that's very kind of you." He indicated the chair across the table from where he had been sitting. "Please, won't you sit down? Would you care for a drop of brandy?"

I accepted this with thanks. "Captain Nuttall," I began as he set down two glasses and a decanter on the table. "I'm obliged to leave Shillington again very soon."

"Ah, yes." He poured out two measures of brandy. "You did say you were planning to live in the town house. We'll all miss you here, sir, but I can quite see why a young fellow should wish to live in the metropolis."

I looked down, swirling my brandy in its glass, uncomfortable at having to deceive yet another person with only my best interests at heart. "The thing is," I said, taking a sip of the fiery liquid. "I've had to change my plans. I'll be going abroad for a time."

A slight frown creased his forehead, but he said nothing.

"I know I can trust you completely with the running of Shillington Hall and the estate here, but I wonder, would you mind liaising with Mr Jennings as necessary regarding the London house and my father's—that is, my other business interests as well? I'm more than happy for you to take on an assistant if you wish to, as it'll be rather more than you're used to dealing with."

He rubbed his forehead, as though to remove the frown that was still there. "Of course, I'm only too happy to do anything I can for you, sir, but, with your leave, I'd like to take on my nephew—and namesake, as it happens—as my assistant. He came down from university last year, and has been working in Bedford as an accountant, but he's dying to get his teeth into something a bit more, well, to use his own word, 'interesting'. I can vouch for him, sir, and so can his current employer."

"That sounds an excellent plan, Captain. Just send for him whenever you like. I'll leave it to you to arrange his wage, and that of Mrs Dear's niece, Alice Cox, who's coming to be nurse to young Oliver. I'm sure you're a great deal more *au fait* with these things than I am." He was inclined to demur, but I waved this aside. "No, no, of course you are, Captain. I have complete faith in you." I smiled at him, taking care to hide my fangs, which had still not completely subsided. "Thank you for the brandy, Captain. I'll take my leave, now. My plan is to travel to London by tomorrow evening's train, and I'll be seeing Jennings before I go abroad, so if you have anything for him, I can take it with me."

Standing up to take my leave, I bowed, but remembered just in time not to hold my hand out for him to shake, in case he wondered why it was so cold. If he thought this odd, he was courteous enough not to show it.

* * * *

The following evening, being anxious not to miss the last train from Luton, I did not feed before travelling, so by the time I arrived at St Pancras Station at a little after eight o'clock, I was ravenous. Instead of taking a cab to Holland

Park, I set off on foot for the nearby Regent's Park. I took my valise with me, having decided, after weighing up the situation, that it need not impede me, and might even assist in hiding my true intent, and afterwards I could go straight on to Holland Park. I was gratified to see a number of folk taking the evening air, and as I approached the trees bordering the area known as Queen Mary's Gardens, I picked up a scent that made my heart beat faster. Under the trees strolled a middle-aged woman in a dark wool mantle over a grey skirt. With her plain bonnet and sober attire, she looked to me like a lady's companion, or perhaps a governess. A wave of excitement swept through me as I sensed the warm blood pulsing in her veins. It was all I could do to suppress it as I stepped up to her and bowed.

"Excuse me, Madam. I wonder, can you tell me if I'm going in the right direction for Victoria Station? I seem to have lost my way."

She smiled, raising large and trusting hazel eyes to mine. Before she had completed her reply, I had her in my power. I led her into the dark shadows of a small copse and untied the strings of her bonnet and mantle, letting them fall to the ground. Her blood was as sweet in my mouth as a summer's day but, terrified of repeating my rampage in Bedford, I was careful not to leave her too depleted. Afterwards, I sat her on the ground, replaced her bonnet and pulled her mantle around her shoulders to keep out the night cold, wondering at my new concern for my victim, and hoping I was perhaps not so great a monster as I had thought.

A short way further on, near the boating lake, I watched from the shadows as a young man bade his sweetheart a tender farewell, gazing after her as she set off across

Clarence Bridge towards Marylebone Station. When she was out of sight, the young man turned towards where I was hiding and I stepped out to meet him. The trick I had used already worked just as well with him and, half an hour later I was able to leave Regent's Park feeling pleasantly replete, and to walk the rest of the way to Holland Park.

As I walked, my heightened senses drank in the cool night air redolent with the familiar aromas of the London streets: the pungent aroma of coal smoke drifting up from numerous fires; the breath of horses pulling hansom cabs and the earthiness of the dung they left behind; the acrid fumes of the more modern motor vehicles; and, above all, the alluring scents and beating hearts of human beings. The blood ecstasy had me half in love with London, almost as though the great city had been a woman pulsating with life and passion, and beckoning me into her arms. All at once, a picture of Emmeline Beaumont came into my mind—sweet Emmeline whom I had left behind it seemed a lifetime ago. My mind conjured up, as though to torment me in my loneliness, her sweet scent, her soft lips and arms, her warm, red hair. Did she ever think of me, I wondered? To my shame, she had scarcely entered my mind since my earliest days in Paris, so lost had I been in the horror my life had become. And now it was too late to put things right. Even if she remembered me with fondness—and I had given her precious little reason to do so—I dared not approach her for fear that any demonstration of affection would lead me to destroy her, or worse, condemn her to my own dark world. At last, I began to comprehend the yearning for companionship that had led Henri to take me into his world.

It was in a thoughtful mood that I reached Holland Park.

As soon as I entered the newly painted door of my town house, I saw Mr Jennings and his various agents had been busy on my behalf. The house had undergone a transformation, with walls recovered, paint and varnish renewed, floors freshly polished, rugs cleaned and furniture polished until it gleamed in the soft glow of electric lamps. In the entrance hall, next to the staircase, a brand-new, modern telephone had been affixed to the wall above a hall table that held a lamp and a new telephone directory. I decided there and then to telephone Mr Jennings first thing in the morning to thank him for his good work on my behalf, to ask him to arrange for the upkeep of both my estate and my young half brother, and to hire a reliable couple to take care of the Holland Park town house and its garden. After that, I could sleep in comfort until sunset.

I spent some hours wandering through the house, admiring all the improvements—of which, I reflected with regret, I should probably never make use—before repairing to the parlour to pour myself a brandy and to write a couple of letters. The first was to Jerome and Lucette, thanking them for their help and hospitality, and reassuring them— though I shrank from the deception—that all was well, and I would soon be resuming my Grand Tour. My next task was to pen a note to Monsieur Lefebvre, apologising for my hasty departure, assuring him of my gratitude for all his help, explaining that news of my father's death had occasioned my sudden return to England, and asking him to communicate with me via Mr Jennings, as I was going abroad for the foreseeable future. Having accomplished these barefaced lies, I finished off my brandy and walked across Holland Park to the mailbox.

Returning home after a pleasant hour or two spent wandering once-familiar streets, I made a survey of my father's library, selecting an old, leather-bound copy of Sir Walter Scott's *Kenilworth* to keep sleep at bay until I could telephone Mr Jennings.

I found myself unable to concentrate on my book, however, and fell to pondering my future. I had told Jerome and Lucette I should be continuing my Grand Tour, but this was not my real intent. Thinking of Emmeline had made me realise, once and for all, I could never go back to my old life. Unless I could somehow find a way to come to terms with what I now was, and to be what I was without becoming a monster, I was too much of a danger to those for whom I cared. The previous night's hunting had shown me the fate I dreaded was not yet irrevocable, yet I feared it might become so, in time. There was only one way I could think of to avoid this. I must find Henri and beg him to forgive and guide me. I could only hope he could find it in his heart to forgive me— either that or to have the mercy to put me out of my misery once and for all. Quite how to find him I had no idea, but there seemed only one place to start, and that was Paris. He had a house there, to which he would probably return, sooner or later. If there was one thing I had in abundance, it was time.

Other Books by Lila Richards

A Different Hunger

In Victorian London, when an ill-advised love affair sees young Rufus de Hunte challenged to an illegal duel, his father, to avoid the scandal this would bring, banishes him to New Zealand to become a remittance man. During the voyage Rufus meets the captivating Serafina Radzinska, travelling with Anton Springer, who may or may not be her father. Despite his uncertainty, Rufus finds himself falling in love with her - even after he discovers both she and Springer are vampires. When Rufus is badly beaten by the vicious Toby Fox, and seems certain to die, Serafina, who returns his love and fears losing him, turns him into a vampire. Rufus's horror and resentment threaten their love, but when they reach New Zealand and Serafina is captured by Viviana Alexandreu, an ancient and powerful vampire seeking revenge on Springer, Rufus must acknowledge his true feelings and find a way to rescue her and to end Viviana's insane vendetta once and for all.

Vicious Circle

When a listener to The Psychic Connection radio programme is emotionally blackmailed by self-styled spiritual teacher Bob Ferris, resident panellists Joss Cherry and Isabel Sinclair decide to investigate. Meanwhile, the remains of a woman's body are found in a creek-bed in Queensland, Australia. Detective Sergeant Declan Kelly's search for

Richard Forster, the last person to see her alive, leads him to communes in Queensland and New Zealand and the flesh-pots of Auckland's infamous Karangahape Road, until his trail meets that of the `Psychic Connection' panel. Their investigations culminate in a dramatic confrontation at the disused church where Ferris attempts to implement his bizarre plans to give birth to the New Aeon.

The Tarot Murders

When a series of bizarre murders based on major trumps of the Tarot rocks the usually staid city of Christchurch, the panel members of radio show The Psychic Connection are drawn into the case when it seems panel member James Myerson may be involved – or even the murderer. Detective Sergeant Declan Kelly (see: Vicious Circle) arrives in Christchurch, on sick leave after being wounded during a stakeout in Queensland, and adds his weight to the Psychic Connection panel's investigation of what the press is calling the Tarot Murders. The murderer's calling card, The Magician, left with each new victim, offers a sinister clue to the killer's identity – if only the panel can solve it in time to prevent the death of one of its own members.

About the Author

Lila Richards lives in one of the leafy suburbs of Christchurch, New Zealand, with two black cats. She works part-time as a sub-editor and proofreader for the New Zealand Meteorological Service. As well as writing, Lila reads eclectically, sews vintage clothes, and collects things, in particular old movies, owls, Egyptiana, and art deco paraphernalia. From time to time she enters the Middle Ages via the Society for Creative Anachronism (an international mediaeval re-creation group), where she transmogrifies into a ninth-century small-holder's widow living in the west of Ireland, and has attained the rank of Baroness.

www.ingramcontent.com/pod-product-compliance
Lightning Source LLC
Chambersburg PA
CBHW021527250626
47154CB00006BA/1999